Enochim

David Kendal Jones

authorHOUSE®

AuthorHouse™ UK Ltd.
1663 Liberty Drive
Bloomington, IN 47403 USA
www.authorhouse.co.uk
Phone: 0800.197.4150

Published by AuthorHouse 09/22/2014

ISBN: 978-1-4969-9117-1 (sc)
ISBN: 978-1-4969-9118-8 (e)

Any people depicted in stock imagery provided by Thinkstock are models, and such images are being used for illustrative purposes only. Certain stock imagery © Thinkstock.

This book is printed on acid-free paper.

Because of the dynamic nature of the Internet, any web addresses or links contained in this book may have changed since publication and may no longer be valid. The views expressed in this work are solely those of the author and do not necessarily reflect the views of the publisher, and the publisher hereby disclaims any responsibility for them.

Image Credit: Samuel Adum Ahenkorah

FOR
Dawn, Zak and Evie
Love
DAviD

"Sanctified imagination"
JH 28/11/04

Contents

I

'The phone's ringing,' Anna shouted as she raced Jamie to answer it. 'I'll get it' she shouted and she got there first.

"Hello, Anna Fisher here" she said in her posh voice. "Hello, Dad Fisher here"

"Hi dad where are you"? Anna asked.

"Just finished my meeting so I should be home about 10.00 p.m. Is Mum there?"

"She's coming now Dad. See you later", she said as she passed the phone to Mum.

"Hi love are you o.k.?" Rachel asked.

"Not too bad", replied Peter

"considering the day that I've had. Are the terrible twins Ok?"

"The same as usual fighting over nothing. Will you be late?" she asked dreading the answer.

"Afraid so. The meeting overran and this awful rain will slow me down. Should see you just after 10.00 pm".

"Ok. Drive safe and I will have some supper ready".

Peter hung up and concentrated on getting home as soon as possible.

"Right you two up stairs, showers and bed" shouted Mum.

'But mum" Jamie tried. 'No buts' came the reply faster than the speed of sound from a mother in no mood for games. Showers over so Jamie and Anna tried the watching TV quietly trick but they were no match for a Mum's radar.

"Off now you two and get some sleep", was the last thing they heard as mum switched off the landing light, waited for their TV to go off and then went down stairs.

It was a truly awful night. The middle of May it may have been but it was dark, windy and raining for Noah. Mum hoped Michael Fish wasn't doing the weather forecast as "he who sow's the poor forecast reaps the whirlwind". Just ask 'Seven Oaks' or 'One Oak' as it's now known.

Rachel busied herself with ironing and then had a shower and thought about some supper. As she passed the phone in the Kitchen it rang. At the other end, sounding as wet as he must have been, was Peter.

"Sorry love. I've got a flat tyre and I'll have to wait for the rain to stop before I try and change it. Don't wait up this could take hours".

"Thanks for letting me know,' Rachel replied. 'Take care and see you soon'

Nothing for it now, so Rachel got herself a milky coffee, that box of chocolates she kept for emergencies and away to bed to watch some late night TV.

The wind and rain weren't letting up but thankfully Rachel can usually sleep through anything when Peter's home. Not tonight. It wasn't long past midnight when she heard a muffled noise down stairs. She stirred, thought about it and decided it was the weather but not when she heard another noise. Now she knew something wasn't right. Rachel grabbed her dressing gown and checked Jamie and Anna before gingerly going down stairs. She had left the front porch light on for Peter but now it was off. That wasn't good and Rachel's first thought was to get back upstairs to the children. Before she could turn to go the Kitchen door opened. With the light on in there and no hall light on Rachel could only see a silhouette of a man. Rachel held her breath as the man ran towards her. As he did she fell back put her foot in his stomach and threw him right across the hall. He flew like a bag of potatoes and mashed the glazed doors as he crashed through them into the Lounge. The noise instantly woke the twins and Anna went into Jamie's room. 'What's all the noise?" she asked.

'I don't know,' replied Jamie. 'Let's check it out.' They got to the top of the stairs and looked down. Rachel heard them, looked up and shouted, "Get to your rooms now and stay there!" As she finished the dazed man had got back to his feet and pulled out a 6 inch dagger and lunged at Rachel. The kids screamed and ran to Jamie's room. Rachel saw the blade of the knife glint in the light of the kitchen. She grabbed the man's arm as he reached her, spun him around and twisted it up his back. She heard the crack as his arm broke and the knife fell to the tiled floor. Rachel bent down to pick up the knife but as she did the man came at her again not seeming to feel the pain of his broken arm that now hung limply down at his side. He kicked Rachel square in the side of the face and knocked her reeling over towards the display cabinet. Rachel felt the blow and saw stars as she fell. She shook her head to try and shake out the daze but saw the mad man coming for her again. This time the knife was in his left hand with his eyes dead, seeming to stare right passed Rachel as he lunged at her.

"You haven't beaten me yet sunshine!", Rachel shouted as she kicked the knife out of his hand, gave him a second kick to the stomach, finishing off with a round house kick to the side of his head that knocked him to the floor. Rachel staggered out to the hall and saw the twins had come back to the top of the stairs. Jamie shouted, "I'm coming down to help Mum."

"No!" she shouted. "I'm ok! I've knocked him out now and I'll call the police." As she said "police", a dark figure came out of the front porch and threw a punch at Rachel. It wasn't a punch. Jamie, Anna and Rachel all saw the flash of the knife as it came down and imbedded itself in Mum's left shoulder. Rachel felt the pain. So did Jamie and Anna. They all screamed as Rachel fell to the floor. The dark figure now looked up at the twins and hissed in a voice that could curdle milk.

"Now I'm coming for you two." Slowly he moved up the stairs.

Rachel shouted "You've come for me not them. Please God leave them alone!"

As she shouted, the other attacker appeared back at the kitchen door and growled "We've come for you all". The man on the stairs stopped and looked down at Rachel. Kitchen man moved towards her with his dagger raised to strike her again.

Jamie and Anna couldn't move for fear. Stair man looked at them and smiled. Rachel crawled to the telephone table in the Hall. It all happened in the twinkling of an eye. Kitchen man threw himself at her. Rachel grabbed for something from the hall table and shouted what Jamie thought was "Be sure you're not faking!"

Suddenly there was a blinding flash of light as Kitchen man fell lifeless to the floor. Rachel moaned and the children heard the clang of something hit the tiled floor. Rachel now lay lifeless at the bottom of the stairs.

The man on the stairs looked again at the twins. "You first and then I'll do for your mother".

He snarled, pulled back his long, black coat and pulled out a 3ft sword and waved it at the terrified two. Jamie grabbed Anna and they ran into their Jack and Jill Bathroom. As they closed and bolted both doors they could hear their mother scream, 'No! No! No! Please God no!!!

Jamie hugged his sister and whispered, "He'll have to get me before I let him get to you". Anna hugged him harder and knew that he loved her as much as she loved him.

Bang! Bang! The mad man rammed the door and ranted "I'll get you, no door will stop me". Jamie knew he was right but didn't tell Anna. They could hear mum screaming "No! No!" and Anna screamed for her mum.

'Not long now until home sweet home Peter thought to himself as he turned off the main road onto the lane that would take him there. The time was approaching midnight but at least the persistent rain had stopped. As he came around the last corner where he could just see the house, something laid across the road was caught in his headlights. Peter did the first emergency stop he'd done since passing his driving test and brought the car to a halt just in front of the obstruction.

Peter got out of the car to see what he had nearly hit. It was a large tree trunk lying right across the lane which no vehicle could get passed. As Peter pondered how to shift the trunk or how far back he would have to reverse to get home another way, he was sure he heard something. He waited a moment and listened intently. This time his ears caught the unmistakable squelch of shoe leather on rain soaked tarmac. As his brain was still processing what he was hearing Peter sensed movement right behind where he was stood. Instinctively Peter fell flat onto the ground and as he did a large axe went sailing passed him and lodged itself in the bonnet of the car. Peter assessed where the attacker was standing and spun around on his hands and swept his legs from under him. The attacker fell and was left sprawled on his back. Peter jumped to his feet and grabbed the axe out of his bonnet.

'Ok twinkle, what's this all about,' Peter asked as he stood over the quivering attacker patting the axe head on his left hand.

'I'll tell you what it's all about Mr. Fisher,' came the reply from a six foot man dressed all in black and carrying a pistol.

'Me and my colleague here have been sent to delay you from getting home whilst others take care of your family.' The words cut into Peter deeper than any axe could. He spun around to look at his home and saw it was in complete darkness. He turned to look back at his attackers and warned, 'If anyone harms any of my family I will bring Armageddon down on your heads.'

'Now, now Mr. Fisher let's not be so dramatic and let's not forget whose got the gun. Come over here you idiot,' the gunman snarled to his still dazed ally.

'Let's see if you can do something right tonight. Set the charge on the car. The axe man pulled a matchbox sized gadget from his jacket and flicked a switch. He then placed the magnetic side of the gadget just by the petrol tank.

'Right, so a tired business man comes home, doesn't see the fallen tree in the lane and skids on the slippery road. 'Boom!' Up goes his nice fleet car in a ball of flames and no one is the wiser.' With that the man pulled the trigger and let off a deadly hale of bullets right at Peter. Peter used the axe head to ricochet the bullets away from himself and as he did so he bounded at the two astounded would- be assassins. He simultaneously punched both in their stomachs and as they doubled over he brought the axe down on their heads. The handle of the axe knocked them both out.

Peter grabbed the two unconscious killers and in turn dragged them over to a drainage ditch in the side of the road. He stood over the lifeless bodies and warned them, 'If one hair of my kids or wife is harmed I will find you and next time I'll use the other end of this axe.' As he finished his sentence he threw the axe down by the side of the sleeping uglies turned and ran down the road to get home to save his family. As he leapt the fallen tree in the road his car exploded into a bonfire night spectacular. Peter couldn't care less about his wheels. His mind was now focused on saving his family.

As the clock in the downstairs hall struck midnight, so the mad man struck the Bathroom door with his sword. Then all those in the house heard the explosion of Peter's car but none except the madman knew what it was. He came to the bathroom door and told the frightened children, 'Bang goes your Daddy. Now it's your turn.'

He struck the door again and the door frame gave way with splinters going everywhere. The twins looked not into the fire red eyes they had expected but ice cold blue eyes.

"Now you're dead," the blue eyed monster snarled and raised his sword over his head. "I do this for you my prince and give my eternity gladly for him!" Jamie pushed Anna under his arm and put his head over hers in a brave but vain attempt to protect her. They closed their eyes prayed to Jesus and waited for the pain.

It didn't come. The man screamed "Aagh" and then silence. The next thing the twins heard was their father's voice. They opened their eyes and saw their dad with one arm around the neck of their would-be killer and the other holding the three foot sword against his heart.

Calmly but with sincerity, they heard their father ask the man, 'Give me one good reason why I shouldn't break your neck and skewer you like a piece of meat on a barbecue?' Peter looked down at his children and then saw two good reasons why he couldn't punish the murderer now but would leave him to a higher power in days to come. Peter relaxed his grip around the man's neck but kept the sword over his chest so he wouldn't try anything. He didn't try anything but he did say something, which actually turned out to be worse.

'You don't scare me Fisher. I knew a wuss like you wouldn't kill a man in cold blood.' The recognition of the man's voice hit Peter harder than a left upper cut.

'Garth!' he shouted! His own surprise got the better of him and Garth took his chance. He punched Peter's hand that was gripping like a vice around his neck. The ring Garth wore on his left hand sliced the skin on Peter's hand. The cutting of his skin and the shock of recognizing Garth was enough for Peter to loosen his grip and allow his enemy to escape. Garth ran away through Jamie's bedroom, passed Rachel who was lying on top of the stairs, downstairs out of the house and into the night.

Peter got his composure back and rushed to hug his kids.

'Are you guys ok,' he asked with tears in his eyes and in his voice.

'We're fine dad, but what about mum?' Jamie asked? Peter had passed her at the top of the landing but with all the strength Rachel could muster she had said just two words.…."the children." With that Peter had rushed to their bathroom and the rest is now history.

They all ran and found Mum just at the top of the stairs with tears streaming down her face and blood streaming down her back. She saw the twins and said "Thank God". She sobbed as she hugged her babies and passed out.

Peter grabbed Rachel. "Jamie, listen to me and do exactly what I say. Get your mobile phone and text gen56 to the number 156".

"That won't work Dad. It's not a proper number".

"Jamie! Trust me and do it". Jamie looked at his Mum and did what his Dad asked. "Anna are you ok", Dad asked "Yes Dad". He gave her a kiss and sent her for a tea towel to put on Rachel's wound. Outside he may have appeared calm but inside Peter was hurting and hurting bad. Jamie grabbed his mobile, typed in gen56 and sent it to 156. The display read, "message sent". "It worked Dad" he said, as he walked back to his parents, "Thanks son. Now help me get your mum over onto our bed".

They carefully lifted Rachel and put her on the bed. Anna followed. Peter pushed the tea towel onto Rachel's wound. The twins could see the pain in their father's eyes and both began to cry. One, two, three minutes passed. Eternity came and went or so it seemed. As the minutes went Peters heart seemed to disappear with them. Suddenly they all heard, "Anyone there?"

Up here", dad shouted, "Quick!" They heard the sound of running up the stairs and then came in a man in a dark grey boiler- type suit carrying two bags.

"Ok! folks time for me to take control. Are you ok Peter?", he asked looking at the cut on his hand.

"Yes. It's Rachel who's been hurt bad'. She's been stabbed. Please help her."

Peter's voice trembled as he gently laid Rachel down on the bed and got out of the way. He could see the worried look in the children's eyes and then said reassuringly, "Don't worry Luke is a doctor and one of the best"

"I sure am kids", Luke said in a slightly scouse accent that they'd heard before during the summer months when Liverpool moves to the seaside.

"Are you two ok?' he asked.

"Yes", they replied, "we're just scared and worried for mum", Peter came over and hugged them both and never wanted to let them go.

"Don't worry you three your mums going to be fine. The wound is nasty and she's lost a lot of blood but I'm sure we can sort her out. Peter you know what to do." Luke then concentrated on Rachel.

"Sure", he replied. "You two stay here with Luke and your Mum. I'll just go and sort the mess". With that Peter went downstairs. Jamie wasn't sure what his dad did next but it involved the phone and some calls. He heard, "That's right. Two up the lane need picking up, one taken at the house and the mess sorting". Peter came back just as Rachel came round and he thought if he smiled any more he would split his head wide open.

"I've made sure Rachel's stable, but she'll need to go to Hospital for a couple of days. Is that possible Peter?" Luke asked.

"Whatever it takes doc. We'll be sound as long as Mums fine".

Within a quarter of an hour the house was full of people who Anna assumed were police and ambulance men although their uniforms were not what they usually were.

She noticed the badge on the uniform but it wasn't one that she recognized or had seen before on 'The Bill'. The lifeless body of kitchen man was taken away, the mess was cleaned up and Mum was put in an 'ambulance' although Anna was disappointed there were no blues and twos going.

For three Days dad did his best but fish and chips gets a bit boring third time round.

No one really wanted to talk about what had happened as they all seemed to agree it was better to wait until mum came home. By Saturday mum was home and considering what she had been through she was fighting fit. The twins thought, "Great. Now our lives can return to normal".

II

The next day Anna, who always wakes up before Jamie, heard dad go out for a run. Nothing unusual in that as dad liked to keep himself fit and always encouraged her and Jamie to do the same. That's why Anna did her riding with her mum and sometimes her Nanas, while Jamie was goalkeeper in a local football team. How they found time to do that and play their musical instrument, God only knows.......well actually, He does.

Anna couldn't get back to sleep now even though it was only 6:30 am so she decided to pop downstairs to have a read. She was sitting in the lounge reading her latest 'pony' book, waiting for dad to come home so they could have breakfast together when she heard dad's mobile 'beep'.

"Funny," thought Anna. "Who would be texting dad at this time of day and why is his phone on anyway?"

Being a cat lover Anna's curiosity got the better of her so she found the mobile but its keypad was locked. No problem, because Anna knew dad's password which was "drum". You could count on Dad's password being "drum" because that's what it always was. Not very secure but at least he never forgot what it was. Dad had chosen it because he liked to play the drums nearly as much as Jamie now did. Although Nana and Pops, Anna's paternal grandparents, were never that fussed when dad played them as a young drummer living at home, especially when he dented the teapot lid as he practiced.

Anna typed in "drum" and sure enough it beat the lock. She scrolled down to 'read message' and pushed the button. What Anna saw meant nothing to her as there were no words just three shapes. Then she remembered the badges she had seen days before on the 'police' and 'ambulance' men that had come to the house the night of the attack. Anna tried to find out the number that had sent the message but all she could ever get was 'sender unknown'. She put dad's phone back and returned to her book.

About three quarters of an hour later dad returned home. After his shower he and Anna enjoyed breakfast together whilst Jamie gave it serious 'zzzzz's' and mum got ready for Church.

When they finally got the bed off Jamie's back they went to Church and got back in time to see the start of the Grand Prix. After lunch, mum and dad relaxed in the lounge with the twins upstairs listening to some music in Jamie's room.

"You know those men who came last Tuesday and attacked us?' said Anna.

'Don't think I'll forget that Tuesday in a hurry,' remarked Jamie. 'For one thing it meant I handed my maths homework in late and Mrs Edwards was not chuffed. And believe me, Mrs. Edwards not being chuffed is not a pretty sight,' Jamie joked.

'Fair enough, but did you notice the badges on the blue light guys who came after the nutters?' asked Anna.

'Can't say that I did with so much going on,' replied Jamie.

'Well I did and they had a logo that I had not seen before but I've seen it again today.' Anna then proceeded to tell Jamie what had happened earlier that morning when he had been sleeping for Wales.

'The logo looked like this.' Anna took a piece of paper and with a pencil sketched out what she had seen as best as she could remember it.

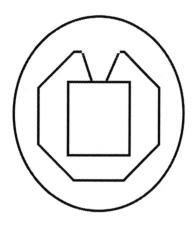

'Not sure what it all means myself,' Jamie said when Anna had finished. 'Why not ask dad about it. I'm sure he won't lie to you,' was all Jamie could suggest.

'Sounds like a plan,' said Anna. 'Let's do it.' They both got up and headed downstairs to see the olds. Halfway down they heard them talking in the lounge.

'Something's not right,' said dad. 'The kids are not twelve yet so why were they attacked? Having a go at us I can just about understand but not them.'

'I know you're right, because I've been wondering about the same thing. Hopefully when we meet Joel and Nathaniel tonight they'll give us some answers,' replied Rachel.

'Who are Joel and Nathaniel,' whispered Anna?

'Beats me,' was Jamie's whispered reply.

Just then mum came through the door and offered hot chocolates all round. No repeating of that question needed. Five minutes later all four are sat in the lounge watching 'Raiders of The Lost Ark' for the sixth time. For some reason mum and dad always seem to find this film particularly funny. Maybe one day Jamie and Anna would find out why.

Over tea dad told the twins, 'Mum and I are going out tonight for a walk so Nana and Pops are coming round to look after you, ok.' No problem there because the children always enjoyed their grandparent's company and to quote Jamie, 'Pops is a legend.' Jamie always had a laugh when he played golf with his dad and granddad and particularly as pops always took the mickey out of dad's swing. 'You know Peter,' Pops would say, 'Your problem is that you stand too close to the ball.........
after you've hit it!' While the lads were golfing, Anna, Nana and mum would go riding.

It was after 8 o'clock when the grandparents arrived and the twins were showered and ready for bed as it was school the next day.

'Ok you two,' Pops said in his usual jovial manner and they both gave him a hug at the same time. He was big enough so you could do that. After giving Nana a kiss they all sat down in the lounge and chatted over tea, coffee and hot chocolate. After half an hour the kids went upstairs to read before going to sleep. But too much was going on, so they sat in Anna's room chispering.

'So who are these friends and what's this logo all about?' Anna asking the question more to herself than Jamie.

'I still don't know but perhaps there's a way we can find out,' Jamie answered with a glint in his eye Anna hadn't seen since he put tomatoes in dad's wellies because he'd moaned he could never find tomato sauce when he had lunch out on site.

'What we'll do is follow mum and dad when they go for their walk and find out where they go and who they meet.'

'Are you serious?' asked Anna. 'If dad found out he'd ground us until we get married and then he'd get really uptight. And what mum would do doesn't even bear thinking about.'

'What else can we do? There's obviously something going on that involves us and we need to know what it is. This way we can get some answers and hopefully be some help to mum and dad in sorting this out.

Anna was not convinced but she could see Jamie was going to go anyway and she didn't want him going on his own. Jamie explained the plan. Go to bed but keep some clothes on. Put the lights out and let the 'olds' think they're settled for the night. Listen out for mum and dad leaving, sneak out through the landing door and onto dad's favourite place in the whole house.........his beloved balcony. Not only was it a great potential fire escape, but it was a great place to sit with a drink and watch the sunset. Once on the balcony they can slide down its legs and onto the patio below. From there, they can slip around the side of the house and follow their parents to wherever. Not a bad idea but was it a good idea?

Some twenty minutes later they heard Nana say,' Be careful you two and don't worry. The twins are safe here with me and your father.'

'Any action from the bad guys and they'll be dealing with an angry granddad which is a worse sight than any angry maths teacher.' Pops had obviously had the word from Jamie about Mrs. Edwards.

The door closed and Anna watched mum and dad disappear down the drive. Just as they reached the crest of the drive before it sloped down to the road Anna snook into Jamie's room through their shared bathroom whose doors had now been replaced.

'They're just at the end of the drive.'

'Ok, let's go.' Jamie jumped out of bed and both he and Anna gingerly made their way onto the landing. They got to the rear door unlocked it and slipped through onto the balcony. Dad loved his balcony with its uninterrupted view out to sea although his view had recently been disturbed by the erecting of off shore wind turbines which Dad called 'a barbed wire fence in his field of vision.' Jamie locked the door behind them and put the key in his pocket ready for their return. Without talking they both slowly slid over the balcony rail grasped the supports with both legs and slowly lowered themselves down. Jamie hit the patio first and put on his torch to light Anna's way down. He put his finger to his lips and then pointed to the side wall. He didn't want to risk opening the gate and letting a 'creak' undo all their good work. Anna understood the signals and got over the wall first. They got to the front of the house and tiptoed across where the cars were parked and then down the driveway. As they got to the road they looked both ways, like they're supposed to, and saw their parents walking down the lane not up.

Whispering, Jamie said as he gave the torch to his sister, 'Keep it shining down so we're not spotted and keep tight to the hedgerow and we'll see where mum and dad go'. They followed mum and dad down the lane and passed the other houses that lived in their hamlet.

'I can't think who they are going to see,' said Anna. 'I thought they might call at Jerry and Mary's but that's up the lane. Do you........'

'Shhhhh....' Jamie cut Anna off in her stride. 'They're going off the lane and onto the old railway track.' The twins followed them onto what used to be a railway line for mineral trains that came from a nearby quarry to iron works down the coast. But this line hadn't heard the clang of wheels on rails for thirty years or more. Having been left derelict for decades it was now a walkway come cycleway come bridleway that led between local villages.

'Dad and me come cycling along here now and again,' Anna quietly said to her brother.

'I bet you don't come at this time of night,' was his quick but quiet reply. 'Any idea where they might be going?' Jamie quietly quizzed his sister.

'The walkway eventually gets to Melden and from there, mum and dad could go anywhere,' Anna whispered back.

'Nothing more to do but follow and see what happens,' Jamie said as he led his sister on. As they walked the breeze touched the trees and made them whisper just like the children. The shadows danced and the lights of Melden went on and off as the tree branches waltzed. At one point the children stopped dead in their tracks thinking they heard someone coming behind them. They waited for a minute and decided it was just the trees and their imaginations. They carried on for a few more minutes just keeping their parents in view. Suddenly Jamie whispered 'Stop'. They both froze as mum and dad said something and then turned off the walkway and up the hillside.

Jamie and Anna looked at each other but thought,' We've started so we'll finish.' Without uttering their thoughts they too left the walkway and started up the hillside. Not far from the edge of the walkway were trees and it wasn't easy keeping mum and dad in sight. They managed to keep up until suddenly mum and dad disappeared.

As Anna caught up with Jamie he asked her, 'Any idea where they could have gone?'

'No,' came the reply all too quickly for Jamie. I've never been here before with dad so your guess is as good as mine.' As Anna finished they both heard a slight sound like a door banging just over to their left. Without a word they both followed the sound and came out of the tree line. There in front of them was a place they had never seen before. Even though they'd lived in the area all their lives they had not been to this place............St. Thomas' Church. There in front of them was a stone built church under its crowning slate roof. Not the biggest church they'd ever seen but no chapel either. They knew it was called St. Thomas' because they walked through its' lych gate past the place where many a Vicar had met the Family and coffin and where there was the nameplate. The other thing Anna noticed was the symbol below the name which was a spear with a set square going across it. What that meant she didn't know but she knew that this symbol, like the other one she had seen recently, meant something and she was determined to find out what. She and Jamie tiptoed down the path through the graveyard and passed the gravestones that all stood at permanent attention. They came to the big oak door that led inside and stopped by the stoup.

'Do you think mum and dad are in here?' asked Anna.

'Only one way to find out,' Jamie said as he grabbed the large iron ring handle and turned it. They heard the latch inside lift and then slowly pushed the door open. They did it slowly not only to keep the creaks down but also because it was a heavy great door. When the door was ajar, they slipped inside and slowly closed it behind them. Then they stood in the silence that thousands of people had heard over hundreds of years. There on top of the steps leading down into the body of this holy house they stood and took in the sights but no sound. The moonlight was streaming through the stained glass window at the chancel end of the church spreading the coloured lights of the image down into the nave. The colours shimmered as a tree behind the window swayed in the breeze. As the twins looked at these living colours they seemed to beckon them down the aisle to where they were rippled like a pool of rainbow water on the floor.

'Let's see if we can see where the folks are,' Jamie said to his sister. 'You go that side,' pointing to the right,' and I'll go along here.' They both moved down the steps into the church and went off to search. For five minutes they each looked up and down the sides of that place but could find nobody. They met up at the front of the aisle just before the choir stalls.

'Perhaps mum and dad aren't here,' Jamie wondered.

'Well I think they are,' replied Anna. This place has such a tranquil atmosphere and it feels comfortable to me that we're here. Mum and dad are here somewhere, I just know it.'

'But where?' asked her brother. 'There's only so many places to hide in here and I can't see where they might be.'

Anna agreed with him but she didn't want to give up yet. She looked around again and her eye caught the raised pulpit where many a preacher had ascended to try and get his congregation to come with him nearer to God. As she set off she told Jamie, 'I'll go up there with the torch and perhaps from there I can get a clue of where they might be.'

'Ok Anna but this is the last try. No joy this time and we better head for home.'

'Fair enough,' and with that she headed up the eight steps to the top of the pulpit. When she got to the top she took the torch and shone it all around the church. The effect was like a lighthouse sending out its saving light in a dark world, just as a church should be.

'Come on Anna, you're wasting time. There's nothing to see. Mum and dad can't be here. We better get going otherwise they will beat us home and then dads' nigglyness will know no bounds.

'Ok,ok just a minute,' Anna starting to show her nigglyness. She swung the torch a couple of more times and then noticed something. The font at the rear of the church, right by the steps where they had come in. From her high vantage point she could look down onto the font and she noticed its shape. It was set on a circular dais with the font itself being octagonal and the hollowed out area for the water being square.

'That's got to be it,' she said to herself and started to run down the pulpit steps. 'Jamie come with me, quick.'

'What's the matter?' Jamie asked as he got into his stride.

'Just come with me,' and Anna led him back up the steps towards the entrance door. 'Look,' she said as she pointed the torch over the side of the steps illuminating the font below.'

'It's a font Anna, so what?'

Look at its shape.' Anna pointed the torch to the circular dais, 'That's a circle, the font's an octagon and the bit in the middle's a square.'

For a moment Jamie's fog wouldn't lift and then the whirlwind struck and blew it away. 'That's the shape of the logo you saw on those guys uniforms and dads phone,' he excitedly said to his sister.

'Give the boy a choccy. Come on there's got to be something around the font that will give us a clue about mum and dad's whereabouts.' The pair headed down the steps and started looking around the font.

'Bring the torch here Anna,' asked Jamie. 'What do you make of that,' he said as he pointed to a stone on the wall beneath the entrance steps. There engraved on this one stone was that logo again. 'Here goes' and Jamie pushed the stone not sure what was going to happen. But happen it did. The stone moved inwards and so did many others to create a doorway.

'This is it,' Jamie excitedly whispering to his sister. He slowly crept into the doorway and could hear voices. He strained his lugholes and could just make out his dad's voice amongst those that were talking. He motioned to Anna to come into the doorway and listen

'You're right, it is dad's voice. Let's go.' They walked down a dark, narrow passageway and followed the increasing volume of voices and then round a corner to the light. As they reached the end of the passageway there was a door that was slightly open and now they could hear both dad and mum's voices. Jamie put his finger to his lip and motioned he was going to go nearer to the door to hear what was going on. As he did so he heard four voices two of which he didn't recognise. He waved Anna to come closer but as she did she caught the torch on the stone wall of the passage and dropped it. Jamie could see it fall in slow motion but could do nothing about it. He knew when the torch hit the floor, the smelly stuff would hit the fan. His parents were bound to hear it come and look and catch them red handed. Before the full consequences of the situation hit home the torch hit the floor. Before you could say 'Deary me' dad was through the door and stood over his children not believing what he was seeing. After a moment to collect his thoughts, Peter asked the obvious question, 'What on earth are you two doing here?'

Not wanting to wind dad up with no answer nor the wrong answer, the twins took a moment to think. Then Jamie dived in. 'We knew something was going on and involved us and we just wanted to find out more.' By this time Rachel had joined the party and gave Anna a hug. She spoke to Peter, 'Come on love, it does concern them and maybe we should have told them a little of what's going on to avoid their imaginations taking over.'

'I suppose you've got a point but they shouldn't be out on their own. Not only with all that's going on but in any case and what about mum and pops? If they find the kids gone with all that's been going on they are going to get in a right state.'

'I wouldn't worry about that if I was you son,' came the reply out of the darkness in a voice that they all knew. Pops came into the light followed by nana.

'What are you doing here dad?' asked Peter.

18

'Looking out for my grandchildren as I told you I would. Mum and I might have retired but we're still on the jazz. There we were watching the news when we noticed two shadows sneaking down the drive. Your mum was up the stairs like a gazelle to check on these two and of course she found them gone. We realised they were following you so we followed them close enough to keep an eye on them and get to them if needs be. A couple of times I thought they had spotted us but they just carried on. As soon as they got hold of the church's door handle we knew they would be safe. Then we left them to it by watching through the side window by the door. When they found the passage and went inside we followed.'

'Don't be hard on them Peter,' said his mother. 'They are just showing the same instincts you had that drove us mad. You know children, I remember when your dad...........'

'Ok mum, no need for anecdote of the day just now. Thanks for taking care of them. As for you two I think you better apologise to your grandparents and say thanks.' No problem there. Jamie hugged his granddad whilst Anna did the same with her nana. Other than from your parents there's nothing feels safer than a hug from your grandparents.

'Come inside you two and meet our friends that you were so keen to discover.' Mum took the twins into the room at the end of the passage where it was warm and light. The room was round with candle lights on the stone walls and on the table in the centre. There was a roaring fire to the right of the door and sat in front of it in two comfy armchairs were two old and soon to be new friends.

Rachel took the twins over to the fire and as she did the two people stood up to greet them. 'Anna and Jamie can I introduce you to Joel and Nathaniel'.

III

'Pleased to meet you,' Nathaniel said as he held his hand out to Jamie and then Anna. Joel did likewise.

'Why don't you two sit over here by the fire,' Joel said as he offered the chairs by the fire.

'Don't mind if we do,' replied Jamie thinking that acting casual might take some of the sting out of the situation and besides getting warm by the fire is always a good option. The twins sat by the fire and watched as Nana and Pops both greeted Joel and Nathaniel. It was quite obvious that their grandparents and these two new friends to the twins were old friends. Not just handshakes but hugs accompanied the 'Hellos'.

'Good to see you. You don't look a day older than went we last met,' said Nana to Joel who replied, 'That's because I'm not a day older since we last met. They both laughed but the joke was lost on both Jamie and Anna....... for now anyway. The adults all found somewhere to sit with Peter and Rachel using the table.

'Right, do you think we had better get back to business?' asked Peter.

'To be honest son, now that the children have met Joel and Nathaniel don't you think we better explain about the Enochim to put the events of recent days into context?' suggested Pops.

'I agree with Ted,' said Joel. 'Seeing as the twins are soon to be twelve, would be told anyway seeing as we are in St. Thomas' Church, what better time and place to tell them about their family history.'

'Fair enough,' agreed Peter, 'if you're ok with this Rachel?'

'I see no reason to delay any longer. Perhaps you'll do the honours Joel?'

'As always, it will be an honour. Are you two sitting comfortably,' he asked as he looked over at the twins, who nodded somewhat nervously. 'Then I'll begin.'

Joel shuffled his chair around so he could look more clearly at the children as he spoke and then he began.

'I'm sure you two have heard about angels at Church,' he asked.

The twins nodded and Anna added,' I actually played one once in a nativity play.'

'I hope you did a good job,' said Joel, 'otherwise me and my friends might get offended.'

'Why's that,' asked Jamie?

'Well, you've read the book, heard the stories and played the part and now you've met the real thing.'

'You're kidding me. You don't mean you're an angel?' exclaimed Anna.

'That's exactly what I mean.'

'But I thought angels were little chubby toddlers with wings, harps and halos.'

'Yes, we've had some bad press that's led to somewhat of a stylised and corny idea of what we're about. In one way it helps to give us a low profile but overall it's a bit of a pain because it obscures the real work we're trying to do. Because people have got this twee idea of what we are about they overlook the real evil that exists and which we are trying to combat. If humans think we're flying toddlers doing no more than singing and scattering flower petals they'll not be watching out for the evil ones who are out to destroy them, but that's for another time.

"Is this appearance of you now as you really are then," asked Anna.

"No," replied Nathaniel. "We take this human form so you can relate to us and if necessary we can fit in unnoticed in your dimension just as the writer to the Hebrews said. But now let's get back to basics. Nathaniel and I are Angels created by The I Am to do his bidding. We were created before your time and dimension existed to do what and go where The I Am commands.

'So you're eternal?' said Anna.

'Yes, in a sense we are but you have to remember keeping time is of your existence, not ours. We are outside your time and dimension so the word 'eternal' has no meaning for us. We exist for as long as The I Am decrees.'

'But you do act in our dimension, don't you,' asked Jamie?

'We certainly do,' replied Joel. 'As The I Am commands so we act and we have done so in your dimension since the very beginning.'

'When you write your biography can I have a copy?' asked Anna, 'because I bet you can tell some stories.'

'We certainly can,' Nathaniel said as he joined the conversation. 'And there's one story we want to tell you now to try and explain how you two fit into all that's been going on. Before your time began but after we angels had been created one of our number decided he was as good, if not better than The I Am. To this day no one but The I Am knows where his distorted belief came from and how these dark thoughts entered one who had been full of light. Sure, he was called Morning Star, he was in attendance to The I Am and was the highest in our angelic order, but he was still a created being who owed his very existence to the creator. However, pride blinded him by his own wisdom and self worth and he altered the centre of his being away from The I Am and onto himself as he had the free will to do so. This putting himself in the centre led him into sin. There is a reason why the word 'I' is the centre of the word 'sin' because that's what it is, putting yourself as the centre of things and not The I Am and His ways. The prince, as he is now known, persuaded others to believe in him and to want the things he wanted. Many followed after him until a third of all angels fell into the Princedom of Darkness. Such rebellion had to be confronted and so war broke out in Heaven.

'Those were dark days,' said Joel as he took up the story. Those gathered in that room could almost see the hurt in his eyes as he spoke.

'Angels who had been friends since their creation were now called upon to fight each other something that was against their very nature. However, because of the nature of our creation, which is different to yours, no angels at that time could be killed. Indeed, until time is no more and the judgement is executed these fallen angels will still live and cause distress and torment in our world and yours. But a lake of fire has been prepared for the prince and his hordes where they will be inevitably sent and punished forever. The war could not be concluded and so the prince and the other fallen angels were thrown out of Heaven. This caused the then created earth to be desolate and void and meant it had to be recreated by The I Am. Once your world was recreated the prince was banished to his own dimension known as 'The Air' where he now resides. Forget the storybook images of him in a fiery hell. He's not there yet. He will be but for now he's free to cause havoc.'

'So he can enter our dimension and cause havoc?' said Anna.

'He certainly can and does. Both directly by his own evil works and indirectly by inspiring sinful people to commit acts of evil or by deflecting them from The I Am, he certainly causes havoc in your dimension. Havoc such as what happened to you two last Tuesday.'

Jamie responded hoping he might be wrong. 'You mean those men who attacked us were inspired by the prince.'

'I mean exactly that,' replied Joel. 'Those who came after you were part of the princedom.'

'But why us and not others?' asked Anna.

'Now that is a very good question that I'll answer now,' Nathaniel said. 'But I won't just tell you the answer, I'll show it to you.' He pulled out a small crystal from his robes and said, 'This is what we call a 'tell you vision'. You see we had TV first.' He asked Peter and Ted to move the table over to the wall opposite the fire. Then the chairs were moved so the wall could be seen. Nathaniel placed the crystal on the table and waved his hand over it. As his hand moved away from the crystal a light shone from it and projected onto the stone wall. Then images surfaced from the light and became a crystal clear picture.

Nathaniel then took up the story and gave commentary over the pictures. 'Seven generations after the fall when the first humans had been led into sin by the prince, mankind was trying to find its way back to The Kingdom. Things were hard because of the judgement brought upon them by their sin and the constant temptation from the fallen.' As Nathaniel spoke The Fishers were looking at the pictures on the wall. They could see a village with quite a few houses where people and animals were wandering about.

Nathaniel continued. 'These people lived after Adam but before Noah. Some followed the ways of The Kingdom but most went another way.' Looking at the pictures, the twins saw some men come to the village, about 50 or so.

These men are actually what we call 'taken',' explained Nathaniel. 'By that we mean they are human beings who have left themselves so open to evil that they have been literally taken over by fallen angels. Because angels are of a different nature to humans there are things we can't do in your physical dimension without using the physical body of someone unless The I Am allows us to take a recognisable human form as He has done now so we can meet you. Anyhow, lets leave transfiguration mode for another time. Just know that we angels were not created to marry and have children. When our number was created it was finite. There was the exact number of angels to do the work of The Kingdom and as we could not die we didn't need to have children. Regardless of this these fallen angels looked upon the women of your world and wanted to marry them and have children. So when the chance came to take over some men they took it. So you see these 'men' entering the village and later on taking a wife. Soon they were having children but these were no ordinary children, they were Nephilim half human and half angel. Because of the mixing of the two different natures these children were different from other human children. They were faster, stronger, more skilled and knowledgeable than their human counterparts.'

The pictures showed these Nephilim children running, fighting and killing.

'These children grew up to become the myths, legends and supermen that you humans still speak of today.'

'Now hold on one minute,' interrupted Jamie. 'You're not about to tell me and Anna that we're descended from these Nephilim are you?' Joel didn't give the panic time to grow in the hearts and minds of these two young people.

'No,' he said with a voice that barely avoided shouting. 'Let me be clear on this. You and Anna, your parents and grandparents are <u>NOT</u> descended from the Nephilim.' The children could almost hear the underlining of the word 'not'. In fact, the Nephilim became such a part of the problem with mankind falling further away from the Kingdom that they were part of the reason The I Am destroyed all but eight living things.'

'You mean Noah's Flood don't you?' said Anna.

'Good to see you didn't fall asleep in that Sunday School lesson. Someone give the girl a gold star.' After all the heavy stuff up until now Joel's humour, however weak it may have been, was a welcome relief.

'So you see you are not descended from the Nephilim.'

As Joel spoke the tell you vision showed the horror of the deluge that wiped out mankind except the eight. Joel clapped his hands and the crystal went onto stand by without wasting any electricity.

'What happened to them,' asked Jamie? 'If they were neither fully angels or human, where did they go?'

'That is the first time I have ever been asked that when I've told this story. Not even your parents or grandparents asked me that when I told it to them. That really is an excellent question.'

'Not just a pretty face me you know,' replied Jamie with a spring in his voice.

'The truth is because they were part angel and part human they couldn't go into the princedom and they certainly couldn't go to Heaven. So they were sent into what we call The Abyss where they are supervised by one known as Abaddon. But because they are neither one thing nor the other the term demon was used to describe them. Not only that, because they thought they have been harshly treated they are the nastiest of all the fallen. They are really out to get mankind and when the prince calls on them and Abaddon releases them you can be sure they will do as much harm as possible.'

Nathaniel jumped back in at this point. 'I think we're in danger of information overload here. The point is you are not Nephilim but the fact that Nephilim could be created concerned The Council of Angels who co-ordinate our work. What they didn't want was a repeat of this episode so they decided they needed people in your dimension ready and able at any time to frustrate the work of the fallen. So they decided to select certain believers to be taken out of your dimension for a time, so they could be trained like angels and then sent back to fight against evil for The Kingdom. Those selected were to come from every nation, people, tribe and tongue that lived on the earth and they would be known as 'Enochim'. Before you ask me, 'Why Enochim?' I'll tell you. Enoch was a man who was removed from your dimension so he could be sent back at the end times to carry out a mission for The Kingdom. Therefore, he came to symbolise those who were taken by The Kingdom for a season and a reason. So those selected for this task became known as 'Enochim'. Nathaniel paused for a moment to let his words plant themselves in the minds of the twins. Then he confirmed to the children what they were already thinking.

'You Anna and Jamie are Enochim.'

'I know this is a lot to take in kids but we're all here to help you,' said Peter.

'Don't forget that me and your dad, not to mention your grandparents, have all been through this experience of finding something out about ourselves that we never knew or could even dream off,' continued Rachel.

'So you're all Enochim,' Jamie said to the two other generations of his family sat there with him in that room.

'Yes we all are,' answered his Nana.

'And Grandma Burnett, she is too?' asked Jamie.

'Yes she is,' confirmed Rachel, 'and so was your Granddad James.'

'This has been some week,' Jamie said as he let out his breath in amazement.' Seven days ago I was an eleven year old looking forward to reaching the dozen. Since then I've been attacked by nutters, met angels and now I've been told I'm descended from some ancient people of hand-picked warriors who fight evil angels for a living after being taken to another dimension and trained by angels. Can I sell this to Marvel comics and make some extra pocket money?,' he asked as always using his humour to hide his nervousness.

'I don't think even Stan Lee would believe this one,' joked Joel.

'So are we going to be taken away to your dimension and trained?' asked Anna not being to sure if she really wanted to know the answer to her question.

'Only if you want to be,' answered her dad. Peter continued, 'Me and your mum had this conversation with Nathaniel and Joel about twenty five years ago and your grandparents over fifty years ago. We all decided to answer the calling of The Enochim but we didn't have to and neither do you.'

Nathaniel took up the conversation. 'Only Enochim who are believers are called but not all respond to this calling and no blame is held against them. They decide to do other work for The Kingdom and that's fine. If the children we approach don't respond we leave them alone and make them think our meeting was just a dream and nothing more.'

'So we don't have to go if we don't want to?' said Jamie.

'No you don't,' Nathaniel assured him. 'It's your choice.

'Look, I'm sure you children have lots of questions but I think its best now if you all head home and sleep on what's happened. Then when you're ready I know your family will be only too happy to answer any questions you have.'

'I know you're right Joel, but there's one question you have to answer for me now because it's been bugging me for days,' said Anna.

'Depending on what the question is, I'll try to oblige.'

'Thanks Joel. Now can you please tell me what this logo I keep seeing is all about?' asked Anna with real feeling. 'It's been on peoples uniforms, texted to dad's phone and now I've found it in a church that was built in the thirteenth century. Please, put me out of my misery and tell me what it means.'

'I think we can do that Anna,' and taking a piece of paper Joel sat at the table.

'Come over here and let me explain this symbol to you.'

Joel beckoned over the children and the olds joined them as well. What you are talking about is 'The Enochima', the symbol for the 'Enochim'. Let me draw it out for you and explain it as I go along. First of all there's the square,' which Joel drew.

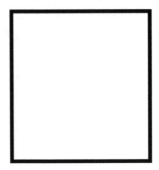

'The square symbolises the earth or temporal, physical things. On the fourth day the material creation was finished, there are four compass points, there are four seasons and four elements being earth, air, fire and water. So the four sided square symbolises your world or dimension. Next we have the eight sided octagon,' which Joel then drew around the square.

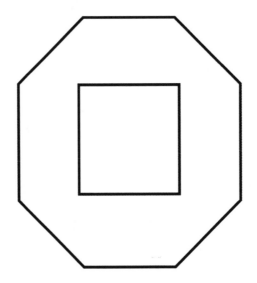

'The octagon is halfway between a square and a circle. As you know the square symbolizes earth or your dimension. An octagon is half way between a square and a circle and for our purposes symbolizes the second dimension or 'Kingdom of The Air' that the prince and his hordes inhabit. The circle symbolizes our third dimension,' and Joel completed The Enochima by drawing a circle around the octagon.

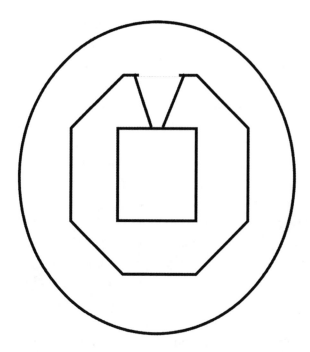

'Circles have since ancient days been thought of as the perfect shape because they have no beginning or end. So they came to symbolize spiritual and other things that are superior to the earthly dimension.'

'I get all that but what are those lines linking our dimension with yours?' asked Anna.

'You don't miss much do you,' said Joel. Those lines symbolize that you Enochim come to our dimension for a time by passing through the second dimension. That time in our dimension is what makes you Enochim different.'

'But how do we get to your dimension?,' Jamie asked.

'That is definitely a question for another day,' said Joel.

'It certainly is,' agreed Rachel. 'Enough now you two. It's way past your bedtime and you've got school tomorrow. Let's all head for home. Thank you Joel and Nathaniel,' she said as she took hold of Anna's hand.

'Say goodnight you two to your new friends,' requested dad. Nothing if not courteous was Peter.

'Good night' came the stereo reply and off they started for the door.

'I'll just have a quick word with the guys before they go. Meet you by the church door,' Peter said to Rachel and the others as they left.

Knowing that Peter's conversation was probably best not heard by the children, the olds nodded and were on their way.

Peter turned to the guys and asked, 'What was that fallen attack all about last Tuesday?'

'To be honest Peter, and as you know that's all we can be, we don't really know. As we all know, under twelve's are not to be considered as warriors until after their twelfth birthday and even then only if they take up the sword. The matter is being considered by The Angel Council and we'll let you know if we get anymore information unless you contact us first over the twins' decision.

'Thanks guys, I appreciate it.'

'And just so you know,' added Joel, 'extra Guardian Angels have been deployed to counter any extra activity from the second dimension.'

'That's good to know. See you soon.' Peter hugged his two friends and as he turned to go they disappeared. Peter met the family by the church door and off home they went.

Not much was spoken on the walk home about the night's happenings to give Anna and Jamie time to get their heads around it but worry wasn't only confined to the children. The parents and grandparents knew full well what could lie ahead for them and these little ones.

IV

The next day was school and for the next week everything was as normal as it could be when you know your parents talk to angels.

Dad said that at the weekend they would all go away to a friend's cottage up in the Lake district and get a chance to really talk through the situation. Come Friday evening the family all set off up north and took the dog with them. The dog was actually an old battered Landrover that for some reason mum and dad insisted on keeping and using for all the mucky jobs. As it turned out it was used for other jobs as well but they didn't find that out until a couple of weeks later. A couple of days before they left dad took the dog for what Jamie presumed was a service but it was back by Friday lunchtime to take them all up north.

They arrived at Mill Cottage at about half past nine and straight away enjoyed the Chinese meal they had picked up on the way. It was then off to bed for the twins whilst mum and dad sat chatting in the living room.

The next day was a trip out organised by dad to try and take the twins mind off things. Anna and mum went riding at the local stables whilst dad and Jamie played golf. In the afternoon they all met up and took a boat ride on Lake Windermere and then back to Mill Cottage for tea.

After tea and washing up the Fishers sat down in front of the open fire and chatted. Soon dad put into words what was already in people's thoughts........The Enochim.

"Listen you two, mum and I know you have had a lot to think about and we're sorry it's all happened like this. We had intended to speak to you about being Enochim soon because of you nearing your twelfth birthdays. Obviously our plans have been somewhat overtaken

31

by events. It's amazing what hassle being attacked in your own home can cause."

"The main thing," mum said as she took over, "is not to feel pressured but to make up your own minds about what you want to do."

"Anna and I have talked a little about it," said Jamie, "but haven't made any decisions as yet. Can you tell us what it's been like for you?" he asked.

"Sure,' replied dad. "You go first love," he said as he looked over to Rachel.

"It was different for me and your Aunty Ruth," began Rachel. "My dad, your Granddad James, died when we were ten years old. Because of that it was left to your Grandma Margaret to tell us about our heritage as Enochim. Grandma didn't wait until we were nearly twelve, she told us not long after dad died because him being Enochim was why he died so young and mum felt we had a right to know why our dad had been taken from us. She told us we were special and had a chance to use our talents in the service of good over evil like she and dad had. She told us the story Joel and Nathaniel told you and like me and your dad are going to let you, she let us make up our own minds on what we should do. As I thought about the centuries of Enochim fighting evil and all the good that did I felt privileged to join in. I think also, because my dad had died in the service of The Kingdom, I wanted in some way to carry on what he had begun. Ruth felt more strongly than me about it so we 'Took the Sword', went off to be trained and came back to fight. We have been on some adventures together and been scared many times but we have always come through. When I met dad I teamed up with him and Ruth went on to be a Guardian."

"A what?" asked Anna.

"A Guardian," answered mum, "but I'll tell you about that some other time. It's not important at the moment."

"Ok," agreed Anna. Going on, she asked, "Why did you do it mum? You could have been killed."

"You're right love and for now me and dad won't be doing it anymore so we can look after you two. Before you were born, I thought it was right for me to use my talents and opportunity to fight evil and help people."

Jamie interrupted. "What's Taking the Sword?"

"That's the phrase we use when people accept the work as Enochim," replied mum. "You take the sword at first and then rest when you have children. Then after your children are twelve you can decide to take the Sword again or do some other work for The Kingdom."

"So if we don't take the Sword you'll have to give up?" asked Anna.

"I won't have to but I will want to," said mum. "I can do other things that are just as important in The Kingdom and will enjoy them just as much."

Dad joined in. "We don't want you to join the Enochim or not, just to let us carry on or not. Even if you do or don't mum and I will still have to decide whether we take up the sword again but that's a decision for us in the future."

"What about you dad, how did you decide?" asked Jamie.

"To be honest, the decision was made for me. You know I have three brothers, one of which, your Uncle Jake is my twin. As you know, Uncles Matthew and Phillip are two years older than me and Jake so they told us all about it after they were trained when nana and pops had taken us to see Joel and Nathaniel. It sounded great so Jake had no hesitations in taking the sword so I thought I better go along. To be fair though, after meeting the angels in The Third Dimension and particularly Teacher Eli, I've never regretted it once. Then meeting your mum was the final up side. I know what it's like having to live up to what you've been born to because even if family try not to pressure you there's always that weight of expectation. Sometimes it takes more courage not to live up to other peoples expectations, take the easy route and give in. Let me tell you though I know lots of people who haven't taken up the sword and have gone on to be real workers and winners for The Kingdom. Taking the sword is just one more option you have more than others who do for work for The Kingdom. It's your choice and no one else's."

Sensing that perhaps things had got a little heavy mum jumped in with her famous 'lighten the mood' suggestion, "Anyone for hot chocolate? Then after that time for bed as it's late and we've got to head home tomorrow."

"I'll have a hot chocolate mum but while you're making it can dad just answer me one more question?" Mum nodded as she left for the kitchen and Jamie asked, "Why is our twelfth birthday so important?"

"The reason for that is when you're twelve that's the year you have to make the decision if you want to be trained as an Enochim or not. The twelfth year was chosen as the number twelve often symbolises government such as 12 Tribes, 12 Judges, 12 Disciples, 24 elders and the New Jerusalem, the centre of Government on the New Earth will have walls 144 cubits high. So it's like in your twelfth year you decide what's going to govern your life from then on. If you decide not to take up the sword after being told of your heritage then you'll be left alone to follow whatever path has been laid out for you in The Kingdom. If you do decide to take up the sword you must be taken to The Third Dimension where the training school is. Otherwise, the fallen can attack you and try to stop you from becoming Enochim.

"So that explains the importance of being twelve but why were we attacked a few days ago?" asked Anna.

"To be honest Anna, we don't know. There was a rule laid down that no Enochim child can be attacked before their twelfth birthday and even then only if they take up the sword. Any Fallen who breaks this rule will be immediately banished to The Abyss until the final day of reckoning. The parents of Enochim children who are on furlough, that is taking a break from active service in The kingdom, are also excluded from hostilities. We've asked Joel and Nathaniel about this and they've said they'll look into it and get back to us. To our knowledge it's never happened before so something's not right for this to be going on. Anyway, don't you and Jamie worry about it at present as either I or your mum will be around until we all know what's going on. Once you've made your decision, either to take the sword or not, then you'll be safe either here on earth or because you'll be in The Third Dimension being trained."

"Thanks dad. I think that's enough information for now," said Anna. They all had their mandatory hot chocolate and the twins went up the dancers to bed. Sleep didn't come easy as both Jamie and Anna were thinking about all they'd learnt and heard over recent days and about what decision to make. As neither slept well that night they were both up early the next morning, even before dad. Soon as they were dressed they went downstairs quietly so as not to wake up their sleeping parents.

"Want some juice?" Jamie asked his sister.

"Orange please," came her reply.

"Fancy a walk and talk?" suggested Jamie.

"Yes. Let's go along the brook and up Mill Hill," replied Anna. Mill Hill was nearby to the cottage that had been given its name. They slowly opened the stable door and pulled it shut so the latch caught as quietly as possible. Out of the yard and down the lane to where the brook crossed under a small stone bridge. They went through the kissing gate and followed the brook for about half a mile. They took the soil pathway that centuries of walkers had taken up Mill Hill. To start off with neither of the twins said much as they enjoyed the crisp, dewy morning and pondered what was going on in their lives. After a few minutes Anna clothed her thoughts with words.

"Have you decided what you are going to do yet?" she asked Jamie.

Jamie took a moment and replied, "I think I am going to take the sword." Anna wasn't surprised by his answer. Jamie went on, "To me it seems a way I can help The Kingdom by fulfilling my Enochim heritage. Not only that to be honest I like the idea of opening a can of welly onto the bad guys particularly after seeing how mum handled herself with those two nutters."

Anna looked away and talked to her feet. "Well I'm not sure about it at all," she almost whispered to her trainers. Perhaps, that's why they're called converses. "I don't mind doing my bit for The Kingdom but I'd rather chose my own path than be pressured on to a way I didn't chose."

"Fair enough," was Jamie's reply, trying his best to sound as if he agreed with his sisters sentiments. Actually, he was a bit disappointed as he thought he and Anna would make a great team but he didn't want to add to the pressure Anna perceived she was under. "Don't forget you can always say 'no'," Jamie reminded her.

"I suppose so' " said Anna, "but because others don't get the choice we get I feel I should take the sword or I'm being ungrateful and letting everyone down."

"Yeah I see what you mean, but the fact you're having second thoughts shows you do have some choice in the matter and at least you're strong enough to make it either way. So whatever you decide it'll be your decision and whatever road you take I'll always be there for you."

"Can you take the sword if I don't?" Anna asked Jamie.

"I think so," was his reply. "I suppose it means I'll be used on my own or paired up with some other Enochim. I'm sure they won't turn me down if I'm on my bill. But don't you worry about me. It's your life and your decision so you must make the one you're happy with not the one you think will make other people happy," Jamie said as he tried to re-assure Anna.

"Thanks Jamie. That means a lot to me." With that the two carried on walking without the talking. The morning was silent except for the babbling, confused brook which seemed to echo the thoughts in each of the youngster's minds.

"What if they won't accept me?"

"What if I fail the course?"

"Will I still get to spend time with Anna?"

"Should I say no to support Anna?"

"Would mum and dad prefer me to say yes or no?"

"Where and what is The Third Dimension?" Jamie's thoughts came crashing into his mind like water hitting the rocks in that babbling brook.

"It's not fair to be pressured into something."

"Will Jamie respect me less if I don't take the sword?"

"Will dad and mum love me less if I don't take the sword?"

"I could get hurt."

"I could help Jamie if I go."

"What should I do?" Anna's thoughts pushed into her mind like the waves of the tide hitting the beach. They soon came to a stile that went over an old stone wall that encircled the top of this ancient hill. Dad had told them that in Roman times this area had been mined for lead even before milling started and that back in the 1700's mining had started again. This stone wall marked the boundary of the mine workings before it all stopped in the late nineteenth century.

"Let's head back and see mum and dad," Anna said to Jamie somehow hoping even saying the words would lead her to an answer even if mum and dad couldn't.

"Sounds like a plan to me and who knows a bacon butty could be mine for the taking," was Jamie's reply. They turned and started to walk down the hill. As they did they met a young mum and her toddler out for an early morning stroll.

"Good morning," both pairs of walkers said to each other along with the obligatory smiles. Anna thought to herself, "There's one mum not getting much sleep." The twins had just walked another few hundred yards when they heard an awful scream.

"HELP!! HELP!! PLEASE HELP ME!!" They recognised it as the voice of the lady they had just passed. Without pausing or discussing the matter, the twins ran back up the hill, over the stile and towards where the screams were still coming from. About two hundred yards beyond the stile they found the mother kneeling by a hole in the ground screaming with all her might, "PLEASE HELP ME!!"

As he asked the question he knew it was a daft one but the words just came out of Jamie's mouth. "What's happened?"

"It's my little boy. He's fallen down this hole and I just can't hold onto him," the woman said with a quivering voice. Jamie knelt down to look into the hole. He couldn't see much because it was so dark. He put his head down the hole and saw the little boy's glistening eyes looking back up at him. Jamie realised the glistening was coming from his tears. The toddler's chubby little hand was hanging onto his mother's for dear life. Jamie spoke as calmly as he could to the little boy. "Can you lift up your other hand and give it to me," he asked. Somehow sensing Jamie was there to help he did just that. "Great. Now I'm just going to speak to your mum." Jamie pulled his head out of the hole and said to the woman, "Let's see if we can pull him out. On the count of three we'll both gently pull. One, two, three." They both gently pulled but the little lad's shoe was caught on a piece of timber sticking out of the side of the hole. As they pulled his little hands started to come out of theirs.

"No!" the woman shouted.

Jamie said, "Stop pulling and please try and stay calm." They did so and managed to reset their grip on the two little hands. Jamie didn't want to be responsible for letting the little guy fall to his death so he thought quickly and spoke just as fast to his sister.

"Anna. Run as fast as you can and get mum and dad. Tell them what's happened and get help here pronto. Quick. Go now!" Anna didn't need telling twice. She was off at a gallop. Jamie started to look around for something he might be able to use to secure the little boy but there's not a lot of rope around at quarter seven in the morning on a hillside path. The mother was losing it now and sobbing uncontrollably.

"I'm going to let him go. I'm going to let him go!" the panic in her voice was readily recognisable.

"No you're not," said Jamie.

"My hand's getting cramp and I'm sweating. Richard's going to fall."

Keeping himself calm and actually impressing himself, Jamie said, "Let me take over holding both of Richards hands." Jamie put his head down the hole again and spoke to Richard. "Hi Richard. My name's Jamie. Listen I want you to help your mum. Your mum's getting tired so I thought I'd take over holding both of your hands. Is that ok?" Richard nodded.

"Thanks Richard. Now I'm going to put my hand next to yours and then you slowly let go of your mums and take hold of mine. Do you think you can do that for me?" Richard nodded again but Jamie wasn't so sure. Anyhow the woman was getting hysterical and if he didn't take over Jamie was scared if she suddenly let go they'd lose Richard so he had no choice.

"Ready Richard? Here comes my other hand." Jamie slowly brought his left hand into the hole making sure he was lying flat against the ground so he could take the full weight. As he touched Richard's hand the little boy immediately did as he'd been asked and let go of his mum's hand. She screamed and tried to grab his hand back but missed and Jamie was left hanging onto Richards full weight. But now the little lad was swinging around increasing the pressure on Jamie's weaker left hand. Jamie panicked and shouted at the woman, "Get off!" As he did he swung Richard towards his right hand and grabbed him.

"Have you got him?" the woman asked.

"Yes," replied Jamie thinking "No thanks to you." Jamie lay there with the life of a three year old boy literally in his hands. "Come on Anna. Where are you," he thought rather than said so as not to fan the woman's hysteria.

Anna was trying her best to get down the hill as fast as she could but she kept falling over on the uneven path. "Where's Black Beauty when you need him?" she muttered to herself as she picked herself up for the third time. It took almost ten minutes to get back down the hill, onto the lane and to get the cottage in sight. Seeing the cottage gave her a second wind. She ran with all her might and banged the door as she went through shouting, "Mum! Dad! Mum! Dad!" Already dressed and wondering where the twins were both parents came out of the kitchen faster than an email on MSN.

"What's the matter Anna? Is it Jamie?" asked dad? Anna was so breathless she couldn't answer immediately.

Mum said, "Take deep breaths and calm down." It took a minute or so before Anna caught her breath and was able to throw out her words.

"We were walking back down Mill Hill and a lady and little boy passed us on their way up. Just after they'd gone over the stile we heard the woman screaming. We ran back to see what had happened and her little boy had fallen down a hole in the path."

"An old mine working," dad muttered.

Anna carried on. "Jamie went to help and tried to pull the boy out but he was caught on something so now he's lying there holding onto the lad for his dear life."

No more explanation was needed. Dad went into organisation mode.

"Rachel ring 999 and get the mountain rescue and paramedics here. Then join me at the dog. Anna, we're going up to help. You stay here and tell the rescue people all you know when they get here. Now confirm to me, the hole is just passed the style on Mill Hill path?"

"Yes," she said with more certainty than she knew she had. Dad was gone. Mum was phoning. Anna slumped on a chair. Rachel finished the call and joined Peter by the dog. Peter just spoke without explanation giving Rachel gear as he did so.

"Ear piece communicator. Body harness. Gloves. Rope. Descent pulley.

Rachel took the gear and responded, "Agreed" No more words just action. They ran out of the yard, along the lane and onto Mill Hill path. As they ran they each put on a body harness. Anna by this time was stood at the door and saw them leave.....just about. She could not believe how quick they were running. Their training and experience shone through as Peter and Rachel got to the stile in three minutes flat. No problem with that, but there was another problem. Richard was losing his grip and Jamie was starting to lose his cool. The toddler's hand was tired and sweaty not a good combination when you're dangling over an old mineshaft. Jamie saw his folks approaching and shouted, "Quick. My grip's going". No words from his parents, just more actions. Whilst running Rachel had tied the rope to her body harness. Peter had attached it to the descent pulley. As Rachel got to the stile she vaulted it with 'some style'. Peter stopped at the style and tied the pulley onto it. Rachel kept running towards Jamie.

"Hurry I'm losing my grip!" shouted Jamie. The shout must have unsettled Richard because he shouted for his mum. As he did he looked up and the slight movement of doing so was enough to move his hands in Jamie's grip.

"No!" Jamie shouted as he felt Richard slipping. He tried to tighten his grip but it was too late. Richard fell from his hands and Jamie thought from this life.

"No!" the young boy screamed as the little boy fell. As Jamies scream flew into the air his mum flew down the hole. Just as Richard fell Rachel reached the hole and without thought for herself jumped in. Seconds later Jamie heard his mum shout, "Got him!" as she grabbed little Richard's jacket and threw her arm around his waist to secure her hold. The shout wasn't just for Jamie but also for Peter. He got the message in his earpiece and engaged the descent pulley. The gears of the equipment gripped and slowly stopped the ropes, Rachel and Richard. Silence followed. The woman shouted, "Is he alright? Have you got him?" Jamie not knowing the answer looked over towards his dad.

"You can tell mum that Richard is safe," Peter shouted over to Jamie.

"Thank you. Thank you," the woman said as she hugged Jamie. Not his favourite past time being hugged by an older woman but Jamie let it go just this once. Meanwhile Peter was talking to Rachel.

"Are you secure for your ascent? Over."

"Affirmative," came Rachel's reply

"Jamie. Come over here," Peter shouted to the son he was so proud of. Not that Peter needed the help but he asked Jamie to help to keep him occupied from his shock and let his son finish the job he had started. Jamie was only too pleased to help.

"When I release the gears on the descent pulley we take the strain and pull your mum and the little lad to safety, ok?" Jamie nodded. Peter released the gears and they slowly pulled the two out of the hole. Rachel came through feet first with Richard clasped tight to her chest as if he were her own. Once safely on firm ground Richard's mum grabbed her little boy sobbing and hugging at the same time.

"Thank you so much," she said to Rachel. The look on the mother's face was all the thanks Rachel, Peter and Jamie needed. Relief overtook Jamie who felt the tears welling up in his eyes. Peter didn't want to embarrass his son but pride overtook street cred. He hugged him and whispered, "Well done mate. I am so proud of you." The words meant so much to Jamie the tears just wouldn't let him keep his cool. And when his mum came up and hugged with the same words being cool was long forgotten.

The cavalry arrived about seven or eight minutes later with Anna in hot pursuit and she got in on the act as well. First dad and then mum passed around the hugs and both parents made sure she knew how proud they were of her as well. The paramedics checked over Richard and then made sure everyone else was ok. When everyone was given the all clear the party proceeded down the hill with Richard on a stretcher. As they walked Richard's mum introduced herself as Joy Palmer.

"I can't believe what you all did," she said. "Without you all, Richard's life would be over and so would mine. Are you trained rescuers," she asked?

"Yes, in a manner of speaking we are," answered Rachel.

"I can't thank you enough," Joy went on.

As they arrived at Mill Cottage the paramedics bundled Richard and his mum into the ambulance and sped off. As they did Peter asked one of the mountain rescue team which hospital they were going to.

"St. Andrews," he replied, "in Kendal." Peter thanked him and after he and Rachel had stowed their equipment in the dog the Fishers all went in for a well earned breakfast. As they ate their wheaty bangs Jamie told his parents how what they had done was fantastic.

"No more fantastic than what you did and if anything you and Anna outshone us both," replied Peter. "You see, me and mum did what we're trained for but you guys acted instinctively and with real guts."

"If I take the sword will I get to do things like that?" Jamie continued.

"It's not all heroic acts and glory but yes there will be days when the buzz is high," answered his mum.

"And will I get to use all the gadgets which I presume came in the dog?"

"You presume right my young sir. Those gadgets in the dog and a few others that would make even 007 jealous."

Later that morning, Rachel rang the hospital to see how Richard was doing. Joy told her he had a little concussion and was badly bruised but a few days rest should see him right. She asked if they would go and see Richard before they left for home and all the Fishers were pleased to do so. When they got to the hospital they found the Children's Ward with Richard sat up in bed watching a video. Joy spoke to Peter and Rachel. "You must be so proud of your children and they way they acted this morning?"

"No argument there," answered Peter.

"They really are a pair of little angels aren't they," Joy went on. Peter and Rachel smiled. After a few more minutes they left the Palmers to let Richard take a nap. Rachel got Joy's telephone number so they could check on Richard's progress.

The Fishers got back to the cottage around four and started to pack for the journey home.

"Come on you two," Rachel shouted up the stairs about an hour later. "I don't know what you're doing up there but it's time to leave."

Anna asked if they could wait a bit longer before they left. Mum agreed and offered everyone the mandatory hot chocolate.

"No thanks mum. Can we just go in the lounge for a chat." When they were seated Anna spoke first. "Jamie and I have had a long think and talk about all that's been going on. After thinking it through I have decided I want to take up the sword. I want to be able to help people like you and dad and I've decided the best way I can do that is to fulfil my calling as an Enochim"

Rachel took hold of Anna's hands and looked her straight in both eyes. "Are you sure you want to do this Anna? No one wants you to do anything you're not happy with and I'd hate to think we're pressurizing you in any way." Rachel was really concerned her daughter was saying what she thought they wanted to hear.

"I'm sure mum. I had my doubts but now I really want to do this for The Kingdom."

"And so do I," Jamie said echoing Anna's words.

"You're both sure about this," asked dad trying his best not to add pressure either way. Without looking at each other the twin reply came instantly from the twins, "Yes." With tears in their eyes the parents hugged their children and to this day neither Peter nor Rachel know if they were tears of happiness or sadness.

V

It was about 7pm when Dad got home. 'I've seen Joel and Nathaniel. They say that we should leave straight away as The Fallen seem to be out to get just us as no one else is being targeted. We're assuming it's because somehow they found out our ancestry and so they're all out to remove us from the Kingdoms work. Now they know who we are Joel says that if you've decided to take the sword you should leave now for the City of Angels.

'But what about school?' asked Jamie. 'Not that I'm fussed but I suppose when all said and done we do need an education.'

'Don't worry about school because you'll be pleased to hear, or maybe you won't, that you won't miss a day, Mum answered. 'When you go for your training you will travel to the City of Angels which is in another dimension where our created time doesn't exist. So you'll leave in one moment in our time and return in the next.

To us it'll be as if you've never been away but for you it will seem like 40 days of our time.

'Now you're just confusing me', interrupted Anna.

Dad took over. 'You will be trained in The City of Angels but that exists outside our dimension which has created time marked by our sun. In the Kingdom to which the angels belong there is no sun or seasons so time is not marked as it is in our dimension. When you are there you won't age or miss anything from earth's time and history. So when you come back you can pick up from where you left off. However, to get you there we first have to travel to The Crystal Sea. From there we'll go to Jacobs Ladder which will take you to The City.

'Sounds straightforward, except, where is The Crystal Sea? What is Jacob's Ladder and how do we get to the City? I'm more confused than a TV Gardener who's shown four spades in a shed and asked to take his pick'

Dad trying his best but also feeling like a TV Gardener replied, 'I don't know where The Crystal Sea is but I know a man who does. As for Jacobs Ladder that's the portal that Enochim use to get to the third dimension where The City of Angels exists. You see because we're human we can't directly travel between our earthly dimension and the third dimension like the angels can. The I Am made us of flesh and bone to live and work in our earthly dimension which is governed by the natural and physical laws that He laid down. As The I Am has made those laws, He won't break them and so we need another way to travel between the earthly dimension and the third.'

Dad continued, 'Do you remember the story of Jacob in The Old Testament?'

'Yeah, I must have been awake for that one,' joked Anna.

'Couldn't have been your Dad telling it then,' laughed Mum.

'Thanks for that family. What's the verse..? 'A Prophet is without honour in his own town.'

'No argument there Dad, but hey, give it your best shot,' said Jamie.

'You know what son, I think I will. Jacob was running away from family trouble fell asleep one night and had a vision. The vision was of a ladder between Heaven and earth with angels ascending and descending on it. That's Jacobs Ladder, a bridge between our dimension and the dimension where angels usually inhabit. So we use Jacobs Ladder to access the third dimension.'

'Do you remember what Jacob laid his head on?' Mum asked.

'Wasn't it a stone?' answered Anna

'Yes it was. When Enoch left to go to the third dimension he was transported by Jacob's Ladder although it wasn't known as that then because Jacob hadn't even been born! Enoch left by using a stone that had been energised to connect the first and third dimensions. n. This stone had been energised when Angel command decided to set up The Enochim. The stone was then split in two with one half left on earth and the other taken to the Third Dimension. The two halves 'connect' when activated and allow transfer between the dimensions. For centuries Enoch's stone, as the earth stone became known after

Enoch's transfer was looked after by The Guardians. It was fought over many times with the most infamous battle being that in The Valley of Achor. It was then decided to let the stone be used by Jacob as a pillow to let it become part of Biblical History to give the Enochim some credibility. So when Jacob used it as his pillow, he had his vision of what we now call 'Jacob's Ladder' the portal between the first and third dimensions. The stone is now safe and looked after by Guardians who keep it in hiding after retrieving it from Jacob still covered in the oil he used to anoint it.

'Where's the earth stone now?' asked Jamie.

'We don't know,' said Mum. She continued, 'Because it's the only way for us Enochim to enter the third dimension it is imperative that it is protected at all costs. If the fallen got hold of it Enoch's People would die out in two generations. To protect it the stone is never kept in any one place very long and is protected by The Guardians.

'You mean like Auntie Ruth?' said Anna remembering what they'd be told up in The Lakes.

'Yes, exactly like Auntie Ruth,' said Mum. She continued, 'The Guardians are some of Enoch's people who have proved they are special enough to guard the stone. It's a real honour to be chosen and we're all really proud of Ruth.'

'So, we need to get to The Crystal Sea, find out where the stone is and then travel through the portal to the third dimension,' Anna said pleased that she had now sorted it out.

'Now you're cooking on gas,' said Dad.

"But how does the stone work?" asked Jamie.

"I don't actually know," replied Dad. "It is activated by those who are called to the third dimension and no one else. So when a trainee like you and Anna touch it the stone activates and opens the portal. I could touch it now and nothing would happen unless for some reason I had been called back to the third dimension, which rarely occurs."

"Has anyone ever be called back to the third dimension?" asked Jamie

"It has been known on very rare occasions but not often." Peter looked over at Rachel and then spoke again to Jamie.

"Anyhow, that's not important now. What's important is that we get you and Anna to The Crystal Sea A.S.A.P."

"How, if you don't know where it is?" queried Anna.

"Because like Dad said we know a man who does," answered Mum. "Now you two off to bed. We've got a busy day ahead tomorrow."

With that Jamie and Anna went to bed but they could here Mum and Dad moving around and talking right up until they went to sleep.

The next day they were all up before dawn despite Mum and Dad being up most of the night before. By 6am they had finished breakfast and Nana Burnett arrived and then so did Nana and Pops. Now the twins knew something was going on.

It turned out that Mum and Dad had told the grandparents they all had to leave and why. Of course the Nanas and Pops had been through it all before but that didn't make it any easier saying goodbye to their grandchildren. The plan was for Nana Burnett to stay and house sit whilst Mum and Dad take Jamie and Anna off to The Crystal Sea and then on to Enoch's Stone wherever that may be.

"You're kidding Dad! We're not going in that," said Jamie with the indignation that comes from being so close to your teenage years when image is more important than life itself and you know everything.

"What do you mean?" said Dad feigning real hurt to his pride. "It's a good solid vehicle and it's been a great friend to me and Mum over the years," as he moved over and patted the Dog.

"But its old, battered and can't go very fast," Jamie added.

"Now Jamie, that's no way to speak about your Father," Rachel said putting her arm around Peter's shoulder and giving him a peck on the cheek.

"Thanks very much. I love you too," Dad said returning Rachel's peck.

"Enough already you two. I've not long had breakfast," added Anna.

With that they got to packing up the dog. Most of the stuff was for the journey to The Crystal Sea wherever that was. Couple of changes of clothes each, bottles of drink and some food. Then Anna and Jamie could only take a back pack each to take to The City. No need for clothes and toiletries as they would be provided on arrival.

"Time to hit the road you lot," Dad said in his best holiday trip voice. "I want to get going whilst road traffic is not heavy."

Tears and hugs all round. Mums and Dads to Mums and Dads; grandparents to grandchildren and eventually grandparents to grandparents. It was a real hugathon. Perhaps it was harder for the grandparents because they knew what was coming. The feelings of doubt, fear, homesickness, worry about your beloved children. They knew it was for the best but the best isn't always easy.

The family got into the Dog and Jamie and Anna couldn't stop waving until they couldn't see their grandparents anymore. That took some time as their grandparents followed them down the lane until Dad was able to put his foot down and take the Dog for a run.

"Where are we going to?" asked Anna.

"We're going to see an old friend of our called Ray Leon."

"Why?"

"We've known Ray for years. He helped us a lot when we were on active service for The Kingdom and having spoken to him a couple of days ago he's going to help us again. You see, Ray is a pilot who owns an air freight company. He flies all over the world and can use his company as a cover to get the Enochim where they are needed fast."

"So he's the one who'll get us to The Crystal Sea."

"Count on it Anna," replied Mum.

"How far away is Ray?" Jamie asked.

"A couple of hours or so, if we get a straightforward journey," replied Dad.

With that they all settled in for the trip with Dad waiting to see how long it took one of the twins to ask, "Are we there yet?"

They hit the Expressway within quarter of an hour and pretty much had the road to themselves until………………………………

Jamie noticed that Dad kept checking his rear view mirror and after a couple of times he looked at Mum raised his eyebrows and slightly tilted his head side wards to get her to look out the back. Mum did and then widened her eyes as if to let Dad know she now knew what he knew.

Jamie looked back and saw two cars which he thought were a couple of BMWs, coming up fast.

"What is it Dad or more importantly, who is it?" he asked.

"No one you know or need to worry about son."

With that the first of the BMW's came alongside the Dog but didn't overtake.

Jamie looked across. The passenger returned his look, smiled and winked at him.

"Dad! Mum!" he shouted, "It's the baddies again!"

"We know son. Thems Bad Mans Wheels You lot, Hang on!!"

As he said it Dad slammed the anchors on. The Dog slowed immediately and the BMW to the side sped off. The one behind didn't and slammed right up the rear of the landy. It was like an apple hitting a brick wall, the landy being the brick wall. The front of the bemer buckled and made the driver swerve all over the road. The car slowed and Dad put his foot down again and left it for dead, or more accurately 'scrap'.

Dad put the pedal to the metal, the V8 kicked in and the Dog became a greyhound after being a Doberman. No sign of the other car.

"Everyone ok," asked Mum?

"No problems back here," replied Anna.

"Right. Let's get to Rays as fast as this V8 will get us there," Mum said as she looked at Dad.

"No argument there," Dad replied. "Full bananas it is. Keep your eyes open for any more guests."

They carried on for another couple of miles and as they passed a service area slip road, the first bemer came out from it like a prat out of hell. As it came up behind them, the passenger leaned out of his window and started firing at them with an AK47.

The bullets peppered the rear door window as Anna ducked and screamed along with Jamie.

"Bullet proof glass; don't you just love it," said Mum.

"Pity we've not got bullet proof tyres because they're coming along side and that's their next target," said Dad more calmly than Jamie thought was proper.

"Oh no they don't. Jamie, move over next to your sister and pass me that Bible off the back seat. As those comedians are driving a 'bema' it's time for 'Judgement Day'. "

As she was talking, Mum moved into the back and took the Bible off Jamie.

"I don't think reading the part about 'love thy neighbour' is going to help," Anna said nervously trying to break the tension. Dad laughed and Mum said "Reading the Word of God isn't the idea but using the sword of God is." With that she opened the back door of the Dog, grabbed the roof rack with her left hand. She stood on the running board and shouted, "The Sword of God! Matter!" Instantly The Bible morphed into a flaming sword. The pair in the bema couldn't have been paying close attention because as they came alongside the passenger looked over at the Dog. As he did, Jamie not only saw his dead eyes glaring at him but his eyeballs growing in terror. Jamie wasn't sure whether it was the flaming sword scaring him or his shouting mother. Then he knew and it wasn't the sword!

As the attacker's car came parallel to the car Dad looked back and smiled at them just as Mum raised the sword and brought it down just below the windscreen on the bonnet. The sword sliced through the metal like a knife through butter. The front end of the car just came away and span wildly creating sparks all over the carriageway as it did. The rest of the car just slowed and slowed and slowed until it came to a stop. Mum got back inside the car, gave Jamie the Bible back and said, "Let's see how AA Home start sorts that out. Not so much a breakdown as a break up."

"Whoa!!" exclaimed Jamie as he gave Mum the Bible back. "I'm not holding that. It could take my hand off."

"Don't be a baby it won't hurt you unless I call on it to become a sword," explained Mum.

Now Anna joined in. "I think you had better explain what this Bible changing thing is all about," she said

"It's quite simple really," Mum started but Jamie interrupted. "It maybe simple but it sure looks deadly."

"It can be only if you're not careful. You see, to give us Enochim some protection from the Fallen we are given the gift of a flaming sword like the Cherubim have."

"The what", asked Anna.

"Cherubim are a type of angel and some of them are warriors who were given a flaming sword to fight with. They were first given them in Eden after the fall to protect the Tree of Life from anyone misusing it and they're still there to this day. You'll learn all this in Angel History Class when you get to The City of Angels"

"If we get to the City", Jamie remarked.

"When, you get to the City," Dad said with a tone indicating he was not mucking about.

"Anyhow, to help us Enochim we have the ability to change The Word of God into The Sword of God if we use the right words," Mum continued.

"The right words being," Anna asked?

"Well, if I am fighting someone who has been 'taken' I take a Bible and say, 'The Sword of God…Taken'. Then when I fight them I don't hurt the person 'taken' but can get rid of the Fallen inside them when I strike across their chest."

"So that's what you said when those two attacked us at home. I thought you said 'Be sure you're not faking' but you said 'The Word of God-Taken' " said Jamie as he remembered that night, not that he'll ever forget it.

"Sure did," confirmed Mum.

"But just then you said 'matter' not 'taken'," queried Anna.

"That's because when I want the sword to deal with something material like the front end of a car, I say 'matter' and 'it does just what I said in the din."

"What happens if you say 'matter' when you should say 'fallen' "asked Anna.

"You don't" said Mum. "That's why we have to be highly trained because if you get it wrong the 'taken' can be hurt or even killed the taken are still flesh and bone like you and me. Even though when they are taken they get stronger they are still human and will die. So as part of the Enochim code we have to swear not to kill any taken or any other people for that matter."

"That must be difficult on occasions Mum," Anna said.

"It is but them's the rules"

"And we're about to put them to the test again," shouted Dad. "Look behind"

They all did and there coming up fast was a BMW with a squashed front end and four taken inside.

"Don't you just hate that ultimate driving machine," Dad said with grudging respect. "Time to take this Dog for a country walk." As he said it Dad swerved over to the left and exited the Expressway where there was no slip road. Down the slope and across the fields dodging the cows as they went. "Let's see if our friends can keep up with this," as he fought with the steering wheel to keep the Dog upright.

"You're not going to believe this, Dad," said Anna, "but they're coming after you."

"They can try but they won't catch us." With that Peter slammed his foot to the floor and headed through a field gate. Shame it wasn't even open! Still the taken came after them. They were nothing, if not persistent.

Field after field and gate after gate they carried on. Then things started to get really tricky as they headed into a wooded area. Dad had to swerve to avoid wrapping himself around the ever increasing number of trees. 'This was one Dog that was not going to wrap itself around a tree,' Dad thought to himself.

"Look out Mum shouted as Dad demolished an old sign. "What did it say?" asked Mum.

"Not sure," replied Dad.

"I think it said 'DANGER QUARRY AHEAD," Anna said.

"Are you sure?" asked Mum.

"Positive," Anna replied as she pointed ahead. There just in front was one big hole in the ground. As Dad looked he slammed on the anchors and turned the landy sharp to the right whilst shouting, "Hang on!!"

The dog turned and as it did two wheels left the ground and Dad shouted

"Lean Right!!" They all did and the vehicle went back onto all fours. They stopped in line with the front of the quarry edge sand about 3 metres from it.

"Everyone Ok?" asked Mum.

"Think so," said Jamie, "although I never thought I'd want to wear nappies again."

"I'm ok too," Anna said.

"You two stay here and I mean 'STAY HERE'," Dad said and he wasn't kidding. "Rachel, we've got to stop that bema going over the edge otherwise those taken are dead.

"You're not serious Dad, are you," because Jamie couldn't understand why he'd want to save the bad guys. Those idiots are trying to kill us and you want to save them? Why?"

"I don't give monkeys about the fallen inside those people but I do care about the people themselves. Those fallen won't die if they go over the quarry cliff but those taken are human like you and me. If they fall 100 metres they're going to die and we can't let that happen."

"If that's true, the fallen won't be bothered to jump out of the car and just let the taken die," argued Jamie.

"No they won't," said Mum. "They need their bodies to get at us so they'll try to keep them alive."

"Maybe so, but they may try to keep them alive to come after us. Enough words, time for action," and Dad ended the conversation.

With that, Dad and Mum grabbed their Bibles and were out of the landy into the wood. Next thing, "The Sword of God......Taken" and they had their flaming swords to hand whilst running back towards where the landy had first turned. They saw the bema bearing down on them and both Mum and Dad waved their arms and started shouting "STOP! STOP! There's a quarry!!" With that three of the doors on the car flew open and three bodies fell out. The driver's door didn't open and the car kept coming.

"No! No!" shouted Peter as he ran towards the car. It came straight at him but he didn't turn aside. As the bema reached him Dad jumped to the side and shouted, "Sword of God.......Matter!" As he did he saw the wild eyes of the driver glaring at him and he swung his sword down at the tyres bursting both the front and rear ones. It was all to no avail as the car kept on and Peter shouted "No!" as he saw it fly off the quarry edge. Silence entered the wood like a mist, cold and foreboding. Within seconds came the explosion and Peter knew that was no big bang that gave life as some think, but a big bang that had taken life.

Peter's moment of peace was short lived as he heard Rachel shout, "Three Taken at 6 o'clock!" He turned and saw three wild-eyed men coming at him with AK47s armed and ready. Rachel joined him and away into the trees they went.

"We've got to pull them away from the Dog and the kids," whispered Dad. He waved two fingers to the right and off they went. After about 20 metres they stopped and looked back. Sure enough the three taken were following those guns at the ready. Peter motioned for Rachel to go left and then upwards. Rachel knew what he meant and moved immediately. Peter went right. The three split up into a line being about 10 metres apart and came towards Rachel and Peter. By the time the furthest one on the left reached Rachel she was three metres up in a tree. As the taken came beneath her she jumped down. She landed right in front of him. As her feet touched the ground, her sword swiped him across the chest and he fell to the floor with the fallen leaving him with an unnatural squeal. Mum checked the unconscious man's pulse and then moved away towards the other two taking the AK47 with her.

By this time the other two had seen what had happened and were now looking up at the tree canopy to try and spot Peter. As the one nearest towards Rachel moved along he trod on someone's foot. Peter shot up from beneath a covering of leaves. "Looking for me?" he asked as he swiped the man's chest. The Fallen left him and the man fell as if dead.

The last taken turned and opened fire on Peter. Peter rolled and rolled until he got behind a tree and caught his breath.

"Got you," Rachel whispered.

She moved towards the man and opened fire. She had aimed at his machine gun and she didn't miss. The gun flew out of the man's hands before he knew what was going on. He looked a t Rachel and grimaced. "I don't need a pop gun to get you." He pulled out a six inch dagger and ran towards Rachel. As he got to her Rachel grabbed a branch over her head swung over like a gymnast and kicked her would be attacker full in the face. He fell back dazed and stumbling. Before he could get his bearings, Rachel was in front of him, her sword raised over her left shoulder. "Tell Azarel he'll have to find better than you amateurs," she said as her sword came down and freed the poor taken from the hold of the fallen.

Peter joined her. "Nice shooting for a girl," as he kissed on the cheek.

"Thank you kind sir," she replied.

"Back to the landy," and with that they were off.

"Anna! Jamie! Are you there?" Mum shouted as they came up to the Dog. No reply. Not the answer they wanted.

"Are you there, you two?" Still no answer. Rachel came round to the back of the Dog and did a 'Lot's wife' when she saw what she saw. There in front of her was Anna being held in a strangle hold by the last of the four taken.

"I'm no amateur," the man snarled. "Now drop your swords!" Peter and Rachel obeyed without a thought.

"You can't kill her. You'll just get yourself banished," Mum said trying to make him realise he was wasting his time.

"Who said anything about killing her or him?" he said pointing at Jamie who was sitting on top of the landy. Now you two I'll kill but these are coming with me and after they reach their twelfth year then who knows what might happen." Peter and Rachel both knew exactly what would happen. "Enough talking time now it's dying time" he shouted. He went to pull the trigger of his AK47 when Jamie shouted "Dad!!" Peter looked and saw Jamie throw a Bible at the chest of the taken. Peter shouted with all his might, "The Sword of God……. Taken!!!" As he did a flaming sword appeared and struck the man straight in the chest. He squealed and fell as the fallen left him for dead. Anna ran to her Mum and Dad shouted over to Jamie, "You son, are the man!"

After a few minutes so everyone could catch their breath Dad took over. "Right, first we'll check over the dog and then we better sort out these taken. Peter checked the tyres and engine whilst Rachel and the twins tidied up the inside.

They then dragged all four taken to lie beneath the same tree on the edge of the woods away from the quarry.

"We're not just going to leave them here are we?" asked Anna.

"Just for a while until Luke and his team can come and get them," assured Mum.

"How will they know where to come," Anna persisted.

"Don't worry. Luke will know exactly how to find them." With that, Mum took off her watch and strapped it to the arm of one of the taken.

"The dog's ok to get us to Ray so let's get a move on," Dad said. They all got into the landy and Dad retraced their drive through the fields and gates until they reached the Expressway. They travelled on the Expressway for about another hour and then turned off towards a place called Hawden. They didn't reach the village because they took a 'B' road with a signpost showing an aeroplane which the twins knew was for an airport. It wasn't actually an airport but an airfield which is a lot smaller. Bouton Airfield had a number of large hangars and two long tarmac runways. There seemed to be a number of companies based there and Dad headed for one on the far side of the airfield. They came to a single storey brick building with a sign in large writing introducing the company as 'Eagle Carriers' and in small writing underneath 'Part of The Large Company.' This was all new to the twins as they certainly had not been here before and as far as they knew neither had Mum or Dad. They got out of the Dog and went straight inside. As they entered the foyer a door opened from the left and out came Ray Leon. He looked about the same age as Dad but still Anna thought he was quite a dish. Over six-foot tall, blue eyes and curly hair. If he hadn't been so old he could have been quite fanciable.

Ray hugged Rachel then Peter. "Great to see you two again. It must be almost thirteen years since I last did. And this must be Anna and Jamie. Thank goodness they take after you Rachel." Ray shook their hands and led them into his office. So this is the man "who does" thought Anna.

VI

They all went into Ray's office and sat down. "You look pretty shattered considering it's only 11 o'clock in the morning,"

"Well, after fighting off four taken and narrowly missing a 100 metre drop into a quarry, I think you'd be fairly shattered yourself," explained Peter.

"Point taken' " Ray replied. Everyone laughed and that felt better.

"Anyhow," Peter continued, "there are four taken out there who need help urgently. We left Rachel's peter with them so you can locate them easily. Neither Anna or Jamie understood 'Rachel's peter' being left there because as far as they knew, Dad was Rachel's Peter' and he was right there with them.

"No problem," said Ray and he left the room for a few minutes. When he returned he sat down again in his leather chair. "It's sorted. Luke and the team will be with those four in no time. I've also notified control about your peter," he said as he looked at Rachel who nodded.

The twins knew what 'Luke and the team' meant but not 'about your peter'.

Ray continued, "Right. Now that's sorted I'll take you into the Pilots' Lounge and sort you out some brunch. Then you two," looking at Jamie and Anna, "can stay in there with the gadgets whilst me and your folks have a chat. Who wants what to eat? Anyone for the full English with me?" He took everyone's order then buzzed his secretary, Trish and as with most bosses, she did the work whilst he got the glory.

The family enjoyed their food with Ray. Then the kids took over the games console although after the morning's events 'Ultimate Warrior Meets Killer Bots' seemed pretty tame. Rachel, Peter and Ray left them to it under the watchful eye of Trish and returned to Ray's office.

"I've had a full briefing from The Colonel about your situation and he's tasked me with getting you and the twins to The Crystal Sea ASAP."

"Any word on why the fallen have targeted Anna and Jamie so soon," asked Rachel?

"Best guess at present is because of what happened with your Dad, James. The fallen don't forget and are out for revenge or to stop his descendants becoming another thorn in their side like him. It seems only your family has been targeted because I'm waiting for two more kids to join us today for the trip and they've had no problems at all. With the scarcity of available 'taken' and them being used being used against you, they obviously mean business."

"What time do we leave?" Peters' voice giving away the urgency he felt inside.

"I've got a scheduled cargo flight to Toronto leaving at 11pm tonight and you'll all be on it. How are you and Rachel about being dropped from the plane to get to The Crystal Sea? "

"Not done it for a few years but falling off a plane is like falling off a bike, you don't easily forget how to do it. I take it the kids will go tandem with us?"

"Yeah, if that's OK with you?"

"Whatever it takes to get them safe as quickly as possible."

"What about this other family?" asked Rachel.

"Will they be OK with being dropped?"

"I hope so," said Ray.

"I plan to assess their situation when they get here and then decide how to proceed."

"Fair enough. I think we could all do with a bit of shut eye if that's alright Ray?"

"No problem Peter. We have sleeping quarters here for the pilots so I'll ask Trish to sort something out."

Sure enough within 20 minutes the family were settled in a four bed room and having a nap.

A couple of hours later Ray snook into the room and roused Peter and Rachel from their nap.

Ray whispered, "The Iqbals have arrived and I'd like you to meet them."

They all met in Ray's office with Adam and Lois Iqbal being watched by Trish in the Pilots' lounge.

Ray introduced Samuel and Anya Iqbal to the Fishers. Turned out that they lived in India where Samuel was a doctor and Anya looked after the children. They had recently come to The U.K. to continue Samuels training but really to be near transport to the third dimension if the children decided to take up the sword. Samuel was a bit older than Rachel, Peter and Anya so he had been to the third dimension a few years before them. Anya had been there the year after Rachel and Peter. Ray's idea of parachuting down to the Crystal Sea was no problem as the Iqbals had seen plenty of active service.

"I suggest we take you all to one of the hangars, get you kitted out for tonight's jump and run through the details with the kids." Ray then buzzed Trish and asked her to bring the children over to Hangar 12. Fifteen minutes later the Fishers and Iqbals were at the hangar. The kids seem to take to each other fairly quickly no doubt because of their similar ages and situation. The fact that Adam liked his football didn't hurt although cricket was his first love. Lois and Anna became friends immediately, just like young girls do. Anna talked about riding whilst it turned out Lois loved her dancing.

Introductions over and Ray started the lesson. They spent all afternoon in the hangar giving the parents a refresher course on parachute technique and teaching the children the basics to make the jump as safe as possible.

At about 5pm Ray said, "OK, lesson over. You all better head to the pilots quarters, have a shower and get a fresh change of clothes. Remember, you can only take a rucksack each to The Crystal Sea. You can get one of the waterproof ones from the stores. Trish will show you where." They all jumped into company MPV and headed back to the main building.

Whilst getting changed, Anna had a word with Lois.

"So you've decided to take the sword. Can I ask why?"

"Nothing special really. Mum and Dad took us on holiday to the Maldives a few months ago and told us all about our heritage as

Enochim. Because India is primarily a Hindu country there aren't many Enochim so both Adam and I thought it was only right to answer the call."

"No doubts at all," asked Anna remembering her hesitation.

"After I had accepted taking the sword I did start to wonder if I'd done the right thing. You know, having to go away to the third, facing the taken and not leading a normal life, but then I thought whose life is normal anyway? We all have to deal with life in whatever way we find it. And we all have demons to fight real and imaginary so why not be prepared and ready to face up to them. If it worked for Mum and Dad I'm sure it will work for me."

Anna felt better after talking with Lois. Doubts were normal and to be expected.

"I'm glad I've met you Lois. I'm sure we'll be friends, aren't you?

"I'm sure we will," and with that the two girls hugged each other.

Ray came to get them all and took them to the pilots' lounge. There waiting for them was a selection of takeaway meals. They all tucked in and afterwards the kids watched TV whilst the olds sat and chatted over coffee.

Ray left about 9:30pm. "Time to go and check the plane for the flight."

"Whose flying us Ray?" asked Samuel.

"Thought I'd better use my best pilot but as he's on vacation you've got me."

Samuel looked a bit bewildered. "Don't worry, Samuel," Peter said. "Rays too modest to tell you he's a top pilot. Before running Eagle Carriers he flew Tornados for The RAF. He was known as 'Ray Gun' because he was 'Top Gun' in his squadron."

"Oh Peter stop. You'll make me blush," interrupted Ray sheepishly.

"Oh yeah, I'm sure. You're the best and you don't care who knows it."

"You may think that but I couldn't possibly comment," Ray said as he smiled and left them to it. He returned about three quarter's of an hour later. "Time to hit the blue you lot." They all thanked Trish and headed to the waiting plane. It was a Boeing 737 converted for cargo flight but with some passenger seats. They all boarded and got buckled up. Ray came back and introduced his co-pilot, Terry, then he briefed the group.

"It'll take us around three hours to get to the drop zone," Ray informed them.

"I'll give you a fifteen minute warning prior to the zone so you can get everything ready. When we get there I'll drop down to 5,000 feet, open the door and out into the black you go." He checked they were all safely buckled up and then up to the cockpit. Anya was never too keen on the take off with that surge of power that takes you to thousands of feet above the ground. The Kids loved it.

"Where are we going, Dad?" asked Jamie.

"The Crystal Sea," he answered.

"Where's that. I heard Ray say he's flying to Toronto and dropping us off on the way. As far as I know there's no place called The Crystal Sea between here and there unless of course he means the Atlantic.

"I'm impressed with your geography son, but why not just wait and see."

No in-flight movie so most got some more shuteye but not Adam. He was a real techie so as soon as he could he was on the flight deck and nothing was going to shift him from there. Ray was impressed with the kid's knowledge of instruments and flight. "If you ever want a flying job you come and see me," he told him. Adam was loving it. Seeing Ray and Terry fly the bird through the night. The illuminated panels. The moving dials. The well rehearsed chatter between pilots. This was for him.

"You better head back to the cabin now mate," Ray said to Adam. The drop zones nearby and you and the rest need to get ready. Tell you what, as you're now my third in command you go back and give the order to kit up." Adam loved it even more. He was now part of the crew and giving orders on behalf of his superior officer. He obeyed immediately. The Fishers and Iqbals all got their kit on. It wasn't too easy moving around after that. What with having your parachute, one of your kids strapped to you, along with a dinghy each in the case of the Dads, they looked like 'Madness' in a music video 'conga-ing' to the jump door. Added to that Ray was now descending down 30,000 feet to the jump level of 5,000 feet so the slope in the floor didn't help.

Back on the flight deck, "OK Terry, we're coming to the zone. Can you take her while I go back and make sure our cargo gets delivered safely."

"Sure skip. No problem but before you go, what's that coming in at 'eight o'clock'?"

Ray took one look at the light approaching and knew exactly what it was. He threw himself back in his seat, stuck his headset back on and shouted over the intercom, "Everyone back there hold on!" As he did he grabbed the controls from Terry. "That's incoming, mate and we've got to avoid it."

"How?" asked Terry who was civilian trained with no combat experience.

"Like this." With that Ray held the aircraft straight and true.

"It's going to hit!" screamed Terry.

"Hang on!" Ray shouted as he threw the Boeing into a sharp dive. The missile flew straight past the cockpit window.

"Great flying Cap," said Terry with relief in his voice. As he spoke there was an ear splitting bang. Ray knew these things come in pairs and the first missiles pal had found its target, the starboard wing. The wing with its fuel tank just blew and was no more.

"Terry! Terry!" Ray shouted at his friend. No reply and Ray knew why. He saw the blood on his shirt and the thousand-yard stare in his eyes.

No time to grieve otherwise they're all dead. "Get out now!!" he shouted over the intercom. Peter tried shouting to Ray but with all the noise he had no chance. He couldn't make his way to the cockpit with all his gear so he had to trust his old friend and leave him to it. Samuel had already got to the door and had opened it. The air came in like a tornado knocking over him and Adam. He regained his feet and shouted to Anya and Rachel, "You girls first and now!!" Rachel looked at Peter who without hesitation shouted, "Go!" Within moments Anya had reached the door and she and Lois were gone into the black. Rachel followed with Anna, Samuel with Adam, Peter and Jamie right after them. As Peter fell through the nothingness he thought of his friend Ray and his friend Terry who had stayed on board to keep the plane flying so they could get out. 'Greater love has no man than he who lays down his life for his friend,' was all Peter could think.

No time to think now as the ocean below came closer, closer, closer and then hit Peter and Jamie. They must have gone down 5 or 6 metres and the cold of the water stabbed like a knife even with their wet suits on. Peter hit the quick release on his chute so that it wouldn't drag them down and kicked for the surface. He broke through with Jamie right next to him.

As they hit the surface Peter could see the fireball that was once a Boeing plunge down and hit the ocean. The explosion blew their ears, blew their minds and broke their hearts. They watched as burning debris floated on the water before it sank.

Peter, holding back the emotion but knowing he had to get a grip, spoke to Jamie. "You OK Son?"

"I think so," Jamie replied whilst chattering his teeth. No time for chattering. Peter pulled the release on the dinghy and within seconds it had inflated. The two of them clambered inside. "First job, find the rest." Peter pulled out a radio and asked Jamie to locate the dinghy's torch.

"Samuel, Rachel, Anya. Anyone there? Over." No reply. He tried again,

"Samuel, Rachel, Anya. Come back please. Over." The silence, broken only by the lapping of the Atlantic on the side of the dinghy, was haunting.

"Are they OK Dad?" Jamie trying to hide his concern.

"They'll be fine. Keep looking out of the dinghy to see if you can spot their torch." Peter thought it best to keep Jamie active to keep his mind from worry. Pity he couldn't do the same for himself.

"Dad! Dad! I can see a light," Jamie shouted.

"Where?"

"Over there to the left," Jamie said as he pointed.

Peter saw it too and it was as if that light entered his very being to bring relief from his dark despair. Peter took the radio again. "Samuel, Anya, Rachel. Come in please. Over"

"Anya here. Lois and Adam on board and Samuel's just bringing Rachel and Anna into the dinghy. Over."

"Thank you. Can you see our light? Over. Jamie, can you shake the torch around a bit please?" No problem there Jamie thought. He just held the torch and let his shivering do the rest.

"Affirmative," came Anya's reply.

"Keep shining your torch and we'll come over to you."

"Affirmative."

Jamie found the oars and they started to paddle across to the others. It wasn't fast and it wasn't easy. The mid–Atlantic swell must have been 3 to 5 metres and in a small dinghy it was like trying to skateboard over Snowdon. Eventually after over an hour of stop/start rowing the dinghies met and were tied together. Rachel and Anna joined Jamie. Peter jumped into the Iqbals boat to discuss strategy with Samuel.

"We should go back towards the debris to see if Ray got out," Peter suggested not looking for an argument. There was a chance his friend had got out of the fireball and he needed to make sure either way.

Samuel wasn't about to argue because he had thought the same. "Agreed, but first let's try and raise those at The Crystal Sea. While we're looking for Ray and Terry they can be looking for us."

"Good thinking Doc. You try and raise them whilst I let my lot know the plan."

Peter hopped back into the Fisher's dinghy and brought his team up to speed.

Samuel got on the radio.

"Samuel Iqbal calling The Crystal Sea. Please come in. Over."

Immediately a reply came over the airwaves.

"The Crystal Sea Here. Good to hear your voice. Over."

"Good to hear from you too," Samuel replied with the relief in his voice saying more than his words ever could.

"Are you and the children safe?" asked the voice.

"Yes. All Iqbals and Fishers accounted for."

Samuel thought he could hear a cheer in the background, but he wasn't sure.

"Great to hear, Samuel. Orders are for you to remain on station to await evac. Crystal Sea One was launched over an hour ago and is now homing in on your 'peter'.

"Now that's what I call service," replied Samuel.

"No credit at this end. Ray Leon managed to get a mayday to us before his plane went down."

"The man's a hero."

"No argument here, Samuel. ETA of Crystal Sea One is about 35 minutes. You OK on that timescale. Over"

"Affirmative. We are near plane debris so we'll go over to search for Ray and Terry but we'll still be on station. Over."

"Roger that, Samuel, but Terry didn't make it. Ray confirmed 'brother at home' during his transmission. Over"

"Roger that." The words stuck in Samuel's throat. He had just accepted that a man who had tried to help him and his family had died trying. Ray Leon wasn't the only hero he had met today.

"Thanks Crystal Sea. Look forward to meeting you soon. Iqbal signing off. Over."

"Likewise, Samuel. Take no chances. Keep safe. Over".

With that the airwaves went silent. All eight of them had heard the transmission. Words wouldn't come. Two men, two friends had risked their lives and one if not both had paid the price.

Samuel broke the silence. "Right. Terry may have gone but Ray may still be here. No time to waste. Terry would want us to save his friend if we can so let's get to it. Us lads will man the oars whilst you girls get the torches and start searching the water."

Peter liked the way this guy thought. Here was someone he could work with and enjoy doing it. They spent over half an hour searching but found no trace of Ray.

"Ahoy, Iqbals and Fishers! Crystal Sea One here for evac." The words pierced the night and were welcome and regretted at the same time. All eight were rescued from the water and taken below to recover. Crystal Sea One was the biggest catamaran the children had ever seen. Not that they'd seen that many except Adam whose techie lifestyle meant he knew about these things. The boat must have been over 30 metres long being painted completely black looking all the world like a floating stealth bomber. The only deviation from its sleek line was the bridge bubble up top with all the other accommodation being housed in the side pods.

Whilst the families showered, changed and ate, the crew of Crystal Sea One used a grid pattern search over the crash area. For two hours they searched in vain. Then Lieutenant Williams, the boat's Captain, came below to speak to the families.

"There's no sign of Ray. We've tried and you've tried. If he survived the impact, which is doubtful, the cold would have got him by now. My orders are to return to The Crystal Sea before daylight so we have to leave station now."

"Thanks Lieutenant. We appreciate you tried." The Lieutenant left but not before Adam asked if he could go up on the bridge. Having got the OK from Samuel and Peter because Jamie didn't want to be left out off all three of them went to the bridge. Even Adam was impressed. Lieutenant Williams sat in his command seat with just two other crews on the bridge. Adam assumed one was for helm and the other for weapons, if there were any. Within five minutes the mighty engines powered up and they left their station, Ray and Terry.

The front end of the mighty catamaran lifted out of the water and if you didn't know better you'd swear you were flying. 25, 30, 35 knots and the engines hadn't even broken into a sweat.

"What's the energy source?" asked Adam.

"Classified," came the Lieutenant's short reply.

"Well, whatever it is, it's out of this world."

"You said it" came the Lieutenant's longer but no more understandable reply although it raised a smile from the crew.

Jamie and Adam sat back and enjoyed the ride which was all too soon over. After about 50 minutes and who knows how many miles they could see some lights in the distance.

"Must be a ship and we're heading for it. I presume we'll transfer to that for the rest of the trip to The Crystal Sea?" Adam said aiming his comments at the Lieutenant.

"Something like that," he replied.

The boat slowed to almost idle speed and came up alongside what Jamie could only describe as a cliff of steel. This ship was enormous. As they slowly proceeded along the side Jamie noticed high up a nameplate which read 'The Crystal Sea'.

VII

They proceeded along the side of the massive hull until they came to a large open doorway that led into the bowels of this monster. The helmsman turned Crystal Sea One into The Crystal Sea. Now Jamie knew what Jonah must have felt like when he went into the bowels of the leviathan. The boat slowly cruised up to a central gangway and stopped opposite an identical craft that Jamie assumed was Crystal Sea Two. He looked over at Adam to ask what he thought of it all but with his mouth open so wide Jamie knew he wouldn't be able to speak. As they docked the outer door in the hull slowly began to close. When it was fully shut the water beneath Crystal Sea One was drained away so that it came to rest in a dry dock.

When the process was completed Lieutenant Williams led the boys back to their families.

"You will not believe this place," Jamie said to his Dad. "It is absolutely massive. I bet you've never seen anything like it, have you?"

"Well, actually we have," said Mum. "In fact we've seen this place before a few times." Jamie then realised how daft he was being. Of course his parents had seen it before, because they've been here before. This massive ship known as The Crystal Sea is obviously a place used by The Enochim and that includes Mum and Dad.

Lieutenant Williams led them up off Crystal Sea One and onto the gangway. As the walked along the Lieutenant introduced the families to a number of people along the way. Jamie was pleased for the chance to stop and stare at the cavernous place they were in. There were the two 'Crystal Sea' boats moored up. Men and women were swarming on and off them probably carrying out maintenance to ensure they were ready for other rescue attempts like the one Jamie had just experienced. There were cranes, little buggies going up and down and a ruck of jet skis tied up at the far end. The noise and activity was bewildering.

"Come on Jamie," interrupted Dad's voice into his bewilderment. They were led away from the cavern along a corridor and into a plush lounge area.

"Can I introduce Neil Johnson?" and with that the Lieutenant excused himself and was off. Neil was a young man probably no older than 25. He wore glasses and had a ponytail but for all that he seemed OK.

"Nice to meet you all," he said as he shook hands with everybody. "I've been assigned to take you to your quarters so you can freshen up and sleep after today's events."

"That's fine but when do we get to see the Colonel to find out what's going on?" asked Dad.

"The Colonel's busy at present and part of that is him trying to make sense of what's happened. He thought it would be better if you all had time to wind down first and then he'll see you later on today."

"It's a good idea Peter," agreed Rachel. "We've all been through a lot, especially the kids, and it'll be good to have some down time."

"Suppose you're right. Over to you Neil. We're in your hands."

"Thanks. I'll take you to your cabins and when you're ready just buzz for me and we'll sort out some breakfast."

Off they went. It took them over 10 minutes and a lift ride to get them where they were going. Both families had three cabins each, one for the olds, and one each for the kids. That sort of foresight really impressed Jamie as sharing with his twin sister was not on his top ten list of 'Things I Love To Do.' The cabins weren't overly big but they were well equipped. Along with the bunk and en suite shower Jamie was particularly impressed with the TV, which had satellite and a games console. After freshening up he went to find Anna.

"Isn't it amazing here."

"Pretty impressive that's for sure. I wonder what the foods like because I'm starving." She must have been hungry because it's not like Anna to be that fussed about eating. Off to Mum and Dad's cabin which was bigger it having a sitting room, bedroom and bathroom. But to be fair there is two of them.

"OK. Let's go and get the Iqbals," said Mum and off they went. The parents seemed to know where they were going and soon found the dining room. Everyone there was pleased to see them and couldn't do enough to make sure they had the food they wanted. About twenty minutes later Neil found them.

"Everything OK?"

"Fine, thank you," Samuel responded.

"Great. After breakfast can I suggest you get some rest and when you're all ready I'll take you up to see the Colonel."

"Thanks Neil. Bed sounds good right now. Come on my two off for some shut eye." Samuel and Anya took their two off back to their cabins.

"Any chance we can get to see The Colonel now?" asked Peter.

"There's no point. He's still got no reliable intelligence to confirm matters and he feels you'll be more use well rested."

"Fair enough. Thanks anyway. Time to go Anna and Jamie," Peter shouted over to the twins who were now playing pool with a couple of the crew.

"Just let us beat these two first Dad," pleaded Anna. Peter loved the normality of the situation and was happy to comply. When she and Jamie had hammered their opponents they all retired to their cabins.

Peters intention had been to sleep for a few hours and then go and see The Colonel regardless of what information he had by then. As it turned out, he and the family were more tired than he thought and they actually slept through until seven the next morning, almost 24 hours sleep. A record for Rachel, Anna and Peter but not for Jamie!

When they eventually got up they showered and headed for the dining room. Anna and Jamie noticed that Mum and Dad were not in their usual clothes. They wore dark grey combat trousers with matching shirts. She also noticed that Mum's shirt had on her left arm the same logo she had seen on Dad's phone and the medical team's uniforms. The only difference was that either side of the logo was a wing. She checked Dad's shirt out and noticed he had the same winged logo. Anna looked at Jamie and pulled a face saying 'Get them two.........ohhhhhh.'

When they got to the dining room the Iqbals were already there and chatting to Neil. The twins noticed they were wearing the same gear as their parents with the same logos.

"Good to see you up, especially you Jamie," joked Neil.

"You see Jamie, I told you your sleeping prowess was legendary," laughed Mum. Jamie wasn't so sure whether he should laugh as well or be worried over how much Neil knew about him. Anyway no time to ponder as a full English required his full attention.

"Have breakfast, then I'll take you all up to the Colonel." Neil joined them with his grapefruit and black coffee.

"How long have you been on board," asked Peter?

"Only about six months. I came straight from university with my human resources degree and am helping in regards to personnel matters whilst I wait for my posting from The Large Company.

"You've not been to the Academy then?"

"Not for me, I'm afraid. I was approached but decided my work for the Kingdom lay elsewhere."

"Good for you, Neil. It's nice to know there are people who realise taking the sword is not the only way to be useful in the work."

"Thanks for that, but it's a pity my parents and twin don't see it that way. They were not best pleased when I turned down the sword and Rob, that's my twin, took it up."

"That's their problem not yours. It's not for everyone and to be quite honest I wouldn't have been fussed at all if those two had your attitude," Rachel said as she looked over towards the twins. "Especially after what's been going on just recently."

"Take your point but it's good to know there are those who are prepared to take the fight to the bad guys. If you've finished we better get up to see the Colonel."

"Sounds good to me," said Peter eager to find out what's going on. They waited another five minutes whilst the Iqbals finished breakfast and Lois and Anna whooped the boys at pool. Of course, the cues were bowed, the table was uneven and Adam's potting the black ball were all just bad luck against the boys. It had nothing to do with Lois' dexterity around the table nor Anna's dead eye shooting.

They all headed off up to the bridge with Neil leading the way into the turbo lift and up to the bridge. They were cleared past the armed guards by Neil and their DNA scans and onto the bridge, or mission control as Adam referred to it. Not a button in sight. Just rows and rows of computer displays and more lights than Blackpool in November.

"Can I introduce Captain Davies?" said Neil. They shook the hands of an elderly man who Lois thought must have been over fifty!

"Pleased to meet you all. How do you like my lady?" Anna thought, 'I've not met your wife, so how do I know if I like her or not?' Fortunately Adam knew what the Captain meant and replied, "She's fantastic, sir."

"Thank you, young man. I do like a man who knows his ships." Adam liked this man. As he spoke to Captain Davies a door opened from the left side of the bridge and out came the Colonel they'd all be hearing about. Not much to look at. If Captain Davies was old the Colonel was positively ancient. Only about 5'6" tall, spectacles, a wiry frame and no hair just a 'polo' around his head. This didn't look like the world's top Enochim, but as the good Book says, you shouldn't judge by appearances.

"Hello Colonel. Good to see you again," and Peter shook his hand as he spoke.

"Likewise," Samuel said as he did the same.

"Ladies, as ever a pleasure," the Colonel said as he kissed the cheeks of Anya and Rachel in turn. "You must be Adam, James, Lois and Anna," he said as he shook the boy's hands and kissed the girls' cheeks.

"Come into my office all of you," as he held the door open and waved them into his centre of operations. This centre comprised of a desk with leather chair behind together with computer and more telephones that BT. In front was a large table with chairs all around.

"Please, do take a seat, all of you." As Captain Davies came through he closed the door behind him.

"Coffee? Tea? Juice anyone?" the Colonel asked.

"Not just now," Samuel said.

"Fine. Before we get started how would you youngsters like a tour of the ship?"

"Yes please," Adam replied for all of them.

"Can Neil take them round Captain?" the Colonel asked not wanting to step on the toes of the ship's master.

"Certainly sir," Captain Davies replied obviously appreciating the Colonel deferring to his authority with regard to the ship. Neil duly left with both sets of twins and the Colonel got down to business.

"First of all can I confirm that the children's transfer to the third dimension is still to go ahead. Delay is not an option for their safety and to allow the Kingdom's progress to continue. I am awaiting confirmation of the current location of the stone and when I have it the transfer will proceed immediately."

"That's good to know but what's all this activity against the children by the fallen?" asked Peter.

"It's not unusual for the fallen to have a go if they can to stop the sword being taken up by new Enochim, but I agree the ferocity and determination on this occasion is very unusual and worrying. Like you I have discussed the matter with Joel and Nathaniel and as yet they have no definite answer. They have now referred the matter up to their Seraphim to see what their take on it is. Until I get some feedback from them I can't answer your question."

"Has it got anything to do with my dad?" asked Rachel.

"Why, who's your dad?" asked Anya.

"James Burnett," she replied.

"You're kidding," Samuel said, not even trying to disguise the surprise in his voice.

"No," Rachel answered not even trying to disguise the pride in her voice.

Colonel Ponting looked over at Rachel saying, "It's a possibility. We know that revenge is a real motivation for the fallen and after what James did they would love to have a go at his family because they can't get to him now. The thing is why haven't they tried before against your mum, you and Ruth?"

"It could just be they weren't ready and now the opportunity has arisen they've taken it," suggested Rachel.

"Maybe. Anyhow, we're trying to sort out the details and when we know you'll know. For the time being, you'll all be safe here with us on The Crystal Sea and until we get the children's transfer sorted."

"Thanks for all you're doing Colonel," Peter said really meaning it.

"No problem. It's my job and my pleasure." As the Colonel spoke a knock came at the door. "Enter."

"Sorry to interrupt Colonel but Neil Johnson has requested that he and the children be allowed into the control room."

"Can't see a problem with that. They've got to start learning about the way we do things at some stage and why not now. Tell Neil his request is granted but that he mustn't take the children into Holds One or Two yet."

"Thank you Colonel." With that seaman Redman saluted and left the room. As he did so the Colonel contacted the control room and Captain Trevelyan to confirm his approval.

"Now where were we?" the Colonel asked himself.

Before he could reply, Samuel took up the conversation. "We were wondering what happened two nights ago with Terry and Ray?

The Colonel provided the explanation. "Since you were shot down we've been monitoring communications and it appears that the missiles came from a Russian destroyer that was mid-Atlantic. The ship's Captain says he doesn't know how or why the missiles came to be launched and is now steaming home to undergo a full diagnostic. To be fair I believe him. Once he realised the missiles had brought down an aircraft, he sent out continuous mayday calls and got to the scene as quick as he could to search for survivors. He didn't find any because we got there first but at least he tried."

"So was it an accident?"

"There are two options, Samuel. One, there was an unfortunate computer glitch that caused the missiles to launch accidentally."

"And two?"

"We had ourselves a 'Jobe'"

"A what?"

"A 'Jobe'. It's rare but it does happen. The fallen are able to affect an inanimate object and cause problems just as they caused a house to collapse on Job's family."

"So you think that's what may have happened?" asked Rachel.

"Seems the most likely explanation considering the fallen's current activity."

"Any news on Ray or Terry?" asked Anya.

"No. it looks like they made the ultimate sacrifice. Rick Parry is using all his contacts to get the details and you can be sure their families will be looked after. We'll be holding a memorial service later on today, so I'll ask Neil to let you have the details."

"We'd appreciate that Colonel," said Samuel speaking for all of them.

"I presume all of you will want to be involved in the children's transfer?"

"You presume right, sir," said Peter.

"Good. Have you been keeping up your training?"

"As best we could without arousing suspicions," Peter continued.

"Same here," added Samuel.

Rachel noted that she would need some refresher flights in The Zeke and Samuel said he would also.

"None of us have flown one for years so some practice would be useful."

"I would like to suggest that you take advantage of the gym and training facilities on board to refresh yourselves and we'll see about some simulator and real flying of the Zekes for you and Samuel. The Colonel closed the meeting and left the four with their thoughts, coffee and training.

Whilst the olds had been having their meeting Neil was giving the twins a voyage around The Crystal Sea.

"The Crystal Sea is actually a converted 100,000 tonne oil tanker that has been used by The Enochim for over twenty years. We use it because it can travel around the world without raising suspicion and it's easier to keep secure from the fallen and their comrades than a land based HQ.

"What did The Enochim use before The Crystal Sea?" asked Adam.

"Going back thousands of years when The Enochim were first instituted, they lived as groups of nomads travelling around for safety. As time moved on a base was set up in a city called Kedesh, that was one of the Cities of Refuge started by Joshua. Later, when Jerusalem became an important City with good communication routes, the HQ was moved there near The East Gate. The problem was that Jerusalem kept getting conquered and the people driven out. The Enochim managed to stay there up until AD 70 when The Romans flattened the place and they had to move out. First of all they went to Rome and stayed until The Empire fell in the fourth century. From there they travelled into the East and set up the HQ at Constantinople and then in Alexandria in Egypt. A base was then set up in Aachen from around 700 AD and by the early thirteenth century the base had moved to Florence and stayed there for about 400 years. By the mid 1700's Florence wasn't the best place to be located for world transport and with the onset of the Industrial Revolution, London was chosen for the new HQ. After the Second World War a land based HQ was seen as risky what with the new airborne bombing so another way to provide a base was thought about. This led to the idea of using a ship that should be safer because it moves around. The first Crystal Sea was commissioned in 1948 and the one we are on now is the third."

"How's it all paid for?" asked Jamie.

"For centuries the Enochim survived by working for themselves or receiving support from the central organisation. In 1878, to take advantage of new technologies, a corporation was set up as a front for The Enochim called 'The Large Company'. This organisation traded for the Enochim and any profits were ploughed back into their work. To assist the company certain theonology was provided to it by the angels just before man's technology was about to develop it and this allowed the Company to stay ahead of the game and be in funds."

"What's Theonology, 2 asked Adam?

"It's technology created and used in The Kingdom, some of which can be transferred to our dimension. I can't say more at the moment but you'll find out all about it soon. Anyway, back to my story. The Crystal Sea is paid for by the Company and is on its books to give it a cover story. Today, the Company is run by Rick Parry who makes sure the work carries on with money available. The Company also owns businesses and provides employment for some Enochim. For example, Eagle Carriers was part of The Large Company. Next year I hope to join the Company at its headquarters in Geneva to do my bit for The

Kingdom. Enough history for now or you'll have nothing to learn in the third dimension. Let's get this tour underway." Neil led them away from the bridge and down two decks.

"You've seen the dining room, cabins and Bridge along with a quick look at The Quay."

"The what," asked Adam?

"The Quay. That's where you came on board in Crystal Sea One yesterday. You know where all the marine vehicles are kept."

"Got you now. Can we go back?" Adam asked dying to try out the technology of those marine vehicles.

"We'll finish off there after we've seen some other parts of the ship." First off they went to the Infirmary. There were about twenty beds including three intensive care beds. There were two operating theatres and a pharmacy that Boots would be proud of. Whilst they were there they met Mrs. Ponting, the Colonel's wife, who it turned out was a nurse working with Doctor Luke Mason.

"Hello again you two," Luke said as he came up behind Jamie and Anna. "Good to see you again. How's your mum?"

"Fine thank you," answered Anna, "and good to see you again. Tell me, is this the hospital you brought mum to?"

"It certainly is. Only the best for your mum."

"So that's why we couldn't visit after the attack."

"Afraid so. Sorry about that, but if you'd visited the game would certainly have been up."

"How did you get mum here so quickly because we're thousands of miles away from home?" asked Jamie.

Luke looked over at Neil. "Have the children been in Holds One and Two yet?"

"No," replied Neil, "and the Colonel says not yet."

"Fair enough. You'll have to wait to find out about that one I'm afraid."

"Time to move on as there's loads to see." Neil ushered his tour group out of the Infirmary and into the Control Centre. Before they could get inside and passed the armed guard, Neil had to get clearance from the Colonel. Once he got it and the DNA scans proved positive they went in.

Adam had been impressed with the Bridge but this was something else. There were three massive screens to the front wall each showing a map of the world. On these maps were reference numbers that must have indicated something. All around the room were personnel working at computer consoles and talking to each other and who knows who else through their headsets. Neil introduced his tour group to Captain Gillian Trevelyan who was watch commander at this time.

"Nice to meet you all," and before Gillian could carry on with the pleasantries, Adam was in there.

"What are those references on the mega monitors?"

"Each reference indicates the global position of an Enochim who is currently on commission."

Neil noticed Adam's puzzled look and explained, "A commission is Enochim speak for a mission for The Kingdom." Adam nodded.

"What sends out the signal to you to give each position? "Adam continued.

"A Global Positioning wrist worn personal Chronograph or Peter for short."

"You mean a posh watch don't you," said Anna.

"That's exactly what I mean. These watches are state of the art GPS technology that allow crystal clear comms and positioning via our navigation satellite known as 'The Star'. Even Adam was impressed that they had their own satellite.

"Why are they called 'Peters'?" Lois asking the question they all wanted answering

"In the Bible it says 'Peter slept on his watch' so some Enochim comedian coined the phrase for our watches."

"So these are the Peters we keep hearing about." Anna continued, "And that's why mum left her Peter with those attackers so you could find them and deal with them."

"Can we have one," asked Adam?

"Not yet," came the Captains reply. "Pass your training and then we'll see what can be done."

"Thank you Captain. Let's leave the Captain to do her job. If you're good, perhaps the Colonel will let you come back again." With that Neil said his thanks and took the group off.

They spent the rest of the morning up top getting some exercise. The exercise mainly consisted of riding around the deck on bicycles to get an idea of the massive size of the ship and see its other sites. Eventually they got to The Quay and enjoyed messing about in the boats and jetskis.

VIII

Over the next couple of days the Mums and Dads kept up their refresher training whilst Adam almost moved into the control room. Jamie and the girls spent a lot of time at the Quay, especially after Neil let them start to use the jet skis. There was a small lagoon in the Quay where the skis could be ridden and fallen off in safety.

They also found out what the other marine vehicle at the far end of the Quay was. Turns out it was a mini submarine called Jonah. It had two crew, a pilot and navigator and space for two other personnel so that it could be used in rescue missions if necessary. When Jamie found out it was going out for a test dive he asked if he could go along. After discussions with Bernard, the dive chief, it was agreed he could with his parent's approval. Dad was all for it but mum wasn't so sure. The solution......Mum went too.

After about an hour of the test dive they were recalled to the ship as the Colonel wanted to see them all. When they finally prised Adam away from the control room Neil escorted them to Colonel Ponting's office.

"Thanks for coming. I thought it would be good to touch base to see how everyone's getting on. Peter, how's your refresher training?"

"Fine thanks. Feels like I've never been away."

Turning to Lieutenant William's, who was overseeing the parents training, the Colonel asked, "Is that how you see it Lieutenant?"

"Considering none of them have been on active commission for over 12 years, they've kept themselves fit and are responding well to the update."

"Are they ready to go back on commission as and when the children's transfer date comes through?"

"Given a couple of more days I would say so," is how the Lieutenant responded much to the relief of Peter, Samuel, Anya and Rachel.

"And how's your flier refreshers going Rachel for you and Samuel" the Colonel continued.

"Not bad at all. It's a pity Ray's not here to help because no one can fly that baby like him but we're getting there," Rachel answering for her and Samuel.

"I'd second that," added Tony Diaggio the Flight Chief.

"Which bit are you seconding?" asked The Colonel. "About Ray or that Rachel and Samuels getting there 'getting there'?

"Both," was Tony's immediate reply.

"I'm glad to hear things are going so well because the children's transfer date has now been confirmed as the day after next. So you've got 48 hours to add the finishing touches. Can you do it?"

"Yes," was the unanimous and immediate reply from the room.

"I like your attitude. Now, I think it's time these young people were allowed into Hold Number One, don't you flight chief?"

"I do Colonel. If they've got to go in a flier in the next couple of days they need to be familiarised with them."

"Thank you chief. Right, what I suggest is that you all have an early lunch and then parents and children all report to the stores to obtain equipment and uniforms. Thereafter meet the flight chief in Hold Number One at 1330 hours. Agreed?"

"Agreed," came the reply.

"Thank you all and happy flying.

With that Colonel Ponting closed the meeting except for, "Oh Peter and Samuel could you spare me a moment?"

The rest left and Lieutenant Williams closed the door.

"It's good news that the children can be transferred very soon but we're all still very concerned about the fallen's activities against them. I've no new hard information but my instincts tell me to expect the worse. That's why the timing and venue of the transfer are not being released to me until the last possible moment. I'll be warning The Guardians to be extra cautious and Peter you'll be pleased to know that Ruth is with them."

"That is good news because she's one of the best," said Peter.

"Ruth being......?" asked Samuel.

"My sister in law and a top drawer Guardian" came Peter's reply.

"He's not wrong Samuel. I have worked with her and she is the best I've seen. As for you two your families will be relying on you so use every moment to sharpen and freshen up your training."

"We will Colonel," Samuel replied with the assurance Peter would have used.

"Thank you gentlemen," they shook the Colonels hand and left.

After lunch Neil took them to the stores where the kids were kitted out with new gear. What they wore was similar to their parents except there were no badges. The gear comprised of combat style trousers and shirts in grey with a waist length padded jacket.

"Where's our belts like our parents?" asked Adam.

The quartermaster was a rather large but friendly man and should have been called the one and a quartermaster. He told them that until they are trained they have no use for a belt because they can't use the equipment that comes with it. When the children joined their parents they saw what they were missing. The Mums and Dads had their belts on with all equipment present and correct. Adam being Adam, had to ask what it all was and his Dad enlightened him. Their equipment consisted of :

A belt to carry their equipment.

1. A device known as 'A Shield'. This was a tube the size of a standard torch. When its button was pressed it created a shield like force field about 2.5 metres high and 1.5 metres wide. This force field would stop most earth dimension material including bullets.
2. A pouch that contained a black leather faced Bible. This Bible was used as any Bible should for reading but all the children also knew it could be changed with the right words in the twinkling of an eye into a flaming sword.

As well as the gear on their belts the parents also had two other bits of kit. The first was known as a helmet although it looked just like a hearing aid and fitted inside the ear for communications. The last piece of equipment was called the breastplate and was a waistcoat worn below the jacket. This was extra body armour protection against any earth dimension weapons the taken may employ. Samuel concluded that the whole kit was referred to as Armour.

'Pretty impressive and when do we get ours?" asked Adam.

"When you've earned it and can use it," replied his Dad. Samuel went on, "Although, I don't know what you others think but a breastplate for each of the kids may not be a bad idea."

"That is a very good idea Doctor," Rachel agreed. Samuel and Rachel went to see the quartermaster who when he was told it was 'doctors orders', supplied the necessary breastplates for the children. The twins saw this extra equipment as good news and bad news. The good news is that they get to wear extra gear and be more like their parents. The bad news is, why do their parents think they need such extra protection?

Now they were all dressed up, they had somewhere to go............ Hold Number One! They'd all wondered what was in there and now they were going to find out. Rachel led them and when they arrived they met a massive steel door. Rachel punched in a code and slowly the door came to life. It moved over to the left and opened into a cavernous metal cave. It was pitch black and no one could see anything. Rachel moved to her left and hit the lights. For a moment the children were dazzled then they were hit and dazzled by what they saw. There right in front of them was a machine the type of which they had never seen before. It was perfectly square and stood on what looked like four wheels, one being on each side, but intersecting each wheel was what looked like another wheel. When the children looked closer they could see that the flier wasn't actually touching the floor but floating above it. The flier was about the overall size of two MPV's put side by side and the machine was covered in what looked like chrome all over having a completely glass dome at its top. Adam noticed that on all the sides were what looked like eyes along with a number of holes that had covers over them.

When Jamie finally got his mouth working again he asked, "What on earth is that?"

"That," his Mum answered is an Ezekiel Flier or a Zeke for short.

"You mean that thing actually flies," Adam interrupted, "but its got no wings and from where I'm standing, no propulsion unit."

"It needs no wings and its propulsion is supplied by nothing ever seen on earth before," continued Rachel. "The flier is based on one used by Angels in their work but its design has been modified for use by The Enochim. Ours aren't as fast as the Angels as our bodies would disintegrate if we travelled at the speeds they do. The other difference is that ours have a dome over the seating position because it still goes faster than a meteorite and if we weren't domed we would be 'doomed'.

For a few minutes the kids just wandered around the flier to try and take it all in. As they got closer they tried to look through the dome inside but it must have been one way glass because they couldn't see in.

"Can we see inside," asked Anna?

"Don't ask me sweetie," replied her Dad. "This is Mum's baby so better ask her."

Anna did and "no problem" was Mum's reply. Mum went over to the flier and pushed open a concealed panel. Inside was a keypad and she typed in a number. With that the dome retracted and the interior became visible. There were four seats each facing out to one of the sides of the vehicle. In front of each seat was a console with what looked like a TV screen and on the seats were some buttons and a joystick.

"Why don't you all try it for size?" said Rachel, "but don't touch any of the buttons."

They all took a seat and wondered what it would be like to fly this bird. 'Adam! Don't even think about it,' shouted Rachel. She had seen him about to press a button which she knew was the ejector seat but he thought was the ignition. 'If you'd hit that you would have been splattered all over the ceiling like one of Anna's Dad's pancakes on Shrove Tuesday. Not a pretty sight.'

'Can you really fly this thing Mum?' asked Jamie.

'I have been known to and so has Doctor Iqbal. Right you and Anna strap yourselves in and I'll take you for a ride. If you and Lois jump out Adam I'll be back to give you a go soon. Are you coming Peter?' she asked.

'I better had in case you get lost and you need me to ask someone for directions,' replied Peter.

'Chance would be a fine thing,' Rachel replied with a smile on her face.

Two minutes later they were all strapped in. Mum did her pre-flight checks and then said, 'Each of the control panels can pilot the Zeke in the direction they are facing. So as your Dad is in the South seat he could pilot us in that direction but only that direction. As you two kids are in the East and West seats you could fly us in those directions. I'm in the North seat so I pilot in that direction. However, my seat is also known as the Master Seat as it is the only position in the Zeke that can control flight in all directions. So the Zeke Pilot or Alpha Pilot always sits up north. I've disengaged all other control stations except mine so only I will fly today.'

'Can you pilot the Zeke Dad?' asked Anna.

'Yes but I'm not as trained or gifted in it as your Mum so the rule is I drive the four wheel fido whilst your Mum flies the four wheeled flier.'

'OK. Everyone ready?'

'You bet,' replied the twins.

With that Mum spoke to the Control Centre. 'Control Centre this is Zeke One requesting clearance for flight. Over'

'Zeke One, this is Control Centre. You are cleared for flight. Over' As the words finished the ceiling started to move slowly to reveal the daylight above it. When the mouth of this metal cave was fully open Mum powered up the flier and closed the dome. No noise was heard and the twins only knew power was on when their screens lit up and the Zeke began to lift. No holiday jetliner take off with the Zeke. No noise. No vibration. No ear popping. Not so much a take off as a float up. They just kept rising and rising. Soon The Crystal Sea looked more like 'The Crystal Puddle.'

As if reading the twins thoughts, Mum said, 'You thought that was impressive, now hang on.' She keyed in co-ordinates into the navigational system known as 'The Star' pushed a button on her seat and then pushed the joystick forward. In an instant Zeke was moving faster than Jamie could describe.

'How fast are we going?' he asked Mum.

'Well, we've just past Elijah One.'

'How fast is that in earth speed?' he realising that 'Elijah One' must be a measure of speed for Angel craft.

'About 2000 miles per hour give or take a few miles and we're not even warmed up yet.'

'What's its top speed?' Jamie asked.

'Well, I've got her up to Elijah Four but I've not had clearance to go any higher.......yet!

'Are we there yet?' Dad asked like a six year old on the way to a birthday party.

'Pretty much,' Rachel replied and then Zeke powered down.

'Where are we?' asked Anna.

'I can't take you any lower or we'll be spotted but check out the screen in front of you.' As they did an image zoomed in that they soon all recognised.

'That's home,' Anna said. 'Can we go down and see properly?'

'Afraid not,' replied Mum. Don't see how I could explain this baby parked on our driveway.'

'So this is how you get transported when you're on a commission,' said Jamie.

'Sometimes if using earth transport is not quick enough,' replied Dad. 'When we were needed a prearranged pick up point would be sent to us and then a Zeke would come and get us. Once on board we could get anywhere in the world in minutes.'

'So that's how you got Mum to The Crystal Sea hospital so quick,' said Anna.

'You catch on quick,' said Dad.

'Fair enough,' said Jamie 'but there's no room in here for a stretcher.

'There is if you take out two or three seats,' Dad replied.

From home they flew over to check on Nana B. and then Nana and Pops. Once they saw they were alright Mum put the pedal to the metal, or whatever Zeke was made of, and headed back to The Crystal Sea.

Then it was Adam and Lois' turn. Anya joined them in the east and off they went. Before clearing the deck of The Crystal Sea, Adam was at it.

'What's this made of?'

'It's a non-earth alloy we refer to as 'Arkov', And before you ask me why it's called that it's because it's the same material the Ark of The Covenant was made of. It's a special alloy that when worked correctly causes the object it makes to levitate, just like The Ark of The Covenant did. Add to that a propulsion system energised by lightning and you've got yourself a gadget that 'Q' would be proud to give 007.'

Adam continued, 'This is all very impressive but how is it you can keep it a secret when these Zekes are flying all over the globe? Surely someone will have seen one, or radar or satellite will have picked one up?'

'You'd think so wouldn't you,' replied Rachel. 'To be honest, on occasions Zekes have been seen. You know sometimes when a person sees a UFO and says it stops and starts instantly, travels at great speed and changes direction instantly? Sound familiar?'

'So they're seeing Zekes.' as the scales fell from Adam's eyes.

'Not all the time, but some of the time,' replied Rachel. She continued, 'As for radar and satellites, well Zekes travel too fast for most systems, but even when we slow or hover we can't be picked up because Arkov is not a terrestrial metal so can't be configured for in human systems.

'I understand all that and it makes sense but why can't the Zeke simply be seen when it slows or hovers by the naked eye or satellite imaging?' asked Adam thinking he may have found the awkward question.

'Before I answer that Adam, can I ask you a question. How do you keep an idiot in suspense?'

'I don't know,' was his reply.'

'I'll tell you later because here we are,' Rachel interrupted herself and put the Zeke into hover mode.

'Check your screens and let me know if I got it right.'

'It's home! Look Mum it's home!' shouted Lois in delight.

'How are you doing that?' asked Adam.

'You saw those lenses on the outside that looked like eyes, well they are cameras that give us all round vision, day or night, whenever we need it.'

'The picture is so clear. I've never seen clarity like it,' said Adam who's not easily impressed. 'So if the 'eyes' are lenses what are the covered over holes that we saw?' he asked.

'Well,' but before Rachel could complete her answer she was interrupted by a call from The Crystal Sea.

'Zeke One come in please. Crystal Control calling. Over.'

'Zeke One here, Control. Over.' replied Rachel.'

'We have received information regarding a commissioned believer who is in imminent danger and is located in the sector you are in currently. Are you able to assist? Over.'

Rachel looked over in the direction of Anya who nodded. 'Crystal Control from Zeke One. We are able to assist. Over.'

'Thank you Zeke One. We are sending over the co-ordinates to your star. Please proceed immediately to position. Over.'

'Understood, Crystal Control. Do you have a sitrep on the believer? Over.'

'Negative, Zeke One. All we know is that it may involve fallen activity. Proceed with haste and caution. Over.'

'Received Crystal Control. Have received details and are en route. Will report in when further details available. So be it.' With that the communication ended, Rachel hit a button and Zeke One responded like lightning.

Anya spoke to her children. 'This is very serious and you must do what I say. When we arrive you must stay in the Zeke and under no circumstances are you to get out. Whatever happens stay in here and no one, human, taken or fallen can get at you. If the worse happens Crystal Control can even fly you back pilotless from wherever we land.'

'But we'll be seen,' said Lois.

'No we won't,' replied her mother.

'Why not ?' asked Adam.

'All you need to know is that we have a system called 'Elisha's Mantle' that prevents us from being seen.'

As Anya finished so did Zeke. Rachel brought the flier into hover mode over a building in Mumbai. She switched on vision to her console and Anya's but not the twins.

'Do you recognise the building?' Rachel asked Anya. There below them was a six storey building set within the heart of the city. All around there were Police and Army with the normally bustling streets cordoned off.

'Not specifically but it looks like some form of Government building. Can you land on the roof?'

'Did John the Baptist get wet?' was Rachel's reply and down they went like a feather falling to the ground. Once they had landed on the roof Anya outlined her plan. 'Initially, you stay here with the children, and I'll do a recce. Once I get a sitrep, I'll report in and we can decide how to proceed.'

'So be it,' was Rachel's reply. Rachel opened the dome slightly and Anya was out and the dome closed again in an instant.

Once on the roof Anya crouched low so as not to be seen over the parapet wall. She hugged the wall until she came to the door leading down to the upper floor. The padlock was no problem. A quick slice with her sword and it melted like chocolate in a frying pan. She carefully and quietly made her way down the staircase before coming to a locked door. After disintegrating its lock, she stopped and listened. No voices could be heard but still she waited. Three minutes later she was in the hallway crouching and listening. She heard muffled voices coming from an office at the far end. She crawled along until kneeling outside the door.

'Are the explosives set?' asked a voice.

'Yes,' came the short reply that for some could have a lifetimes repercussions.

'Excellent. It's a pity all the people on the other floors got out but at least we'll take out Davindra and a few extras just for the hell of it. He and the other man laughed. Anya just got angry.

'The timers are set for three o'clock to give us time to make our escape through the basement,' the second man said.

'Good.' You and the others have done well. The Ruler will be pleased. Now we just wait for these futile humans to play out our little game. They will be none the wiser just thinking Davindra and all the others are more casualties in their war on terror.'

Anya had heard enough and headed back down the hall. At each office door she waited to listen and see if anybody was in there. Eventually she came to a main office that had windows into the hallway. She looked in and saw two heavily armed men watching over a group of about twenty people. Which one was Davindra? She didn't care because her job was to save them all if she could. Anya headed back to the stairwell that led up to the roof.

Whispering she called up Rachel and gave a full report on what she had learnt. Her communication was relayed to The Crystal Sea who informed them that Davindra was crucial to upcoming work for the Kingdom in India. He has to be saved but not at the expense of the others.

'Understood Control,' was Rachel's reply.

Rachel updated Anya who had time to assess fully circumstances and decide how to act.

'We can assume the four terrorists are taken allowing for the reference to the ruler. We must take them out and as we don't know where the bombs are we had better lead out the hostages and then return to collect the taken and get them and us away from here. It's 2:45pm so time's short. Rachel you better get here and let's get this show on the road.'

'So be it,' came Rachel's reply. She spoke to Adam and Lois and told them whatever happened to stay put.

'No earthly explosion can damage the Zeke. If it happens just sit tight. If me and your mum can't get back to you Crystal Control will fly you out.'

The dome opened and she was gone. She met Anya at the bottom of the stairwell. 'I'll take the two with the hostages whilst you deal with those two in the end office. You go first so the two with the hostages are distracted to give us more chance to protect them from harm.'

'You've done this before Anya, haven't you?'

'Once or twice,' replied Anya with a smile on her face, 'Once or twice.'

'For the Kingdom,' said Rachel.

'So be it,' Anya responded. They left the stairwell and each took up positions outside the doors to the two offices. Swords drawn and active Rachel awaited Anya's signal to go. She didn't have to wait long. 'Go,' Anya whispered. Instantly Rachel was though the office door. She found the leader sat behind the desk with surprise in his eyes. He went for the pistol by his side but as fast as Rachel shouted 'Taken!' her sword was across his chest and he was comatose. As she turned she saw the other one pull himself up after being floored when she had kicked in the door. He trained his machine gun on her and pulled the trigger. He was fast but not fast enough. Rachel had seen it coming and had deployed her shield. The bullets bounced off like rain hitting the ground. The bemused would be killer stopped and before the thought of what was going on made its way across his mind, Rachel was across the desk and her sword was across his chest. Two comatose taken meant her job was done.

As soon as the noise of Rachel kicking in the door reached the two guards with the hostages they turned to see what was happening. As they did Anya demolished her door and took out one of the taken as she ran towards the hostages. The other, realising what was going on pulled his trigger to fire not at Anya but the hostages. One was hit but before another bullet could rip into flesh Anya was in front with her shield in place and deflecting the deadly hail. As the bullets came so did the terrified screams of the hostages. The taken pulled his trigger harder as if that would give the bullets the extra power to pierce Anya's shield. The word 'futile' came to Anya's mind as Rachel came through the hole where once a door had been. The taken turned just as Rachel gave him a flying drop-kick to the chest, he fell back with his gun still firing. The bullets bounced off Rachel's breastplate as she fell on him with her sword and sent the fallen one out of the taken back to where he belonged. As the silence fell on the room so did the magnitude of what had just happened hit the hostages. The screams were replaced with tears and then Anya's voice. She spoke in fluent Hindi and although Rachel couldn't understand the words, she understood its tone. Calming. Authoritative. Caring.

'Rachel, I've told them we've got to get out of here now. Its 2:53pm and those explosives won't wait. You get those taken all together in one place and I'll get the hostages out via the ground floor.' Anya spoke again to the hostages and then she was off. She had the wounded woman over her shoulders in a fireman's lift and led the group down the stairs to the ground floor lobby and freedom.

'Who are you?' asked a man.

'Police Special Forces,' Anya replied.

Another said through her tears, 'Thank you.'

'No problem,' Anya said, 'just doing my job and loving it.'

She then turned to the group and asked,' Who's Davindra?'

'I am,' came the reply from a man who couldn't have more than five feet tall but who Anya knew was to be a giant in the Kingdom.

Anya spoke to him. 'Can you slowly go out the door waving your white shirt as a flag? Shout loud and clear that you are the hostages coming out. Now that we've saved you from those terrorists we don't want our own side shooting you.'

'I will and thank you.'

Anya replied, 'No, thank you for what you will do for the Kingdom.' Strange words Davindra thought and how in the coming days he would think over them. He took off his shirt and left the building. He shouted, 'We are the hostages! Don't shoot!' His fellow prisoners followed him but not Anya. She checked her peter and saw that it was 2:58pm. Running as fast as she could Anya got up to the sixth floor by 2:59pm. She found Rachel had moved all the unconscious released into the main office.

'There's not much time, Rachel. We better get the first of these up to the Zeke.' They each put one of the released on their shoulders and headed to the roof stairwell. As they went, they heard it and looked up as to where the noise was coming from. Not only was the noise coming down from the ceiling but the whole ceiling was coming down with it.

'The explosives must have started and one's above us,' shouted Rachel. As they moved to shelter themselves and the two released with them they saw it. Zeke One was coming down through the ceiling.

'What on earth...' and before Anya could finish the sentence the dome opened and she saw her son piloting the flier.

'Adam what do you........'

'Not now Mum. It's three o'clock and the explosions are about to start. Get in,' he shouted!

Anya and Rachel didn't need time to think. They threw in the two released just as the explosions started all around. It was like being in the middle of a firework display on bonfire night as well as being on top of the bonnie with Guy.

Come on! Get in!' shouted Lois. Neither Anya or Rachel took any notice. Even though fires and noise were raging their only thoughts were to get the other two released. They ran through walls of fire and falling debris to reach them. Anya was hit by a roof beam but she carried on. They threw the lifeless bodies over their shoulders and ran back to the Zeke. As they got there Adam opened the dome having closed it to protect those already inside. Rachel and Anya jumped in with their sleeping passengers and Adam shut the dome. Just as he did the building began to collapse around them, the once proud edifice turning into a mass of rubble before their very eyes as the outcome of evil took its toll. Zeke One just hovered amidst the carnage. Those on the ground below ran for cover not even knowing the flier and its passengers were there.

After what seemed like minutes but was only seconds there was silence. No one spoke until Adam said, 'So that's how it felt in Jericho when Joshua blew into town.'

All those awake laughed and eventually so did Anya although she was going to have words with Adam about flying a machine without her say so.

'Move over chief,' Rachel said as she went up north and took control of Zeke. 'You can tell us later how you came to be flying this baby but for now let's get home.' Rachel punched in the co-ordinates for the Crystal Sea and headed back to base.

IX

'You better tell me all about it,' said Colonel Ponting. 'How is it you knew how and when to fly the Zeke?' Adam couldn't tell from the Colonel's tone whether he was mad or not so he just got on and told him what happened. He, the Colonel, his Dad and Mum were all in the Colonels office having a debrief over the incident in Mumbai yesterday. By now everyone on The Crystal Sea had heard about the goings on and the Colonel needed all the details.

'I'd heard Mum and Mrs Fisher talking over the comms about the situation so I knew they only had until 3pm to get the hostages and themselves out of the building. By 2:55 me and Lois were getting concerned so I listened in via the Zeke's comms system to what Mum and Mrs Fisher were saying.'

'And you knew how to do that because……?' the Colonel asked.

'Well, its fairly straight forward. You just enter the Zeke comms system and select the communicators of the people you want to listen in to. Once selected, you patch it through to your console and there you go.' As he finished, Adam thought perhaps it would have been better if he hadn't answered with such matter of factness and then maybe the Colonel wouldn't have rolled his eyes back so much.

'But,' the Colonel explained, 'You need a security code to clear yourself to enter into any system on the Zeke, so how did you do that?'

At this point Adam knew he was in trouble and looking over to his Dad didn't make him feel any better.

'You better tell the Colonel, son,' was all the help he got.

Knowing he was about to get in trouble Adam just looked down at the floor and said, 'I saw Mrs Fisher enter her code so I just used hers.'

'Not good Adam,' replied the Colonel. 'I'll let your father deal with that one.'

'Thank you Colonel and be assured I will.' Adam knew the tone his father had used and it didn't bode well.

Before Adam could carry on, Colonel Ponting contacted Crystal Control. 'Colonel Ponting here.'

'Yes Colonel. Captain Bradshaw, watch commander. How can I help?'

'Thank you Captain. Can you contact flight control and instruct them to issue new systems access codes to Rachel Fisher?'

'Affirmative and understood Colonel. Bradshaw out.'

'That'll please Mrs Fisher,' the Colonel said sarcastically as he turned and looked again at Adam. 'Please continue.'

'I heard Mum say the hostages were safe and she was heading back up to Mrs Fisher. I checked my watch and saw it was 2:58pm. The explosives were set for 3pm so I figured Mum and Mrs Fisher were running out of time. I couldn't just sit there and do nothing and then Lois shouted, 'Do something, Adam!' So I did. I put the flier onto manoeuvre power and powered up the missile system.'

'And you knew how to do that because….,' asked the Colonel.

'Whilst waiting for Mum to come back I had been checking out the fliers systems.'

'Foolhardy initiative is the best way to describe that I suppose,' is how the Colonel saw it and Adam thought he almost detected grudging respect in his voice.

'I armed two missiles at their lowest level and fired through the roof. Instantly the roof collapsed and I saw Mum and Mrs Fisher. Then the explosives started so I opened the dome and shouted for them to get in the flier. Before they would they threw in the two taken, ran off to get the other taken and then got in. I closed the dome and the building collapsed. As the dust and rubble settled we just sat there watching but not being watched. It was unreal. There we were with a bird's eye view but no one down below took any notice of us. Then Mrs Fisher came over, took over and flew us back here.'

'Quite a story, young man. Now let's just consider what's happened. You stole an authorisation code and used it illegally. You flew a flier without clearance. You fired missiles without consent, but you also probably saved the lives of six people which has to count for something. On this occasion I am not going to note a black mark on your record but no more heroics until you're trained, OK?'

'Yes sir.'

'Thank you Adam for being straight with me. You're dismissed.' Adam left and the Colonel spoke to Samuel and Anya. 'Clever lad you've got there and to be fair his actions did help to avoid a possible catastrophe.'

'Thank you, Colonel,' they both replied with the same tone of pride that as a parent himself the Colonel could detect.

'Now back to matters in hand.' The Colonel hit the intercom and asked that the Fishers be shown in. When the Fishers joined them the Colonel continued.

'Tomorrow at 03:00 hours three fliers will leave the Crystal Sea. Rachel you'll take Zeke One with your family when your new authorisation codes are through.' Rachel looked quizzically at the Colonel but before she could ask he said, 'You'll find out soon enough. Samuel you'll take Zeke Two with your family and Lieutenant Williams will take Zeke Three with two pilots to bring Zekes One and Two straight back. Co-ordinates will be in the Zekes systems but let me give you details of where you're going.' The Colonel turned his chair to face the rear wall and as he did he grabbed a remote control unit. He hit a button and down came an LED screen. More button pressing and the screen came to life as the Colonel said, 'Here's a presentation I made earlier.'

The Colonel stood up and pointed to the screen as he spoke. You leave at 03:00 hours and head for New England. The fliers will lead you to a small isolated farmstead whose specific location you don't need to know. On arrival you will land in a copse to the north east of the farmhouse as shown here.' The Colonel pointed to the screen as he spoke. On landing you will be met by two guardians who will escort you to the house and then onto Jacob's Ladder. You will wait for the children's return and then signal Crystal Control to send back the fliers. Any questions?'

Samuel went first. 'Weather conditions, Colonel?

'It's going to be a clear calm night so on the ground manoeuvres should be straight forward.'

'Any chance the bad guys might make an appearance?' was Peter's question.

'Normally I'd say no but after the events of recent days I can't be sure. Information to date does not indicate the transfer site has been compromised. However, I suggest you assume there could be problems and act accordingly.'

Silence until the Colonel spoke. 'Right if there are no more questions you better get back to your refresher training. Can I advise you take the children with you to get them used to acting as part of the team and to build up their confidence. For the Kingdom.'

'So be it' was their unanimous reply and off they went. For the next 24 hours, both families trained together. They were allowed to use Zekes One and Two to practice getting in and out as fast as possible and even to do flights to make the twins feel more comfortable. Samuel watched Adam closely and although tempted he didn't let him fly.

One of the flights was used to drop off the released back to their homes. They all lived in or near Mumbai. The procedure was to keep them sedated whilst on The Crystal Sea and then transfer them by flier to where they came from. Identities were obtained by checking DNA against governmental records which The Large Company had access to as the Company had designed and installed the software. The released would be dropped off usually near hospitals or Police stations and kept watch over until someone found them. Once it was certain they would be looked after, personnel would return to The Crystal Sea. Peter explained to the children that on this occasion as the taken had been involved in criminal activity but were unharmed, they would be left near the central police station in Mumbai. Then an anonymous phone call alerted police to their involvement in yesterday's activities and their whereabouts. Peter continued that as the taken had allowed themselves to be used they were responsible for their actions. Therefore, they had to be dealt with by the laws of the country in which they had acted. Jamie wondered about what happened to the taken who had attacked them?

'On that occasion we decided not to get the police involved as it would have drawn attention to us and awkward questions might be asked,' explained Dad. 'Although local members of The Kingdom were informed that these people had got involved in unwise activities to let themselves be taken. Hopefully these local members could lead onto the right path to avoid further problems.

Explanations and training over they all slept well that night, exhaustion overcoming apprehension, just as The Colonel had hoped.

'What was that?' shouted Jamie as an alarm went off in his cabin. He looked at his watch and said to himself, 'It's no o'clock in the morning so why are they waking me up?' No sooner had the thought crossed his mind when he heard Dad's voice. 'Get that bed off your back. Get showered and meet us in the canteen in 15 minutes. Don't be late.'

Not wanting to get Dad officially niggled Jamie got to it. As he came out of his cabin he met Anna and off they went to get the other twins.

'Excited?' Anna asked Lois?

'Sort of, but a bit scared as well.'

'Don't worry about it sis. You've got me looking after you, so what can possibly go wrong?' As he finished Lois and Anna looked at each other and smirked.

'Ah, come on girls. Seriously. I'll keep an eye on you.'

They all went down to the canteen and met up with their parents and Neil.

After supper, it was time for pool and the girls practice paid off because they opened a pack of in your face as they whooped the boys yet again.

After this very early breakfast they all returned to their cabins to get ready to leave. The twins couldn't take anything with them because the portal of Jacob's Ladder was too narrow so only they and their clothes would get through. Rachel and Samuel left the cabins first to carry out their pre-flight checks on the Zekes. At about 1:30am, Peter and Anya left to sort themselves out. They thought it best not to let the twins know that they were having to check weapons and tactics in case of attack.

Dad said as he left, 'Neil will come for you in about quarter of an hour and bring you down to the fliers. Make sure you're set to go straight away. We're on a tight time schedule. He kissed Anna, hugged Jamie and left with Anya for the quartermasters.

All four children got together in Adams and Lois' cabin.

'What do you think it will be like?' asked Jamie.

'Dad says The City of Angels is amazing. It's massive and all the buildings are pure white.'

'That's what my Mum said to Anya, but its so long since she was there she can't really think of the words to describe it. I suppose we'll have to see it to believe it.'

'I'll take some impressing but I can't wait for the transfer by Jacob's Ladder. Can you believe that we're going to another dimension? It's mind blowing.' Ever the scientist, Adam was hyped by the thought of a new experience.

'I wonder what the training will be like and what about this 'gifting' process. What's that all about. I asked Dad but he was pretty vague.' Jamie spoke the words to know one in particular hoping that any of the other three might have a take on it.

Anya was the first to reply. 'My Dad says it's not for them to explain. Their parents couldn't tell them. We've got to wait for our teacher to tell us.'

'Never thought I'd look forward to school but that's one double lesson I won't mind going to. I might even stay awake!' With Jamie's words came a knock on the door. Neil's Voice followed.

'Time to go you lot!' Neil came into the cabin with a look that to Anna seemed to be made up of worry and jealousy. 'It's 1:45am and this is one flight you can't be late for.' Neil checked their clothing and led them off to the fliers.

They headed first off to Hold Two from where the Iqbal family were flying. The Colonel and his wife were there, so was Luke.

'Just came to wave you off. I won't wish you luck as you don't need it.' Then the Colonel started the hugging off by hugging Anna and then 'all hugs' broke lose with everyone getting involved. As the Colonels wife hugged Lois she said, 'Hugs for everyone. One size fits all.'

The 'hug fest' over and the Iqbals boarded their Zeke.

'See you over there,' shouted Peter and then the Fishers left for their flier. At the same time, Lieutenant Williams and two other pilots boarded Zeke Three so thay could bring Zekes One and Two back.

'All settled down and strapped in?' said Mum, 'Then I'll begin.' Anna held her breath as the flier lifted off and then she held Jamie's hand.

The flier soon reached its cruising height then Mum said 'Hang on.' The joystick moved forward and so did the flier. As it was dark you couldn't get the sense of how fast they were flying until they crossed over onto mainland USA. The flier descended silently and relatively slowly to keep the noise down. As they went down the lights below came up and Anna thought of herself as an angel being placed on top of a Christmas tree. The descent stopped and Mum moved the flier slowly forward on temporal thrust power,whatever that was but it sounded good when mum said it. The lights below disappeared as the flier moved away from whatever settlements were below and into the country.

'Are we there yet?' Jamie couldn't resist.

'Nearly,' said his Dad sternly, 'Now be quiet.' Jamie knew this was not a good time for humour so he didn't say anything more.

'Zeke One to Zeke Two, do you copy? Over.' Rachel spoke quietly but clearly into the radio.

'Zeke Two here. We copy. Over,' came Samuels reply.

'What is your status Zeke Two? Over.'

'We have landed as arranged and await your arrival. Over.'

'Copy that, Zeke Two. We are coming into land now at your co-ordinates. Over.' Rachel stopped speaking and started landing. The ground came up and Zeke One nestled just above the grass.

'Everyone stay here. I'll go and link up with the Iqbals.' He turned to Rachel, 'Do you have them on scope?'

'Sure do, she replied. 'They're about 200 metres to the north west.'

'Good enough.' With that, Mum opened the dome and Dad left. He waited to let his eyes get accustomed to the dark and then headed through the woods crunching the grass as he went. 200 metres later he stopped. He knelt down, checked all four compass points then whispered into his headset. 'Zeke Two, do you copy? Over.'

Anya replied, 'Affirmative. Over.'

'Good to hear your voice, Anya.' I've checked the surroundings and you're clear to disengage 'Elisha'. Over.'

'Affirmative. Over.' Instantly, Zeke Two appeared out of nowhere just to the left of Peter. He reached them as the dome opened and Anya disembarked.

'Let's get your family over to Zeke One and then we'll rendezvous with the Guardians,' suggested Peter.

'Sounds like a plan to me,' answered Anya.

They headed back to Zeke One and stopped just before Adam ran into it because you can hit what you can't see.

'Rachel. Peter here. We're outside the flier. Please disengage 'Elisha'. Over.' No sooner requested than received. Rachel opened the dome. 'Time to leave you two.

Let's go, quick and quiet.'

They joined the group by the trees and watched Zeke Three appear out of the night. Its dome opened and without ceremony or noise, Lieutenants Redman and Wilder disembarked. They acknowledged everyone, got into Zekes One and Two and everyone watched as all three Zekes were mantled and then they presumed, flew off into the night.

"Right, now we're on the ground, Anya and I take command. Anya, let's put the plan into action.

With authority and experience in her voice, Anya said, 'Everyone stay down and stay quiet. Peter, I'm happy the area is safe at present. I'll scout the perimeter whilst you contact the Guardians. '

'Thanks Anya.' Anya left and was gone like a shadow on a sunny day, only quieter. Peter knelt down but still kept a lookout. Then he spoke into his helmet.

'Guardians, this is Jacob here, do you copy? Over.' Jacob was the groups call sign.

'Jacob, this is Guardians here. We copy loud and clear. We have your peter position and are proceeding to join you. ETA 3 minutes. Over.'

'Thank you Guardians. Be advised that Anya is working point on our perimeter. Over.'

'Received and understood. Over. We have Anya's peter position and will approach via same. Over.'

'Thank you Guardians. Jacob over and Out. Peter calling Anya. Over.'

'Anya, here Peter. Over.'

'Did you copy the Guardians transmission. Over.'

'Affirmative. Will link up with Guardians and rejoin you as one. Over.'

'Thanks Anya. Over and Out.' Jamie went to ask his Dad how many Guardians there would be but Peter put a finger to his lips to show no talking.

Without noise or warning, Anya and the Guardians came up to Jacob. There were four Guardians all wearing the same gear as the parents except there were no wedding rings and each had two Bibles. Anna recognised Aunt Ruth but didn't dare say anything to her. Ruth looked at her and smiled then whispered to her, 'Good to see you too.'

Ruth hugged Rachel and introduced everyone else. Ruth took over command. Jamie didn't know it then but Guardians have seniority. They all knelt down in a circle except for the three other Guardians who set up a triangular perimeter and kept watch.

Ruth whispered, 'We are set up in a farmhouse about half a mile from here. We'll head straight there and link up with the others. I'll take point with Jed. Sarah and Mel will cover the flanks and Peter and Anya will cover the rear. All clear?' everyone nodded. 'Move out.'

Ruth stood up and joined Jed. Samuel told the twins to stay close to him and Rachel. Ruth checked everyone was in position and then gave a waved signal to move forward. They moved through the woods which wasn't easy in the dark nor when you were following quick moving silhouettes out in front. Fortunately, Samuel and Rachel had done this before so they kept the twins up with the troops. The night was crisp and clear with a full moon. Jamie thought, 'I could get used to this' but Anna wasn't so sure. It took about ten minutes and Jamie guessed without them the olds would have done it quicker. They came to the edge of the woods and Ruth signalled for them all to kneel down and Adam heard her mumble something into her headset. The Guardian at the other end of the headset heard her clearly.

'Ruth here. Come in David. Over.'

'David here. Over.'

'We have Jacob with us. Is the coast clear? Over'

'Affirmative. Over.'

'Received. We are coming into your position from the East. Over.'

'Copy that. The kettle's on. Over.'

'You sir, are a gentleman. Jacob coming home now. Over and out.' Ruth beckoned for the group to stand up. They did and were soon moving out of the woods towards a light in the near distance. The light became a farmhouse and then a window. As they reached the house Ruth led them to the back door and to a warm glow of the stove and the warm welcome of The Guardians. Now they were out of the open Jed, Mel and Sarah could introduce themselves properly along with David.

Ruth seemed to be in command because before things turned into a party, she issued further orders.

'Jed you go and join the others in the barn. You three get your refs then go and relieve the compass point perimeter guards.'

'How many of you are there,' asked Adam.

'Guardian troops come in twelves,' replied David. 'We rotate duties so we have four to guard the stone, four to guard the perimeter and four to eat sleep and be merry, all on eight hour shifts.'

'You must get tired pretty quick,' said Anna.

'We get used to it and don't forget its one month on and then two months off. Not as many days off as teachers but hey who does except Father Christmas.'

'Thanks, David. Now you kids get some eats and I'll chat with your parents.' Ruth, obviously not being one to argue with, was obeyed straight away by the twins. The sight of pizzas, juice and chocolate didn't hurt either.

'Let's grab a coffee you four and chat.'

'It's good to see you Ruth,' Rachel said as she hugged her sister again.

'And you sis but let's get these kids safe first and then we can spend some time together. In fact if that husband of yours can stand it I'm on furlough next week, so I can come and stay.'

Peter heard every word, as he was meant to. 'You can come anytime you like now sis because I've got satellite TV and ear plugs.' As he said it he put his arm around his sister in law and they both knew he was kidding. To be fair they really respected each other and would do anything for each other.

Ruth, still in command mode continued, 'I suggest we all finish off our supper then head straight to the stone. The sooner these kids are with Eli the better. The group nodded its approval and Samuel said, 'Agreed.'

The chat was broken by a call to Ruth from one of the perimeter guards. 'Ruth its Joe here on the south side. Do you read me? Over.'

'Affirmative, Joe. What's the story? Over.'

'I thought I heard something over to my left. Over.'

'Thinking you did is no good to me Joe. Did you hear something? Over.' The silence was louder than any reply. Ruth tried again. 'Joe, come in. Over. Come in Joe, over.' No reply. 'All guardians this is Ruth. Code Red. I repeat, code red. All guardians not with the stone report to the farmhouse now! You lot get ready to move out on my command. We will head straight for the barn and get the children to Jacob's Ladder. Anya and Peter, give the children close cover and the rest of us will provide a perimeter. Draw swords!' The assembled adults did so and awaited Ruth's next command. It wasn't a long wait. As Ruth held her two Bibles in front of her chest she shouted, 'The Sword of God!' As her two Bibles flamed into action so the others shouted, 'The Sword of God!, and the room was emblazoned with the light of The Word of God.

No Guardians came to join them from outside. 'We wait no longer. We go to Jacob's Ladder now. For the Kingdom!' Ruth shouted and they all replied, including Jamie, Anna, Adam and Lois, 'So be it!'

Ruth opened the rear door, looked out and then followed her stare into the darkness. The others followed with Peter and Anya sticking close to their precious charges. As the whole group came out they couldn't believe what they saw. The four perimeter Guardians were all fighting against four, five even six attackers all at once. Their two swords flashed in the dark night leaving trails like the tails of meteors. Joe sent one fallen back to Abaddon as the lifeless body of the released fell at his feet. The attackers saw the children and locked their stare onto them. One shouted out, 'Get them!' Joe turned and looked at Ruth. Before he opened his mouth Ruth knew what he was going to shout and then he shouted it. 'Get those kids out of here!' As Joe shouted a dark figure lunged at him from behind and Joe fell to earth like a meteor.

'No time now get to the barn!' Ruth shouted as she herded the group past her over to the large timber building that was now surrounded by wailing attackers. Jamie noticed that some of the attackers didn't look like what he'd seen before. They were different with no lifeless staring eyes. As he thought about this he heard David shout, 'We've got Goliathim here!' Jamie didn't understand what David meant but he certainly understood Aunt Ruth's worried look of surprise.

'Enochim, let's get these children to Eli now! No one stands in our way! For the Kingdom!' With that they all waded into the howling mob surrounding the barn. Their swords flashed like lightening leaving unconscious, lifeless bodies everywhere. But the more they took care of the more came at them.

'Jed! Get that door open now! I don't want to be fighting taken and Goliathim all at once and that group of Goliathim are all heading our way.' Realising she had to do something about those attackers, Ruth shouted, 'David, Mel! Take care of those Goiliathim!' Instantly, the two of them left the group and sheathed their swords. Jamie then noticed they stopped, knelt down and got something out of their back packs. He couldn't see clearly but suddenly things started flying through the air and those Goliathim started falling like......well Goliath.

'Come on.' Ruth's voice penetrated Jamie's concentration as he and the others flew through the disintegrated barn door. Obviously, Jed can hit a barn door with his sword. As they got inside, amidst the hay and farm tools, Jamie saw four Guardians standing in a square formation with eight swords drawn.

Again, Ruth took over. Adam wasn't sure, but it could have been her tenth commandment.

'Guardians draw shields and make a protective wall around the stone with the children in the centre!' No sooner had the word 'centre' left Ruth's lips, the job was done. All six Guardians activated their shields and an impenetrable wall was built around them and the stone. The taken and Goliathim came rushing in with madness in their eyes and murder in their minds. They reached the wall but this was no Jericho.

They began hammering at it and screaming, 'We'll get you and those children!!'

Inside the wall Ruth said, 'Parents, say your goodbyes and get those children onto Jacob's Ladder, NOW!'

The waters of the Red Sea could be held back but not the tears of fathers, mothers and children. The parents knew they had no time to waste. Their children's lives were worth more than sentimentality. Rachel hugged Anna and said 'I love you.'

This was repeated eight times then Samuel shouted, 'You must go now! Adam, stand over the stone and open the portal. It will take you to safety and it will bring you back to us. Do it now!' Adam obeyed his father and his curiosity. He looked at this stone. It was about the size of a melon. 'How could this inanimate piece of God's earth transport him to another dimension?'

'NOW ADAM!' his father shouted again.

'Stand over the stone.' Adam did so and immediately he was bathed in a warm glorious light which seemed to enlighten his whole being. Then he noticed the light split into the seven colours of the rainbow. As he looked to try and take it all in he realised he was rising up and up and looking down on the scene below. Then it was gone and so was he.

'Now you Lois. Get on the stone.' Lois hugged her mother and did as she was told. 'Thank God they're safe,' Samuel whispered to Anya as he tried to hold back the tears. But the taken and Goliathim needed holding back as well. They were still battering the wall and more were joining them.

'Quickly Anna. Follow your friends and remember we love you,' Rachel said as she placed Anna on the stone. She was gone.

'I can't leave you and mum, dad, not like this. You'll be killed,' Jamie's anguished voice almost failing as he spoke.

'You must go son. Please, do it for me and you mum, go now.' Jamie hugged his Dad and Mum, hoping it wouldn't be the last time he did. He stood over the stone and as the rainbow encircled him he looked down and saw the wall of shields collapse.

'No!' he shouted and then they were gone.

X

Was he rising or was the earth falling? Adam couldn't tell. As he rose up Jacob's Ladder he felt he was leaving behind all he knew, understood and loved. Those feelings were both exciting and sad at the same time but before his thoughts had time to cross his mind, he had crossed into another dimension.....the third. Suddenly he juddered like you do when you're asleep and you experience a falling sensation. Everything stopped and he found himself sitting on a floor in a room. As his eyes got accustomed to his new surroundings, a voice asked 'Are you alright?' Adam thought he recognised the voice but he wasn't sure. Obviously, travelling between dimensions plays havoc with your hearing.

'If only I'd had a boiled sweet when I got on the ladder' he thought to himself. Anyway, he managed to reply, 'I guess so.' Adam rubbed his eyes, blinked and looked up to see Joel standing there in front of him.

'It's good to see you, Joel. Is Nathaniel here as well?'

'I sure am,' Nathaniel answered, 'and it's good to see you here in one piece.'

'You mean I could have got here in pieces,' Adam said with therapeutic humour.

'It's not happened yet,' Nathaniel replied, 'But there's always a first time.' Their conversation was interrupted by the sound of a rushing wind as Lois appeared out of nowhere next to Adam on the floor next to him.

'Nice you could make it sis. 'You'll be pleased to know, Joel and Nathaniel are here with us and soon so will Anna and Jamie.'

'You're not wrong,' said Joel as the wind got up again and then there sat Anna.

'You OK Anna,' asked Lois?

Anna took a moment to reply as her ears cleared themselves and she cleared her throat.

'I think so but I'll know better when I can see again. Is Jamie here yet?'

'Unless someone's left a door open I do believe that's him coming now,' Adam said as he heard the rushing wind again. Sure enough where there was wind there was Jamie.

The three others sat there and watched Jamie rub his eyes and shake his head to let him acclimatise himself to where he now was.

'Am I there yet,' he asked to no one in particular. The other three answered together, 'Yes.'

'Are you all OK,' asked Joel?

'Yes,' all four replied as one.

'If this carries on you'll all be joining one of our choirs,' said someone in the corner who none of the children knew. Everyone smiled at the comment and the unknown friend introduced himself, 'Greetings to you. My name is Eli and I will be your teacher whilst you here in The City of Angels.'

'The where..?' asked Adam.

'You have arrived in The City of Angels, which as you know is in the third dimension. This is where The I Ams Angels live when we're not out on a mission for the Kingdom. Enough questions and answers for now, I should think you're all pretty shattered after your journey.'

'Adam maybe shattered, but pretty...' quipped Jamie. The girls laughed but Adam for some reason, didn't.

'Thank you James for that insight,' replied Eli. 'Can I suggest that Joel and Nathaniel take you to your quarters where you can rest for now and we'll speak later.

Eli looked over to Joel and Nathaniel who both nodded their heads and replied,

'Certainly Teacher.'

'Come on you lot, follow us,' Joel said as he stepped onto the platform where they were all sitting. The children hadn't noticed before but they were all sitting on a raised area that was about a metre off the floor of the room they were in. This stage where many dramas had been played out over the years was in the centre of the room and was completely clear, like glass. Beneath the glass was what looked like a rock and Adam guessed it must have been a duplicate or part of Enoch's Stone that was still left on earth in the first dimension. Looking around the room Jamie saw that it was circular and on the doors was a large reproduction of the symbol Anna had first seen on Dad's phone and that was on their parents uniforms. There was nothing else in the room except for two large angels with swords drawn. Even Adam was too tired to ask what it all meant so when Joel and Nathaniel had lifted them all to their feet, they just went quietly.

'This way,' said Nathaniel as he led them to the door. 'Can I suggest you put these on as its very bright outside. 'These' were sunglasses but not like ones the children had seen before.

'But it's night time isn't it?' asked Adam.

'It was when you left earth but here there is no night only day,' explained Joel. 'You'll learn all about it soon enough but for now just put on the shades.' Adam was too tired to continue his line of questioning and so like the other three he put on his shades.

When they got to the door with no handle it opened automatically without even an 'open sesame.' Joel wasn't kidding. The light hit them like an explosion in a daylight factory. For a few moments the children were all blinded and stood still.

'Are you OK to carry on now?' asked Nathaniel.

They all nodded and proceeded to follow their two guides along a corridor to another door.

'Right, we're going outside now where it's even brighter,' warned Joel.

'Not possible,' replied Jamie. 'The only thing that could possibly be brighter than this is Stephen Hawking and he's not here is he?'

Even Joel and Nathaniel laughed but it was Adam who really appreciated Jamie's scientific humour.

'No he's not yet but you never know,' answered Joel. 'Seriously though, it will get brighter so be prepared. 'Right, here we go,' and Joel opened the door. He hadn't lied to the children before and he wasn't starting now. They hadn't believed it possible but it was even brighter. The only saving grace was that there was a cooling breeze that really refreshed them. When the twin's eyes had got used to the new level of light they all looked to see where they were. They were standing in a colonnade with arches that ran all along the rear wall of the building they were in. Beyond the colonnade was a large park-like area with grass so green and smooth they could have been stood on the baulk cushion of a snooker table. Jamie had been to The Millennium Stadium in Cardiff but this park made that look like the 'Century Stadium.'

This time Lois beat her brother to it and asked, 'What is this place?'

'You would probably know it as a school field,' replied Nathaniel. 'It's part of the school we have for you Enochim and it's where you will do some of your training and where you can relax and enjoy yourself.

'So I take it this building behind us is the school,' Adam added.

'All Saints Enochim School to give this centre of excellence its full title. This is where you will spend a lot of your days with teacher Eli and other tutors who will be teaching you new skills prior to your 'gifting'.

'Our whatting,' asked Anna.

Joel interrupted and called a halt to this line of conversation. 'I think we're getting a bit ahead of ourselves. All will be revealed in good time but for now, let's get you four settled and rested.' He led them across the park, a journey that must have taken fifteen minutes or more. When they reached the far side they came to a double gate in the wall. As the group got close to the gate it opened automatically and led into a courtyard area behind a three storey house.

'This will be you home for the next forty days. As you can see it is right next to school so there's no excuse for being late, is there Jamie?'

'You know me so well,' he replied. Once inside the house the two angels gave the twins a tour. On the ground floor were what the children would have known as a lounge, dining room, sitting room and kitchen. The kitchen had cupboards but no cooker or fridge but as it turned out it or the children needed neither. They did notice there were bowls of fruit, bread and a selection of fruit juices. The ground floor accommodation also had a bathroom to match the other four in the house.

Anna thought of it first and ran upstairs like a child looking to choose its bedroom in a new home. Lois was quick to realise what she was doing and soon followed. By the time the two boys twigged it was too late and the girls had already chosen their rooms on the first floor leaving the boys to occupy the two top floor bedrooms. As it turned out it didn't really matter as all four bedrooms had en suite bathrooms although the girls had less distance to travel to the kitchen but they were nearer school.

'Right, I can see you lot are sorted. Can I suggest you get some sleep and we'll call later to see how you're getting on. You'll need to close the shutters on the windows to keep the light out as we have no night time here.' With that, Joel and Nathaniel left them in the kitchen and left them to it.

'Can you believe this place?' said Adam as Lois poured him and the others a glass of juice.

'When we were upstairs I had a look out of my bedroom window there are loads of houses just like this one and I saw lots of people,'

'You mean Angels,' interrupted Anna.

'Fair enough,' Adam continued, 'Lots of Angels walking and talking in the streets.'

'Well it is The City of Angels so I suppose that's to be expected,' added Jamie.

'Listen, I don't know if it's late or not because my watch has stopped. What time have you got,' Lois asked the others?

They all checked their watches and found theirs had stopped as well.

'Of course,' Adam shouted. 'Of course our watches have stopped. We're no longer in our dimension where our time exists. We're in the third dimension where it exists differently. Isn't that incredible?'

'Maybe so, but how do I know when it's breakfast time,' Jamie said wryly.

'Never mind that now. Whatever 'time' it is, we're all shattered so let's get to bed and I'm sure Joel and Nathaniel will come and wake us when they're ready.' Anna's plan seemed reasonable so they all finished their juice and went to their rooms. After freshening up they found some clothes in their wardrobes including pjs. Ten minutes later they were all giving it serious zzz's.

The next thing any of them knew was a tapping on their bedroom doors and the words, 'Time to get up.'

Jamie, as sharp as ever, came back with, 'As there's no time here, it can't be time to get up.'

'Not bad considering you've just woken up Mr. Fisher. Now get that bed off your back, get organised and meet us downstairs in fifteen of your minutes.' Jamie heard the others moving about so he thought he better join in.

In fifteen of their minutes they were all downstairs sitting round the large kitchen table with Joel and Nathaniel. Fruit juice all round.

'Anybody like anything else for breakfast?,' asked Joel.

'Bacon butty wouldn't go amiss,' Jamie said more in hope than expectation.

'That I can't help you with I'm afraid, James. In this dimension, any animals we have are not used for food. They don't have a Kingdom of their own but are part of our Kingdom, so as we all exist together we're not about to start eating them. Not only does the lion lie down with the lamb but with us. The food we eat is plant based and let me tell you even the 'other Jamie' would be impressed and enjoy it.

'Point taken. So how about some cereal and toast then?'

'No problem young James.' Joel got up and went to the cupboards in the kitchen and took out everything he needed. Joel took the other children's orders and soon they were all enjoying their first meal in the third dimension.

After breakfast Joel took them out into the rear garden and explained how the rest of their day was planned. This time they didn't put on their sunglasses as their eyes were getting use to the light.

'We're going to take you back to All Saints where Teacher Eli will give you a run down on your course and you can meet your other tutors.'

'Sounds fascinating,' both Jamie and Adam replied the only difference being, Adam believed what he said.

'Are we going to have to walk through the park again to get to school?' asked Lois.

'I'm glad you asked me that because it gives me chance to explain how you can get around the city. Nathaniel, if you would be so kind,' and with that, Joel let Nathaniel take over.

'The city of Angels is bigger than any city you have in your dimension on earth. It's so large that I can't describe it using dimensions from you dimension, if you see what I mean. Enough to say that it is big, very big. Now we angels can get

around by walking, flying or 'rapturing'.' As Adam went to open his mouth, Nathaniel looked at him and he closed it again.

'Rapturing is when we transport ourselves to any destination that we decide we want to go to. Joel would you demonstrate.'

'With pleasure.' Joel led them all through the gate back into the schools park. He looked over at the school building that was visible in the distance. He said to the children, 'You see the high tower at All Saints over there...' as he said it he disappeared and suddenly they could just see a figure on the roof of the tower waving his arms frantically.

'That's 'rapturing'' said Nathaniel. As he said it Joel re-appeared next to them.

'At the moment you can't rapture,'

'What do you mean 'at the moment?' asked Adam.

'That's for another time. So because you can't rapture 'at the moment' you're allowed to use our horses to get around the City.'

'You're kidding,' squealed Anna in delight. 'You've not got horses here have you?'

'We most certainly have and they are the most beautiful and well behaved horses you will ever meet.'

'Can I see one now,' asked Anna?

'I don't see why not,' said Nathaniel. He led them over the grass to the right hand side and opened the gate into the adjoining property. It turned out that next door was a stable yard with stables circulating a cobbled courtyard. As Anna looked intently around she saw the most beautiful pure white horses in the stalls. Unable to contain her excitement she ran straight over to the first horse and stroked its head. The horse didn't flinch at all. In fact Anna thought it smiled but she couldn't be sure.

By this time Lois was at the next stall doing what most girls do with horses loving it to bits.

'I see you've met Milk and Honey' said a voice behind the girls. They turned to see an angel not much bigger than they were but wider, with less hair and red cheeks around a smile almost as wide as the horses.

'They're beautiful aren't they,' he continued. Can I introduce myself, my name is Philip and I'm in charge of the horses in this district.' The girls thinking they had done something wrong stopped stroking Milk and Honey and Lois said, 'We're sorry sir for touching the horses.'

'No, no,' Philip replied instantly. 'They love being touched and if they're happy, so am I. Please, carry on,' he said as he moved next to Lois and said to Honey, 'You're fine aren't you girl.'

'Can we go for a ride, sir?' asked Anna.

'Only if you call me Philip,' he replied as he smiled.

'Can we go for a ride please, Philip?' asked Lois.

'You certainly can.' Philip took them over to the tack room that was in the rear right hand corner of the yard and he fitted them out with silver riding hats and boots.

'You won't need whips,' he said. 'Our horses are so in tune with us they will act on our commands without being forced to.'

They all saddled up and Philip led them to the park. 'Let's see how fast we can get to school.' With that he gave the command 'walk on' and his mount called Breeze, immediately walked on. The girls followed Philips lead, soon were up with him and before they knew it they were galloping across the park. Neither Anna or Lois had ridden like that before with such confidence in their horse's ability and their own safety. The cool air kissed their faces as they rode to school like the wind.

Back in the courtyard, Jamie and Adam stood watching as the girls became smaller and smaller in their vision.

'Not bad if you're a girl,' said Jamie. 'I don't suppose you've got a Mazda RX8 in a stable somewhere have you?'

'No, but perhaps this might do instead,' Nathaniel said as he walked over to a large double-doored barn to the left hand side of the yard. He swung open the doors and inside were what Adam could best describe in his own mind as chariots, but what chariots. They were two wheeled, had a wrap around seat, and a double overhead reins arrangement that gave the ability for twin horsepower thrust.

'Not bad,' said Jamie, 'But where's the CD player?' After they laughed Joel and Nathaniel helped the boys set up the chariots and then tacked up two horses each. Jamie got 'Thunder and Lightening' and Adam 'Fire and Brimstone.'

Joel jumped on with Jamie and Nathaniel with Adam. They got out of the courtyard into the park and Nathaniel said, 'Right, after the count of three let's see who can get us to school the quickest.'

'Ready?'

Both boys nodded. 'One, two...........Three!!'

And they're off! Welcome ladies and gentleman to the inaugural running of the Enochim Gold Cup. It's a lovely day to be racing chariots and the speed these two young charioteers are going even Elijah himself couldn't beat them. Adam with Fire & Brimstone is slightly ahead but Jamie with Thunder & Lightening is sticking with them. Ohhh, Adam nearly made that tree into match sticks and his chariot into a Lada but he's still going strong. It's neck and neck as they come to the Babbling Brook and there up.........................

and over to the other side. Adam had a slightly better landing so is now leading into the final straight. The crowds are up on their feet cheering, well three of them are, as these two latter day Ben Hurs or Ben Hims if you will, race to the finish. The line approaches and ....it's Adam over first!!

'Well done lads, that was great,' said Joel.

'Great? It was double bifters,' replied Jamie trying to catch his breath.

'I don't know what that means but it sounds like you both enjoyed yourselves.'

'Nathaniel, I haven't had this much fun since I won our school record for completing a calculus test!'

'Easy Adam, I didn't think it was that good,' he replied. Even Adam was impressed that angels knew what sarcasm was.

'I take it we've all finished our horsing around for now,' came a voice from behind them all. Joel and Nathaniel knew who it was and the twins turned to look and see the angel they had met last night in Jacob's Room.

'We have Teacher Eli,' replied Joel respectfully.

'Well in that case, perhaps you could show my new students to my room.'

'At once Teacher.' Nathaniel followed his words by ushering the children into the colonnade and through a door into the main building of All Saints.

'What about the horses and chariots?' Anna asked.

'Don't worry Philip will deal with them and he'll have them back at the end of school today to get you home. Now come, we don't want to keep Teacher Eli waiting.' The two angels led the children along the corridor and up three flights of stairs to the second floor. They took a right hand turn and came to a door that didn't open automatically.

'This is Teacher Eli's Study and you must always knock and wait before you go in,' instructed Joel. He did just that and waited.

'Who's there?' came the reply to the question of the knock. Jamie was tempted but looking at Nathaniel, who knew what he was thinking he decided silence was the better part of humour.

'It is Joel and Nathaniel with your students, Teacher Eli.'

'Come,' and in they went. The children looked around and were amazed with Jamie worried by the number of books on the shelves. Looking around the twins saw Teacher Eli sat behind a desk so large they thought it could have been re-cycled from Noah's Ark. His chair must have been Goliath's in another life. Then they saw the window. Well it wasn't so much the window as what they could see out of it. Teacher Eli recognised their amazement as he had seen it so many times before on the faces of other Enochim.

'Impressive isn't it?' Teacher Eli said as he rose and went over to the window. Come over and get a closer look.' The children didn't need a second invitation as they moved to the window and the picture it contained. There in front of them was The City of Angels. Massive. Enormous. Titanic. Gargantuan. BIG!! As far as their eyes could see there were buildings of different shapes and sizes all gleaming white in the light. Amongst this collection of buildings were angels all moving about. Some walking some flying and some just disappearing and re-appearing to who knew where?

'Does it ever end?' asked Adam.

'The City does have limits but I can't define them to you as the dimensions of your dimension are inadequate to describe what exists here.' Teacher Eli left the children just enjoying the view for a couple of minutes whilst he chatted to and the dismissed Joel and Nathaniel.

'Now children, come and sit down. You'll get to see more of the city tomorrow.' Both sets of twins sat down on chairs set in a circle and all facing Teacher Eli.

'That's better,' began the teacher. 'Before we go any further, can I explain that I don't want our time together just to be another school term for you. You are here out of choice and therefore I believe it is my duty to respect that fact and not force you to learn but encourage you to want to learn. During our time together I want to give you 'The Three R's'......Respect, Reasons, Rules. Now we've got that clear let me tell you how our time together will work. You will be here for forty of your days whilst we train and gift you as Enochim. Out of those forty days there are only twenty four days scheduled for formal teaching sessions with the rest of the time being for you to teach yourselves.'

Anna shuffled in her chair and Eli knew instinctively she wanted to ask a question but was afraid to do so. He looked at her with kind eyes and asked, 'Do you want to ask something dear?'

The words surrounded Anna like a hug and she no longer felt scared to ask. 'All it is sir, how do we teach ourselves?'

'Please Anna call me 'Teacher'. I hope you will teach yourselves because you will be so energised about the work you can do for The Kingdom that you'll want to learn. My task and that of my fellow tutors who you will shortly be meeting is to awaken the desire that exists within you to want to do all you can for The Kingdom. See by asking that question you've already started learning for yourself.' Anna knew he was right and wanted to learn more.

'I think what I should do now is explain to you 'Alpha Time'. I take it you've all noticed your watches have stopped?'

'Yes Teacher,' they all replied.

'And that's because........?' Teacher Eli threw out the question and Lois batted it straight back.

'Because in this dimension there is no time like in our dimension.'

'Good answer Lois but not quite right. There is time here as much as we understand what has past, what we are doing now and that things will happen in the future. But we do not keep time like you do in your dimension. That's because our dimension has no seasons as created by the sun and moon on earth. Now as we angels are created outside of what can best be called temporal time we don't need time keeping.'

'Then how do you know when to do something,' asked Adam?

'We follow The I Am's bidding as it comes, however and whenever it comes. Suffice to say, His word is our action, but let's not get too theological now.

At this point, all you need to know is that we don't work by time but we know you find it easier to as it's what you are used to. Also, as there is no day, night or seasons here we can't refer to things as 'today,' or 'tomorrow. Therefore, to help you Enochim that come here we have developed 'Alpha Time'. Let me show you.' Eli stood up and pointed at the blank wall that was behind his chair. Instantly a three dimensional clock appeared although as they were in the 'third dimension' that was to be expected.

This is what we call a 'Holygram' which you probably know as a 'hologram'. Yes?' they all nodded because they'd seen 'Star Trek'.

'We use these holygrams all the time here to explain things more fully for you. This holygram shows an Alpha Clock. The children looked and saw........

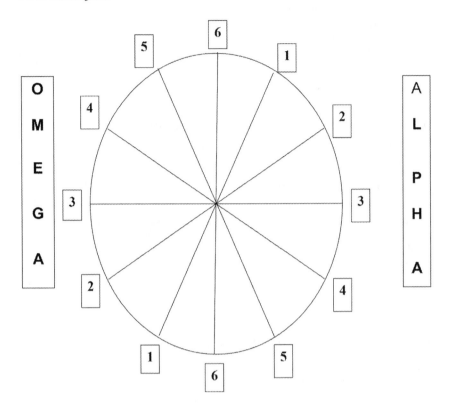

Teacher Eli continued. 'The idea behind 'Alpha Time' is to give you Enochim something as a reference point. As there's no day or night we can't have am and pm so instead we have 'Alplha and Omega, The Beginning and The End'. As you can see the Alpha clock is divided into 12 points with each one equating to two hours of your earth time. So for example, 'Alpha 1' is your 2am and 'Omega 3 is your 6pm. There's only one hand to point to whatever time it is as we don't bother with seconds and minutes. Anything we do always happens 'on the hour'. When something is about to happen we like to say, 'The hour has come'. As an example you should get up at least by Alpha 4 and be in school by Alpha 5. Alpha lessons finish by Alpha 6 and Omega lessons start at Omega 1. School finishes by Omega 2 and you should be in bed by Omega 5. Simple isn't it?'

'I suppose so once you get used to it,' replied Adam not wanting to appear slow.

'So what time is it now,' asked Lois?

'Now that's an excellent question. For us angels it doesn't matter but for you Enochim we would say it is Alpha 5/6 because it's between those time stations. That's as accurate we need to be.'

'Well Alpha time should suit Jamie,' said Anna, 'As his time keeping is always a bit 'ish'.

'Hopefully it will suit you all while you're here.' Eli waved his hand and the holygram disappeared. 'To help you here's an Alpha watch each,' and Eli handed over a timepiece to each of them.

'Because we don't have time like you do nor days and nights tomorrow never really comes, so we just give each alpha and omega you are here a number with this being your second day. Don't worry too much about it as Joel and Nathaniel will keep you in order. Right, that's enough for today as it's you first full day here. Joel and Nathaniel will look after you for the rest of the day. Can you be back here at Alpha 5 tomorrow?'

They all nodded and thanked Teacher Eli as they left. Outside the door were there two chaperones who led them back down to the park. They went home for lunch and then spent the rest of the day in the stables next door, the girls grooming and riding the horses and the boys playing on the chariots. Omega 5 came round all too quickly and so did sleep. Even though tomorrow wouldn't be another day none of them could wait for it to come to see what other new things they would experience.

XI

'And there was light!' Joel shouted as he pulled back the shutters in the boy's room.

'What are you doing?' asked Jamie. 'It can only be 'no o'clock' in the morning.'

'Actually it's Alpha 4 and as you know things start on the hour here in Third Heaven, so the hour has come for you to get the bed off your back and get ready for school.'

'So that's where Dad got 'bed off your back' from,' Jamie answered Joel as he got the bed off his back.

'I'll have to have words with your father; stealing an angels catchphrase can't be right,' Joel answered back with what Adam thought was a wry smile.

'Two of your hours to School and you don't want to keep Teacher Eli waiting on only your second day, do you?'

'Certainly not,' Adam replied as he raced to the bathroom to freshen up.

'Only thirty eight more days to go I suppose,' Jamie whispered as he put the bed back on his back to wait for Adam to finish.

Joel left them to it and met Nathaniel on the first floor landing after he had finished waking the girls up.

Within 30 of their minutes all the children were downstairs enjoying breakfast. This time it was cereal and fruit juice all round. As it was only Alpha 4/5 they popped next door and played with the horses and chariots until Joel came to get them just before Alpha 5. No need to worry about being late as the horses and chariots got them across the park and to All Saints on time. Once there they found their way to Teacher Eli's study and waited to be beckoned in. 'Come' came instantaneously and by Alpha 5 they had all taken their seats.

'Thank you for being on time as you squares would say,' and with that Teacher Eli began 'The First Lesson'.

'Today you are going to meet your tutors and then this omega Joel and Nathaniel will be giving you a tour of The City. I will be overseeing your training but the day to day teaching will be carried out by four tutors. There are four subjects that these tutors will be covering and these:

Transport – The Eagle
Defence – The Lion
Communications/intelligence – The Man
Service – The Ox

'Each of these areas will be taken by a respected and highly trained angel and these are they.' At that moment four Angels appeared in Teacher Eli's Study from nowhere. Well actually from their respective studies but the twins didn't figure that out until lunch.

First to introduce himself was Zechariah who was to concentrate on transport, a subject that turned out to be a lot more interesting than it sounded. Zechariah was a tall, thin Angel with a wiry frame and short hair which was unusual. It turned out he preferred this haircut as his hair wouldn't get in his eyes when traveling faster than light through a black hole. Not only was his hair unusual but so were his clothes. All the Angels so far had on white flowing robes, whereas Zechariah wore what could best be described as a fitted jumpsuit although it was still brilliant white.

Next came Micah who was to teach defence. Nothing thin and wiry about Micah. He must have been over seven feet tall, if only the twins could use earth dimensions. Not only that, he had muscles that even his clothes couldn't contain as they bulged out and could be seen even through his robes. Once you managed to stop staring at his muscular frame and took a glance at Micah's features, you saw the contradiction of a gentle, smiling face with a body that seemed to scowl at you. Micah was used to the Enochims surprise and returned their curious looks with a smile and a gentle 'Hello.'

Micah continued, 'You lot look in quite good shape for squares but in my experience there's always room for improvement.'

'Room for improvement' now there's some words that can strike terror into any young persons mind', Anna said. Teacher Eli looked over with a look that said 'Quite funny that, but not now'. Anna 'heard' the look and became a 'doer not just a listener'.

'Don't worry, no Enochim have ever died yet from my training........ although one of two have come pretty close,' chuckled Micah.

Jerahmeel was the third to introduce himself and he did so in English and then Hindi much to the pleasure of Adam and Lois. Jerahmeel was going to teach communications and 'intelligence'.

'Now that's something Jamie could use' thought Anna, but remembering Teacher Eli's previous look she decided to keep this further evidence of her 'top class humour' to herself. Jerahmeel look liked the classic angel with his long blond hair and deep blue eyes. If Lois hadn't have known better she would have thought he made his living in 'Bollywood'.

Last but not least was Uriel, the smallest of the four and unusually he wore glasses. 'Good morning children,' Uriel said in a quiet voice yet one which carried authority. Uriel had the look of a professor what with his long flowing white hair with the widest parting in that Jamie had ever seen.

'I am Uriel and my areas of teaching are angel and Enochim history to explain your service in the Kingdom. I know it sounds a bit dry but I'll try and make it as interesting as possible. By the way, I know what you're thinking, 'How can an Angel be shortsighted and need glasses?''

'Well that's interesting,' said Jamie, 'You can mind read as well.'

'Not really,' replied Uriel, 'it's just that after so many of your centuries dealing with Enochim, you get to know how they think. Anyway, because of what I teach I just thought it suited my image better to be 'bespectacled' just like a lot of your earthly 'profs', hence my 'vision expression'. And before you ask, Adam, 'no' I have never left any of my pairs of specs in your dimension on a plate to be found by just anybody.'

'Are you sure you don't read minds,' asked Adam?

Uriel chuckled and with that turned to Teacher Eli to acknowledge he had finished his introduction.

'Thank you, Zechariah, Micah, Jerahmeel and Uriel.'

All four nodded with respect with their heads to Teacher Eli and answered in unison 'Teacher' with a tone that confirmed their admiration for him.

Teacher Eli then turned to the children and asked 'Are there any questions?'

Adam jumped straight in just as Eli knew he would and asked, 'Teacher Jerahmeel, what exactly does your teaching on communications and intelligence involve?'

'Good question Adam but before I answer it can I ask that you do not refer to me as 'Teacher'. Only Teacher Eli is referred to in that way. For the rest of us, we are happy for you to call us 'Tutor'.'

'Adam nodded and all the other children took note as well.

'Now to answer your question, communications and intelligence or 'Comtel' as we call it involves the theonology we use to keep in contact and to obtain intelligence for the work of The Kingdom on earth. It's important that you understand that The I Am is all knowing but because in His wisdom he has set limits on the earth we must use other ways of obtaining our information unless He deems fit to provide it to us.

'I can understand that,' said Lois going on to ask, 'but what's Theonology?'

'Theonology is the term we apply to all equipment provided by The I Am for us Angels and you Enochim to do our jobs. Such things as The Zeke Fliers you have flown in, the energy source used by our equipment, the 'Peters' you use as personal communicators and locators and so on. In regards to our intelligence work we obtain that from many sources including undercover work so we help you with learning how to disguise yourselves and how to infiltrate 'enemy' targets without being identified. There are other areas of our work too but perhaps that can wait until later.'

'Thank you Jerahmeel. Any other questions for the tutors' asked Teacher Eli?

'I have one for Tutor Zechariah,' said Anna. 'Can I ask do you teach us on the horses?'

'I do teach you on the horses and chariots and hopefully you'll really enjoy it especially when we're training for Phillips Cup, but more of that later.

Teacher Eli brought things to a close for this session. "Right, I think we've done enough this alpha so let's break for lunch. After that you children can meet Joel and Nathaniel at the park entrance at Omega 1 and then go for a tour of the city.'

With that the children went to the refectory for lunch and tried to take in not only their veggie burgers but also all they'd learnt that morning. By Omega 1 they were all raring to go for their tour of Angel City. When they got down to the park entrance, Joel and Nathaniel were waiting with two chariots each being pulled by Thunder and Lightning and Fire and Brimstone.

'Years of doing these tours has taught us the best way to enjoy them and understand the city is to do it by air.'

'Seems reasonable' said Adam, 'so I suppose you're taking us to a 'Flier Port' to get a flier and give us an aerial tour?'

'As ever Adam, logical and reasonable but on this occasion you're off the mark,' replied Nathaniel. You girls come with me and you lads go with Joel,' said Nathaniel. Once they were all aboard the two chariots, the angels shook the reins, flames came from the rear of the chariots and they took off and ascended faster than Richard Branson after a ballooning world record.

'Now that is 'Chariots of Fire'. Seen the film, got the tee shirt now taking the tour,' Jamie said certain it was just his humour and not words to cover his nervousness. Soon they must have been thousands of feet in the air but none of them felt at all cold.

'If we were in our dimension we'd be dead by now due to cold and lack of oxygen,' remarked Adam.

'It must be being so cheerful that keeps you going,' responded Joel.

At what must have been 3000 metres high, both the chariots leveled off and drew close to each other. No turbulence, no wind, no cold and maybe just a few jitters from being so high up and yet not contained in a pressurized metal tube.

'Great view isn't it,' asked Joel. By now all four had risked looking down and couldn't believe what they were seeing. There below was the most gigantic city they had ever seen, it was perfectly circular and at one end it seemed to border land made of pure glass.

'Now Reverend Thomas Cook would like to organize a tour here wouldn't he,' joked Joel. The children turned to him and were about to fire off the whole nine yards of questions when Joel raised his hand in defeat before the barrage began.

'Before you bamboozle me with your questions let me show you this and explain a few things to you.' With that he unfurled a scroll from his robe and laid it across the front of the chariot. There before them was a schematic of Angel City.

'Now let me explain a few things,' and off Joel went.

'The Angel City was prepared by The I Am for His angesl before your creation was even started. As we were intended to be immortal to be able to carry out His every command, we needed somewhere to be based from and this is it. Unlike your cities and now your mega cities, Angel City was planned and built once for a set population of angels and has not needed to be altered since, except for after the rebellion.

'So what is the population,' asked Adam.

'Enough,' was Nathaniel's quick reply.

'How much is 'enough',' Adam persisted.

'As I'm sure your parents have said to you on many occasions,' enough is enough,' Nathaniel answered. He continued, 'To be honest we don't know the number of angels as that was decided by The I Am and we don't question His decision or doubt His provision by counting. King David did that and look where it got him!'

'Ok. Point made about numbers but what's this rebellion you mentioned,' asked Lois?

'It's not time for your history lesson yet but I suppose you need to know about the rebellion so I can explain about 'Lo Debar.'

'Lo what?' asked Anna.

'Right, before I confuse you more than your mum does over Maths homework, just look down at the city. Do you see it is circular but towards most of the edge of the city there are empty places. Those empty places we call Lo Debar and that's where the third of angels who rebelled against The I Am used to live. After the rebellion there were many places dotted all over the city that were abandoned and so to regularize the city again, all the remaining angels moved towards the centre and left empty places on the edge.' With that Joel pointed to his schematic and showed with his finger the two areas now called Lo Debar.

'You guys need to know that you do not go there,' Nathaniel added quite firmly in a tone reminiscent of Teacher Eli's. 'Lo Debar' is a place of great sadness to us angels as it reminds us of where our fellow angels used to be and how they have fallen and now follow the prince of the air. We don't go there and we expect you not to, ok?'

'Ok,' they all replied.

'Why's it called 'Lo Debar,' Jamie asked?

'Lo Debar means 'no pasture' and it reminds us angels of the blessings we forfeit when if we turn our backs on The I Am just like the third who fell.'

'Right, enough on that let's get back to the rest of the city, you can see it's somewhat like a wheel with a central hub we call 'The Circle'. He pointed to the plan and then over the side of the chariot to the real thing. 'In this central ring are a number of buildings including your School. There's also Angel Head Quarters where The Angel Council of Seven is based, the Library and 'Wings'.

'Wings,' Adam asked?

'I think you'd enjoy it there. Essentially it's a place where angels meet socially to relax and get to know each other. We don't often get there because we're so busy but you lot should be able to a few times whilst you're here. Hopefully, we might get there tonight to have some meribah and try some manna.'

Adam looked the question and Joel replied 'Later.'

'Carrying on with the tour, you'll see that radiating from the circle are twelve segments and each of these are districts occupied by the 12 families of angels. Each of these families is named after its head with names that you may recognize. Look again at the plan and you'll see the names and districts for each. The four did and there they were in clockwise order:

Judah

Issachar   Zebulun

Asher   **Simeon**

Dan   **Reuben**

Naphtali   **Gad**

Benjamin   Joseph

Levi

'And those names are……..,' asked Nathaniel?

'The Twelve Tribes of Israel,' answered Lois.

'Not quite but very, very close. They are the Twelve Sons of Jacob who mostly became the twelve tribes although Joseph became two tribes through his sons Ephraim and Manasseh.

Joel continued, 'In each of the family's districts are the barracks for one of Twelve Legions, with each Legion being named after its 'family'. The barracks are right next to the ring so that their commanders are available to the Council of Seven as they are needed.

'These Twelve Legions being….' Asked Jamie?

'Just like your SAS, or SEALS or Special Forces. They are the cream of the trained angels but Uriel or Micah will explain all that to you.

'What's that motorway dissecting the whole of the city,' asked Lois?

'I'm glad you asked me that', said Joel. 'That 'motorway' is called Straight Street and it leads from the Garden Gate to Fair Haven Harbour. Look again at the plan. The area outside the city is called The Garden because that's what it is. It's a beautiful place with grass, trees, babbling brooks, flowers, whatever your imagination tells you that 'paradise' is then that's the garden.'

'Can we go there,' asked Anna, more in hope than expectation.

'No reason why not,' replied Nathaniel to her surprise, 'As long as you go with one of us. Not because it's dangerous but because more than one Enochim has got lost out there. We'll arrange something before you go home.

'Thanks,' Anna replied excitedly.

'Getting back to the Garden Gate, that's in the district of Levi and the angels there act as gatekeepers. Once you enter the gate you are on Straight Street which eventually leads you to the Harbour through the circle'.

'So if there's a harbour, what we are seeing at the north of the city is a sea, a crystal sea.' Adam was certainly on form now.

'Spot on my young friend. You sir shall have a choccy tonight. That is indeed The Crystal Sea you can see there.'

'Where does it lead to,' Anna asked hoping her eagerness to learn might get her a choccy tonight.

'Somewhere you cannot go to whilst you are in still in this dispensation. You see The Crystal Sea surrounds the throne of The I Am and until all things are fulfilled you cannot go there. No Adam, don't ask. Now's not the time and I'm not the Teacher. Suffice to say that those who are called to the throne can go via Fair Haven if that is how The I Am decrees it. Although most angels are simply called to the throne and rapture there before you can even think about 'twinkling your eye'.

Nathaniel jumped in, 'Right Joel's given you the basics, how about we have a flying tour around Angel City to really bring it to life for you.

'Sounds like a plan and one I like,' Jamie responded.

'Buckle up and let's see what these babies can do.'

All four Enochim 'clunk clicked to have a safe trip' and they were off.

They dived straight down to 'Straight Street' and flew along just above ground level. Straight Street must have been 50 metres wide with massive pillars either side. Joel took their chariot over to the left hand side whilst Nathaniel and the girls were right over to the right. Jamie wondered about all those poor pedestrian angels who would get in the way but no accidents happened. Either they'd been warned there was an Enochim tour on, or those angels can 'rapture' quicker than the chariots can move. As they flew along, Jamie could see the houses that the angels must have lived in. They were all only two storeys high and were pure white. There were windows but no glass in them and they all had flat rooves no doubt because there was no rain. The chariot slowed and suddenly took a sharp left turn. Now they couldn't see the girls and were traveling along a narrower street than before. The chariot seemed to be bearing ever so slightly left.

'Where are we now,' asked Adam.

'We're in one of the side streets running off Straight Street. These side streets are all circular and eventually circle round back onto Straight Street. You'll see there are just more angel houses on these streets.'

The chariot picked up speed and soon they had half circled back onto Straight Street. The boys looked over and saw the girls over to their left and waved. The chariot slowed again and Nathaniel asked Jamie if he wanted to drive.

'Is the pink panther pink? You bet I do.' Nathaniel handed over the reins and Jamie took over.

'Just keep the reins straight and let the horses follow their noses dead ahead.'

'Where are we heading,' Adam asked Nathaniel?

'To Fair Haven so I can show you the Crystal Sea. You better let me take it from here Jamie otherwise the girls will beat us, and none of us want that, do we?'

It may not have been what they wanted, but it was what happened. And not only that, it was Anna driving when their chariot got to the harbour.

'I think we may have found out which one of these four is going to be a pilot,' Joel pointed out to Nathaniel.

'I think you could be right,' he answered.

'Anyway, what do you think of our harbour,' asked Joel The children looked out and saw a massive circular harbour wall stretching into the sea of glass. It looked all the world like a massive magnifying glass. The sea itself was dead calm and at first Lois thought it was solid. Joel seemed to know what she was thinking.

'It is you know. Go on, put your hand into it. Go on.'

Tentatively Lois walked a nearby slipway to the sea. She knelt down and put her hand towards the water. As she did, she could see her reflection more clearly than she had ever seen in a mirror. It spooked her for a moment but then she let her hand slowly touch the sea. As she touched it's surface it felt just like ice but it wasn't cold.

Once again Joel read her thoughts and answered her unspoken question.

'The Crystal Sea leads directly to the throne of The I Am. So as not to cause disturbance in the presence of The I Am the water is frozen like a crystal and is as blue as a sapphire. That's how we get its names, The Crystal Sea or Sapphire Sea.'

Seeing the students had probably learnt enough for one day Joel suggested they all head off home.

'Home's a good idea. I think we've all seen enough for one day,' agreed Jamie. Joel got the girls into his chariot whilst Nathaniel loaded up the lads. Then they were off straight down Straight Street. No sooner had Anna asked, 'Can I drive' than they were back at home.

'I think it's a bit late to go to Wings tonight so we'll take a rain check on that and maybe go tomorrow night.'

'Joel's right. You guys get some rest and we'll see you back at School tomorrow.' Nathaniel made sure they got in safety and then he and Joel were off and Rachel was sure they were racing.

After showers and tea the four sat in the lounge talking about all they had experienced during their second day.

XII

Day four dawned and so as it happens did the school term at All saints. Joel and Nathaniel came to wake the children as usual at A4 and made sure by A5 they were at school.

First of all they went to the refectory where they had a chat with their two chaperones.

'Today you start your first session or as we call it your first 'Season' at All Saints.' Joel continued,' you'll have 6 seasons in all with each one lasting four days. After each season you will get a two day break to relax and hopefully revise and practice the things you have learnt,' he said looking over in Jamie's direction.

'What you looking at me for,' asked Jamie.

'No particular reason,' smiled Joel.

'If you work it out you'll see that overall you have twenty four days of teaching with fourteen days off, including four days right at the end before you go home. Let me give you a timetable that hopefully clarifies this all for you.' Nathaniel handed each of them a timetable with the Seasons, Days and Tutors all marked out.

'You'll see from your timetables that you have one session a day with different tutors who will teach and train you in their certain subjects. So for example, today you have Uriel this Alpha teaching you about angel history then tomorrow you start your training with Jerahmeel on comtel. Then tomorrow.......'

'Thanks Nathaniel, we get your drift. But do we get coursework and/or homework,' asked Jamie with almost a quiver in his voice?

'Yes, do we,' asked Adam with more of a spring in his voice.

'That depends,' answered Joel.

'On what,' Jamie asked just before Adam.'

'You,' came Joel's reply. 'If you want to go to the Library and do more research or you want to practice your self defence, or if you want to fly the Zeke, then you can. It's entirely up to you. We can't and we don't want to force you to do anything. You're here because you want to be here not because you have to be. We understand that so it's our job to encourage not discourage.'

'So things are fairly relaxed then' Jamie said with surprise bordering on relief.

'Yes, pretty much but we usually find Enochim once they get into their calling, they try much harder because they want to not because they have to. If you give somebody something to believe in they try their best to put that belief into action.

'I hate to break into this pep talk but aren't we going to be late for Tutor Uriel's class. It's already gone A5,' pointed out Lois.

'Thanks for that Lois. You're right but Uriel knows we always have this 'pep talk' on the first day of term so he's happy if we're not dead on A5. Although I don't recommend you're late any other day. Everyone OK with what they've heard so far?'

They all nodded and so off they went to Uriel's study. On reaching his door they heard, 'Come in' before they'd even thought of knocking. They trooped in and Tutor Uriel was standing waiting to greet them.

'Welcome. Please find a seat where your comfortable and then I'll begin. The four looked around at a study that really lived up to its name. There were more books that you could shake a stick at and as for swinging a cat, you couldn't even get the moggy into the room!

'Sorry about the mess but that's the way I like it,' apologised Uriel with a smile.

'To be honest, Tutor, I appreciate the mess because it makes me feel at home, but all these books can't be healthy,' added Jamie.

'Thanks for that Jamie, but I hope after our time together you'll come to love books as much as I do.'

'Now that's wishful thinking to the nth degree,' responded Jamie with a laugh.

'Can we sit on this sofa,' asked Lois?

'Of course my dears please make yourselves at home,' and the girls sat on a large chesterfield like sofa that couldn't have been made of leather. Adam found himself an armchair and Jamie sat in what he would call a 'beanbag'.

'Is everyone comfortable,' Uriel asked. They all nodded and Uriel began the first lesson.

'Great. First can I say I always deem it an honour to teach those who have chosen to take up the sword. Your calling is not an easy one as I'm sure you're finding out even now with missing your parents.' No one replied vocally but they all agreed he was spot on.

'What I hope to do in our time together is not to 'teach' you but to 'interest' you in matters relating to us angels and how you Enochim fit into The Kingdom. If I succeed, you will develop this interest and teach yourselves as much as you want to know. Have you all been given your timetables..?' The children answered by nodding and 'Yes'

'Good. You'll see that we have six sessions together and at these I will discuss with you matters you need to know and hopefully you will join in as much as you can with as many questions as you can. The only daft question is the one that isn't asked.'

As he was talking Uriel was making eye contact with each of the four and putting them at their ease.

Adam, never one to be slow in coming forward got in with the first question.

'Can we take notes?'

'Yes,' replied Uriel. 'In fact you'll find notebooks and pencils on my desk for each of you if you want them. Who would like one?'

Remembering their first days at primary school and wanting to look eager to teacher they all asked for pad and pencil and Uriel duly obliged.

'Don't worry if you don't actually use them but I appreciate the thought,' and Uriel winked at Jamie. 'Either this guys good, very good or he's seen my school record' Jamie thought.

'Ok' lets get started. What do you know about angels,' Uriel asked?

'They are Messengers of The I Am replied Anna.

'Excellent answer, thank you Anna. You see the word 'angel' actually means 'messenger' and that is what we were created for. But we angels carry The I Am's message in many ways not just by telling people things. We carry His message by carrying out His judgement, by helping people and even by fighting.'

'So when you are stuck on top of a Christmas Tree like a fairy you're not really like a 'fairy,' Jamie commented.

'I tell you what Jamie, you ask Micah if he's a 'fairy', replied the Tutor.

'Jamie actually is making a good point with his 'interesting' sense of humour, because 'squares' have got this sugary idea about us angels. Yes we can be gentle and loving as we minister to those in The Kingdom but just ask the angels at Sodom and Gomorrah or The Passover Angel how gentle they were. Before our Fall we were only gentle and loving but when the First Great Battle happened, love and gentleness had to be left behind.'

Is that when the prince rebelled and took the fallen angels with him,' asked Lois?

'Exactly Lois and thank you for your contribution. We angels were created aeons ago to serve the I Am with Michael The Archangel as our leader, Gabriel as his deputy and lucifer the one between The Godhead and his angels. He was created with great beauty, being wise, skilful, with many blessings and was even allowed to walk on The Holy Mountain amongst the most precious stones. But then one day pride diseased him as he took his eyes off his maker and concentrated on himself. There is a reason why 'I' is the centre of the word 'pride'. This 'cherubim', this bright morning star', this 'lucifer' began to believe he was a god who should be followed, obeyed and worshipped. To this day no one except The I Am knows how, why or when this dark thought was born in his mind. But whatever caused it, its effect was that lucifer rejected the way of The I Am and began to follow his own way and persuaded others to do the same. Those who had been created just like him to do the bidding for The Kingdom now wished to have that Kingdom under their control. Even though they were not all powerful, all knowing and ever present as is The I Am, they thought their limited power, incomplete knowledge and partial presence gave them the right to be as God. With their battle cry, 'We can be as God is', their rebellion and apostasy was complete." Uriel paused and then continued.

Right this seems a good time to use the 'tell you vision' and let you see what happened. Have you experienced a 'tell you vision before?'

'Jamie and I saw a short one with Joel and Nathaniel,' replied Anna.

'Is that the one about the Nephilim,' asked Adam?

'Yes,' she replied.

'Must be a favourite because we've seen that one as well.'

'OK, so you know what a 'tell you vision' is about but the ones you've experienced so far are just for viewing. Up here at All Saints we can actually put you in t he vision so it's actually like you're there.'

'Kind of like a virtual reality show,' Adam suggested.

'Pretty much, but with ours you don't need headsets. All you need is to see what's going on realising you won't be able to talk to each other or me. Just enjoy the show and I'll bring you out when its time.' The girls were a little apprehensive but the boys couldn't wait to get on 'tell you vision.'

'Sit back, relax and enjoy the ride.' Uriel went to a keyboard on his desk with what looked like twelve coloured stones. He pushed a number of stones in sequence. Looked up at the children, smiled and then dramatically pressed one more. There was a blinding flash and as the scales fell from the children's eyes they were high on a hillside looking down on a scene they could hardly take in.

'I cannot understand how it's come to this,' said Michael to Gabriel and the other five angels sat around a circular table that was set within a tent like the ones nomads use in the earthly deserts.

'How did we and our brothers get to this stage when we are facing each other on opposite sides of this valley?' Michael stood and walked to the door of the tent. He looked out towards the scene outside that he was describing. There in, what became known as the Valley of Decision, were two armies the like of which had not be seen in the creation before. Set on two, opposing hillsides were the armies of The I Am and the ruler. You could easily tell which army was which. The Army of The I Am were all arrayed in brilliant white and standing still. The number of those there had not yet been devised and never would be. As far as the eye could see were angelic warriors filling every available space. And Michael knew his army extended well beyond the sight of his vision. And yet with all those present no sound was made. No words were spoken and many looked as though they could cry at any moment.

This great army arrayed in white consisted of foot soldiers stood at attention with flaming swords in their hands. The swords had their points touching the ground and both of the angels hands holding the scabbard. There to the flanks of the foot soldiers were the horsemen and charioteers. The horsemen were seated on powerful horses. Some of the mounts were coloured white, some red, others black and the remainder grey. Different colours but all had the same powerful muscles, majestic stance and keen eyes not flinching. Many of the riders carried their flaming swords but many also had bows with flaming arrows stood to attention in their quivers, waiting to go to war.

Looking up Michael saw the silver fliers that one day would amaze a man called Ezekiel. In each of the fliers were four angels each facing a different direction. There were discs on the fliers that were covered in what Ezekiel would describe as eyes. The fliers were perfectly still, motionless. They filled the air so that if there had been a sun, it would have been blotted out.

Michael looked at the army he had been created to command and despaired that he and they would now be in eternal battle with others he had once commanded. For there across the valley were a third of the angel population who had once been happy to obey The I Am and his captain but who now obeyed another. And there he was, at the head of his army, Lucifer, the first of the fallen. Still he had the face of an angel with light seeming to come from 'this bright morning star.' But there behind him were those he had tempted to rebel, with the evidence of their rebellion etched in their countenance. No more did joy come from their faces but despair and hate. Their rebellion had torn them from the reason for their being and without that, they were in torment. Their faces distorted with the pain they now felt and the hate which this fostered towards those they had left behind. Their eyes were dim, their brows furrowed and their mouths grimaced in a silent scream. No longer did they stand tall as they had once, but now the burden of their choice weighed them down and they stooped. Just like Michaels army, there were horsemen, charioteers and fliers making up this army of the ruler. But unlike Michaels army, even the horses seemed to be sad with the lot that had now become theirs. Not only were they carrying their riders but the burden of opposing the one who had created them. No shiny coats and flowing manes falling over eyes that sparkled. These mounts looked old before their time.

For sometime Michael surveyed this vast army of the fallen and didn't recognise those who he had once broken bread with. Then he saw Abiel who had served with him and trained others. There was Hananel, who had shared many a meal with him and discussed the works of The I Am. And he was certain he spotted Reuel who could pilot a flier better than most. There he was, up in the air with others who had deserted their calling, taking their equipment with them. As he looked, recognising brothers and friends became impossible as the tears began to fill his eyes. He looked down for a moment to compose himself and then returned to his seat to address the brethren with him in the tent.

These seven in the tent made up the Angel Council who were appointed by The I Am to administer the affairs of his angels. Michael couldn't help feeling that perhaps they had failed in their duty by allowing lucifer to fall and take others with him. But none of them had been admonished by The I Am and so they had faith to believe this tragedy must be for a reason.

'We may not understand how this has happened, but we have been called here today to do battle with the enemy of The I Am. Our enemy is mighty but our Lord is almighty.'

As one, the six shouted 'Hallelujah' and those outside the tent on both sides of the valley heard their shout. Those on the Lord's side were encouraged by it. Those on the far side of the valley were shaken by it for they knew the power of those who opposed them.

'Our command is to engage the enemy in battle and see how they react to fighting their brothers.'

All six responded with, 'So be it!'. Again the Lord's army felt fire in their hearts as they heard the shout. The enemy felt cold all through their being.

'I will lead the army into battle as is my honour and you will be at my side. Three on my right and three on my left. We will march across the valley and if the enemy should withhold its arm we will surround them and await further command. If the enemy does not withhold its arm we will fight for The Kingdom.'

As Michael finished, the ground shook with the sound of 'SO BE IT!!' which came from all in the Lord's army.

Michael stood and the rest of The Council stood with him. They left the tent each taking their swords as they did so and sheathing them. The Seven moved outside and not a word was heard from the massed ranks of that angelic army.

Michael, Gabriel and the five appeared at the front of the army and all waited. Michael took his sword out of its sheath and knelt down on one knee with his forehead pressed against the swords handle. As he did so, all others on the Lord's side immediately did the same. Not a sound was heard until...........

'Come on Michael. There's no point in praying to your God now. I'm your god so why not come over and bow before me.' Lucifer spoke with a shrill voice that cut the air and into the hearts of those still on the Lord's side. Still Michael and his army knelt in silence.

'Look, I think he is scared,' Lucifer said as he turned to his followers. They all laughed nervously and were encouraged by Lucifer's disrespect to the Archangel and his God.

Michael rose and all around him rose with him. He raised his sword and shouted with the power of rushing waters, 'FOR THE KINGDOM!!!!!' All on the lord's side returned his words with the power of many rushing waters, 'SO BE IT' and they all advanced into the unknown.

Quietly without saying a word this vast army that could not be numbered moved towards Lucifer and his cohorts. No sound was made. No words were spoken. No cries to try and unsettle the enemy. Just a massive white army moving forward in golden silence.

As they reached the valley floor the enemy launched an attack on their silence with blood curdling screams that would echo down the ages. They followed their screams down the hillside to meet their enemy. As the two armies engaged each other, the battle to win each other over was lost.

Suddenly the screams of the fallen were matched by the clash of swords of fire against each other. From the skies came the squeal of fliers dive bombing with bolts of fire coming out from between the wheels on these unearthly craft. The cavalry angels charged each other with horses colliding as their rider's swords did the same. There was the scream of arrows tearing through the air searching out a foe to pierce. Never before had there been fighting between angels but now the die was cast but none were cast to die.

Angels were not created to die and so this fight to the death could not happen. As swords, arrows and fiery bolts found their mark no wounds were inflicted. No casualties were brought low. No angel died. Michael knew this and he knew the idea behind the battle was not to kill angels but to kill the idea. The idea that angels could forsake their calling and follow another. Now he knew, as The I Am already knew, that the fallen had been given their chance to repent but had decided to continue on in their rebellion. The Valley of Decision had seen its decision made and its name given.

Michael didn't know for how long the battle went on but he came to a point when he knew it couldn't continue. He had fought his way past the ranks of fallen and was now engaged in a desperate sword fight with lucifer himself. He looked into those dead eyes whose light was now shrouded in darkness and knew there was no way back for this cherubim. For a moment he felt what could have been sadness but this was soon engulfed by his love and loyalty for The I Am. He fought with courage and skill scoring with blows that would have killed any mortal man. But this was no mortal man. He was of a creation superior to what mortal man would be. A creation whose torment could only be inflicted at the word of The I Am.

Suddenly, the command came to Michael that he and his army should stop fighting. With the authority of the Archangel he stopped, held his sword high above his head and shouted 'BE STILL!!' Automatically, every angel, including all the fallen stopped at the sound of the voice of The Archangel. Silence descended once more to the valley.

Then, without warning, lucifer thrust his sword into the chest of Michael. The first murderer withdrew his sword but no wound appeared in Michael's chest. Michael glared at the one who had stood with him as the universe was brought into being. His emotions ran from anger, to disgust, through to despair and finally arrived at sadness. He turned his back on his would be killer and walked slowly back across the valley. He walked through the massed ranks of angels and fallen who parted like the Red Sea would for another of The I Am's commanders. The other six of the Council followed him as did all the white army.

The fallen stood and watched as not only their friends departed but also any hope they may have had of returning to their former lives. lucifer ranted after Michael. 'Come on, let's finish this now!!'

No reaction and all fell silent.

The troops returned to their stations and awaited their next command. Michael and the Council returned to outside the tent and all stood and waited to see the fallen would do. Michael took a moment and then began. Silence returned to the valley. Michael looked across at the fallen to await their reaction. He hoped for repentance, a falling prostrate in sorrow, anything to bring them back to their place. What he got was lucifer baying for the blood of all those not on his side.

The silence was broken by the ranting of the old deceiver.

"Let our hate be our energy to overcome those who oppose us. Shall we fight,' he screamed to his followers'

'Yes our prince,' they responded!

'Shall we win?'

'Yes our prince,' his angels responded again.

'To victory!!!!!' and with that lucifer led his men across the valley.

Michael's army stood firm and silent as the legions turned to face their foe. As the fallen reached the legions Michael's voice boomed out over the valley like a trumpet.

'Be Still!!' Everyone obeyed the command of the Archangel.

'You who have rebelled are no longer to remain in this Heaven. You have chosen to follow this dragon, this ancient serpent, this devil, this satan who has deceived you and will deceive others. Your fate is sealed and the time is set for your condemnation. But until all things are completed and time is no more you are banished to the air where your prince will rule for a time until the glorious appearing. Be gone, endure your rebellion knowing there is a lake of fire prepared for your punishment.

As Michael finished pronouncing the judgement all the fallen were completely encircled by the angels. Knowing their very existence now depended on it the fallen began to fight as never before. Spurred on by the hate they now felt, the fallen slashed with their swords at the angels for all they were worth. But now they were worth nothing. Their fighting was futile as the angel lines held and none could escape. Lucifer stood in their midst howling that he would one day ascend high over them all. As he did he was the first to fall from heaven into eternal exile. He fell to the earth then all the fallen followed in an instant behind him and were gone.

The battle was won but the war had only just begun.

In another instant the children were back in Uriel's study. The tutor gave them a moment to compose themselves to try in some way to take in what they had just experienced.

'Are you all OK,' he asked?

'Considering we've just witnessed the most immense battle in universal history, not too bad,' Adam was the first to reply. 'That was the most amazing thing I have ever experienced,' he continued.

'Thanks for that Adam. How about the rest of you, did you all understand what was going on?'

'As I understand it,' Anna said, 'that was the battle over good and evil when satan and all his followers were thrown out of heaven.'

'Couldn't have put it better myself,' Uriel responded. You and others need to realise that satan and his hordes are not in hell yet but 'in the air'. He is prowling around like a lion to see who he can ravage in your world. One day, he and his followers will be in a fiery hell, but that day has not come yet. The last thing I would like to add is that we angels still feel the sadness over what happened to our brothers. I don't think we'll ever get over it until all things are completed and we enter into the new Heaven and a new Earth. I hope you now understand a little more of our history and how we and you have come into conflict with the fallen. This seems a good time to end our first lesson. Please go for you lunch. If you want to come and see me with any questions before our next lesson, my door is always open.'

'Thank you Tutor Uriel for that experience.'

'Thank you Lois for your kind words.'

The children left Uriels study but couldn't wait to get back for more. 'I tell you, if all school was like this, I'd be a professor by now,' Jamie said as they headed for the refrectory.

XIII

After what they had learnt that Alpha, the four couldn't really concentrate on doing more work in Omega. So when they had finished lunch, they all decided to spend the afternoon at the stables with Philip.

The girls helped with mucking out whilst the boys cleaned the chariots.

When they had finished, Philip suggested a ride through part of the city.

'Great idea,' said Adam, 'but I can't ride.'

'To be honest, I'm no Frankie Detorri myself,' added Jamie.

'No worries,' Philip said. 'These horses are fully in tune with their riders and they'll look after you.'

'If you're sure, then I'll give it a go,' replied Adam.

'Count me in,' Jamie said, not wanting to be left out.

Soon enough they, or rather the girls had tacked up the horses and the five off them trotted out of the stable yard into the street. There were a few angels around who smiled and said 'Hello' as the 'cavalry' passed by.

As they rode along, Lois asked Philip about 'Philip's Cup which she had heard about..

'Philip's Cup is just a bit of fun. Every now and then, two riders are picked from each of the 12 districts to race around the city. The competition starts at the sixth street away form The Circle and gradually moves into the centre with the sixth race being the final. The last four to finish in each race are out of Philip's Cup until we end up with four riders in the final. The final is raced around The Circle with the winner being the first to complete the circuit. Nothing serious, just a bit of fun.'

'Can anyone enter,' asked Lois?

'No. each rider is asked by the Constable of each district to represent their district. It's quite an honour.'

'Constable? Why do you need police up here,' asked Anna.

'We don't. The word 'Constable' comes from the words 'Count's Stable' which referred to the person or 'Count' who used to run a stables. The idea of someone being in charge and making sure the rules were followed was adopted by The Police and used to describe their officers as 'Constables' the abbreviated version of 'Count's Stable'. So we are just using the original word for those angels like me who run the stables here.'

'So do you get to chose who runs for The Circle,' asked Lois.

'Actually, The Circle has never put up two riders because I look after the horses for the Angel Council and you Enochim. So it's been thought that it wasn't fair for the Council members to ride because they would be bound to win and no Enochim have ever asked to enter.

'Me and Anna would love to have a go if it would be allowed,' Lois continued.

'I tell you what, if you to can show me you're good riders, I'll have a word with Teacher Eli and see what he says.'

'Thanks Philip,' both girls replied.

'How about you two boys, do you want a go,' asked Philip?

'You must be joking,' said Jamie. 'I can't even deal with a clothes horse, never mind a real one.'

'That goes for me to,' continued Adam. 'Best leave the horsing around to you and the girls.'

'Fair enough,' and with that Philip led them on for the rest of their ride. They all enjoyed a quiet Omega having a chat with each other and taking in the sights of the city. They got back to the stables at about Omega 3. After the horses had been safely fed and watered the four said goodbye to Philip and headed home.

Lois and Anna were excited about trying out for Philips Cup whilst Jamie was excited about tea. Tea was over when Joel appeared to see if they were all ok.

'It's a lot to take in about the First Great Battle isn't it,' he said.

'It certainly is,' answered Adam, 'but the 'tell you vision' certainly makes it clear what it's all about.'

'You angels must find it hard to have lost all those friends through the rebellion,' Anna commented.

'Very hard, but it was their choice and now they and we have to live with it,' Joel said with the sadness shaping the words he spoke.

'Enough of this or you guys will be getting upset about not being with your folks.'

'To be honest, that's not easy. Even with all the amazing things we are seeing and learning here, we're all still worried about the way we left our parents in the middle of that attack.'

'Of course you are but don't forget, your parents are highly trained Enochim and I am sure they'll be fine. And remember, Teacher Eli has promised to send them help that will make a difference.' Joel let his words settle into the minds of his young charges and then continued.

'Who's up for a night out at 'Wings',' he asked?

'I'm up for it,' Jamie replied first. 'Come on you guys, it'll be fun.'

'Couldn't hurt to take our minds of things for a few hours I suppose,' Anna added.

'Count me in,' Lois said. 'Come on Adam time to let your hair down,' Lois turned and spoke to her brother.

'Well I don't want to be left here all on my own and it would be good to experience everything this city has to offer. Ok, I'm in.'

'Now don't get too excited Adam,' joked Joel. The tea things were cleared away and off they went, down the street to 'Wings'. It was a lovely balmy evening reminding the squares of long summer days at home. They chatted as they walked along with Anna and Lois wondering how Philip would be checking on their riding for the Philips Cup.

They could hear Wings before they saw it. The low chatter of voices wafted through the air like mist in the early morning. As they got nearer the sound of music intermingled with the voices to create an invitation to go in that couldn't be refused.

As they turned the corner they could see a single storey building that resembled the old town halls they had all seen before, even Adam

145

and Lois with the legacy of The Raj. There were seven corinthian pillars to the front leading into a large auditorium with more angels in that you could shake a harp at. Some angels were sat at tables drinking, others stood whilst some were actually dancing towards the front where there was a raised stage area. There was laughter all around and angels were coming and going as their commissions dictated.

'Everyone seems to be having a good time,' noted Jamie.

'That's the idea. These angels are always carrying out commissions for The I Am in many times and places. Not to mention being called to the Throne to join the choirs and multitudes in worshipping The Almighty. When they are on furlough, angels will come here to spend time with friends and relax until the next commission is given. Anyone like a drink,' asked Joel?

'What is it,' Lois replied?

'It's not alcoholic that's for sure. We all saw what happened to Noah and that's somewhere none of us want to go. The drink we have here is a mineral water called 'Meribah' that comes from the Garden. Try some, I think you'll like it.'

Joel went over to the bar whilst the children found a table and sat down. Joel returned with a tray having five glasses on it, each filled with different flavours of Meribah. Lois had apple flavour, Anna strawberry, Adam lime and Jamie peach.

'No complaints then,' asked Joel?

'No way. This stuff is absolutely lovely,' said Anna.

'Good, I'm glad you like it. When you come here you can have as much as you like.'

'Can you get food here as well,' asked Jamie?

'Yes but it's angel food and you might find it a bit rich. It's called Manna. It'll be ok for you guys as a snack now and again but I suggest you stick mainly to your Daniels diet whilst you're here.'

'Can I try some now,' Jamie asked as if he hadn't heard what Joel had just said.

'Don't see why not,' and Joel went off to get some.

When he returned Joel was carrying a golden bowl filled with some white stuff that they all took to be manna. Jamie tried it first. He took a piece of the small white round piece of manna that reminded him of the sugar icing his Nan put on her cakes. When he tasted it, the manna melted in his mouth with a sweet taste he thought reminded him of honey.

'Well, what do you think,' asked Joel?

'That sir, is what I call a snack,' and with that Jamie proceeded to enjoy another disc of the manna. Seeing no ill effects befalling their brother and friend, the other three joined in and enjoyed their snack. The dish was soon finished and although more was asked for, Joel decided they had enjoyed enough for one night.

After a while chatting the girls decided to go for a dance down the front with some of the angels. The music was being provided by a band of angels called 'Cloud Nine.'

'That music's pretty good,' remarked Jamie.

'Well those guys have being playing together forever,' joked Joel.

'And not a harp in sight,' remarked Adam.

Joel laughed, 'Yes, that image has somewhat haunted us angels for a long time. Most people see us as rosy cheeked, chubby cherubs playing harps and flying around with a permanent smile fixed on our faces.'

'When in reality, you are highly trained warriors who carry out difficult commissions all over the universe fighting the fallen who hate you with a vengeance.'

'I couldn't have put it better myself,' answered Joel. 'I don't suppose you play any instruments do you,' asked Joel?

'Not a harp,' said Adam.

'Anna and I play instruments because Mum and Dad did, I mean 'do''

'Yes you definitely mean 'do',' Joel said firmly. 'So what do you play,' he continued.

'I play the drums and Anna plays the guitar and does a bit of singing.'

'You don't sing then?'

'I had a great voice before they invented tunes,' Jamie replied to Joel.

After laughing, Joel asked Adam about him and his sister.

'I play keyboards, Lois plays a bit of guitar and has the voice of an angel,' was Adams reply.

'Ok let's see what you can do,' and Joel went off down to the front. A couple of minutes later when Cloud Nine had finished the song they had been playing, Joel stood up and said a few words.

'Welcome my friends to Wings tonight. Is everyone having a good time?'

'YES!!' was the unanimous reply.

'Great. Well I've got a special treat for you all. At great cost all the way from the first dimension I have four young people who are going to play for us here at Wings today. Friends and fellow angels I give you 'The Squares!'

A round of applause swept the place as all eyes turned to look at Adam Lois, Anna and Jamie. Somewhat surprised by Joel's words, the four were not sure what to do.

'Come on you four, don't be shy.' Joel along with everyone else there encouraged them to come forward. The girls got to the front first and the boys joined them presently.

Jamie went to the drum kit and saw it was 'pearly white with cymbals that looked as though they could certainly 'resound'. Adam was impressed with the 'Yahweha' keyboard as was Anna with the 'Godson' guitar and Lois with the 'Defender' bass.

'What songs do we all know,' asked Adam?

'How about 'I Believe',' said Lois. They all nodded.

'You count us in Jamie and we'll play it in C,' Adam said.

Lois took to the front and told the crowd, 'We've suffered for our music and now it's your turn.' With that Jamie gave them a four beat count in and then they rocked the joint. Lois certainly did have the voice of an angel and Anna's guitar solo was a blast. 'The Squares' and the audience really enjoyed the song and the place really took off when Cloud Nine joined them up front and they jammed the night away.

At Omega 5 Joel had to call a halt to the festivities as he knew 'The Squares' had to be round at All Saints in the Alpha. As they left, lots of the angels thanked them for their playing and told them, 'Come back anytime.'

For the first time, all four felt they were stating to fit in with The City of Angels and that Omega, they all slept better than they had since arriving.

XIV

Alpha 4 in the third dimension seems to come around as fast as 7 am in the first dimension. No alarm clock, just an angel called Joel. Jamie decided he actually prefers the alarm clock as that doesn't up end your mattress and turf you out on your bedroom floor.

'Yeah, yeah I know, 'get that bed of your back,' Jamie complained as once again he found himself not lying in but 'lying on' ....the floor to be exact.

'You know you love it,' joked Joel.

'Tell you what. Get up with Adam tomorrow and I'll leave you alone.'

'I'll give it some thought and get back to you,' Jamie said as he closed the door on the Bathroom and went for his shower.

By the time he had got downstairs, he was on his own.'

'Making myself look this good can't take that long,' he thought.

'Where are the others,' he asked Joel.

'Adams gone off to the library to see what new things he can learn. The girls are just along the way with Phillip and the horses. In fact, they've been their since Alpha 3.'

'I didn't even know there was an 'Alpha 3'' quipped Jamie. He had his breakfast and joined the girls at the stables. Whilst they went for a ride on Milk and Honey, he looked over one of the chariots.

'Tell you what,' Phillip said, 'if you come after lessons today and clean it, I'll take you for a ride.

'It's a deal,' replied Jamie.

Cometh the hour cometh the angel. As Alpha 5 approached Nathaniel arrived with Adam to get them all to school. All four actually rode to school to start getting use to riding horses as they realised riding would form part of their training.

When they met Nathaniel at School he walked them to where tutor Jerahmeel was waiting for them This time the children did not go up stairs to where they assumed Jerahmeels study would be, but stayed on the ground floor.

'Tutor Jerahmeel has asked me to take you to his lab for today's lesson,' explained Nathaniel. Adam could hardly keep the smile on his face or his thoughts to himself. Eventually his thoughts escaped through his words.

'Now this I am going to enjoy.'

When all five reached the door, Nathaniel knocked and they all waited.

'Come,' soon came the reply from inside. Nathaniel showed the children in and closed the door behind him as he left. All four looked around and were amazed that Jerahmeel seemed to have more gadgets than Apple. There were benches covered in what seemed to be handheld P.C.s and what Adam took to be miniature cameras. There were bits of metal strewn around along with more wires and tools. On the walls were shelves that boxes with writing on none of them could understand.

'Take a seat where you can find one,' Jerahmeel suggested. Easier said than done in this Aladdin's cave.

'I know it's a mess but it's my mess and that's the way I like it. Everything is to be done in order as you know and this is my order,' he said as he smiled and sat in front of them on a stool.

'I like to give my classes their first lesson here in my lab so from the start, you students can get hands on with our kit.

'I'm liking the sound of this already,' added Adam.

Bit of a technogeek are we,' asked Jerahmeel?

'I am the original 'technogeek'' replied Adam.

'Then I think you and I should get on like a re-booting computer,' he said as Jerahmeel looked and smiled at Adam.

'Right, let's get down to business. As you know I am tutor Jerahmeel and my area of expertise is Communications and Intelligence or 'ComTel' for short. The logo for my department is the silhouette of a man's head so any documents in the library you want about my subject will have that logo on it. Anyone, other than Adam, have any idea what we might cover in our time together?'

Not quite Adam but the nearest you'll get so Lois answered. 'I presume you'll tell us all about how we can communicate with you angels and each other.'

'And the 'intelligence' bit is possibly how we gain information to help us carry out our commissions,' was Anna's contribution to the answer.

'Both good answers. Thank you ladies. You are both right. My job is to let you in on the secrets of what we call 'Theonology.''

'Theo ...what,' asked Adam.

''Theonology' is the term we use to describe the technology we have been given by The I Am to perform our duties for Him. Any guesses as to what sort of things 'theonology' includes, he asked?

''Peters'' was Jamie's quick reply.

Adam followed up with, 'Zekes and swords of fire.'

Lois added, 'Chariots and shields.'

Anna completed the grand slam with, 'Jacob's Ladder.'

'All excellent answers. Thank you. You have all obviously picked up some things over the last days and that's great. Keep it up. We tutors can teach you so much and point you in the right direction but it's for you on your own to develop and expand your knowledge.' Jerahmeel got up and walked over to a cluttered bench over to his left.

He rifled around for something and the children heard him mutter, 'Ah there you are you little tinker.'

He looked up at his charges and asked, 'Who knows what this is?' he removed his left hand from on top of his right and offered it towards all four of them.

'It's a 'Peter',' Jamie answered first.

'Well done, but I suspect you other three knew that too.' He looked across at them and got his answer from the nodding of heads.

'The Technical term for this is........' Before he could answer himself Jerahmeel was cut off in mid flow by, 'Global Positioning System Wrist worn Personal Chronograph.' Adam wasn't trying to be clever, he was just excited about what he would learn and about what he had already learnt.

'The title of 'Technogeek' is not wasted on you young man, is it. But next time you want to answer remember it's rude to interrupt. Put your hand up and I'll give you a go.'

'Yes tutor,' Adam replied.

'Adam is right about the 'Global Positioning System Wrist Worn Personal Chronograph' but let's stick to 'Peter'. Jerahmeel continued, 'The Peter is made up of a flexible arkov compound that in you dimension is indestructible. You can drive over it, burn it, throw it out of a plane chuck it in the sea, even sleep on it Jamie and you will not break it. The only problem is that you can lose it. We are actually ready to introduce a new 'peter' that is no longer a watch but a micro transmitter that will be injected just below the skin. Then even your Mum won't be able to lose it,' Jerahmeel said as he looked over at Anna and Jamie. Both looked suitably bemused but Jerahmmel said,' You ask you Mum next time you see her.'

'So it will be like those chips that vets put into animals for identification if they get lost,' commented Adam.

'Exactly like that,' replied the tutor. 'Only ours will be traceable globally not just in a vets surgery with a hand held scanner.'

'How will the new peters be powered because it's not easy to hide even an AAA battery under your skin,' Jamie said.

'True,' Jerahmeel answered with a smile. 'The new peters will be powered by a mixture of kinetic energy and the electric impulses generated by human muscles.'

'You know, I understand the muscle one because I do P.E. at school but 'kinetic' ' Jamie quizzed.

'Kinetic is energy created by movement. So as an Enochim moves, he will be generating power to run his 'peter'.

'Bit of a design problem there tutor. Jamie's not known for his over use of movement so his might not work,' joked Anna. They all laughed except Jamie for some reason.

'When do we get our new peters,' asked Adam?

'Probably in a couple of years. We have to be careful not to release theonology into your dimension too quickly because if it gets found by those who are not Enochim, they could exploit it for their own ends. But more than that, it could cause mankind's technology to jump forward too quickly and unbalance the flow of time and history.'

'Has that ever happened,' asked Lois?

'Well sort of,' replied Jerahmeel.

'What happened,' Lois continued.

'What you would call 'a long time ago' we were instructed to deploy a Zeke into your dimension to transport an Enochim on a commission to another part of the globe. Now we are talking what your historians called 'pre-history' so transport was pretty much none existent except for the odd horse and 'shanks' pony'. That's why it was necessary to deploy the Zeke. The only problem was that when we got to the first dimension, a stranger stumbled on the rendezvous. I was able to instigate the Elisha immediately but not before the stranger caught a glimpse of the interlocking wheels.

'And that caused a problem because......' asked Adam?

'Well up until that time, no one had invented the wheel. So the glimpse the stranger got of our wheels sparked off his thinking. It took him some time but eventually he came up with the first wheel and the rest as they say 'is history'.

'Did that cause an unexpected jump in technology then,' Adam posing the question again.

'I can't be certain because what happened must have been in the will of The I Am but all I do know is that when I returned I was hauled before The Council and was told in no uncertain terms, to be more careful in future. So that's why, I make doubly sure no theonology hits your dimension until I am certain it should and has double clearance from The Council. Now back to your peters. You don't need them up here but when you return and have your debrief you'll be issued with your own, along with all your other kit.' With that, Jerahmeel put the peter he was holding down and moved towards a cupboard at the back of his lab.

'Could you all come over here pleased,' he asked the children, and they all duly obliged.

Jerahmeel opened the cupboard and as he did he spoke.

'You've all seen the gear your parents were wearing when they escorted you to Jacobs Ladder?'

'Yes,' some replied, whilst others nodded.

'That gear is used by Enochim when they are on active commission and expect trouble. We call it 'Armour'. Your defence Tutor Micah will be showing you how to use the armour but as its theonology, it's my job to introduce you to it. The first piece of this armour is the 'Helmet'' at which point Jerahmeel opened his closed right hand to show the quartet a small object that resembled more a hearing aid than a helmet.

'I've got to tell you Tutor, with my big head, there's no way I'm going to be wearing that helmet,' quipped Jamie.

'Looking at your bonce, I'd have to agree with you,' and with that, Jerahmeel batted the ball of Jamie's wit straight back at him.

'It maybe called a 'helmet but as you can see that's no longer what it is. It is actually a communicator that allows transmission and receipt of verbal communications.'

'A radio,' Anna clarified.

'Exactly. It fits in your right ear whereby you can hear communications. It also has a built in microphone that picks up your voice when you speak. Jamie, stick this one in your ear and go outside.' He gave the 'helmet' to Jamie who did as he was asked. Jerahmeel then placed another helmet in his ear and spoke.

'Do you read me Jamie, over?'

'He hears me,' Jerahmeel said to the remaining three whilst giving the thumbs up.

'If you can hear me, bang on the door,' Jerahmmel said out loud.

'Bang. Bang.' Came the response.

'It's working then,' Jerahmeel winked as he spoke to the three.

'Now Jamie, I want you to stand on your hands up against the lab door until I say stop.' Jerahmeel winked again and took the helmet out of his ear.

He continued,' I know you're all stood there wondering why it's called a 'helmet'.

'Well actually, I was wondering if I could ride Honey this afternoon but as you've mentioned it, perhaps you better explain,' was Anna's reply with a coy smile.

'O.K. I will. It's called a helmet for the simple reason that when your technology first allowed us to use the communicators, we hid them in helmets so, the name stuck even to this day.' As Jerahmeel finished there was an almighty 'BANG' outside the lab door. They all rushed to see outside and found Jamie in a heap in the corridor.

'Sorry Jamie. I forgot to tell you to get back on your feet,' Jerahmeel said as he and all the others laughed.

'I bet you did,' was Jamie's sheepish reply.

'Everyone back inside and we'll continue,' and Jerahmeel led them all back to his cupboard.

'Right we've done the helmet, now the belt.' Jerahmeel held out a black belt that had two pouches on it one was circular with a tube like device and the other was square being the size of a small book.

'The belt is again made of flexible arkov as are its pouches. Do you know what these are in the pouches,' he asked the class?

'The tube is 'The Shield' and the small book is 'The Good Book', Adam answered.

'Couldn't have put it better myself. Someone's being taking notice of what they've seen. Again, Micah will be training you in the use of these items, my job is to introduce them to you.'

'Is the good book active as a flaming sword,' asked Jamie?

'Not at present for you Enochim because you're not on commission. However, we Tutors can instigate them as and when we need to for training purposes, like now, The Sword of God, Fallen!!' As Jerahmeel shouted those words they had all heard before the book in his hands transfigured into a flaming sword. As it did so Jerahmeel started to twist and throw the sword around his body until the sword and he became a white blur. He stopped as quickly as he had started.

'I'm no Micah but not bad for a comtel tutor,' he said as he slipped the small book back into its pouch with the dexterity of an old time gunslinger.

Jamie thought to himself, 'Dear me. How good must Micah be?'

'Anyone know what the last bit of kit is,' asked Jerahmeel?

'The breastplate,' Lois replied before Adam could get his mouth into gear.

'Very good Lois and here it is. Why don't you try it on for size,' were his words as Jerahmeel threw the breastplate towards her. Lois caught it and soon had it wrapped around her body.

'Just like the body protectors we wear for riding back on earth,' she told everyone.

'Maybe so,' said Jerahmeel, 'but can your rider's body protector protect you from this. In a flash he threw a divers knife at her chest and it bounced off like hail off a car windscreen. The knife fell to the floor and it was so sharp, it stood to attention as it stuck rigid into the floorboards.

'Don't tell me,' said Lois, 'it's made of an arkov compound isn't it?'

'And that young lady is ten out of ten for you,' came Jerahmeels reply.

'Right, I think that's enough for today. You now all understand about how theonology works. Next time I'll be talking a little more about the intelligence side of things. Don't worry Jamie, you can cope with a bit of intelligence.' Jerahmeel continued, 'Remember, my door is always open so if any of you want to come and ask me anything or do some extra reading or whatever, feel free.' Adam was about to speak but Jerahmeel put his hand up to stop him.

'I'll be here all day if you want to come back Adam.'

'Thank you Tutor, I may just take you up on that,' came Adam's reply.

The group said thank you to their tutor and found Joel waiting for them outside the door of his lab. They all headed back to the house for lunch.

After lunch, the girls and Jamie decided to go back to the stables whilst Adam went off to spend some more time with Tutor Jerahmeel.

Phillip welcomed the three back with the smile and a hug. The girls set about grooming the horses whilst Jamie tinkered with one of the chariots.

At Omega 2, Phillip asked them all if they wanted to go for a ride. All three accepted the invitation and once saddled up they had a hack around The Circle.

'What a lovely day,' commented Anna.

'To be honest, they're all lovely days,' said Phillip.

'I suppose that means that because things here are always so pleasant you don't really appreciate it as much as us squares who aren't here all the time,' Jamie said.

'There is something in that,' accepted Phillip. 'Although, we angels have experienced sadness when our brethren fell, because we don't live with suffering in our world day in and day out, we haven't got the understanding of it as you have. I suppose that's why The I Am uses you to spread his Kingdom in your world as you can relate to the sufferings your fellow human beings are going through whereas we angels can't.'

'I never thought of it like that before, but you're right. Those who experience suffering are best placed to share that experience with those who have only seen it from the outside.' Anna continued, 'There was a man our family knew who within two years had lost most of his family to death through illness. At the time you could see the sadness in his eyes hear the pain in his voice. But as he got stronger the light in his eyes began to shine again and his words came from a voice strengthened in the crucible of his despair. Through his suffering was able to comfort those around him who were going through similar difficulties far and away better than any others of us could.'

'So even the cloud of suffering in your dimension can have a silver lining. It helps you to help others until the time comes when time goes and suffering is no more.'

'I suppose you're right Phillip,' was how Jamie entered the conversation. 'But is that why suffering occurs?'

'Let's be clear, I'm no expert on this but I did hear Teacher Eli talking about these things once. His take on it was that suffering entered the world when mankind's parents fell into sin with the prince and unleashed al the troubles that sin brings. It's not what was intended for humankind. You're supposed to be like us and not die of old age, disease and accidents.'

'Or at the hands of other people?'

'Exactly, Anna. Sin's done it all through the temptation of the evil one. He and his kind hate The I Am so much, that they know the best way to hurt Him is to hurt you.'

'I get that but what about these natural disasters that occur,' asked Jamie?

'Hundreds of thousands killed by a Tsunami. Thousands killed by an earthquake or a volcano blowing its top. Famine and flooding that kills instantly or by destroying people's food or homes. You can't blame those on mankind, can you.'

'Well, perhaps some of this ecological stuff that is killing people now is caused by your misuse of His creation. Don't forget, The I Am said, the next time He will judge thee earth' He'll use fire and what do you think 'global warming' is?'

'So, in a sense, mankind is being judged for not looking after the creation He gave us,' added Lois.

'Seems a reasonable assumption. Your earth can feed and house everyone on it. The reason it doesn't is because mankind is not following His guidelines for everyone to help their neighbour.'

'OK, I get all that about the ecological stuff, but what about natural disasters. You can't lay all those at our door can you' said Jamie.

'Not directly,' was Phillips intriguing reply.

'How do you mean, 'not directly',' asked Anna.

'The way Teacher Eli tells it is that mankind was the pinnacle of creation but still part of and in harmony with it. When creation was finished it was good. But when man let sin in, that rebellion against The I Am that harmony was shattered. Through that shattering all of creation was effected badly and now groans under the weight of it. That disharmony leads to the 'natural' disasters you now see in your dimension.'

'So sin not only brought death and disease to man but also to the creation,' concluded Jamie.

'Exactly that. So you see the suffering you undergo both from man's inhumanity to man and creations upset is all traced back to original sin of the first humans caused by the original sin of Lucifer.

'I've got to ask,' said Adam, 'otherwise my credentials as the science geek will be shot. What about all this evolution stuff?'

'You mean the 'theory' of evolution I presume,' replied Phillip. 'Again I'm no Teacher and you should ask Teacher Eli. But I know a lot of people get hung up over this and suggest many ideas to explain the evidence that now seems to be apparent. Some suggest that after The I Am created the Heavens and Earth in Genesis 1 verse 1 chaos was caused to it by lucifers fall to earth. During this time dinosaurs and other anim,als came and went and fossils were created. Then The I Am moved over the waters and started Creation that Adam and Eve knew. Some others ask, 'How long were Adam on Eve on Earth before they fell? Long enough for the evidence now available to be created? Still others suggest the Earth was created at an age, just as Adam was created as a man not a boy. Teacher Eli says that The Book you have is not a science book although it never contradicts the scientific discoveries The I Am has allowed you to make so far. The main point as The writer to the Hebrews says, 'By faith we understand that the universe was formed at God's command.' We don't need to know how God did it, just that He did it.'

'Thanks for all that Phillip, but I'm not afraid to admit that I'm suffering a bit with missing my folks and that's due to us being here which I suppose indirectly is due to original sin as we are here to learn how to fight in the war against darkness.'

'We're all suffering,' Lois said as she wafted a smile over to Jamie.

He continued, 'I'm really worried because as we left them down there, those evil ones were overwhelming them. I'm scared they might not have survived.' As he spoke, Phillip could hear the tears welling up in his voice.

'Listen Jamie, don't you worry about your parents nor you Lois about yours. Don't forget that I have met them and taken rides with them just like this. I know how brave and well trained your parents are and believe you me, the thought of not seeing you guys again will keep them alive. I'm not a parent myself, but I've seen on many occasions the things human parents will do for their children and it's nothing short of incredible. Hold onto that and don't forget, Teacher Eli has told you he's sending them help and I know that help will do the business.'

'Thanks Phillip,' said Anna. 'But we all still miss our parents so much and there are weeks to go before we get back.'

'I tell you what, let's go to the Library,' suggested Phillip.

'Not sure that's going to take our mind of things,' Jamie offered.

'We'll see.' Phillip kicked his horse into a trot and they all followed. Not long, probably within a few minutes, they were all stopped outside a magnificent building

on the direct opposite side of the circle from 'Wings'. There were twelve steps leading up to the large wooden doors that were open and had no locks or handles on them.

Phillip knew what they were thinking and said, 'No need for door furniture because these doors never close. Knowledge is always kept open for everyone at anytime.' They followed Phillip threw the open doors into a massive circular foyer with an atrium that Jamie would have said went up to the stars, if there were any to see.

'Will you wait here for a moment whilst I go over and talk to my brother angel.' Phillip raptured off.

'I wish they'd warn us before doing that,' said Jamie. 'Any more of this sudden rapturing and I might get a sudden rupture.' Phillip and re-appeared over to their left at a large desk with an angel sat behind.

'Hope he's gone no fines to pay,' joked Anna.

A few minutes later, Phillip returned and beckoned the three children to follow him. They all went to the back of the foyer and down a long white corridor. About half way along Phillip stopped and spoke them.

'In this library are copies of the books about The I Am that the world can't hold along with a few others. There are more stories and storeys in this building than you ever imagine. But there is one book not kept here and if anyone can let me know which one it is, there'll be a reward. Anyway back to the business at hand. You can come here to the library but only when accompanied by one of us angels.' Phillip moved over to the wall as he continued talking

'For what I want to show you we need to go up. Now I can just rapture but you can't at present which means I'd just leave you all behind. So many of your millennia ago, to allow you Enochim to get to other parts of the building, these were installed.' Phillip waved his right hand and a panel silently slid back to reveal a circular cylinder In the wall.

'What is that,' asked Anna.

'It's what we call a 'Tornado Tube,' explained Phillip. 'What you do is, you get inside and us angels can then send you to the place in the building we want you to go to.'

'And that is done how,' Anna continued.

'Actions speak louder than words so why not get inside and I'll show you.' Phillip said as he took Anna by the hand and directed her inside.

'Right the door will close and you'll be transferred to the storey I want you to go to. When you get there, just get out of the tube and wait for the rest of us to join you.'

As Anna went inside and turned to look at her companions, the door silently shut and she was all alone. Outside, Phillip had exposed a small square panel out of the wall with what looked like twelve coloured jewels set on it. He pushed four of the jewels in order and then opened the door so Lois and Jamie found Anna gone. What they hadn't seen inside the tube was when suddenly as Phillip hit the last 'jewel' a powerful, warm wind had risen and taken Anna to somewhere they did not know.

'Where is she,' asked Jamie with a little anxiety colouring his voice.'

'Don't worry, she's fine. The 'tornado tube' has just transported her to the storey I want to show you. Tell you what, to prove it, you go next Jamie because I'm sure Anna will feel better seeing a friendly face, even yours.'

Jamie got inside the tornado tube and soon found himself looking at Anna who was waiting for him as the door opened.

'Isn't that fantastic,' she said. 'Alton Towers, eat your heart out.'

'Impressive, but it's made a right mess of my hair,' Jamie laughed as he joined Anna outside the tube. The door closed and before you could say, 'Beaufort Scale', both Lois and Phillip had joined Anna and Jamie.

'Everyone alright,' asked Phillip?

'Top drawer,' replied Anna.' Any chance we can do that again?'

'Not right now, but you'll have to if you want to get back home tonight,' said Phillip. 'Come on, over here is what I brought you here to see. Phillip led them over to a large table that was set amidst a clearing in the forest of books surrounding them.

'Take a seat and I'll be back shortly.' The children sat down as Phillip went over to a shelf and took a large, square book off the shelf.

He brought it back to where the children were sat and let it fall open by itself as he laid it on the table. As the book fell open all the children looked to see what they could see. What they saw was not what they expected.................photographs!

'Does any body recognise anybody,' asked Phillip?

The children looked some more and then Anna asked,' Is that you Lois?

'It can't be,' Lois answered but to be honest it did look like her, but she was with people she didn't recognise. Then the scales fell from Lois' eyes.

'That's not me,' she exclaimed, 'That's my Mum!'

'And there we have a choccy for the young lady,' Phillip said.

'On this storey is the story of The Enochim. We keep all the histories here along with pictures of all those Enochim who have been here before.'

'So you've got our mum and Dad as well,' asked Anna.

'We sure do, as well as Lois and Adams Dad, not to mention your grandparents, great grand parents, great great grandparents and......'

'Thanks Phillip, I think we get the gist,' Jamie interrupted fearing Phillip was going to keep this shaggy dog story going for some time yet.

'Can we see the other pictures,' asked Anna.

'Of course you can.' Phillip left them again only to return with a trolley load of books and albums.

Up until Omega 5 they enjoyed seeing the pictures of their families when they had been to Angel City and although it didn't take the pain away, the memories they kindled warmed their hearts a little.

XV

'Adam! What's happening? We're falling like a stone,' screamed Lois.

The flier was now taking a near vertical dive and if they'd been in their own dimension, Adam would've thought they were falling to earth. As it was they were taking a nose dive into The City of Angels, but how did the two of them get into this situation?

The 'day' had started normal enough, well as 'normal' as it could do bearing in mind these four youngsters were in another dimension spending time with angels in a city where night never fell. It was the usual start to the day with Joel's alarm call, breakfast then a ride to All saints. When they arrived, Nathaniel took them up to Tutor Zechariah's 'study'. Although when the kids arrived it wasn't what they expected. Instead loads of books on shelves and papers on a desk there were no books and no desk. The furniture consisted of a number of armchairs, settees and a low coffee table.

"Come in. Good to see you all," Zechariah said as the children came into the room.

"Make yourselves comfortable. Anybody want a drink?" they all declined as they'd not long had breakfast. Zechariah grabbed himself a bottle of chilled meribah from his drinks cooler, which was actually a bucket of ice. He banged the top off on his coffee table and sat himself down.

"I think you'll find my teaching methods a little more flexible than my fellow tutors," Zechariah telling the kids what they already knew.

"Us fly boys tend to take life a little less seriously than others although we take flying and safety very seriously. Now this is what our time together is all about....getting about. My job is to teach you squares how to use different forms of transport both temporal and non-temporal."

"Does that include horse riding," Lois asking the question Anna was about to.

"It certainly does little lady." Both Lois and Anna smiled.

"I suppose that big old softy Phillip has had you out riding already has he?"

"Yes," Lois replied.

"Good. All the practice you can get is excellent. We'll do some more structured riding in our sessions and that includes you boys as well. You don't need to be John Wayne but you have to know how not to fall off."

"Who's John Wayne," asked Adam?

"Ok, I'm showing my age. He was a Hollywood cowboy who could ride. But hey, history is Uriel's thing so don't fret it. I take it you guys have had a familiarisation flight in one of our temporal Zekes?"

"Yes sir," answered Adam.

"Tutor will do Adam."

"Thank you sir, I mean tutor."

"Right, as you've already been riding our horses I think we'll have a flight in one of our Zekes."

"Excellent," was Anna's reply just before Adams.

"Nathaniel told me about you Anna. He seems to think you could be the groups 'dualpha'.

"What does that mean," she asked.

"Well, all of you will learn to fly a Zeke but one out of each pair, or 'testament', will be allocated as the 'alpha' pilot. This means, they will do most of the flying. However, on some occasions you will work in a team of four, known as a 'Gospel' and when this happens there has to be a recognised alpha pilot. Because that pilot is the 'alpha pilot' twice we shorthand the name of the position to down to the 'dualpha' being an abbreviation of 'dual alpha' because that person is alpha pilot for the testament and the gospel that is on two occasions.

"So each pair has its alpha pilot and each 'gospel' has its 'dualpha' pilot," confirmed Adam.

"You're not wrong young man," was Zechariahs reply.

"Why is a pair called a 'testament' " asked Lois?

"There are how many 'testaments' " answered Zechariah with a question?

"Two. So a pair is known as a 'testament'. Got it. So I suppose a four is called a 'gospel' because there are four gospels."

"And there you have it," said Zechariah with a smile.

"How are the alpha pilots chosen," asked Adam?

"Usually it becomes obvious to the Enochim and us tutors what each child's gifting is. There is no competition. If there is some uncertainty, I make the decision and that's that. But I haven't done that for about five hundred of your years so let's hope I'm not due for a choice very soon. Don't forget, there are two areas of work, one for each of you. Usually, the alpha pilot is not the defence specialist. So if you mostly fly, you don't mostly fight."

"So it's very much a team effort, with each of us having our specialisms to bring to the 'testaments' and the 'gospels'"

"That Jamie sums up the whole thing. Strength in numbers. That's why you Enochim are always twins. By the way, all Enochim are twins but not all twins are Enochim. The way of The Kingdom is to send its workers out in pairs so that how it's been from the beginning. How did you guys get to The Third Dimnension," Zechariah asked?

"By Jacob's Ladder," came Lois' reply.

"And what do you know about Jacob," he asked?

"He was a shepherd," offered Jamie.

"Can't fault you there, but what else?"

"He married Rachel and Leah," suggested Anna.

"This is all good stuff, but it's not what I'm after. Who was his brother?"

"Esau," Adam answered knowing he was right.

"And……" Zechariah looking for more.

Finally the penny dropped with Lois who remembered from a Sunday School lesson years ago that, "They were twins."

"Right," said Zechariah. "Any other twins you can think off," he asked?

"Then the pound sterling dropped with Jamie. "Thomas, one of the disciples, he was a twin."

"Now that is an answer straight from the top drawer."

"Are you saying that Thomas was an Enochim," asked Adam?

"Well, he was a believer and a twin so what do you think," replied Zechariah.

"But he's probably the one who brought the message of The kingdom to India," said Lois.

"So, a great worker for The Kingdom, a believer and a twin. Perhaps I'll leave the rest up to you. Ok, I'm starting to sound like Uriel and that will do this fly boy no good at all. I tell you what, let's have a drink and then we'll pop down to the Flier port and start some flying lessons."

They all had a bottle of chilled meribah then headed down to the flier port. Of course, to keep their training going, they had to ride which for Anna and Lois was no hardship. As they rode, Lois asked Zechariah about 'Phillips Cup.'

"It's only a bit of fun. Each district elects two riders to ride for them and then there are six races to the circle to find a winner."

"Why is it named after Phillip," asked Anna?

"Well, whenever horses are needed for some big job in The Kingdom, Phillip is used because no one knows horses like he does. So when Elijah needing picking up, it was Phillip driving the chariot. When the cavalry was sent to assist Elisha, Phillip was in command. And you just know who'll be one of the four horsemen of the Apocalypse don't you?

"Phillip," came Anna's reply.

"And there you have it. A hole in one. So because of all Phillips horsing around, when someone came up with the idea of a bit of a fun horse race, to name it after him seemed to be the only way to go."

"Was it your idea to 'have a bit of fun'," asked Anna?

"You're getting to know me now aren't you young lady."

"Can we enter," asked Lois?

"I don't think it's against the rules because there aren't any rules. But you girls don't live in one of the districts but in the circle which usually doesn't put a pair of riders forward. Also, it could make the math difficult. I'll have a chat with Phillip and we'll get back to you." They carried on their ride and soon came to the flier port.

Adam couldn't believe what he was seeing. Everywhere he looked there were silver, shining Zekes. Some were flying around, others were taking off or landing but most were just static, levitating above the ground.

"Can I see where the Zekes are repaired and maintained," he asked.

"No," came Zechariahs instant reply.

"Why not," asked Adam somewhat downcast.

"Because young man unlike in your dimension these vehicles don't have built in obsolescence. The only service these babies have is service for The Kingdom."

"So even when my mum drives one of these things and prangs it, she can't do any damage," noted Jamie.

"You would be right Jamie if your mum had ever pranged one of these. She may not be able to reverse park but your mum can fly one of these babies as well as any Enochim I've seen to date." As Zechariah spoke, another angel walked up to the mounted group of riders.

"Can I introduce my 'wing man' to you. This is Abel one of the best fliers we have.

"Hello" they all said.

"Hi kids. Good to meet you. I see you've survived Zechariah's first lesson, so that means you should survive anything from hereonin. As a teacher, Zach's a great flier."

"I taught you everything you know," retorted Zechariah to Abel who laughed.

"To be fair guys, that is true. Now who's flying with me and who's with the great Zechariah?"

"I'll take the two girls with me Abe and you can have the lads."

"No change there I see. He always pulls rank on me so he gets the beauty and I get the brawn."

"And the brains," added Adam.

They all dismounted and followed Zechariah and Abel over to a couple of fliers. They looked just the same as those on the Crystal Sea only there was no dome over the cockpit. Abe 'raptured' into his machine and helped the lads follow him.

"You guys sit east and west and I'll take north." They all sat down.

"I understand that you know the basics of how our babies operate is that right?"

"Yes Tutor," was Jamie's reply.

"Please guys, just call me Abel. I know me and Zechariah kid around but at the end of the day he really is our best flier and only he is due the title tutor."

"Received and understood Abel," Jamie replied.

"Right, what we are going to do is talk about the controls of the flier and then we go for a spin. Now turn and face your screens. All the controls are exactly the same at each station except for two extra switches on the north face. Anyone know what those two are?"

"One is the master control switch for the north face to have complete control of the craft," answered Adam

"Spot on. Now the other switch is this one marked with a 'T'. Not to complicate matters at present let me just say you do not use that button at present. What don't we do," asked Abel?

"Use the 'T' button the lads replied.

"Right, first of all, are either of you chaps left handed?"

"No," they replied.

"That saves a bit of messing about with the seats because if either of you were we've have to get an ehud in here."

"What is an 'ehud'," asked Adam?

"An ehud is a seat built for a left handed pilot with the control positions reversed," answered Abel. "Any how, neither of you are lefties so we can proceed. There are five control buttons on the left hand arm of your seat and a joystick on the right. The joystick is for steering the flier just like you would with one of your earth planes. The control buttons on the left side of your seats are coloured coded for use and there are five, one for your thumb and one each for your other fingers. Going from right to left and starting with your thumb," Abel motioned for them to place their hands on their controls and follow him.

"The Green button for your thumb is used to give you thrust to move the flier forward. Any idea why it's green?"

"Because green means go and that button let's you go forward."

"Couldn't have put it better myself, Jamie. Green also stands for your earth or your creation so it can symbolise the fact that by pressing this button it allows you to travel all over your dimension. You press the button and you keep increasing speed. Once you stop pressing it, you will continue to travel at the speed you reached. When you press it again you will slow down until you stop and levitate. The next button for your index finger is blue and this gives you vertical motion, that is height because......." Abel waiting for an answer.

"The sky is blue," answered Adam, not wanting to disappoint him.

"Excellent. The longer you press the button, the faster and higher you go. Once you stop pressing it you will levitate and if you press it again, you will descend.

Now the clear button is your 'Elisha' which......."

"Cloaks the Zeke so it can't be seen," answered Jamie.

"This really is very impressive. Nice to see you guys took notice when you flew in your temporal Zekes."

"The red button...."

"Is not to be used by you yet," was Abel's reply to Adams question. "The red button activates the missile launchers which are used only as a last resort. More about that in a later season. Now the black button activates the eyes of the Zeke. These eyes give you all round visibility even in the dark. Also, they have what you would call an 'x ray' capability in that they can see through solid objects."

"Can I ask a question Abel?"

"Of course, Jamie. What is it?"

"I understand how these buttons all activate the features of the Zeke but how do you control the features once their activated. For example, how do you know how high you are? Or how fast you're going? Or where to fire your missiles?"

"That is an excellent question Jamie and brings me onto the other feature you will see at your position, the control screen. When you activate any feature, its capability appears on the screen. So for example, as you ascend the screen gives you altitude. As you move forward you get a speed reading. When you activate the cameras you get a live feed to your screen. And so on. Of course, as there is usually two of you in the Zeke, one will be flying and the other dealing with vision and munition as needed. Although, the alpha or dualpha pilot needs to be able to fly and activate other features all in one go so that's why there more highly trained."

"How do you deal with more than one camera image," asked Adam?

Another good question. Rather than tell you, let me show you." Abel moved east to Adam's position and activated his console. He pressed the black button and the screen lit up with four images each of which were numbered. He touched the screen with his finger to select an image and instantly the images became holygraphic floating above the screen. The screen then filled with four more numbered images on the screen from other cameras. Abel touched the screen and those images became holygraphic and were replaced by four more images.

"This could go on for some time," said Abel. "Just so you know, if you use any camera in darkness it automatically switches to night vision."

"Which camera is for 'x ray'," asked Adam?

"Camera 10 because........."

"10 in roman numerals is a 'x', replied Adam with a smile.

"Very good. Now it's time we took this baby out for a flight. Who fancies a go," asked Abel knowing what the answer was to his question. All three buckled up into their seats and Abel took control.

"Gentlemen, if you look in the right hand side pocket of your seats you will find earsets. Please place them in your ears. You will find they are a perfect fit as we knew you were coming." The lads did as they were told.

"Now, we are about to have a test flight where I will retain complete control. Is that understood gentlemen?

"Yes" the gentlemen replied.

"I am alpha pilot and I have control. Please confirm you understand this and all other instructions by replying 'confirmed' each in turn."

In alphabetical order Adam replied "Confirmed" and Jamie followed him. Abel took control and first of all closed over the dome to protect his 'square' passengers. The flier then moved upwards and into the heaven, or the Third Heaven to be more precise. As the boys flier lifted off so did Zechariah with the girls in their flier. They rose over the city and then flew out over The Garden. The girls looked out and saw green hills, trees, streams, flowers and understood why it was called 'The' Garden. All through the flights both Abel and Zechariah talked the children through the manoeuvres they were performing.

"I hope you're taking notes girls because it's your turn next," said Zechariah. The girls looked at each other wondering if they should be until Zechariah put them out of their misery.

"Don't panic. You'll soon pick it up and there are no exams," he re-assured them. After about half and hour of Earth time, so Adam estimated, they all returned to the flier port. Then for the rest of alpha, time that is, nothing to do with the pilots, the children all spent time in what Abel called 'ground control' of the fliers. This meant that they each took turns in controlling the flier but only at ground level at minimum height and with minimum thrust. Then Abel and Zechariah took turns in taking each of the children out on low level flights to build up their confidence.

"That's what I call a good alphas work," said Zechariah at lunch time. "I know you guys normally get omega off for personal study and down time, but if you want to come back and do some more flying you are more than welcome."

Anna even beat Adam in saying she would definitely be back. The other three all said they would do as well. After lunch,they all rode back to the flier port and carried on practicing their flying.

By omega three it was time for finishing but they all wanted to carry on. Adam asked if he and Lois could take a flier up by themselves and Jamie and Anna asked the same. Zechariah and Abel spoke for some moments and decided that as their first day had gone so well they would let them. But they could only go on a low level flight and not leave the flier port.

"Confirmed" all four answered in unison. After they had all strapped themselves in their respective Zekes, Zechariah gave the signal for their lift off. Anna and Adam were in the north seat of each Zeke and complied as requested. Both Zekes rose slowly up. Once they had reached 300 of their earth feet, they each went their separate ways. Adam with Lois to the left and Anna with Jamie to the right.

"Permission to go to 500 feet," Adam radioed to Abel.

"Confirmed," came the reply. Adam depressed the blue button slowly but suddenly he heard Lois scream. The scream made him look over at his sister who had cut herself on the buckle of her seatbelt. By losing concentration momentarily, Adam put more pressure on the blue button so that the Zeke shot up into the air. Adam didn't notice the reading on his screen until it read 7000 feet. The shock of seeing that figure caused Adam to tap the screen to make sure the reading was correct but he missed the screen and hit the 'T' button by accident. Then it all happened, or rather it didn't. The Zeke stopped dead and began falling like a stone.

"Adam what's happening. We're falling!" Adam didn't have a clue what was happening. He tried pushing the blue and green buttons but nothing would arrest their suicidal dive down to the city. Their speed was increasing and now the g forces were pushing them back into their seats so that trying to regain control, even if Adam knew how to, was nigh on impossible.

Suddenly Abel was there. He had seen what had happened and he immediately raptured into the flier. As he did, he hit the 'T' button then grabbed the controls at the west station and brought the Zeke under his control. Without saying a word, he piloted all three of them back to the flier port. The children, especially Adam who really wanted to be an alpha pilot if not a dualpha pilot, were worried about what would be said. When they landed at the port, Abel waited a moment and then quietly spoke.

"Who can tell me what just happened?"

Lois thought she better answer as Adam had being pilot and she thought her independent account might go down more easily. "I cut myself on the seatbelt buckle and screamed. As I did Adam tried to help me and them the flier lost all power and started to fall."

"Do you know why it started to fall," asked Abel with his tone giving away that he already knew the answer.

"No we don't, honestly," replied Adam.

"Well somehow the 'T' button was pressed at the north station. 'T' stands for 'temporal' which is used when the flier exists in your dimension not ours. So the fliers configuration was all wrong and it couldn't continue flying here. You don't know how the button was pressed," Abel asked Adam

"I must have done it by accident when I tried to stop the flier going higher and higher."

"Seems like we've had ourselves a narrow escape but at least the lesson has certainly been learnt, don't touch the 'T' button." Just then Anna and Jamie came rushing over to see how their friends were.

"Are you ok," Anna asked.

"Except for a cut on my hand and I bit shaken, I've never felt better," replied Lois.

"That is definitely enough flying for today," said Abel. You guys head off home with the horses," he said to Anna and Jamie. "I'll drop these two off in a flier and get Joel and Nathaniel to take care of them." The Fisher twins rode home and met up with their friends soon enough. Considering the day they'd had even though they had been flying they all decided to give 'Wings' a miss that night.

XVI

It was the fourth 'day' of their first season and although the children were enjoying their lessons, they were all looking forward to some time off. But before time off, it was time to have their first lesson with Micah.

By Alpha 5 the children were at All Saints tying up the horses. Micah met them at the park entrance.

"Good morning children, as you squares would say."

"Good morning tutor," they all replied.

"Thank you. You don't need to go inside today because a lot of our work is carried out in the park where we've got more room. Let's go and sit over there by those trees and have a chat before we start." They all followed their tutor and to be honest, when your teacher is as big as Micah you don't need asking twice.

Micah sat on a bench that encircled the largest tree in the copse and the children sat down on the grass in front of him.

"You all sitting comfortably," asked Micah?

"Yes thank you" replied Lois and all their behalfs.

"Ok, before we get into the technical stuff, there's one lesson you must all learn from the out set. What I will be teaching you is defence. You will learn skills with the equipment we give you but it is for defence not attack. You do not go looking for trouble but if it comes your way you will defend yourselves. The golden rule is 'you shall not murder.' What's the golden rule," Micah repeated for effect.

"You shall not murder," came the fourfold reply.

"Has any Enochim ever broken the rule," asked Jamie?

"Sadly they have. There have been occasions when death has come from action by an Enochim which was not their fault. In those

174

circumstances an Enochim must lay down his sword and no longer be on active commission. He then works as a Nethinim for The Kingdom."

"What's a Nethinim," Anna asked?

"We'll let Uriel sort that one for you as that's his subject area not mine. To get back to an Enochim who kills. When such a tragedy happens, the Enochim must face the law of the land where the action happened."

"Can Enochim join the armed forces if they want to," asked Jamie?

"No," came Micah's firm reply. "It was decided at the outset of creating the Enochim that it would be unfair to allow their special skills and strengthening to assist in wars between nations in your dimension. The other problem would have been that you could end up with Enochim fighting each other which would do your people no good at all. What Enochim can do in those situations is to carry out a commission that could influence the outcome of a war if The I Am decrees it."

"What about other members of The Kingdom. Do they fight in our wars," asked Adam?

"The sad truth is that they do," replied Micah. "It's sad because wars are not the way of The Kingdom for mankind but as your race has fallen away from The Kingdom, wars are inevitable. So if a rightly appointed Government declares war and calls up members of The kingdom to defend their country then it is right that those Nethinim obey the law."

"What are these Nethinim you keep mentioning," asked Anna?

"Uriel will give you full details but basically Nethinim are the majority of the people of The Kingdom who are not Enochim. So Nethinim obey the law but those in Government who declare a war better realise they will be judged for what they do."

"Is self defence a good excuse for war," asked Jamie?

"There is no good excuse for a war," replied Micah, "but self defence is certainly an acceptable reason to defend yourself if need be by war. It's what Teacher Eli calls the 'Two Sword Principle'. When The King asked how many swords his twelve disciples had the reply came 'two'. The King then confirmed that two was enough for the twelve. Now two swords for twelve people is not enough for them to go on the attack but it lays down the principle that the twelve must be able to defend themselves, which they can do with two swords. So the 'Two Sword Principle' was adopted allowing for self defence."

"So is the war you are in with the fallen one of self defence," asked Jamie?

"Exactly," replied Micah. "The fallen started it not us so we are acting in self defence as you are in your dimension." Micah was really pleased about the discussion they were having but thought it now best to leave the rest to Uriel and move on to what they were supposed to be starting on their first day together.

"I think that's enough discussion for now and if you want to we can always carry it on some other time. I think we better move on to my introduction of your defence classes but before we do, what's the golden rule?"

"You must not murder," came the quadraphonic reply. Micah got up and led the children back towards the rear entrance to the school. They followed him into the rear lobby and through into the main hallway. Micah went over to a door on the left hand side and waved his hand in front of it. The door opened and he beckoned the children to follow him inside. There in the room was a row of ten lockers with benches set in front.

"Please find your locker," Micah asked. The children looked at the lockers and each soon found their own name on a locker door.

"Anna, will you try opening Lois' locker." Anna carried out her tutor's instructions but to no avail. The handle to the locker door would not shift.

"Perhaps you would try opening your own locker now Lois." Lois went to her locker, turned the handle with no problem and opened the door.

Micah explained, "All your lockers have the same security which means only you can open your own. If you will all do so now and take out the equipment you find in there." The children did so and found inside the theonology Jerahmeel had introduced to them a couple of 'days' ago and which their parents had used on the night of their transfer.

"I trust you all recognise what you have taken out of your lockers," continued Micah. "Can I ask that you all put on your equipment and then join me again outside in the park. Micah left the children to put on their belts, breastplates and insert their 'helmets'. As soon as they'd all done so, they re-joined Micah in the park.

"Not bad. You got here in less than five minutes 'square' but you're going to have to speed up when you go on active commission. Now will you all please follow me." Micah led them around the side of the school building to a training area. There in front of the four were human sized dummies, targets, an assault course and other things that they didn't recognise.

"This is where we will do the majority of our training and where you can come yourselves to work out if you so wish." Micah motioned for the children to sit down at one of the benches in the training ground.

"Adam, who's in charge here," asked Micah.

"You are tutor," came the reply.

"Adam, who's in charge here," Micah asked again.

Adam, not sure if he'd got the first answer wrong, thought for a moment but decided he had been right. So again he said, "You are tutor."

For the third time, Micah asked, "Adam who's in charge here?"

Adam was panicking now thinking he can't be wrong, but wondering why he'd been asked the same question a third time. But all credit to the twelve year old, he stuck to his guns and said for the third time, "You are tutor."

"Thank you Adam," replied Micah, who then proceeded to carry out the same interrogation of the three other children. All three gave the same three answers as Adam and then awaited Micah's response.

"So we all agree that I'm in charge," asked Micah?

"Yes tutor," came the reply.

"So that means what I say goes."

"Yes tutor."

"Good. Now don't any of you forget that the training we are about to start could be very dangerous so for everyones safety you will at all times do as I say, is that clear?"

"Yes tutor."

Micah pulled out the good book he had in the belt he was wearing and shouted, "The Sword of God. Matter." Instantly the book transfigured into a flaming, two edged sword. Micah then swung it over his head and brought it down right between where Adam and Jamie were sitting. The bench split asunder and the ground where the sword hit had a gaping hole with burnt grass. All four fell to the ground shocked about what had happened. For the minutest second, Jamie wondered if the fallen had found him and Anna again.

Micah spoke in hushed tones as he re-transfigured the sword to a book and in one swift movement returned it to its pouch.

"That bench could be you. These swords are dangerous and can kill in the wrong hands or if used in the wrong way. That's why what I say goes. Is that clearly understood?"

"Yes tutor."

"Can I apologise for scaring you like that but I find it's the best way of getting the point across. Right, bring another bench over here, and we'll get started." Adam and Jamie pulled over another bench and they all sat down.

"As part of our time together I will be teaching you defence techniques and how to keep your square bodies in shape. Without fitness any defensive techniques are a waste of time. It's no use me teaching you how to use a sword or defend yourself with a shield if after two of your minutes of action you are out of breath. You need to exercise and eat the right stuff to be 'the right stuff'. Up here in the third dimension we are aware of the poor diet many kids are now eating. Fast food is the fast way to poor health. And by the way, exercise doesn't involve sitting down for hours on end in front of a computer or television screen. If you don't move, you don't improve. Tell me, how active are your parents?"

"Our mum and dad are always out running or swimming or hill walking," answered Lois.

"Ours are pretty much the same with a bit of golf and horse riding thrown in," added Anna.

"And how's their diet," Micah continued.

"Lots of fresh fruit and vegetable with some meat thrown in," said Jamie and Adam confirmed the same for his folks.

"Good, so they're pretty much keeping up with the Daniel Diet we taught them up here."

"Can you explain the Daniel Diet," asked Adam, who's not one to shy away from a question.

"The Daniel Diet is one based around fresh fruit and vegetables as used by Daniel many of your centuries ago. When he was taken into exile, he didn't want to eat meat offered to pagan idols so he and his crew just ate fruit and veg. After some weeks, there was a competition between the meat eaters and the veggies and who won?"

"Must have been Daniel and his crew," offered Jamie.

"Exactly," confirmed Micah.

"So does that mean we have to be vegetarians," asked Lois.

"Not unless you want to be," said Micah. "In our dimension we don't eat animals because our bodily make up is different to yours. But in your dimension, after the fall, animals were given as food to help build up you're temporal bodies. Before the fall animals weren't used for food and when all things are complete, 'The lion will lie down with the lamb.' " However, you were not given animals to mistreat them, which does happen in your dimension. So making a stand to improve treatment of animals by not eating meat is understandable. Whilst you're here with us you will be on Daniels Diet of fresh fruit and vegetables but when you return to you dimension, the choice will be yours. But whether you eat meat or not, I hope you will still keep up with the fresh fruit and vegetables, ideally eating five a day of either."

Micah took a breath and continued. "So part of our training will be for fitness so you are able to fight for The Kingdom when called upon to do so. I hope to see a lot of running, riding, sports and if you want, some work over in the gym which I'll show you later. Ok, you've got the point over fitness but as I've started with the sword, let's carry on with that. Do you all know how to obtain your sword?"

"Yes tutor."

"Good. But you also need to know how to configure it to the use you want to put it to. Our flaming swords have three configurations which are Matter, Taken and fallen. Matter has a white flame, Taken has a blue flame and fallen has a red flame. The old red, white and blue. The Matter configuration is used to deal with any material item in your dimension."

"Any material item," asked Adam.

"Any," replied Micah, "including flesh and bone. So that's why you have got to be careful how you configure your sword before you use it. If you get it wrong, someone could easily die. Let me show you." Micah led the children over to the three human like dummies set in what Adam presumed was an arkov framework.

"You will see that each dummy is a different colour relating to each configuration of your sword. Now if I configure my sword to matter," which Micah did, "it will deal easily with the white dummy." Micah produced his sword faster than the kids could see and as they blinked, he had sliced the dummy in two.

"Now watch." Micah then struck at the fallen dummy but nothing happened. But when he struck out at the taken dummy, it to parted like the Red Sea in front of Moses.

"You see, people who are taken by the fallen are still made of matter. So if you wrongly configure or use your sword, you are going to kill them. So don't do it."

Micah returned to the red dummy and shouted "fallen!" with that the sword became a flaming red and struck the dummy which disappeared.

"When you strike a fallen with the red blade, you can't kill them because they like us are not made like you are. But what you will do is send them back to their own place from where they can't leave for six of your days."

"So if we come across a fallen, we can use our sword with no fear of killing them," said Jamie.

"Exactly," confirmed Micah. "But it is very rare that you Enochim meet taken in your dimension. It has happened in exceptional circumstances but not often.

"So what happens to the taken," asked Lois.

"As long as you configure your sword correctly, and strike the taken across the chest you will not harm their bodies. But what you will do is release them from the power of the fallen who has taken them, and send that fallen back to 'the air'"

"From where he can't return for six of our days," added Jamie.

"Correct," Micah confirmed. "Now for this Alpha I want you all to practice your sword configuration on these dummies. You each have your own rack and I'll be here to supervise. The rule is when I say 'Draw Swords' that is what you will do. When I say 'Sheath Swords' that is what you will do, is that understood?"

"Yes tutor," came the quick fourfold reply that Micah enjoyed so much. Up until Alpha 6 the children practiced with their swords. A few times they each got the configuration wrong because Micah hadn't told them that as the dummies repaired themselves they would sometimes change colour and so need a different configuration. Eventually the four picked up on this and by the end of the session they were all getting it right, although Lois and Jamie were quicker than their siblings.

"That was a good alphas work you four, but time for lunch. Now you know that you can come here to practice like with you other subject tutors but must only do so if I'm around. Don't worry about letting me know because when you open your locker I get a signal and I'll come down and join you."

"Can I come back this omega," asked Jamie?

"Of course you can."

"Can I come as well," asked Lois?

"The more the merrier," replied Micah.

Anna thought she better mention that she was going flying that omega so couldn't make it.

"No problem Anna. You do as you are led. Right, before lunch, let me just show you where the gym is." Micah made sure all equipment was put away and then he took the children inside All Saints. They went past the locker room and down the Hall and into the first door on the right, which was the gym. It was kitted out with the usual equipment including the weights, rowing and running machines along with the mandatory bikes.

"You can come here anytime you like to work out and that includes you Adam," Micah said trying to encourage the less sporty of the gospel. Adam smiled hoping that would be enough to keep Micah of his back, but deep down, he knew it wouldn't.

With the gym located and the lesson finished they all headed down to lunch. As Micah ate with them, all four made sure they had at least five pieces of fruit and veg.

That omega Jamie and Lois returned to do some more training with Micah whilst Adam and Anna headed down to the flier port where they got some more flying in.

By Omega 3 they were all back at the house for tea and chat. Then down to Wings for some deserved r and r to start off their two day break after their first season of tuition.

XVII

The children's two day break went all too quickly. No sooner had they closed their eyes on day 7 than day 10 arrived and they were off again to see Uriel to start off their second season. But not before Jamie had been out for a run and the girls had sorted out the horses. As for Adam, well Jamie tried to get him running but he wasn't up for it just yet.

By Alpha 5 they were in Uriels study wondering where they might be going today.

"Morning children," Uriel said as they entered his study. "I hope your first season went well and you enjoyed your time off."

"Yes thank you tutor," replied Lois.

"Excellent. I thought this Alpha we would look at us angels and how we are organised and if we've got time, consider how you Enochim are organised. From our last lesson you all understand the origin of us angels and how the prince and the fallen developed and were dealt with." All four nodded and Adam said, "Yes tutor."

"Ok," Uriel continued. "Some revelation has been given in your dimension over us angels but a complete explanation has not been given. For whatever reason, The I Am does not want to give the full story of us angels to you. Bearing this in mind, what I tell you this alpha will not go beyond what has been disclosed in your dimension but I hope will explain in general terms, what has been revealed.

Uriel stood up and the kids excitement grew thinking they might be experiencing another 'Holygram'.

"I know what you are thinking, but no Holygrams today," Uriel said to the disappointment of his students. He went over to the blank wall in his study and as he turned again to face the children, a chart appeared on the wall.

THE THRONE

Seraphim   Cherubim

(6 wings)   (4 wings)

Onaphim

Authorities   Dominions   Powers   Principalities   Thrones

The Archangel Michael

The Angel Gabriel

The Angel Host including The 12 Legions

Referring to the chart, Uriel asked the children what they recognised on it. First to answer was Anna. "The Archangel Michael". Then came Lois with, "Angel Gabriel", those nativity plays paying dividends now. Then Jamie came up with a belter of a statement. "Weren't Cherubim used to guard the Tree of Life after Adam and Eve sinned."

"That really is an excellent answer Jamie, Thank you," said Uriel with real sincerity in his voice. "How about you Adam. Any bells ringing," Uriel asked?

Adam thought for a moment, straining to remember something from his Sunday school lessons. That a right clanger peeled in his head. "Weren't Seraphim around in Isaiah's day," he asked?

"They certainly were Adam. Once again, that is an excellent answer." Uriel sat down as he finished congratulating Adam and then proceeded to explain the chart as clearly as possible, within the parameters of The Book available in The First Dimension.

"First of all I need to let you know that the layout of this chart does not necessarily define a hierarchy within the angel society. There are ranks and divisions of responsibility but as The Book in your dimension does not clearly define these, other than The Archangel is over other Angels, then I am prevented from doing so. The Throne you see is that of The I Am who rules over all. The Seraphim around The Throne are high ranking angels with six wings who are particularly concerned with purity before The I Am and His worship. The Cherubim have four wings and are particularly concerned with guarding the holiness of The I Am and are available at a moments notice to be sent out to defend this holiness. The Onaphim are there to attend The Throne of The I Am and be of service in His Court. At anyone time there are Seven of these angels before The Throne, there being two Seraphim and Cherubim and three Onaphim to attend to the threefold Throne of The I Am. Any questions on that," asked Uriel?

No one spoke until Jamie said, "I think we're all clear on that tutor, thank you."

"Thank you Jamie, then I will continue. The five entities you see thereafter are the divisions of angels given specific areas of work within The Creation. Once again The Book in your dimension does not define those areas so therefore I cannot. Enough to say that these angels carry out their work as The I Am commands, when, where and how He commands. Then you have Michael, The Archangel. He is also referred to as a Prince and has command over many angels. He is most notably a warrior but also has the task of watching over the chosen people. Then we have Gabriel who I'm sure you all know from your Christmas stories. He is particularly used as a messenger to bring The Word from The I Am."

Adam asked, "Isn't Gabriel an Archangel?"

"The Book only speaks of 'The Archangel' when referring to Michael and never uses the plural 'Archangels'. Thus, I can say no more than that." Uriel took a moment and then concluded, "To finish off we the Angels of which I am one, come under the direct authority of The Archangel and others who The I Am decrees have authority over us. Does all that help to make things clear in your minds about the make up of the angel organisation," Uriel finishing this part of the lesson with a question. "Please tell me if there is any confusion and I will try to clear it up. But remember, I cannot go beyond what The Book says."

There were a few moments silence before Lois spoke. "The main thing seems to be that there is an order of angels which functions to organise the work of The I Am. We need to know that organisation exists but not the particular details of its set up."

"I couldn't have put it better myself Lois. Thank you."

Encouraged by Uriel's kind words, Lois continued. "Is part of the reason that the details of Angel society are veiled so that we won't be come to hung up on it and be deflected from the authority of The I Am?"

"That could well be part of the reason. It doesn't take much for you squares to over complicate matters and miss the main point. We angels do not want to be venerated by you because we are simply created servants for The I Am and don't deserve any form of hero worship."

Jamie then asked about 'Guardian Angels.' Uriel explained that Guardian angels do exist but principally for members of The Kingdom. They act when prompted to do so in ways that could effect those outside of The Kingdom indirectly.

A few more moments silence and then Uriel said, "Let's move on. He stood up and carried on with the lesson. "Can anyone tell me where the prince fits into all this?" Uriel wasn't really expecting a reply to his rhetorical question, but he was to be presently surprised when Anna spoke up.

"Wasn't he one of The Cherubim," Anna said as more of a question than an answer.

"He certainly was young lady and that has to be the best answer today. How did you know that," Uriel asked.

"Well, when your dad takes classes on The Book, you get to go and some things stick."

"Brownie points to you and your dad. Next time I see him I must shake his hand. Both you and your dad are spot on. The prince used to be called 'Lucifer' and he was one of the princes of Heaven like Michael. But as we all know, he became so full of himself he thought he could become like The I Am. Last lesson we saw the horrific consequences of that and the battle that threw the prince and his hordes into down to the earth and into 'the air'. The prince is a ruler and he has set up his own organisation modelled on that of The I Am with his own Authorities, Dominions, Powers and the rest. But his 'principality' is of the air and your world and no matter what he tries to do, the prince is doomed to destruction. Nevertheless, he shouldn't be under estimated. With his ruthlessness, deceit and pride along with his many and violent hordes, he has to be reckoned with and that my friends is where you Enochim come in."

Uriel paused for a moment and then quipped, "You see, I don't just throw these lessons together." The humour was well placed to break the tension in the class that had built up listening to these mighty truths. The four gave out nervous laughs and shuffled a bit in their seats.

"I tell you what, let's call it an Alpha there. We've covered a lot of ground so far and we can continue next time."

Jamie spoke up, not only surprising his classmates but also himself. "to be honest tutor, I am finding this fascinating and I wouldn't mind carrying on with the lesson this Omega."

Uriel was chuffed and asked if the rest wanted to and his 'chuffness' increased when they all said they did.

"Ok, it's nearly Alpha 6. How about you come back at Omega 1 and we'll move onto The Enochim." They all agreed and set off for lunch.

After there 3 veg and 2 fruit, they were all back at their places in Uriels study, ready for the next instalment.

"Good to see you back. Now this shouldn't take too long and it will actually mean we're ahead of ourselves in what we need to cover. Before I start with the Enochim I better just complete the picture of the angel organisation by mentioning the twelve legions. I take it you've been on your trip over Angel City with Joel and Nathaniel?"

They all nodded. "So you know the city is divided into twelve districts named after........." Uriel waited for the answer and Anna did not disappoint.

"The twelve sons of Isaac."

"No school boy error there with the twelve tribes of Israel. Well done, Anna. You obviously listened when you were given the sightseeing talk. The 12 legions are the best of the best out of all the warrior angels. The best fliers, horse riders and defenders. You do not mess with the legionnaires. Just so you know, both Micah and Zechariah are legionnaires."

"Thanks for the word," Jamie said to his tutor.

"No problem. The twelve legions are used whenever special weapons and tactics are required and they do not lose. As you will, recall from last seasons lesson, they were the ones who finally executed the order to ban the fallen to the earth and the air. The fallen, nor any earthly army are any match for the angel hosts and certainly not the twelve legions. When time ends and the judgement is executed, you will find the legions leading the way behind The King as Conqueror. Each legion is commanded by an angel named after one of the twelve sons and they come under direct command of Archangel Michael. Ok that completes our brief description of angel society. Everyone got to grips with that?"

"Yes, tutor," said Adam, adding, "Are the twelve legions the ones who were ready to rescue The King when He was executed?"

"That is correct. That day was even worse than the first great battle. The one who could save mankind was slain by those He wanted to help. But the legions were ready to defend Him if He so wished. I can see it now," and as Uriel said that s, so could the children. As their tutor spoke, a Holygram appeared and they saw all he was speaking about.

"The City of Angels became still and silent. And not only that, for three of your hours, complete darkness fell over the city which is always light. And there stood along Straight Street with their heads bowed was every angel from the legions with a tear in every eye. They would have gone to aid The King quicker than you can have the thought but the call never came. The King followed the path laid out for Him and it cost Him His life. The darkness lifted after three of your hours from the city but for three of your days the darkness stayed in our hearts. Then the command came and the legions left to escort The King back and to His Throne."

The holygram left as soon as it appeared but was replaced by the smile on Uriels face.

"So that's the twelve legions and angel society." Uriel paused and then said, "You know, I think that will do for today's lesson. You've taken a lot in and I don't want to over face you. Let's 'call it a day. I tell you what, I suppose Zechariahs on at you to keep your riding up, isn't he?

"Yes tutor," answered Lois.

"Well how about we all go and see Phillip and take a ride around the city."

"The children were a little surprised that one who they thought of as not a 'sporty' tutor was up for a ride, but it wasn't their place to argue. As they left his study, Uriel, closing the door said in a voice they could all hear, "Oh by the way, I'm a legionnaire to."

When they got to Phillips stables, he was more than happy for them all to go for a ride and even asked if he could tag along.

"We would be honoured if you joined us," Uriel assured Phillip.

"Thank you tutor." Phillip went on, "Could I suggest that as the children haven't yet been into the garden and there are two of us with them that we take a ride out there.

"That is an excellent idea constable," replied Uriel.

"To save time and give the children some driving practice, can I further suggest that we take two of the chariots rather than horses."

"You really are on a roll this Omega, aren't you Phillip, "Uriel said with a smile in his voice. The next quarter Omega was spent getting two of the chariots ready and then tacking up the horses. Once they'd done that, Phillip asked the girls to drive to the Garden and let the boys know they could drive back so they wouldn't get upset. Phillip went with the Iqbals whist Uriel went with the Fishers. The two chariots were guided out into the park and Phillip gave a quick lesson on piloting them.

"What you need to do is get the horses up to a fast gallop. When the crystal on the front of the chariot turns red then you push it and that will 'fire it up'. The fire from the rear of the chariot will launch it into the sky and you just steer by using the reins and as the horses alter course, so will the chariot." It sounded simple enough but all four thought it couldn't be that easy.

Phillip and the Iqbals went first. "That's it Lois, get them up to a fast gallop. Right, watch your crystal. Right we're at orange .....now red. Hit It.!" Lois did and immediately they all felt the thrust as the fire kicked in and they were airborne. Lois was really surprised how smooth the steering was and how responsive the horses and chariot were to her steering.

As soon as the Iqbals had flown out of the park, the Fishers followed under Uriels guidance. No doubt about the fact Uriel had done this before as his instructions, as ever, were clear and precise. The Fishers could soon see the Iqbals ahead of them and Uriel couldn't resist saying, "Follow that chariot." Anna did and like her friend in front, she had no problem driving her fiery chariot.

"Right, landing can be a little tricky," Phillip told Lois who thought he could have chosen his moment and words a little more carefully.

"What you need to do is press the crystal which will start to decrease the power from the fire at the rear. This in turn will make you descend. As you come near to the ground, the horses are trained to start galloping so you will hit the ground running. Ok Lois if you're ready, press the crystal. Lois did so and as she did it started to change colour from red and the chariot slowed down. The slow descent was smooth and gradual but soon enough the ground started to come up and meet them. Just before they hit the ground, the two horses started to move their legs so as they touched down the chariot continued to move forwards.

"Text book landing Lois. Well done. Can you bring us to a halt just over by the trees by that brook." Lois did so and neatly parked the chariot by the copse. Not long after, Anna brought her chariot into land and parked right along side Lois'.

"I don't know why in your dimension, men say you ladies can't park or drive," commented Uriel.

"You've obviously not met my mums friend Charlotte," joked Jamie.

After they'd untacked the horses and left them grazing, they all went for a walk along the brook. The Omega was warm and the babbling brook was accompanied by the rustle of a breeze in the trees. After a while they all sat down to enjoy the scenery.

As the group chatted, Adam commented that, "Such a beautiful garden must remind the angels of the first garden called Eden.

"I don't wish to be picky," said Uriel, "but the garden wasn't actually called 'Eden' but the land in which it was located was known as 'Eden'."

"Thanks for the 'garden tip'," joked Jamie. He carried on. "Can you tell us where Eden is located now on the earth," he asked?

"Who said it's still on the earth," replied Uriel.

"Well I assumed that because it was originally located on the earth and that in Genesis we are given geographical clues with the four rivers, that it still was."

"You make a fair point but if those clues were still relevant, how come no one has found the garden and the Cherubim in it?"

Adam joined in. "My dad pointed out that the clues given in Genesis are no longer usable because the earths topography was altered after Noah's flood. So the rivers mentioned will have changed their courses and the Garden can no longer be located by them."

"Your dad is right but I wonder where he heard that," Uriel said as they all realised the answer.

"So where is the Garden of Eden now," asked Anna?

"If I were to tell you that the word 'Paradise' means 'beautiful garden' would that give you a clue?"

"Are you telling us that Eden is now here in The Third Dimension," asked Adam?

"Rather than me answer that question, let me give you a few facts to think about. When those who are part of The Kingdom leave your dimension, they have to go somewhere. The King, before the Fall, used to walk in the Garden with your first ancestors. Whilst He was in your dimension, The King was recognised as 'the gardener' and He didn't object to that. When the thief died on the cross he was told by The King, 'Today, you will be with me in Paradise.' When Paul came from your dimension to ours, he saw and heard things in 'Paradise' that he couldn't repeat. Now if there was no one in 'Paradise' or 'The Garden', he couldn't have heard or seen anything.'

"So you are telling us that the Garden of Eden is now in The Third Heaven," suggested Adam.

"Yes, but it was not always so. Perhaps it's easier to show you than explain it to you. Can all of you come here and sit around me now." The children did as they were asked.

Uriel continued. "In your dimension you have 'Virtual Reality'. I want to use what we call 'Spiritual Reality' to show you what happened aeons of your time ago. All of you close your eyes and listen to my voice." The children did as they were asked.

"Now I want you to imagine a beautiful garden like the one we are sitting in now. Lush grass. Crystal clear water flowing in a stream. Majestic trees. Colourful flowers of all kinds." As Uriel's voice drifted into their ears, the minds of the children drifted to Eden. Uriel continued.

"Your first ancestors lived in this beautiful place without death because sin had not yet entered their world. Time meant nothing then with 'a thousand years being like a day and a day like a thousand years'. Then one day, the prince led the first humans away from The I Am and out of the garden into darkness. The Tree of Life was to be guarded by Cherubim with flaming swords and still is to this day. Because sin was now stalking the earth bringing death with it as its companion, two places had to be found to hold those who die and leave your dimension. So Sheol was created with Hades to hold those who die outside The Kingdom. For those who died in The Kingdom Eden was transported into Sheol and became known as Paradise. For millennia the dead would go to one of those places, their fate having been sealed by the choice they made in your dimension. And thus it continued until The King conquered death. He was the only one who could do it. He died on the cross with The twelve Legions and all the rest of creation outside your dimension looking on. As he gave up His Spirit he accompanied the thief to Paradise. Whilst there He told all those in Hades that He had won the victory and had made the way possible once more for eternal life in The Kingdom."

Uriel paused to allow the children to see the Spiritual reality of what he was talking about. Then he continued with the history lesson.

"On the Third Day He rose again to life in your dimension proving who He was and providing assurance of eternal life to those who come into The Kingdom. As He rose again, others rose after Him as a symbol of the new life that he had inaugurated. But the resurrection of these others also pointed to the coming removal of Paradise from Hades into The Third Heaven. After forty more days, The King ascended back into His Glory taking all those who had died in The Kingdom with Him and so emptying Hades of all those but the lost. The time had not yet come when the citizens of The Kingdom were to be changed to be like The King as that would only happen when The I Am decrees it. So the

New Eden was placed in The Third Heaven where those who depart your dimension hear those words from their King, 'Today you shall be with me in Paradise.' The angels take them there to join other believers who have past and to walk with 'The Gardener' in 'His Garden'.

As Uriel had spoken, the children had seen the spiritual reality of his words. As he finished they all opened their eyes and felt comforted by what they had experienced. For a few minutes all four just sat there, listening to the waters of the brook pass by and the new thoughts in their minds. Adam was the first to speak as he started to grasp the enormity of what he had heard.

"So, all the dead are somewhere, either in Paradise or Hades."

"That is exactly so," confirmed the tutor.

"Can they leave either place," Adam asked?

"It can and will happen but it is very, very rare. Even when it does, it can only happen with the express permission of The King."

Jamie jumped in with a question about the fallen. "I presume the fallen aren't put into Hades with the others are they? Joel told us early on that the demons are held in The Abyss, so is that where the rest of the fallen are?"

"No. As you say, the demons or Nephilim are in The Abyss only to be let out when Abaddon decrees. The majority of the fallen are in the air with the prince to do his evil bidding. They are not yet in the fiery hell called Gehenna but will be thrown there at the end of time when The King executes His final judgement. Those fallen who came to your dimension and fathered the Nephilim have been imprisoned in a place called Tartarus as punishment for that particular rebellion. They await their final judgement in that dark, cold dungeon. I hope that explains the present situation other than that for the one who betrayed The King who was sent 'to his own place.'

'But what about those people in our dimension who aren't part of The Kingdom. Do they go to the fiery hell to be punished,' asked Anna?

'This is a difficult situation to address. The first thing to say is that the fiery hell was created for the devil and his angels not human beings. The I Am wants all to be saved but won't over rule your free will because he wants your love and devotion as free beings not robots.

But if there's no punishment to be avoided, why did The King have to die? The problem for many is accepting that a God who is love would purposely send people to eternal torment as indicated in Chapter 20 of The Revelation in The Book you have been given. What I can point out is that the devil and his angels are created differently to you so a fire that torments them 'physically' doesn't necessarily effect you humans physically. At the very least those outside The Kingdom will be banished there so perhaps their 'torment' is to be separated from God with the fallen.

Having said that, you can probably think of evil people in your time and through history who should be punished for the great sins they committed. Even you humans with your defective consciences know it's unfair that wrongdoers go unpunished. Perhaps that's why when The King told the story, not the Parable of The Rich Man and Lazarus, The Rich Man was in torment in the fire. So there is room for punishment for some individuals. Maybe the best way to leave this is to trust in The I Am to do what's right.

Uriel stood up and said, "Don't try to analyse what you've experienced too quickly. It's best to meditate over these things and let the answers be given to you in due time. Not to mention it's nearly time for your tea. How about you lads take us home."

They all walked back to where the chariots had been parked and soon had the horses back in harness. Having seen what the girls did to get them into the Garden, the boys soon had everyone airborne and heading back to All Saints Park. When they arrived it was no quick tea as the chariots and horses had to be sorted first.

By Omega 4 they were all having tea with not much chat as the days lesson and field trip, or 'garden trip' started to sink in. Some how now, death for those in The Kingdom didn't seem as daunting but what about those outside The Kingdom with the prince?

XVIII

The rest of the second season had been taken up with more defence and flying practice with Micah and Zechariah, including missile training. The children had also spent more time with Jerahmeel concentrating on more maintenance of their equipment.

After the two day break, which really wasn't a break at all because the children kept honing their new found skills as they had been inspired by their tutors. Jamie even found himself going to see Jerahmeel to discuss how best to store his equipment when back in the first dimension.

The third season didn't start as usual with Uriel because he had let his fellow tutors know he was ahead of schedule due to the 'lesson' he and the children had in The Garden. Accordingly, Micah snook in an extra lesson to start the children off on a hand to hand defensive technique used by angels that was called 'Archangel'. It was called that because it had been developed by The Archangel Michael to overconme opponents when weapons aren't readily available or to use to ensure you don't kill somebody. Micah accepted Adams term of 'martial art' for 'Archangel' but emphasised that its only purpose was defence not attack.

"Michael when he first described the technique to us angels said that, 'You must think before you strike with the intelligence symbolised by man, you must have the strength of the ox, the speed of the eagle and the courage of the lion.'"

Micah went on to demonstrate all the 24 moves and throws that formed the basis of 'Archangel'. Thankfully he didn't expect the children to learn them immediately, just by next season. He passed out tablets with all 24 moves on and suggested they practice in pairs until they had all 24 moves down. In answer to Jamies' question, Micah said there was no reason why the girls can't be paired with the boys.

"Archangel allows so called less strong combatants to overcome 'stronger' opponents by using their opponents strength against themselves." The rest of the session was taken up with all five practicing Archangel with the practice overlapping into the afternoon. As they finished Micah explained that they would still have their session in two days time as scheduled.

"Todays session replaced Uriels because you are ahead of yourselves in his classes. So we'll meet as usual on this seasons fourth day to carry on our defence training and look particularly at shield work."

The next day, the children met with Jerahmeel who this season wanted to concentrate on undercover work.

"We angels have been used on occasions in undercover work but this is very rare. Normally, Angel Command expects you Enochim to carry out you own covert operations as you deem necessary." Jerahmeel went on to explain that certain theonology is released to The Enochim prior to general availability in the first dimension to assist in such activities.

"For example, you Enochim will be getting access to new materials to assist in facial disguise along with real time language decoders that can be worn inside the ear allowing you to decipher overheard conversations not in your natural tongue instantaneously." Of course, Adam was fascinated by all this and stayed behind after class to try and understand the mechanics of 'The Pentecost' chip which made immediate language decoding possible.

Day3 of season 3 saw the troops back flying with Zechariah. By this time all four were becoming competent at flying the fliers, but Anna and Adam seemed to be heading towards becoming 'Testament' fliers. Who would be the 'Gospel' flier, was yet to be determined. After their Alpha session with Zechariah he took the girls aside for a little word.

"I've been speaking to Phillip about your request to take part in his Cup. I think he's pleased that after so many centuries some of you Enochim have had the 'hutspa' to ask. Not only that, he and I are both impressed with the way you look after your horses with such dedication."

"Thank you Tutor," said Lois, "But really it all comes out of our love for horses and it is not work to us."

"Both Phillip and I appreciate that, but it's still a credit to you. Anyway, Phillip has suggested that you both take part in some training with some pairs from the other twelve districts and we'll see how things develop from there."

"Thank you tutor. When do we start," asked Anna?

"How does Omega 4 today sound," replied Zechariah.

"It sounds just fine," answered Anna.

After lunch, not to continue impressing Phillip but simply for the love of it, the girls went to the stables and spent their time grooming the horses and riding through the park. At Omega ¾, they headed off for some tea but were back in the stable at Omega 4 to meet Phillip.

"You girls are never way from here are you," he quipped. "But I'm not complaining. Before we leave to meet the others, do you remember what I told you how we run the races for Phillips Cup?"

"If memory serves me correctly, two districts race at a time and the winner goes forward to the next race until only two teams are left for the final." Lois completed her answer.

"Couldn't have put it better myself," said Phillip. He continued, "Anna, where are the races run?"

"If my memory serves me correctly, you start at the third circular street away from The Circle. After each round your move a street nearer The Circle until the last two teams run in the final around The Circle."

"Once again, I couldn't put it better myself. Now the first round will be held at the end of this season on the first day of your two day break. The next round will be at the end of next season and so on until the fourth and final round at the end of your time here. The Cup is not run every time Enochim are here but only once every hundred of your years. So not many Enochim get to see it, never mind be in it."

"So our parents didn't get to experience it," noted Anna.

"Just so, young lady, so you will have a real story to tell them when you return. Now, if you're ready, we'll ride out to meet the teams taking part in this centuries Cup." They all mounted up and rode out of the stables into The Circle. Soon the horses were up to a mighty gallop, faster than any horse either girl had seen run, let alone ride themselves. But as they and their mounts were in real harmony, there was no fear just exhilaration. The three went zooming past the first street beyond

The Circle. Soon they were beyond the second street and Phillip stated to slow everyone down to a steady canter. As they continued, the girls could see in front of them the junction off Straight Street with the Third Street beyond The Circle. There on the junction was a group of about twenty horses and their riders. On thinking about it, Lois realised there would be twenty four horses and riders, two from each of the City's twelve districts. In fact when they arrived at the group there were actually thirty six riders and horses as each of the districts constables were there as well.

When he arrived, the girls could tell Phillip was held in great honour by all those present, almost like a hero Anna commented to Lois later on before they went to sleep. After informal welcomes all round, every one hushed to listen to Phillip.

"Welcome, my fellow angels and riders. Good to see you all. I see you constables have chosen your riders and horses well for this Cup. As you know, no rider can compete more than once in The Cup so it's good to meet new competitors to our little race. May I introduce to you the two young Enochim who have asked if they can take part in the race. Firstly over to the far right can I introduce Lois." All present as a choir in unison said "Welcome".

"Sat next to me on Milk is Anna." Again the unified refrain of "Welcome came from all present.

"Thank you Brethren. Now let us all ride together as we get to renew our friendships before we cast lots for the first race." Phillip whispered to the girls, "We'll be going slower than usual so you shouldn't have any trouble keeping up" With that, Phillip flicked his reins, turned his horse on its shoes and led the cavalry away down Third Street. Anna and Lois had never ridden so fast in all their lives nor even in their time in The Third Dimension. The houses and buildings went by as a blur until such speed was reached that the buildings weren't seen at all. Both Anna and Lois hung onto their reins not wanting to fall off. It wasn't the thought of hurting themselves that kept them on their horses, but not wanting to let Phillip down. They needn't have worried because their horses knew exactly how each of their riders were coping and always corrected their stride as needed so neither girl even came close to falling off. After a time, which Anna nor Lois could determine, the cavalry came to a halt. The whole troop surrounded Phillip to wait for his further words. Before Phillip could start, Lois and Anna walked up to him on their horses.

"May we have a word Constable," asked Anna.

"Certainly girls. What is it?"

"Can I ask on behalf of Lois and myself that we be excused from the draw for the first race. After having seen the speed you angels travel that is 'slow' we know we couldn't keep up and we don't want to endanger any riders or horses by getting in the way."

"Thank you very much for your considerate words, Anna. I am sure all of us here appreciate your honesty and your real interest in the Cup. Perhaps your suggestion is a sensible one because none of us want to see anyone get hurt, particularly you and Lois." All present nodded their approval of Phillips words. Then without any prompting aloud round of applause rang out from the assembled throng.

Phillip motioned with his hand for quiet and said, "I would like to suggest to you friends that both Anna and Lois be appointed as stewards for the race to assist me in adjudication." No words of affirmation were needed as everyone took the second round of applause to be giving agreement to Phillips proposal. Not really knowing what being a steward meant Anna and Lois still thanked everyone as it seemed the polite thing to do.

Phillip continued. "We will now chose the teams for the first race." Phillip took a small bag of his belt and put his hand inside. He took out two highly polished stones. Each of the stones had a black side and a white side.

"for the benefit of our guests, I will explain how we use these Urim and Thunnim to decide who races when and who. The girls listened intently as Phillip explained how the stones would work.

"I will put the stones back in their pouch. I will then ask in order of the sons of Jacob as to who will be in the first race. So my first question will be, 'Should Reuben be in the first race?' I then turn the pouch upside down so that the stone fall out onto the ground. If both black sides land facing upwards that is 'Urim' which is a 'No'. If both white sides face upwards that is 'Thunnim' which is 'Yes'.

Lois asked the obvious question, "What if a black and white side each face upwards?"

"That is neither 'Thunnim or Urim' and means 'No reply'. So we move on to the next district and so on until all races and competitors are decided. Is that understandable to you girls," Phillip asked?

"Yes Constable," they replied.

"Good, because you can both share the asking of The Urim and Thunnim." Phillip passed over his pouch to Anna and asked her to pour out the stones after he asked the first question about Reuben. She did so and the answer was 'Thunnim' so that Reuben was in the first race. Lois took over for the next question but got 'no reply'. Not until Gad's question was the first race sorted. It took some time but eventually all twelve races were decided.

"Thank you for your help girls," Phillip said as he replaced the pouch with its Urim and Thunnim onto his belt. "Can I also thank all riders and Constables for their attendance and I look forward to seeing all of you at the first race soon." Phillip bowed to his friends with the words, "For The Kingdom." His 'friends' did likewise and quick as a twinkle were gone, riding off back to their districts.

"Did you enjoy that," Phillip asked the only two of his friends now remaining with him.

"Yes constable, very much," replied Anna." I can't wait for the race. When is it by the way?"

"The constables and riders will await to be summoned but just so you're prepared I can tell you it's at the end of your third season on the second day you have of and starts at Omega 3. Can I suggest that you come to the stables before then so we can get ready and be at the starting point in good time."

"It will be our pleasure," answered Lois. By now it was heading towards Omega 5 so Phillip was keen to get his charges and chargers back home. They all mounted up and rode like the wind back to The Circle. The girls were soon home in bed getting excited about the coming races and wondering how they would be helping Phillip.

The next couple of days couldn't go quick enough for the girls who were eagerly awaiting race day. But before then they had more riding and flying practice with Zechariah which actually they really enjoyed as they had their first solo flights, one of which was over The Garden.

On the last day of the season they had their second session with Micah on shield training. To set them up for this session, Jerahmeel had taken time to show them the theolonology they would be using earlier in the season.

"This is your shield," he had told them. It didn't look much like a shield to them. It was a small cylindrical object about six inches long and about 3/4 of an inch in diameter. When Adam switched his on, before he was told to do so, all it did was shine like a torch. A very bright and useful torch, but still just a torch.

"Not much protection from this,"Adam commented.

"Not when you use it like that and without being told what to do," answered Jerahmeel. The sense of his tutors words was not lost on Adam who from then on waited to be told what to do before doing it.

"Jamie, would you please come here." Jamie was happy to comply with his tutors request.

"Will you just hold the on/off switch until I tell you when to stop." Jamie did so for a few seconds until Jerahmeel said, "Thank you."

"Now will you switch your 'torch' on by pushing the switch and not sliding it." As Jerahmeel spoke, he looked over at Adam who understood the repeated sentiment allied to his tutors look. As Jamie switched his 'torch' on as Jerahmeel requested, what looked like a highly polished pane of glass emanated from his 'torch'.

This 'window' was six foot high and two foot wide.

"That ladies and gentlemen is your shield. Anna, will you throw your stool at your brother." Jamie was somewhat taken aback by Anna's lack of hesitation and willingness to do so, but he needn't have worried. Anna threw the stool with some gusto but it just bounced off Jamie's shield, missing Jerahmeel by only a few inches.

"I'll get you next time," Anna joked with her tutor.

"We'll see," he replied. "Anyway, Jamie try this for size." Jerahmeel immediately drew his flaming sword and in an instant slashed at Jamies shield. Not even a scratch as the sword bounced off.

"As you can see, not even a flaming sword can penetrate this shield so there is nothing in your dimension that can. This shield theonology is based on the same theonology that protected Daniels friends in the furnace. Nothing will get through it."

"Couldn't that cause problems if someone else manages to get hold of your shield," asked Adam.

"Good question and here's the answer. Jamie, throw your shield over to Lois please." Jamie did so and as soon as he let go of the handle, the shield disappeared. Lois tried to re-activate it but with no success.

"You see, before I gave Jamie his sword I calibrated it to his DNA so only he can activate it. That's what safeguards it from being used by the wrong people for the wrong purpose." Jerahmeel then calibrated all the other childrens shields so by the time of Micahs last seasonal session, they were all set to go.

"Right, you've got your shields and I presume Jerahmeel has told you all about them." The children nodded.

"Good. Now my job is to show you how you can use your shield." As Micah finished speaking suddenly there was a scream and out of nowhere came Phillip driving a chariot. As the children watched in disbelief, Phillip rode straight at Micah to run him over. In an instant Micah had deployed his shield and fell backwards onto the ground making a ramp which Phillip, his horses and chariot proceeded to ride over. The chariot must have travelled over thirty feet before Phillip landed it safely on the grass.

"Now that's just one way you can use your shield. Whether it's a chariot or a four by four, it will take the weight and protect you."

"Surely we can't hold the weight of a chariot and a four by four," said Lois. "We'll be crushed."

"We, or should I say 'Jerahmeel' thought of that. Can you all stand and deploy your shields." The children did so.

"Now, have you noticed that the opposite end of the shield cylinder has a button you can depress." The children hadn't but now they did.

"Make sure you are all stood squarely in the middle of your shield. Here's a little tip. You can use the advantage you have over Adam and Eve. If you put the cylinder directly in front of your belly button, you'll know you are centred." The children didn't get the Adam and Eve reference until they asked Uriel about it, but did as they were told.

"Now hit that back button hard." The four students did and as they did, two 'legs' came out of each side of the shield, four foot up from its bottom edge.

"Fall backwards and see what happens." The children did and each of them found they were lying perfectly safe under a see through ramp.

"Stay there and don't move," Micah shouted. Suddenly, Phillip came thundering back with his chariot although this time he was joined by three more, driven by Joel, Nathaniel and Zechariah. Each charioteer rode towards their assigned target and proceeded to run over one of the children. The shield and its legs took the strain and afterwards Adam confirmed "I didn't feel a thing."

Having real confidence in their new piece of theonology the children were shown other ways of using the shield.

"One of the most effective tactics is to use the shields you as a testament and a gospel have. If as a testament you need to protect each other, you twist the back button clockwise. This will increase the width of the shield and make it semi-circular. Then back to back you can stand together and be enclosed in a protective cylinder." As Micah spoke, Joel and Nathaniel who had remained for the rest of the session, demonstrated what the tutor was explaining.

"As a gospel you can turn your back button anti-clockwise which lengthens the shield and makes it into a triangular shape. All four can then come together to be inside a protective pyramid." As he spoke, he Joel, Nathaniel and Phillip demonstrated the gospel pyramid. For the rest of the session all eight of them practiced shield manoeuvres. That Omega it was more hand to hand defence practice along with some flying. Then the two day break the girls had been waiting for so they could see the first race in Phillips Cup.

The first 'day off' everyone spent some time with the horses, then Jamie and Anna went flying, Adam popped over to see Jerahmeel and Lois did some reading at the Library. Then they all met at Wings at Omega 4 and had a pleasant evening, chatting, drinking meribah and playing a little music.

The following day, the girls spent with Phillip and the horses whilst Adam and Jamie did some self defence training and flew a bit. There was no danger of the girls being late for Phillip because they had been with

him all day. Early Omega, the Constable sent them home for a shower
and to change but they were well back before Omega 4. When they
returned, Phillip had got Milk and Honey harnessed to a four seater
chariot they hadn't seen before. Phillip asked Anna to drive.

"it's just like driving the two seaters you have used already. We'll
leave as soon as our guest gets here," Phillip said. There wasn't a long
wait until Teacher Eli joined them.

"Don't be nervous Anna. I've not been in one of these yet that has
crashed and in any case, tutor Zechariah tells me you are all flying very
well."

Once everyone was settled in the Phillip asked Anna to proceed.
She did so keeping a close eye on the crystal. As soon as it hit red she
punched it and off they flew from a perfect take off.

"Tutor Zecharuiah is not lying is he," Teacher Eli said to Phillip.
Phillip smiled.

"Not that he would anyway," continued Teacher Eli.

"Where to Constable," Anna asked Phillip.

"Milk and Honey know where. Just let them lead," came the reply.
As they flew both girls noticed other chariots and horses joining them.
Soon another four seater came up along side them with Adam flying
and Jamie and Zechariah as the passengers. Before long the chariots
reached the start/finish point and hovered above it. Phillip asked Anna
to take them down to about ten of 'her feet'; above ground level and
then level out. Without blinking or thinking, Anna did so. Zechariah
watched and thought to himself how well the children were picking
up their training.

Phillip bent down and thanked her. The Constable then stood up
to his full height and addressed the assembled crowd.

"Welcome friends." No microphone or megaphone but everyone
heard every word.

"Thank you for coming to this running of Phillips Cup. I have seen
this Cups riders and they all look extremely capable to me. Our first
race will be between Reuben and Gad." Cheers rang around the crowd.
Jamie wasn't sure, but he thought he saw a Mexican wave.

"Will all four riders please come to the start." A hush descended
over the crowd as four magnificent white horses walked forward. They

all lined up to a golden strip laid in the street and waited. Phillip looked over to a nearby chorus of trumpeters stood on a balcony overlooking the start. The chorus master nodded to Phillip and the trumpeters raised their trumpets.

Phillip raised his arm and shouted, "Let the races begin!!" He dropped his arm, the trumpeters blew and the horses shot off like bullets from a gun. Having been primed by Phillip, Anna immediately ascended the chariot so that they could get a clear view of the race. As they looked down they could see the four horses racing away. As they did, Lois noticed they were changing lanes with the horses taking turns to go on the inside and outside of the street.

"Why are they changing lanes," she asked Phillip?

"The inside lane is a shorter route than the outside so that's the favoured lane. Each pair takes it in turn to use the inside lane to try and stay in front."

The race continued at a breathtaking pace with first Team Reuben then Team Gad taking the lead. The crowds were cheering on their teams but Phillip and Teacher Eli remained quiet and neutral as they were overseeing the race. Not long after it had begun, the race was over with Team Gad taking the honours. No 'in your face' victory antics here. Both teams took the applause and gave each other embraces.

"It's not the winning, but the taking part," explained Phillip. Anna descended the chariot again so Phillip could start the next race. In fact, Phillip asked Teacher Eli to do so. The same procedure was adopted and then Levi and Issachar 'got it on'. Another exciting four races after that with the eventual winners being Gad, Issachar, Dan, Judah, Zebulun and Joseph. Not only that but each one of The Enochim got to start a race and that made them feel like winners as well. When Joseph had beaten Benjamin in the sixth race Lois took over flying and it was all back to Wings for the after race party where everyone was invited. The party went on for 'hours' but eventually the children had to admit defeat as they had school the following day.

Lying in their beds the girls discussed how much they'd enjoyed the day.

"I can't wait to tell mum and dad about this," said Lois.

"Me neither," concurred Anna.

"I'm sure they're all ok," Said Lois and some guilt hit her about enjoying themselves when they'd left their parents in the first dimension battling for their lives.

"I know you're right," said Anna.

"How," asked Lois?

"Because teacher Eli whispered to me during race three that 'mum and dad will be really jealous that they never saw Phillips Cup but you have.' He then continued, 'be sure you tell them when you see them' and then he winked at me. So if Teacher Eli knows we're going to see mum and dad, that's good enough for me."

"And me," confirmed Lois. With that they both lay down to sleep and each dreamt of winning Phillips Cup.

XIX

The fourth season began straight forward enough although it wasn't going to stay 'straight forward' or even just 'forward'. Uriel took the children to the Library and reviewed what they had already discussed. Micah kept them practicing their sword, shield and self defence skills whilst Zechariah had them flying and riding until they couldn't tell the difference.

Omegas were taken up with more of the same but Lois and Jamie concentrated on Micahs work whilst Anna and Adam kept their interest in transport moving. At the end of most 'days', Wings was the place to be, although on one late Omega Zechariah had them night flying. Not an easy thing to do when there's constant light but Jerahmeels theononlogy can deal with that. Special full face helmets are available to create the conditions of night flying. Wearing these helmets with their night vision visors cut out all light and gave the pilots a realistic impression of night flying which they would come across in the first dimension.

Anyway, the girls were particularly looking forward to their two days off so they could be involved in the second round of races in Phillips Cup. But when Jerahmeels session was postponed to be the last one of the season, the children should have known something was up.

Having gone to the laboratory as usual at Alpha 4, the children made themselves comfortable until Jerahmeel arrived. They didn't have long to wait. The children noticed that their tutor seemed a little more serious than usual. Once he had sat himself down at his stool, he began what would turn out to be, a momentous session.

"The fourth session of the fourth season here at All Saints is always a special lesson for you Enochim. Today we are going to discuss and experience one of the most exciting pieces of theonology that you Enochim have access to when on special commission. But first of all, I want to take time to discuss just that.........time." Jerahmeel adjusted his posture and continued.

"As you know, here in the third dimension time does not existas you understand it and means nothing to us. But your dimension is governed by time, your time which is finite. Your time had a beginning and will have an end."

"When did our time start," asked Adam?

"Back when creation was undertaken, the planets and stars in your dimension were set to allow time to be divided into day, night, seasons and years."

"But at what date did time start," Adam asked again?

"No date can be given because although time started at creation, the clock didn't start running until the fall. Until then, time meant nothing because sin hadn't caused death and destruction to blight the human race. Only after sin did the clock start ticking. And there are only two recorded instances when the clock was stopped or turned back."

"And those were," asked Lois?

"That can be your homework to find out," came the disappointing reply from her tutor.

Adam took up the discussion again. "So before time was marked, our earth with humans on it could have been around for millennia."

"Even longer than that. Millions of millennia," confirmed Jerahmeel. "As a learned man in your dimension once said, 'it's all relative'. If your life has no end, a thousand years can seem like one day and one day like a thousand years. That learned man gave us the following example; 'When you sit with a nice girl for two hours, it seems like two minutes. When you sit on a hot stove for two minutes, it seems like two hours. That's relativity.' So times length is relative from where you are experiencing it."

"So to you in this dimension it means nothing," Jamie speaking to clarify what he was thinking."

"Pretty much," confirmed Jerahmeel. "But because we are outside your dimensions time and not constrained by it, we can enter your dimension 'at any time'."

Adam was the first to twig what Jerahmeel was talking about. He took a moment and then blurted out, "Are you talking about time travel? I thought that was impossible?"

"Maybe when viewed from your dimension but not if you come from our dimension. As I said we are outside your time so we can drop into your time at any point in history. What you might call 'Ballistic Time Travel'.

"Can you explain that please" asked Lois.

"Certainly. Have you all heard of ballistic missiles?"

"Yes," came the reply.

"Ballistic missiles are called that because they use a technique whereby they are fired at a high point in your atmosphere and then drop back down onto your planet to hit the intended target. So with 'Ballistic Time Travel' we in the third dimension can 'drop' into your time at any point if we need to do so."

By now, Adam was beside himself with excitement. "Now hold on," he said, straining to speak as fast as his thoughts were developing. "If you can drop into our time at any point from this dimension, and we are here in this dimension that means we can be dropped back at any point in our time."

"You know what, I think the boy's got it," Jerahmeel answered with a smile.

Anna jumped in now, not being able to contain her own excitement. "So we can time travel?"

"Within certain constraints, yes," Jerahmeel confirmed. The tutor now went over to his board for the first time. As he spoke, he wrote. "There are three rules in regards to time travel in your dimension that apply to all of us, Angels and Enochim alike. We call them 'The Time Trinity'. With that, Jerahmeel began to write.

1. **You can only travel back in time and not forwards.**
2. **You must not change anything in the time you travel to.**
3. **You must only use the technology and theonology available in whatever time you go back to.**

"Before you ask, let me explain the reasons behind these three rules," said Jerahmeel before Adam could start questioning him.

"We are not allowed to go forwards in your time because that would allow us to know when The King is going to return. The return of The King to your world is the universes best kept secret. It will occur in the future but none of us know when. But if I were allowed to go forward let's say to the year 2150, not that I know whether the year 2150 will ever occur, I would know The King couldn't return before then and that sort of clue we can't have. We are given signs to watch out for to warn us when The King returns but no more than that."

"So we can only go back to a time that has already passed in the first dimension," Adam said thinking out loud.

"Yes, that's pretty much it," confirmed Jerahmeel. "Now moving onto the second rule, that's been set because once history or 'His Story' has taken place, it can under no circumstances be altered. If history were to be altered it would have effects that none of us can imagine. As we look at history and see the awful things that have gone on, we're all tempted to think, 'what if?' but we have to rely on the greater knowledge of The I Am who knows all that has past, all that is happening and all that is to come. He sees the big picture and we have to trust and let 'His Story' take its course." Jerahmeel let his words register for a moment and then Lois asked the next obvious question, "So if we can't alter history, what's the point of going back?"

"We go back as a teaching tool or to experience things directly so we can better understand what is happening in your present," was Jerahmeels reply.

"Has anyone ever gone back to change history," asked Anna.

"Other than me and the wheel, not that I'm aware of. But there was one famous occasion when an Enochim went back to protect history from being changed for the worse by those in the princedom."

"Who and when," asked Jamie?

"That is not a story that I am at liberty to tell. Uriel usually covers that event in his overview of the history of The Enochim."

"We've not had that yet," commented Adam. Jerahmeel for a moment looked a little surprised as Uriel normally gives the history of The Enochim as his first session to set the scene for the rest of his teaching. Then realising who was in this class he understood why things had probably changed. Jerahmeel regained his momentarily lost composure and continued, "I'm sure you'll be getting to that next."

Jerahmeel moved back towards the words on the board and concluded his explanation of the rules with number three.

"I hope the reason for the third rule is fairly obvious. Any ideas," the tutor asked the class.

"Well, It would be a bit unfair to go back to 70 Ad with a bazooka and stop the fall of Jerusalem or it would cause problems if you gave Abraham Lincoln a bullet proof vest to stop John Wilkes Booth," Jamie said surprising himself how much history he remembered.

"Exactly right. So on the rare occasions time travel is permitted for you Enochim, you can only use what technology and theonology already exists at that time. Are those three rules clearly understood," Jerahmeel asking so that no excuses could be given if they were broken and questions asked of him and his teaching. To be doubly sure, he went round the class and got each student to confirm their understanding with 'Yes'.

"Good. Now us angels can drop into your time line by simply being sent there on a commission. But because the physical bodies you squares have are not the same as ours another way has to be employed to get you back in time. Anyone any ideas how you Enochim travel back in time.?"

The tutors question hung in the air for a moment until Lois beat Adam to the answer.

"Jacobs Ladder," Lois offered as an answer with more confidence than she thought was advisable.

Jerahmeels reply matched Lois' hope more than expectation.

"Absolutely spot on Lois. Well done. Can you go on for a further ten points and explain your answer," he asked?

"Well, Jacobs Ladder has been available I presume through all of our time so it's always available as a doorway to the past. We know our bodies can survive travel through Jacobs Ladder so that must be how we do it."

"Thank you, Lois. A well thought out and explained answer. Lois has 'hit the crystal on the red'. In the rare event that one of you needs to go back, you will be brought to the third dimension by Jacobs Ladder.

Then after you are briefed for your commission, you will be sent back to the first dimension the same way you left. Then when your commission is completed, you come back here to us and then are sent back to your own time in the first. Sounds straight forward enough, but can anyone see a problem with the procedure?"

This time Adam was in there like an angel out of Heaven. "The location of Enochs Stone could cause delays, because it moves around the Earth to protect it. So for example, if your commission was in Australia and the Stone was in Denmark, you've got some travelling to do."

Lois continued Adams thinking. "Not only that, but if you are sent back to 1805 you don't have any planes to move you around, only ships and trains and that will slow you down as well."

"Thank you, Master and Miss Iqbal. You obviously understand how this works. So you can see, each 'retro' which is what we call a travel back in time, has to be planned allowing for the time you are being sent back to."

"And also for any opposition you might get from the fallen."

"And also for exactly that as well, thank you Jamie. So as many clever men have suggested, this time travel thing is not straightforward and has to be dealt with very carefully."

"Yeah, you've really got to take your time over it," added Jamie.

"Thank you young Fisher." Jerahmeel started to bring that Alphas lesson to a close, or so the class thought. "It's nearly lunch time so we'll stop now and then could you all get back here at Omega 1 so we can carry on with the lesson." This surprised the children somewhat as they each had plans to do other things that Omega. No one said anything, but Jerahmeel knew what they were thinking.

"I know it's unusual to have an Omega session but this one I think you will find interesting. If you get back here in time perhaps you'll find out what being 'in time' really means." With that Jerahmeel dismissed the class for lunch.

By Omega 1 all four were back in their seats in the laboratory. Jerahmeel soon joined them and sat down.

"As you know, here at All Saints we try to make your learning interesting by getting you involved in your own education. Actions don't only speak louder than words, they teach louder than words as well. With that in mind, to help you understand this Alphas lesson on time travel, this Omega we are going back in time." The children couldn't believe what they had just heard and looked excitedly at each other. Lois gasped audibly and Jamie said "Wow."

"The question is, where do we go.?" Jerahameel wasn't really looking for an answer to his question but before he could answer it himself Jamie jumped in.

"Is there any chance we could go back to The Great War? The one thing I've always actually enjoyed in school is History and I am fascinated by The First World War and how its effects still linger in our dimension today."

After having regained his composure, Jerahmeel thought for a moment and wondered if Jamies idea wasn't a bad one after all.

"Usually I take my students back to Roman times or to Africa in the 1800's or once we went to' The Wild West' in America. But never have we been to a war zone. For one thing it's got to be pretty dangerous and you must understand, once you're back in your dimension the clock starts ticking again. This means you start to age again and you can be injured or even killed. If that were to happen it would effect the time line from where you came. Having said that, yours is an interesting suggestion Jamie. I tell you what, you wait here whilst I go and speak to Teacher Eli and see what he says." With that Jerahmeel disappeared having no doubt raptured up to Teacher Elis study.

"Can you believe this, "Adam said to his compatriots. We are actually going to travel back in time. Up until today I just didn't think it was possible but now....."

"And this may not be the only time we do it," added Jamie. "We could end up going on commissions who knows when and where. I'm really getting into this Enochim thing."

"Don't get too excited, Jamie," Anna said to her brother. "Don't forget that it is pretty rare for Enochim to go back in time. Perhaps we'll find out why when Uriel tells us all about Enochim history." As Anna finished speaking, Jerahmeel returned.

"I've spoken with Teacher Eli and he agrees with me that granting Jamies request could be very useful in your education. So we will be going back to The Great War but at a date, time and place set by me."

"Fantastic!" Jamie shouted not being able to control his excitement.

"It certainly is but let's not forget the three rules which are.......?"

Lois obliged. "We go back. We don't change anything and we only use what we find there and then."

"Thank you Lois. We all got that class?"

"Yes tutor," came the unanimous reply.

"The fourth rule for today is, you do what I say, when I say and how I say. Is that clear?"

"Yes tutor," came the fourfold echoed reply.

"Right, let's go to The Ladder Room. Follow me." The children had no choice but to do as their tutor asked them. Although they'd been at The Ladder Room once before, they were a bit pre-occupied then having just switched dimensions for the first time. If they'd been asked to find it again none of them could have done so which actually was good because they were not allowed in there without express permission from Teacher Eli and only then if accompanied.

Having followed Jerahmeel out of his laboratory they went up the stairs to the seventh floor. No lifts or escalators here as up and down stairs was a good way to keep fit so Micah reminded them every chance he got. When they got to the seventh floor landing they turned right, went along the corridor and recognised The Ladder Room by the two giant angels stood outside on guard. There were two wooden like doors with what the children thought were metal hinges and handles. They also noticed an 'Enochima' on each of the doors.

Jerahmeel greeted the two angels formally with, "I am tutor Jerahmeel. I am here with Adam, Anna, Jamie and Lois with the consent of Teacher Eli to enter the Ladder Room."

The right hand angel responded, "Your words have been confirmed. Please introduce each person as they pass and enter the room."

With no small talk, Jerahmeel motioned for the children to join him at the door. Then he introduced each in turn to the right hand angel. As he did so, the angel looked at each child's face and then at the unfurled scrolled he was holding. Having done so he said, "Enter".

This happened with all four children as the left hand angel looked on, with his sword drawn and poised for use. After Lois entered, Jerahmeel followed and the double doors boomed shut behind them. Each child had been relieved to get passed the two menacing angels astride the doors not realising there were four stationed inside the room itself. Two were stood by the raised glasslike platform that was placed over half of Enoch's Stone and which was the first thing to greet the children when they first arrived in the third dimension. Once again, swords were in hand, ready for immediate use. As the other three entered and stood by Adam they noticed the other two angels stood over in the right hand side of the room. Jamie whispered to Adam, "What are those two over there standing by?"

"Looks like some sort of control panel," Adam whispered back. Then Jerahmeel entered the room and spoke again to the assembled throng of his fellow angels.

"Greetings. May I introduce Adam, Anna, Jamie and Lois." All four angels acknowledged the children and the children did likewise to the angels.

Jerahmeel then turned to the children. "You no doubt remember this room but not its details. May I just refresh your memories. Over there is the crystal platform which receives and transmits you Enochim between the dimensions. Below is half of Enoch's Stone that links to its other half in your dimension and creates the way between the dimensions." Turning to his right and walking towards the right where the other two angels were stationed, the tutor continued.

"Over here we have the control panel which dictates the times when you Enochim travel between dimensions. Come over and look," and Jerahmeel beckoned the children over. They reacted somewhat cautiously, not forgetting the four angels and their swords, poised and ready. As the children walked, the angels watched.

"Come on, don't be shy," Jerahmeel picking up on the children's caution, said to encourage them. When the children got over to their tutor he got them to stand around the panel on the wall that he was stood by. They could see that it was a square panel made of what they presumed was gold. On it were what looked like twelve jewels ranging from looking like, emeralds, to sapphires and rubies and other colours in between. Jerahmeel began his explanation.

This panel is used for setting the time for Jacobs Ladder to send you back to in your dimension."

Adam had to ask, "How does it work?"

"I can't tell you that. Only one angel is allowed to use the panel to keep its secrets, secret."

"Why all the secrecy," asked Jamie. "Surely nothing can go wrong here/"

"That's what we always thought until 'The Wolf Episode'."

"The what episode?"

"The Wolf Episode," repeated Jerahmeel. Something happened over fifty of your years ago that made us alter things here and improve security. Before then, there were no guards nor encrypted control panel with only one operator. But after what happened with The Wolf, we had to upgrade security to make sure it didn't happen again."

"Any chance you could explain this to us in more detail," asked Anna.

"I would," said Jerahmeel, but then Uriel would not be chuffed and we would have time to go back in time."

"In that case then," interrupted Adam, "shall we get on with it."

"Yes, I think we shall Adam. When Gedaliah gets here, we'll get started. As he spoke, Gedaliah got there.

"Hello Jerahmeel. This must be Adam, Anna, Jamie and Lois," he said as he introduced himself and shook all their hands.

"Shall we get started." Jamie thought it cool that someone who had a time machine didn't seem to want to waste much time.

"Yes, thank you Gedaliah. Perhaps you will brief the children over the transfer."

"My pleasure. Shortly, I will activate Jacobs Ladder and set co-ordinates for a time in your dimension. Then each of you will enter the transfer beam individually in alphabetical order and be transferred to your dimensions Enochs Stone. On arrival you will be met by the Guardians and you will do what they say. Jerahmeel will follow after the last of you has transferred. Any questions?"

The children thought they better not ask any so as not to give the impression that their tutor had not briefed them properly earlier.

"Good, then we'll begin. Will you all please stand on the crystal platform with Adam and Anna nearest the circle etched over the stone." The children did as they were asked. Gedaliah moved over to the control panel. He pushed a sequence of 'gems' and then the rainbow beam appeared form Jacobs Stone.

"Are you ready Adam and the rest of you?"

Almost stuttering through excitement, Adam replied "Yes."

"Then let's get this show on the road." Gedaliah punched a 'gem' and shouted "Go!" Adam didn't need a second shout. He jumped in the beam and was gone. Anna, Jamie and Lois followed in quick succession and then they and the rainbow beam were gone.

Going through the rainbow beam was still as exciting the second time around and just as quick as the first. Before he knew it, Adam was at the other end being shouted at by a Guardian.

"Quick, off the stone!" Adam jumped down onto the ground as Anna appeared behind him. He moved over to the corner of the room he and Anna had entered and watched as in quick succession, Jamie and Lois joined him.

"Good evening, my name is John Morris and I'm the leader of this Guardian troop. We asked for some help but I must admit I'm surprised that you four have been sent. May I ask who you are?"

The children introduced themselves and explained why they were there.

"I don't suppose you've got any Legionnaires following you by any chance have you," asked John?

"Not that we are aware of sir," replied Jamie. "Tutor Jerahmeel said he would be following us but now I think about it, he didn't say when. Can I ask why you need some legionnaires?"

"Certainly my boy. As you can see I have the usual twelve Guardians in my troop," and John introduced the five with him in the room, being Marie, Elizabeth, Boris, Pierre and Andre.

"The rest of the troop are outside the house providing a protective perimeter."

Somewhat concerned by the phrase 'protective perimeter' and remembering the last time the group were with Guardians and the stone, Lois asked, "Why do you need a protective perimeter? We're not going to be joined by some fallen are we?"

"Not that I'm aware of," John tried to re-assure her on that point "but we could be joined by some advancing Germans who may not understand that we're not part of the enemy. You see, this is August 1914, a war has just been declared and we are between the British and German lines. For a couple of days now we've been caught in the crossfire and we haven't been able to get the stone away to safety. So we sent a message to Colonel Foster to see if we can get some help." As John spoke, the children could hear the whistle of gunfire and the boom of artillery shells exploding nearby.

Noticing them listening to the sounds of war, John commented, "in only a few days of fighting we've witnessed death and destruction of soldiers, horses and even local people not involved directly in the war. This war looks like it's going to be the first one to use technology to kill many, many people. There'll be nothing great about this war I just hope it's the last world war we see." Remembering their lesson on the three rules, none of the children thought it wise to tell John about The Second World War that would follow this 'war to end all wars.'

By now, dusk was falling. The gathered group heard excited people outside some speaking French while others were speaking English.

"What's happening," Elizabeth asked John?

"Let's see if Steven knows." John picked up a telephone, wound it up and waited for a reply.

"Pretty impressive technology," John commented to his guests.

"Yes sir," Adam replied trying his best to sound impressed.

"Steven, John here. What's going on ? Over." The group waited as John listened and then said, "You and the rest of the troop better join us here. Over."

John put the receiver down and spoke to the expectant gathering. "Looks like the British are retreating and The Germans are coming. We can't risk being caught with the stone so we're going to have to fall back with the British." Looking at his new charges John said, "You four will have to come with us. I presume Jerahmeel knows what he's up to." John then issued orders to his Guardians. Andre, Pierre and Ernst," who had just entered the room, "Can you get the stone down to the truck in the street. The rest of you form a cordon around our guests, get them in the back of the truck and then create a perimeter around it. All understood?"

"Yes," all eleven Guardians and children answered.

"For The Kingdom," John said and was met with the rest echoing his words. As gunfire was happening all around joined by its sister artillery fire, the group headed into the street. Jamie thought, "There are millions of bullets to be fired in this war with the names of millions of people on them." What met them was mayhem. People running every which way. Mothers clutching young children in their arms and fear in their eyes. Fathers pulling carts with meagre possessions in them. Bodies were lying in the street and Lois saw something in a burnt out house she couldn't recognise and preferring to leave it that way. Soldiers were running stopping to fire now again and then shouting, "The Hun's coming. Run for your lives." Jamie thought again, "If this is the 'glory of war' you can keep it."

Once safely in the back of the truck with the stone, four of the Guardians joined them. Two more were in the front and the other six followed in another truck. The convoy sped off down the street trying its best not to run down those 'fleeing for their lives'. Suddenly there was an almighty explosion; just to the left of them a house had been hit and it simply fell as if it were made of cards. The rubble flew across the road like bullets and knocked over both of the trucks. After a few moments Anna came around and heard Jamies words before she saw him. "Are you ok sis?" Anna managed to say "Yes" as Jamie helped her out of the overturned truck and onto the side of the road. Ten of the Guardians joined them but John and Pierre weren't there and Elizabeth had been hurt. Without taking a breath, Ernst took command.

"We need to get the stone and keep moving away from the canal and the German advance. Boris and Steven, get the stone." The two guardians complied immediately. Just then John came out of the dust and smoke all around and cried out, "Move now! They're coming down the street!" As he spoke, the children looked and could see cavalry moving down the street with swords drawn. The air was filled with the screams of the horsemen, the crackle of gunfire and the boom of shells.

"Where's the help John had asked for," wondered Jamie.

Then silence.

Everything stopped.

The guns, the shells, the horsemen, the screams.

Nothing could be heard.

Then nothing could be seen except a midday bright light that illuminated the night sky and shimmered in the smoke filled air. Everyone stopped and looked up. There in the sky hovering above the scene of mans carnage were the angels of The I Am's peace. No bullets, shells or warriors could penetrate the barrier these unbeatable warriors made and all fighting and death stopped in that town.

Having come back to his senses, Jamie said, "Now that's help."

John had no time to admire the spectacle although he did have time to whisper 'Thank you' under his breath.

"Let's move now," he ordered. Everyone obeyed. Boris and Steven had the stone in a sling, the children were placed around it and then the Guardians around them. The group ran out of the town away from the light and out into open farmland.

"Off the road," ordered John and 'off the road' they all went. They rushed through the field of wheat until John held up his hand for everyone to stop. Looking back, they could still see the light over the town.

"Right you four quick, your transfer back to the third is about to take place."

"How do you know sir," asked Adam?

"Let's just say it's a perk of the job," John answered. "Steven. Boris, get the stone on the ground now. Children, positions." Having done this twice before, the Fishers and Iqbals knew their 'positions'. As the two guardians laid the stone on the ground, the rainbow beam appeared.

As Adam got into it, he could hear John ask Anna to thank the angels when they got back."

As Lois disappeared into the beam, the guardians reset the stone in its sling.

"We'll wait until morning and then head back into town to see if we can get some transport. Alpha can take the first watch." Six of the guardians took up positions as a perimeter whilst the others tried to get some rest.

Just before dawn John and Ernst headed back into town and found a truck left behind by The British and not yet found by the Germans. Ernst managed to get it started and they headed back to their troop. The road out of the town was pot marked with shell craters so Ernst had to take it easy to avoid damaging the truck. On the edge of town, Ernst swerved to miss a rather large shell crater and as he did so, he gave the town sign a glancing blow and left it swinging loosely on its bolts.

As the truck left the sign behind, John glanced back to see it swing in the morning mist. But he could still make out the towns name.......... 'Mons'.

XX

Arriving back in the Ladder Room, Jerahmeel was there waiting for them with the others.

"Everyone back," Gedaliah checking because as the angel in charge of transfers it was his responsibility to 'count them all off, and count them all back home'.

Jerahmeel confirmed to his colleague that all had arrived and then he spoke to the children "Good to see you all back safe and sound."

"That was amazing," Jamie said when he had shaken away the slight disorientation transfer between dimensions causes.

"We have actually been to 1914. I actually experienced what it's like to be in the middle of a war."

"So have I and I can't say I enjoyed it. People were dying down there," Lois added with real emotion in her voice.

"I agree with you Lois," Jamie thinking he better explain what he was thinking so that no one got the idea he was saying war was something to be enjoyed. He continued, "If everyone could experience what we've just been though in a small way, perhaps they'd think twice, three times or even four times before going off to war."

"Especially politicians," Adam suggested with what Anna thought was actually some passion.

"This is exactly the reaction we want to see from our students when history is brought alive to them. You've been made to think about things and that's really good."

"By the way Jerahmeel, was that you we saw down there lighting up our night sky," asked Anna?

"It might have been and maybe I'll let you ponder on that one," he answered.

"I presume the guardians got away alright with the stone because we're here today, but did all of them get way safely," enquired Lois.

"Perhaps I'll let you find that out by yourselves in the Library if you want to. "Now," said Jerahmeel, "It's the end of a busy session and season and there is the second round of Phillips Cup in two days, so how's about we all head home." With that Jerahmeel turned to Gedaliah and thanked him for his assistance.

"My pleasure," responded Gedaliah. "See you at the races and then he waved goodbye to all and left the room. The remaining guards stood silent and watchful. Jerahmeel thanked them but didn't wait for a response as he knew he wouldn't get one. He ushered the children out of the room and led them back down to the park.

"You can find your way home from here children. See you next session and with that Jerahmeel left them. The children mounted their horses and rode off back to their house all chatting about the incredible journey they had just taken.

"I've got to find out if John and his troop got away safely," Lois told the group. "So after tea I'm off to the Library.

"We'll all come with you," said Adam and they all did.

They found out from the librarian where the Enochim histories were kept. Off to the sixth floor via the tornado tubes and down to the History section. They soon found the histories and Adam eventually found 1910 to 1915.

They flicked through and didn't even stop to find out why the Titanic was mentioned in 1912.

"Here it is," said Lois and she started to read the text out loud.

"At the outbreak of The Great War, Jacobs Stone was caught up in the hostilities around the town of Mons. The troop of John Morris was tasked with getting the stone out of Europe to America. As they travelled across the continent they reached Mons but then war broke out. Transport was severely disrupted with railways commandeered for army movements and roads clogged with panic stricken civilians fleeing the fighting. The troop were held up for days in Mons, the place where the first and last Allied soldiers would die in this catastrophe that would rob the world of a generation of its young men. As the Germans advanced on the retreating British forces there seemed nothing else to do but make a run for it. As night fell, he troop loaded up the stone and fled in two trucks. As they reached the edge of the town shell and bullet fire raged around them. A breakthrough by the German forces was imminent with the chance the troop and its precious cargo could be discovered. Without warning a direct hit on a house blew rubble like shrapnel across the road on which they were travelling and knocked over both trucks. The guardians managed to retrieve the stone but as they tried to leave the town, soldiers were almost upon them. As all seemed lost, help came from the third dimension. To assist in the safeguarding of the stone angels were sent to stand between the two sides of this man made war and allow the troop and the stone to reach nearby fields and safety. The angels were not there to take sides but just to save the stone.

Retuning to the town the following morning the troop managed to find new transport and make good their escape to the coast. However, the wounds that Elizabeth Eastwood had suffered became infected and she left the first dimension before reaching Great Britain." Lois lowered her voice and whispered, "The rest of the troop made it to America by October where the Stone remained for the rest of this war." Lois could read no more. The silence remained for some minutes before Jamie spoke.

"Elizabeth gave all for The Kingdom and also taught us that this is not a game. It's life and death."

"It's eternal life and death," Anna added.

"I think we've had enough history for one day," said Adam. "How's about we head home and have a quiet night in?" All agreed but as they were leaving a thought crossed Anna's mind about her granddad Burnett. "Wouldn't his story be here in this archive somewhere.?" Doing some quick sums she reckoned he would fall in the 1930 onwards records. She headed there and was just about to pull out the records for 1950 to 1955 when Nathaniel appeared.

"I agree with Adam. I think you've all had enough history for one day. How about we leave granddad Burnett for another time?"

"Maybe you're right," agreed Anna as she put the volume back on the shelf. She joined the rest of the group and so didn't notice Nathaniel take the 1950 volume with him as he raptured away.

For the next two days the children carried on with their extra curricular studies and did manage to enjoy the second round of Phillips Cup. This was after Teacher Eli reminded them where Elizabeth was now living and how she'll be glad to know the children were thinking of her and her sacrifice.

The fifth and pen ultimate session started with a session from Jerahmeel concluding his round up on the current theonology available to the Enochim. This included fist aid kits with spray on skin, bio computers and a fuel component that can soup up any terrestrial vehicle. Sessions two and three of this second to last season were spent flying and fighting with Zechariah and Micah.

Session four was Uriels.

"Morning children. How was your field trip last season?"

"Interesting but thought provoking," replied Jamie.

"Just as it should be," Uriel confirmed. "To continue the historical theme, this session I'm going to run through the set up and brief history of you Enochim so you all understand why and how your people got to where they are today. Now normally, we would have covered this by now but this group is not quite as 'normal' as usual."

"Why is that," asked Anna?

"I think I'll let Teacher Eli answer that question. But for now, let me give you some background details."

Uriel settled himself in his chair and when he was sitting comfortably, he began.

"The Kingdom is divided into Nethinim and Enochim. The Nethinim are all members of The Kingdom who are not Enochim and they are by far the larger number of souls. The word 'Nethinim' means 'Temple Servants' and is used to describe these members of The Kingdom who serve day and night in the Temple which can symbolise The King. You Enochim must never forget that the Nethinim are essential to the progress of The Kingdom and it is your job to protect them when needed by the gifts you have been given. The Enochim are not superior to the Nethinim, nor the Nethinim to The Enochim. You are all servants of The Kingdom and each other."

"What are those outside The Kingdom called," asked Anna?

"Lost," came Uriels one word and powerful reply.

Uriel paused for a moment and then continued.

"I take it you all know why your people are called Enochim," Uriel said as he began.

"Because Enoch was the first man to be taken to the third dimension to wait until he's sent back to do job for The Kingdom later," answered Anna.

"And he's still waiting now in The New Eden for the call to be sent back. "Thank you Anna. Anyone know how Enoch was taken?"

"By Enochs stone that we still use today to access Jacobs Ladder to get to this dimension." This time Lois answered.

"Good. Now let me give an idea of the set up for you Enochim that has lasted for millennia. The Enochim are represented in every people, nation and tribe of your world. When one of you Enochim decide to take up the sword you are sent here to the third dimension. Here as you know, you remain for forty of your days to complete your initial training on the four areas of........."

"Transport, defence, communication and service," answered Lois.

"But what you don't yet know is that when you complete your forty day training you are awarded your wings."

"Like the ones our parents have on their gear under the Enochima"

"Precisely, Adam. That is the first grade of The Enochim and it is known as 'Onaphim'. Most Enochim are at Onaphim level but some show exceptional skill and courage and are taken to the next level. Anyone know what that might be called?"

Remembering the previous session on The Angels, Jamie took a guess at 'Cherubim'.

"Well done Jamie. As you have rightly realised, the three grades of The Enochim are named after those of the Angel Divisions. To gain Cherubim level an Enochim needs to return to here for a further three years training and if he or she passes they get two more wings placed under their Enochima."

"Like Aunt Ruth," Anna said, not sure if her words were a statement or a question.

"Exactly like your Aunt Ruth who is a what?"

"A Guardian," answered Jamie.

"Right. So all Guardians are...........?"

"At Cherubim level," Adam answered.

"Now you're getting it," said Uriel.

"Has anyone ever got to Seraphim level," asked Jamie?

"Only one up to now," answered Uriel.

"Enoch." Jamie came straight back with the answer without thinking.

"Correct," confirmed Uriel. "To date he's the only one. Seraphim level takes forty of your years to train for and only he has done it so far. So he is the only one who can wear three pairs of wings under his Enochima." Uriel took a sip of water and asked, "Everyone with it so far?"

"Yes tutor," all four replied.

"Good. Now I understand that all four of you have already come across some 'Taken'. Jamie and Anna were attacked by some and you, Adam and Lois, saw them in action in Mumbai. Is that right?"

"Yes tutor," Adam answering for all four.

"So you all understand how these taken can be very dangerous. Do you know why we call them taken?"

"Because they've been taken over by evil ones," Lois said confidently.

"Correct. Thank you Lois. The taken occur very, very rarely. They are human beings of your dimension who have let themselves be open to evil influences by dabbling in things that The Word tells you not to. Once the evil gets a hold, if it is not checked, it's ultimate effect can be to let a persons personality and will be overcome by that of one or more evil spirits. I need to re-emphasise that this is very, very rare and many peoples lives have been damaged by some attributing their behaviour to having been taken. Such a diagnosis if incorrect will cause great harm and only those with the specific gift of discerning spirits should exercise judgement and exorcise judgement."

"Are there any signs we can look for to consider if any we come across are someone we think might be taken," asked Jamie?

"Often the taken have increased knowledge and strength, some have a vacant stare and some even have strange voices. But the real test is how they act to the name of Jesus that is spoken in love. If they react violently to hearing The Kings Name, that is a pretty good indicator. Of course, if they go around attacking you, that's also a pretty good indicator. If you are attacked by someone and you're not sure, I'm sure

Micah has trained you to transfigure your swords to 'Taken' because if they haven't been, a strike from you will not harm an 'untaken square'.

"Is it possible for us to be taken," asked Anna?

"Never," came Uriels emphatic reply. "Once you have the Spirit of The Kingdom in you, He can't be removed and certainly not by an evil spirit that hasn't got anything like the power He has."

"That's good to know," responded Anna. She went on, "Can I ask, was it just the taken who attacked Jamie and I, because the one who tried to kill us didn't seem to fit the description you've just given."

"Garth," Uriel whispered under his voice. He carried on, this time with what Anna took as a hint of sadness in his voice.

"Anna has made an excellent observation and asked an excellent question. The question Anna asks leads me now into telling you about 'The Goliathim'." The children recognised that the word probably came from the name Goliath but all decided to wait and see how Uriels explanation panned out on the Goliathim.

"The Goliathim are descendents of The Anakim and Rephaim. You remember the first Nephilim were killed off during The Flood? Sadly that wasn't the end of them. After mankind re-established itself on the earth, second dimensional beings once again managed to infiltrate them and create new mixed race beings. The first of these was named Anak and so as no to draw attention to themselves like their Nephilim ancestors, they became known as Anakim with some referred to as Rephaim through their ancestor of this name. Because they have Anakim 'genes' they and their twins are able to be trained to a high standard by the prince in your dimension and then be sent out to thwart The Kingdom. These Goliathim are very dangerous and should not be under estimated. Because they are of your dimension, they can keep their identities secret and you may not know what they are until it's too late. Always be on your guard and when you come across them, as you will, treat them with respect. Many Enochim have been defeated by Goliathim and some have been killed."

"But we can defeat them," asked Jamie, hoping for the right answer.

"You can and have."

"What do you mean," he asked?

"When you and your sister were attacked, it was a Goliathim who tried to kill you."

"So dad actually beat one of them," said Anna.

"He did and had done so before and no doubt, will do so again."

"Can I ask why they are called 'Goliathim," Adam asking the question only he was brave enough to do so. "Does it have anything to do with Goliath?" Adam was really doing a giraffe now and sticking out his neck.

"You can and it has," answered Uriel to Adams relief. The tutor then went on to explain.

"The most famous descendent of Rephaim was Goliath who came from a city called Gath. Due to this and the way you Enochim defeat The Anakim they became known as Goliathim to you."

"But, Goliath didn't have a brother," queried Anna.

"His brother's name was Lahmi and he too met a nasty end," answered Uriel to this reasonable query.

"Ok, but if we defeat a Goliathim but we don't want to kill them, won't they keep coming back," asked Jamie?

"They will unless they are deheaded."

"But we're not allowed to kill them, so how can we 'behead' them," ask Adam?

"I said 'dehead' not 'behead'. The Guardians have special stones that if they can strike a Goliathim with in the middle of their forehead, removes their extra powers that they have and makes them 'human' again. Before you ask, David was not Enochim, just a great shot. Only a Guardian can 'dehead' a Goliathim as it takes real skill to hit the right spot and lots of training."

"About three years," said Jamie. He went on. "Are there enough Guardians to deal with all the Goliathim?"

"There are only ever seventy two Guardians in your dimension at any one time. They are chosen from all Enochim as the most skilled and with the right character to be a Guardian. It's not an easy job. All Guardians chose not to marry as they couldn't do their job if concerned over husbands wives and children. If they decide to marry, they relinquish being a Guardian and someone else takes their place. When chosen, they come here for their three years training and then are sent back to replace the Guardian who is retiring or who has left your dimension permanently. The seventy two Guardians each work in troops of twelve, having four months on commission and then eight months off each year. Whilst they are not on commission, any Guardian can be put back on commission to replace another Guardian who may be out of action for some reason."

Having done the math, Adam decided to ask the question. "If the Guardians troops are twelve strong and work for four months at a time, that only equals thirty six. So what are the other thirty six doing?"

"They are guarding something else."

"What," Lois asked her tutor?

"The Ark of The Covenant," came her tutors reply.

"You are kidding. Does that still exist," asked Adam?

"Of course it does because it was made of a combination of elements we call Arkov which as you know is indestructible. The Ark has to be guarded and kept form the fallen, because it is a powerful piece of theonology. It is indestructible, it can kill and it is a place where The I Am met with mankind. The fallen would love to get hold of it to see if they could use it against The Kingdom or hold it ransom."

"So that's why mum and dad always enjoy 'Raiders of The Lost Ark'. They know the real story," said Jamie.

"Yes," said Uriel "And the real story is that just before the Babylonians defeated the Jews about 597 BC, The Ark was spirited away through Hezekiahs tunnel by the Guardians and from then on it has kept moving around your planet to keep it safe. Some think the Ark is now in Ethiopia and it is true it did spend some time there but it never stays in one place permanently as that would be unsafe. The Guardians have kept The Ark moving for centuries and will continue to do so until they are called home."

"So the Guardians share the duty of keeping both Enochs Stone and The Ark safe."

"Exactly so Lois," replied Uriel.

"Can I ask why there are seventy two Guardians?"

"You certainly can Jamie because that leads me into the story of how the Guardians came to be formed and the great cost they paid when first they took over the stewardship of the stone. If they hadn't sacrificed themselves, none of you would be here today. In fact rather than tell you what happened, let me show you."

XXI

It was after lunch when the children returned to Uriels Study. He thought it best they all have a break before he continued on with the history of The Enochim. Once they were all seated Uriel waited a moment until the holygram came into being and took all five of them back to pre-history. They saw a crowd of many warriors sat around a desert oasis and armed with what looked like normal earthly swords. Uriel explained that because The Word of The I Am had not been written down yet then it wasn't possible for these Enochim to transfigure it into flaming swords. So until the written Torah and Talmud were ready, that is The Jewish Scriptures, Enochim were provided with temporal swords that they transfigure into flaming swords with the words...............

"The Sword of God," answered Jamie.

The holygram continued.

The warriors were wearing camel hair tunics with leather belts around their wastes. They were all sat around the water hole talking to each other when one of their number, a man got up to speak. As he did so he was joined by a woman.

"My name is Kenan and this is Adah. You seventy Enochim have been brought from all the peoples of the world and commissioned to retrieve Enochs Stone to protect The Enochim. The fallen know it exists and want it badly. If they can get it they can destroy our people and will have potential access into the third dimension. Enoch's Stone has to be put into our possession and kept there. The journey and battle we are about to undertake will not be easy. For we wage war not only against flesh and blood but also against evil from the heavenly places. We must use all our strength, skills and faith to defeat our arch enemies.

If any do not consider they can meet the challenge, they should leave now." Kenan waited in silence and not one of the seventy stirred. Then one of the women stood up and said,

"I am Joanna of The Negev and I am willing to give all for The Kingdom. Are you with me?"

The crowd responded with,"Yes! For The Kingdom!"

Kenan spoke again. "Thank you my friends. Now we must get provisions and make for the desert of Aven to the Valley of Achor and the stone of Enoch." All those there knew that the places Kenan had identified were dreadful places of wickedness and trouble. Places where The Kingdoms Laws had been thrown away and where mankind and the fallen preyed on the weak for their own satisfaction.

One of the men, Jared, asked why the stone was in such a place?

"Often the best place to hide something from your enemies is to hide it with your enemies. They wouldn't think of looking for the needle in their own haystack. Are you still with me," Kenan asked?

"For The Kingdom," came the seventy fold reply.

"We rest here tonight and then tomorrow our journey begins. We will divide into testaments and travel separately into the Desert of Aven meeting to the east of the city of Nimrod in three days at dawn on the eastern ridge of the Valley of Achor. We will not travel in our usual testaments just in case we meet those of our enemies that might recognise us. Being with other partners will also help to build up relationships that will help us in battle. I and Adah will travel to where the stone is with a cart, retrieve it and take it away to safety. Maleh and Eve will obtain a cart and we will use Eve's horse to pull it. You will all watch from the sides of the valley and give us support if we need it. Questions?" None were forthcoming as darkness was now falling.

"Mahel, you take your troop for the first watch. The rest of you, eat, rest and create your new testaments with those you have today met as friends and with no one you already know. For The Kingdom!"

"For The Kingdom," came the reply.

The seven foot tall Mahel, who was Kenans twin, although not identical as Kenan was a mere six foot three, stood up and eleven others followed to create the protective perimeter around those remaining. The remnant shared their food and drink around the fire and then settled to sleep to enjoy their last night before their journey for the stone began.

Dawn followed quickly the watches of the night. After breakfast Kenan sent off his troops in their testaments to meet some three days later at the Valley of Achor. He and Adah travelled together.

As they rode, they talked. They had only met two days ago when Joel and Nathaniel introduced them to each other. They had been chosen to lead this commission due to their courage and skill. The task of retrieving Enoch's Stone was commissioned by the angels to them and then they were left to work out the strategy for accomplishing the commission.

"Where is your twin," asked Kenan?

"She died some four years ago. We were sent to save a tribe who were being terrorised by the fallen and their followers. No problem in defeating them but my twin Zillah was exhausted from the battle. As we left there to travel on to our next commission her tiredness overcame her and she fell from her horse jumping over a stream. She died in my arms that day."

"I'm sorry. Didn't you think to come off commission and do other work for The Kingdom after your sister died?"

"I would be lying if I said I didn't consider it but I decided the best way to keep Zillah's memory alive was to keep doing what I do best for The Kingdom. So I teamed up with Enosh to form a new Testament after his brother was killed in the battle of Salem. "

"Your parents," Kenan asked?

"Both gone to the grave now. They worked hard for The Kingdom and taught me and my sister well. I look forward to meeting them all again when my time comes. What about you," Adah asked Kenan?

"Both parents still alive but no longer on commission. They have a farm near the coast by Joppa. Mahel and I try to get to see them when we can but being on commission keeps us busy and away."

As they came over the ridge of the hill they were met by a horde of nasties brandishing stones, slings and axes. There were twenty if not more. The horde were surrounding a family of about ten or so people, including young children. They were taunting them with words as they struck them with sticks. One of the horde saw Kenan and Adah and let out a blood curdling scream.

A man who made Mahel look like a toddler strode forward.

"What have we here? More weaklings to have fun with. Get them!" the horde rushed the two riders not knowing who they were dealing with.

Kenan shouted, "Kill no one but let no one escape." Both he and Adah charged the oncoming horde, they and their horses not flinching. They each took two of the enemy out with kicks whilst on their horses. Kenan turned and charged again whilst Adah did a somersault dismount landing on two more hapless barbarians, knocking each out cold. The battle continued with Kenan on horse back and Adah on front. At one point, Kenan grabbed Adahs arm and swung her around, sending more of the enemy into the land of nod. Within minutes the battle was won but they lost one of their adversaries. The man who had been guarding the tormented ran for safety rather than take on these two strangers who he knew he could not defeat.

The Enochim untied the tormented family and tied up the defeated horde. The family could not thank Kenan and Adah enough for saving them from a certain death. Kenan told them they could repay them by making sure they kept their tormentors tied up for the next two days.

"Feed them, give them drink but don't give them their freedom," was Kenans request.

The family were so were happy to repay their saviours in whatever way they could. Kenan was pleased to have helped but concerned about the one that got away.

The Enochim spent the night with their new friends as Malek reached the City of Nimrod. Malek had lived there for years and had soon joined one of the ruthless gangs that scoured the nearby countryside looking for people to rob and kill. This time he had something fresh to sell to the King of the city, a story about two strangers who could easily defeat a gang of twenty and yet kill no one.

He went to the palace of King Gog and demanded to see his 'highness'. At first the guards wouldn't let him past, but after he told them his story they thought Gog would want to hear it as well.

Malek was taken through the courtyard into the Kings House where he followed the guards and the noise of music and laughter into the Kings Hall. He was taken forward to the King and knelt down in front of him whilst the captain of the guard whispered in Gog's ear.

Gog wiped the saliva from his beard and looked at the kneeling Malek in front of him.

"So you have a story to tell me do you? If I don't like it, it will be your last." Malek knew Gogs reputation and realised too late he shouldn't have come. There was no going back now, so he told his story. To Maleks' surprise Gog started to listen intently without saying a word. When someone interrupted Malek, Gog waved his hand and one of his guards knocked him out senseless with one punch.

"Go on," the king said to Malek. The reluctant storyteller resumed his tale and when he finished, everyone sat in silence for a minute waiting for Gogs reaction. Suddenly the King rose and shouted,

"All of you out now, except the captain, and Malek. Captain, send for the Chamberlain now!" His orders were obeyed and within five minutes only Gog, Malek, Lamech the captain and the small, weasel faced Chamberlain Mago were present. Gog made Malek tell the story again and then spoke to his Chamberlain.

"Sounds like we have Enochim in our midst. What are they doing here?"

"They don't usually come so close to Nimrod," the weasel replied. "They're up to something."

"What should we do," asked the king.

"Double the guards on the walls, quietly," the chamberlain said looking at the captain, "And let's see if we can't spot if these do gooders come to our fair city. If we spot them, we wait and follow them to see what they will do."

"Captain you have your orders."

"Yes my King," the captain bowed and was about to leave when Malek spoke.

"What about me, my King?"

"Captain, take him away and let have leave the palace with his just reward." The captain did as he was bidden. He took Malek to the Kings treasury and as the informant wondered at the wealth there, the captain gave him his reward and let him leave the palace through a fourth floor window.

For two days and nights the guards watched from the walls and nothing. Then on the third night, the guards on the east wall spotted a lit torch for a moment down below.

"Put that out," Kenan whispered as strongly as he could.

"Are the seventy here Mahel?"

"Yes," his twin answered.

"The cart and horse?"

"Just down the slope with Eve."

"Good. We leave for the Valley now. Adah are you ready?"

"As I'll ever be," she whispered.

Kenan whispered and motioned with his arm, "Move out." Mahel led the way down the slope away from the city walls and onto the well beaten track that led to the Valley of Achor. When they reached Eve, Adah and Kenan took the horse and cart.

"You and Eve re-join the others and remember what we've discussed. The brothers hugged as did the girls and then departed from each other. As dawn broke, the troop were on the ridges looking down into the valley below. All they could see were thousands and thousands of stones and rocks below. Without asking how they would find Enoch's stone, Adah and Kenan moved down the valley side. The seventy watched as they reached the valley floor. She stopped for a moment, looked up at the sun as it rose and then walked towards it. Five, six, seven minutes, the seventy watched. Then Adah stopped, stooped and signalled to Kenan. He soon joined Adah with the cart and then they loaded something onto it. As he stood up he sensed something surrounding him. He looked and saw there on the ridges surrounding the valley were hundreds and hundreds of armed warriors. Chariots, cavalry and infantry. As Kenan watched, one of the horsemen left the ranks and rode towards him. He stopped some twenty feet from Kenan and spoke.

"Give Gog what you have and live. Refuse and die. If you do not lay down your weapons by the time the sun clears the top of the valley or you will be attacked and annihilated." The rider turned and fled back up the side of the Valley. As he did so, Kenan raised his sword and shouted, "The Sword of God." His sword turned into flames. The troop on the valley sides recognised the signal and as one came running down to join their brother and sister. As they did so, Adah unbridled the horse, slapped it and watch it speed away up the other side of the valley.

As the troop reached the two on the valley floor, they formed a circular perimeter around the cart and its precious cargo.

Without waiting for the sun to rise further, Gog broke his word as he always did. He raised his arm, stood up in his stirrups and shouted, "Kill them all!"

The blood thirsty throng needed no encouragement. They knew that these Enochim would not kill them but try to defeat them without death. The hordes ran and rode down from all sides of the valley, wailing as they did. The Enochim stood their ground and transfigured their swords. As the hordes came down, suddenly they were joined by hosts of taken who had been sent to ensure the carnage. The Enochim would find their fight harder by having to switch their swords between matter and taken. The battle was joined and it was vicious. The Enochim way of avoiding death to others would lead to their deaths. Enoch's people fought bravely and killed no one, but soon the first Enochim fell. Eventually after three hours of relentless fighting the Valley of Achor fell silent as Mahel, the last Enochim standing, fell under the blows of ten soldiers. He fell down to the valley floor and silence fell down into the valley.

Gog and Mago rode down the valley to view the scene of their victory.

"There must be over sixty Enochim here", Gog stated, almost hearing the folk songs that he thought would now be sung about him and his famous victory. Mago was more interested in what these 'fools' has died trying to protect. He moved over to the cart with Gog right behind him.

"Is that it," Gog sneered. "A lump of rock. These people shed their blood for that."

Mago was by now never surprised by the ignorance of his 'king'

"My lord do you not realise what we've got here. This is Enoch's Stone. It is a gateway into Heaven itself." Gog may have been a bit slow but he was not stupid. He knew what Enoch's Stone was and he knew what power it could give to him.

"Captain, get a guard around this cart now." The captain obliged. "Take this cart and stone back to Nimrod. If you lose it, you lose your life. Am I clear?"

"Yes my King. What about these Enochim?"

"Leave them to the vultures and wolves. Graves are too good for them." The King mounted his horse and escorted the stone back to his city. When there, the stone was placed in the Treasury with a permanent guard whilst Mago tried to unlock the stones secrets.

Night fell in the Valley of Achor. The vultures had started their feast and the wolves were soon to join in. As darkness enveloped the valley, something other than a wild beast stirred. Up on the north side of the valley, Eve slowly came out from behind a rocky outcrop.

She looked down on the scene of carnage and fought to keep back the tears. "No time to grieve," she told herself. "Thank you all. May your days in Eden be blessed." For a moment Eve almost wished she could have joined her brothers and sisters and then she remembered Mahels words.

"One of us has to survive to save the stone. Are you willing to sacrifice your death and live to carry on the work." Knowing that Mahel would sacrifice his life, Eve had no doubt she must do as he asked. He told her that if the troop had to go to the aid of Kenan and Adah, that she must remain on the northern valley ridge. Then, Adah would send her horse back to her assuming the enemy would let what they thought to be a scared animal run away from the battle. Eve must take her horse and when she considered it safe to do so, leave the valley and get to safety. Eve had waited until darkness started to fall and until she was sure the enemy weren't coming back before she broke cover. She reached into one of the saddle bags laying astride her loyal mount and looked at what was inside. It was the size of a melon. She took hold of the true Enoch's Stone and stopped to say good bye once more to her friends.

"Bless you all. Today you are in Paradise and I look forward to the tomorrow when I shall join you." She mounted her horse and without turning back, she left. Eve travelled for days through the desert away from Nimrod until she came to the city of Ur. There she waited until joined by other Enochim. She left the stone with them. The Stone travelled on through the world as did Eve. But her heart was left in the Valley of Achor with her seventy one brothers and sisters.

From that day it was agreed that Enoch's Stone needed special protection and so The Guardians were formed. As a Memorial to the Seventy One who died and the one who completed their mission, the number of Guardians was set at Seventy two. The rest is 'His Story'.

For some minutes the children just sat there trying to take in what they had seen. Uriel let them to do so, not wanting to speak until one of his students did. Jamie spoke first, but not to his tutor but to his fellow Enochim.

"What we have seen makes you realise this is no game. We are involved in a war against evil and some of us are going to get hurt and maybe even pay the ultimate price. We should never forget the sacrifices others make for our lives and freedom with us carrying on their memory and battle being the best memorial we can give them."

Uriel was pleased with Jamie's words and his sentiments. He had heard them before, but it was always refreshing to hear young people grow up and accept their responsibility to those who had gone before and for what they had done.

"I don't know about you lot, but for me what I've just seen means I am going to train as hard as I can with the time I've got left here, to become the best Enochim I can." Lois' words were echoed by her three friends.

Uriel now spoke.

"Thank you Enochim for your words and assurance of your ongoing action. I don't call you children any longer, because what I have heard tells me you have now grown up. Being grown up means you leave childish things behind and accept your responsibilities to The Kingdom and Mankind. All four of you have now done that and I thank you for it." Uriel took a moment and then continued.

"Today has been a turning point for you all and I'm sure you could all do with a break now. So let's draw this session and this season to a close."

As Uriel got up to close the session Anna asked one final question.

"Before we finish isn't there some other history you need to tell us," she asked remembering Uriels earlier comments in the Alpha about their group not being 'normal'.

Uriel stood up and answered his young Enochim.

"You are right Anna, there is something else in your history as Enochim and as a family that you need to know, that all of you need to know. But I have been commanded by Teacher Eli that he will deal with that history with you before you leave and when he feels it's right to do so. Can I ask that you be patient and await the Teachers words on the matter."

Anna appreciated Uriels straight answer and let the matter drop. They all said their goodbyes and the four returned home.

No Wings that Omega as all were shattered and hit the sack early. Their minds reminded them all night about what they had learnt and led them all to rise early even though they now had two days off.

They all practiced riding, flying, defence, spent time in the lab checking theonology and even Jamie hit the books in the Library. All four new that Uriel's words about a change in their lives were true and now that had to show it to themselves and others. Little did they realise then how much of a change it would prove to be.

XXII

The first day off was filled with more training and learning for the four. Adam and Anna concentrated on flying whilst Lois and Jamie on Defence. But all four also found time to hit the lab and the library.

That night was the semi final for Phillips Cup when Reuben, Judah and Issachar would compete for the two places in the upcoming final. Once again Teacher Eli joined Phillip in his chariot, but this time, Phillip had asked Jamie and Anna to assist him. The race went off without a hitch and led to Reuben and Issachar coming first and second to be placed in the final.

"Does that mean that Reuben is going to win," asked Anna?

"Not necessarily," answered Phillip. History tells us that the placings in the last round don't always indicate how the horses and riders will be placed in the final. To be sure, Reuben have looked strong this time but the final race around The Circle is different to the street races we have already had and can turn up some surprises."

"How are you two this Omega," asked Teacher Eli?

"Fine thank you Teacher," answered Jamie.

"Yesterdays session with Tutor Uriel is always a difficult one for you Enochim, but he told me you all handled it very well."

"It wasn't easy seeing how our ancestors sacrificed themselves for The Kingdom. It makes you thankful that they did but challenges you as to whether you would do the same."

"Your answer shows maturity Jamie. As yet you may not know how you would face up to the challenge but you're on the way to being able to deal with it by knowing it will be a challenge. How about you Anna?"

"The same as Jamie really. It makes you think and hope and pray you'll live up to the challenge and what your forefathers did. It's never easy learning these sort of truths. That old saying 'The truth hurts' really is true. But we need to learn these things so we can be encouraged by them or perhaps learn from a mistake and avoid repeating it." Eli was heartened by what he was hearing and thought the time may just have come.

"Time for Wings I think," suggested Phillip.

"You know Constable, I think you're right. May I drive," Eli asked?

"It would be an honour Teacher." Eli took the reins and drove them all to Wings. The race party was already started with Lois leading the singing. They had a great night and all went to their beds, well the Enochim did, weary but contented.

More training and learning the following day before the last session started.

"Not long now," said Adam as all four were reading in the Library. They had spent all Alpha and more training and had all agreed to hit the books that Omega to brush up on their technical and historical knowledge. Adam was reading the maintenance manual on the Zekes. Lois was checking out some historical battles and their tactics. Jamie was engrossed in a digest of great Enochim escapades. Anna started riding 'The Big Book of Horses' but soon found herself heading towards the Enochim history section. She had still been wondering about, ".there is still something else in your history as Enochim and as a family that you need to know."

What had Uriel meant. Anna had concluded it could have something to do with her dead grand father. Having done the math and knowing grand dad James had been born in 1930 she reckoned any books between 1942 after he was twelve, and up to 1973 when he died, may hold some clues. She knew the Enochim histories were in volumes covering five years each and so went to find 1930 to 1934 but couldn't find it. She looked for all the volumes up to 1973 but for some reason they were missing as well.

"Jamie come over here for a minute," she whispered remembering her Library protocol. Jamie joined her and she explained what she had been doing. Jamie looked for the volumes and he couldn't find them either.

"Perhaps someone's doing homework and has got them out for reference."

"Possible I suppose but I can't see the Librarian let them take them away from here." Jamie was thinking to himself that Anna was probably right when he heard,

"Are you looking for this?"

He and Anna recognised the voice being that of Teacher Eli. Jamie turned to look at where the voice came from and Anna leaned to her left to look beyond her brother at the one who had spoken. There stood just at the end of the bookshelf was Teacher Eli holding one of the missing volumes. Anna could see it was it was 1950 to 1954.

"That's one of them", she said. "Why has that one and the others been removed from the shelf?"

"That was at my request and can I apologise to you, your brother and your friends. We always try to be fully open with Enochim when you spend time with us but sometimes circumstances dictate we have to be careful as to when we're fully open. This is one of those times."

"Has it got to do with our grand dad," asked Jamie? Eli knew it was time.

"Yes Jamie it has. Your grandfather did a great work for The Kingdom that eventually cost him his life. Because of what he did he has gone down in Enochim folklore and is always remembered with honour. The sadness is that your parents or Nana Burnett could not tell the full story of his life without giving away your heritage before it was time for you to learn about your family and yourselves. Not only that, your grandfather asked me if I would take on the responsibility of telling future generations of his family the story, a responsibility I have been privileged to carry. So it was I who told your mum and Aunt Ruth about their fathers great work and now it is time for me to fulfil my responsibility again and tell you. And if The I Am wills it, I will be telling your children and your children's children and all generations of your family until there is a New Heaven and a New Earth."

Jamie and Anna were getting a bit overawed now by what they were hearing. Eli noticed it in their eyes and spoke gently to them. "Don't be afraid. What I have to tell you needs to be told and I am sure will help you. Let's go to my study and carry on there." By now Adam and Lois had seen Teacher Eli talking to their friends and wondered what was occurring. They both came over and could sense something heavy was happening. Eli turned to them and spoke.

"Hello you two. I hope you don't mind but I, Jamie and Anna need to go for a little talk."

"No problem Teacher," answered Adam.

"Can they come too," asked Anna?

"Are you sure," Eli responded?

"Well, they need to learn all about Enochim history and I think it will help to have our friends with us. What do you think Jamie?"

"Sounds like a plan I can sign up to."

"If you're both sure and Adam and Lois want to join us, I would be happy for them to do so."

Lois could sense Anna would appreciate the support and so said she would be happy to go along although she hoped she wouldn't be imposing. Adam followed his sister's lead and so all four rode from the Library back to All Saints and Teacher Eli's study.

When they arrived, they went straight up to the third floor and joined the teacher in his study.

Thank you for coming on your day off. What I am about to tell you has been passed onto all Enochim for decades and will continue to be so until your commission is finally complete. It's a story about a man who showed great courage, commitment and dedication to carry out a commission for The Kingdom that when he undertook it, knew could well kill him. James Wesley Burnett was born on May 7th 1930 to Felix and Margaret Burnett. He was born in the country in North Wales and had a younger twin called Andrew Sankey Burnett. The family lived happily in North Wales until fathers job as a train driver took him down to London in 1933. The family lived near Euston Station where Felix worked from and although times were hard, they were still happy. When the boys learnt of their Enochim heritage in April 1942, they both immediately took up the sword hoping that as there was a world war on, they could do their bit by working for The Kingdom. Not only that, it meant that Felix and Margaret could get involved again in commissions. The family had many adventures all over your world which you can read about in The Histories if you want to.

1945 saw the end of the Second World War but not the family's commitment to the cause. They carried on in the new atomic world that had now emerged helping The Kingdom and its Nethilim to find and secure their place. When James was sixteen he decided to join the Police service as a cadet whilst Andrew carried on in Grammar School because he wanted to go onto University and become a Doctor.

James loved being a Policeman and by 1948 he was a Constable. He also carried on his commissions for The kingdom and by 1950 he was noticed by the then Chief Enochim, Colonel Waldren. He was recommended by him for appointment as a Guardian. The recommendation was approved and when approached James was pleased to accept as long as he could continue as a Policeman. For a time that seemed like it was going to be a problem until another Enochim Chief Superintendent Marcus was given the job of setting up his own undercover squad to fight organised crime. When James was seconded to the squad it meant he could go in communicardo for months at a time with everyone assuming he was on an undercover mission.

Now that James' cover story was in place he could be transferred to the third dimension for his three year Guardians training. The transfer was arranged for September that year. Enochs Stone was now in Scotland and James bought his ticket and packed to go. It was a rainy morning when his dad, mum and brother saw him off at the station. They were proud that the family had its first Guardian but worried about the tough, nomadic and dangerous life James would now be living.

"You take care of yourself," Andrew said as he hugged his twin. "Make us proud."

"And you make us proud by becoming the doctor we all know you can." 1950 wasn't a time when 'real men' spoke about their feelings but James and Andrew loved each other and didn't care who knew it.

Father shook his son's hand. "I am so proud of you son. But you take care and come back to me and your mother."

245

"I will sir." James' dad didn't expect to be called 'sir' but James wanted him to know how much he respected him and that whatever he achieved he would always be his dad, the man whose authority and guidance he would never ignore.

"Thank you son." Felix knew what James' words meant but perhaps James would never know how much they would mean to him.

With tears in her eyes Margaret hugged her eldest son.

"Look after yourself James. I love you." James had for the last twenty years known that but it was good to have it confirmed again.

"All aboard," the guard shouted to the Guardian and everyone else on the platform.

"Time to go mum," and James had to prise himself out of his mothers grip. He got onto the overnight express, found himself a compartment and lowered the window. As he saw his parents either side of his brother Andrew he shouted, "Look after them bro!"

"I will and you look after yourself," Andrew shouted back. The guard blew his whistle, waved his flag and James was off. He waved as long as he could see his family through the steam and tears. Then he sat down wondering what lay ahead. After dinner in the Restaurant Car he spent time in his compartment reading the Daily Mirror before settling down to sleep for the night. The rattle and motion of the train soon had him asleep.

Before he knew it the guard was shouting, "One hour to Edinburgh! One hour to Edinburgh!" Sure enough, one hour later the train pulled into the splendid Waverley Station. James got his suitcase and left the platform and the station. Once outside the station he was looking for something unusual and then he found it. You didn't see many Scotsmen wearing a rose in their caps but there was one. The man noticed James and came up to speak to him.

"You don't get many of these to a pound," he said with his Scottish brogue and pointing to his rose.

"I bet you don't up here in bonny Scotland was," James' reply.

"Good to meet you James. I'm Cameron," the short, stout Scotsman said shaking James hand with a grip that could have squashed rocks.

"Good to meet you Cameron."

"Right, let's get a move on. I have a car over here that we'll use to get you to where you need to be." Cameron grabbed James' case and led him over to a four door Morris that looked like it had been in the wars, because it had. Discoloured paintwork and more dents than you could shake a hammer at. Anyhow, it beat walking. It didn't take them long to reach a large Victorian villa on the edge of the city. But James did notice that Cameron was a bit twitchy and kept checking his rear view mirror.

"Everything ok Cameron?"

"No problem. It's just that the troop have been a bit concerned we may have been under surveillance and we're just a jumpy. We should have moved the stone a week ago but needed to hang on for your transfer. Any how, you're here now so we'll soon get the show on the road." They reached the villa and James noticed at least four of the troop on perimeter duty assuming the rest were with the stone. Cameron rushed him inside and to the cavernous study over in the right hand corner of the ground floor. As they entered, they were met with five flaming swords.

"My we are jumpy," said James.

"Sorry about that," said Jules as she introduced herself and extinguished her sword.

"Cameron said you were a bit twitchy which I suppose is better than being complacent. Tell you what, let's get me transferred and then you can get on the road."

"Agreed. Troop, protective perimeter. The stone is about to be activated." As Jules gave the order there was an almighty commotion in the Hall. Screaming, breaking glass and shouting. The door to the Study burst open and everyone in there recognised the Goliathim and taken they had come across before.

"Get to the stone. We'll keep them occupied," Jules shouted.

"Let me help," James shouted back as he transfigured his Word into a sword.

"No! Our job is to get you to the third dimension and your job is to go. Now go!" James knew when a woman shouldn't be argued with and this was one of those times. He stood astride the stone and it activated. But as he did, two of the enemy burst through the Guardians surrounding it and grabbed James as he stood in the rainbow beam. All three were transferred to the stone room. For a moment all three were disorientated and as James started to come round he felt a sharp blow to the back of his head. He wasn't knocked out but he was dazed. Even so, he could make out one of the enemy punching buttons on a panel in the stone room. Then he was manhandled away from the stone and thrown off the platform onto the floor. He could just make out the rainbow beams and two figures in it as he finally passed out.

"James. James." The words wafted through James dizziness until he recognised the one who was speaking his name.

"Is that you Joel?"

"Is Stanley Matthews a footballer," came the reply.

"Yes that's you Joel. The angel who put the 'un' in 'unfunny'."

"Nice to see you again as well. How are you feeling?"

"Like I've been hit by a doodle bug but I'll live."

"Ok. You rest here for a while and I'll come and get you later." No argument from James. He just lay back and let his bed do the work. When he awoke some time later, he showered and went downstairs soon realising he was in the Enochim house not far from All Saints. This time Nathaniel met him and after breakfast escorted him over to Teacher Eli's study.

"Good to see you Teacher."

"And you James. Are you feeling better?"

"Yes thank you although I would be grateful if you don't tell tutor Micah about this. Don't think he's going to be too impressed that I let those two enemy hitched a ride up here."

"Micah knows and you can rest assured that he nor anyone is holding you to blame for any of this."

"Is the stone safe?"

"It is. After the transfer Jules and her troop overcame the attackers and now they are en route to a new safe place."

"So what is this all about Teacher?"

"As you know, we angels do not have complete knowledge and only know the things The I Am allows us to know. Applying what we do know as far as we can tell, the two who transferred with you have used the stone to go back in time."

"To when, where and what for?"

"It seems they have gone back to Vienna in 1909."

"What for?"

"We think it's to do with the one we know as 'The Wolf'"

"Who's he?"

"If I tell you that the German name Adolf means 'Wolf' would that give you a clue?"

"Do you mean Adolf Hitler?"

"Yes I do. We call him 'The Wolf' because it kind of describes the way he was. Wild and ruthless. Not to mention, during the 1920's when he didn't want to be recognised he called himself 'Herr Wolf'. And when he was waging the Second World War his military headquarters was known as 'The Wolf's Lair'. So we call him 'The Wolf.' " James knew all about this 'wolf' and knew if those guys got to him, it wouldn't be good.

"So why do you think they want to see Hitler back in 1909?"

"Myself and Uriel have pondered this and have concluded it has to do with 'The Spear of Destiny.'

"Now you have lost me. What's Hitler, Vienna and this Spear of Destiny got to do with each other?"

"Well in 1909 both Hitler and The Spear were in Vienna."

"Fair enough," replied James. "I think you better explain to me what you think this is all about."

Teacher Eli cleared his throat and having been joined by Uriel began a story that was about to change James' life.

"When The Christ was crucified, the centurion named Longinus, who some think was of one of the Germanic tribes and supervised the execution, pierced His side to make sure He was dead. The spear he used became known as The Spear of Destiny and a belief grew up around it that because it had pierced God, that whoever possessed this spear could rule the world. The journey this spear has made is supposed to have included being used by Emperor Constantine in the fourth Century to make the Roman Empire Christian. Then Charlemagne is said to have used it in the Eighth century to bring him success. This 'success' continued with Henry IV in the eleventh century to create his 'Holy Roman Empire.' By 1424 the spear is in the hands of Sigismund of Luxembourg who sells it to the town of Nuremburg. It stays there for centuries but to save it from capture by Napoleon, it is smuggled to Vienna.

"Along with 'The Wolf.'

"Exactly James. Now Hitler spent some years in Vienna yet a cloak exists over much of the time he was there and what he did. But some believe he went to the Hofmuseum in Vienna where he was intrigued by the spear and the supposed power it could give the one who possessed it. Now if you remember your history what was the first foreign country that Hitler took over in 1938?"

James knew and loved his history and replied, "Austria."

"So in 1938 when Hitler had taken over the land of his birth and it what did he retrieve?"

James was on a roll now. "The Spear of Destiny."

"And where do you think he took it?" James' roll had finished because he didn't know.

"He took it to Nuremburg which was the spiritual home and powerbase of The Nazi Party."

The magnitude of what Teacher Eli was suggesting started to dawn on James. "So those barbarians were empowered by this spear and the havoc that man has just reeked in my world is based on the power he got from it?"

"No," came Eli's immediate and emphatic reply.

"How are you so sure?"

"Because the spear is a fake. It is not the spear that pierced the side of The Christ."

"You're certain of this," James asked looking for re-assurance?"

"Absolutely positive. Don't forget, when The King died The Legions were there and we saw all that happened. We know the spear that caused the wound was destroyed soon after. So we are certain that sometime in your future this 'Spear of Destiny' will be proved to be a fake."

"That's good to know. But if the spear of destiny is a fake with no power, why is it so important to the wolf."

"The spear itself may have no power but the belief it generates has enormous power."

"So it's not the spear that has the power, but the belief in it."

"Exactly so."

"Got it so far. But if I remember my training I am not allowed to go back and stop Hitler coming into contact with this spear as that could drastically alter history. It's tempting to go back and stop that madman starting a war that will kill fifty five million people but I'm sure you won't let me."

You're right, we won't let you do that. But our concern is that those two who have gone back will stop Hitler coming into contact with the spear and thereby change the course of history for the worse."

James got the train of thought now. "So you're saying, if history is altered around Hitler and the spear, things could have been even worse than they were?"

"Yes. You see because Hitler may have believed in this relic and other occultic influences it was one more thing that he let tempt him into the evil he executed. Everyone has free will and so is responsible for their own actions. So we should all avoid things that lead us into temptation so we don't fall even deeper into sin. Hitler's willingness to support racism, intolerance and the use of violence to achieve his goals along with his other misguided beliefs all led him over to the principality of the air. His sins and those who followed him are their own responsibility for which they will be judged."

"Not only that," Uriel jumped into the discussion now, "If he hadn't believed in his own ego and the spears power he may have acted differently. You see if Hitler hadn't had so much confidence in the spear and himself, he may not have invaded The Soviet Union in 1941, or perhaps he would have supported more his scientists in developing rockets and an atom bomb that could have drastically altered the course of the war and it's outcome. The Nazis may actually have won and then more than the fifty five million who did die could have died."

"So we need to make sure Hitler comes in contact with the spear and let history take its course."

"That's it."

"It's incredible to think that this one object could have such an effect on world history."

"I think I better correct your thinking on this. The spear was only one element that contributed to way the wolf and his henchmen acted.

Other factors like the outcome of World War One, economic depression and hatred of communism and the Jews also played their part. But it seems to us that because a lot of the Nazis belief system was based on 'supernatural' beliefs, the system it created and the people within it left themselves open to being taken over by evil."

"How do you mean 'supernatural' beliefs," asked James?

"Well, not to get too technical, Nazi beliefs such as the idea of a super race or removing the weak or having one leader who must be obeyed, stem from age old traditions. Not only that, but Hitler himself came to believe that he was some kind of 'messiah' who had been sent to save the super race and the world from darkness. Initially he saw himself as a herald for someone else. He was 'the drummer' who was announcing the coming of one who would be the world's saviour. But somewhere along the line he started to see himself as that saviour. Maybe he looked at his life and saw that providence had made things happen that indicated he was this 'messiah'. He probably thought because he was born in 'an inn' that is Braunau am Inn on Easter Saturday 1889 when symbolically the real Messiah was 'dead' meant he was the one who would overcome. Perhaps as he eventually thought of himself as some kind of architect had a meaning. The Greek for 'architect' is 'arkitecton' which can also mean 'carpenter.' Then he remembered how during the Great War on many occasions he was spared death whilst others around him died. The fact he started his 'ministry' to the world at the age of thirty in 1919 mirrored another one who started His ministry at the same age in his life. He saw his Reich lasting for a Thousand Years echoing the Millennial Kingdom of another King. And who knows it could be relevant that in The Book of Revelation Gods people are beheaded by evil forces. Did you know that the Nazis guillotined more people than were beheaded in The French Revolution because Hitler thought it was a degrading way to die. Maybe the powers of darkness thought they could use his misguided beliefs and perhaps they did. How else can you explain how the uneducated son of a lowly customs official born in a backwater could rise to lead one of the great nations of Europe. This failed artist who could only reach the rank of corporal was to become a military leader who for three years would have the world stand in awe at his victories. Here was a loner who could speak to thousands at a rally or millions through the radio or newsreel and inspire a loyalty that those people would kill for and die for. Could he have been energised by something outside of himself? In Scripture those who are taken over by evil sprits whether permanently or intermittently show certain signs."

"Such as," James asked?

"Often they become physically ill as Hitler did. They behave abnormally as Hitler did. Their voice can alter which seemed to happen when Hitler spoke to those tens of thousands of his followers. On occasions such people can show unusual knowledge and perception which Hitler showed in how successful he was in his early military campaigns. And there is no question he had no time for God. These things aren't proof but make you think.

Eli continued. "Anyway,with these circumstances and this man in place the powers of darkness might have thought they could get a system in place that could remove the Jews and so be able to frustrate the plans of The I Am for The End Times. In 1933 the nightmare began and would leave millions of Jews and others the Nazis hated, dead. But Hitler was not the 'anti-christ' who was to come. His seven years of tribulation starting with Austria in 1938 and ending in an obliterated and divided Berlin and Germany in 1945 was not The Great Tribulation. Hitler must have forgotten that his party number was 555 and not 666. He tried to become greater than the dark forces would allow and so he fell and took his country with him. Even his death leaves you wondering about his motivation. Hitler killed himself on April 30th which for centuries has been a revered pre-Christian pagan festival called in Germany 'Walpurgisnacht'. On this night witches are supposed to meet up and await the arrival of the devil. Fires are lit just like the one that consumed Hitler's body. You have to wonder if Hitler chose this date deliberately? Perhaps some day we can talk about this more depth but not now."

"Just to consolidate the point Teacher Eli is making let me finish with this. You know what the symbol of Nazism was don't you," asked Uriel?

"The Swastika," James replied.

"Right. But did you know that this is an ancient symbol that stood for light or the sun and that for sometime it was used by Christians as a symbol for the Cross of The Christ. You can still see it today on some ancient graves in Rome. The Nazis took the swastika for their own and altered it's meaning from light to darkness"

"Let me show you something else about the swastika," said Eli. The teacher took a piece of paper and drew......

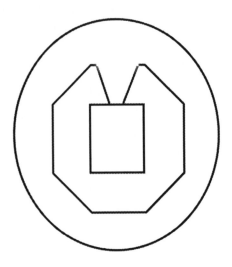

"Do you recognise this James?"

"Of course, it's the Enochima."

Teacher Eli took his pencil again and then drew something James recognised all too easily.......

Teacher Eli asked, "Do you see any similarities between these two symbols?"

James looked and pondered but the pupil didn't see what the teacher saw.

Seeing that the scales hadn't fallen from James' eyes, Teacher Eli put him out of his misery by explaining.

"If you look at both symbols carefully you will see you have the same shapes." James had a scale falling from his eyes experience.

"Yes, I can see them now, a square and circle but no octagon."

"You're right there is no octagon but how may sides does the octagon have," the Teacher asked looking to tease learning out of his pupil.

"Eight," was James' immediate and correct reply.

"And how many lines make up the swastika?"

It took James a moment and then he got it, "Eight?!"

"Well done Mr. Burnett. Now what does this mean?" No reply.

Eli continued, "To be honest we're not sure if there's a meaning either. What we do know is that Hitler gave great thought to creating this Nazi banner and even refers to it in his book with some explanation. But maybe there is another explanation and he was trying to use ancient symbolism to show that this world system symbolised by the square can be greater than the spiritual realm illustrated by the circle. But to do this you need to have the overcoming of man at the centre of all you do shown by the swastika. If this is the case the history that followed this banner shows that by letting man win by following his own way is no victory. Any way we're not sure if there is any connection and maybe if you get chance you could ask the wolf yourself?"

"This stuff is pretty heavy to take on board," James finally speaking as his mind came back online. "But what's it got to do with me, here and now?"

Teacher Eli paused for some moments knowing the gravity of what he was going to ask James. Then his thoughts had to come out in the words he needed to use.

"We need you to go back to 1909 and make sure these two 'werewolves' don't change history."

James thought for a moment and then asked, "Werewolves?"

"Sorry, James. After World War Two finished some Nazis set up a covert group to carry on their work and called themselves 'werewolves'. We presume these two who sabotaged your transfer and have gone back are part of that group."

"They are more than likely Goliathim as well," added Uriel to Eli's words.

"Ok. I get that someone has to deal with this but why can't the Guardians or other Enochim who are there deal with it?"

"Because the history we have just given you is their future and we can't risk divulging it to them otherwise directly or indirectly it could lead to them changing what's laid down."

"Ok then, why not send me back to just before my transfer and let me stop these two getting into the rainbow beam."

"We can't do that either. Because it's already happened. It is now part of history that cannot be altered. The only way to deal with this now is to send you back to thwart the plans of these werewolves."

James could see the logic in what Teacher Eli was saying. He asked if he could have time to think this through which his Teacher and Tutor were happy to give him. James went down to the park behind All Saints and spent quite some time wandering over it's grass, looking at the magnificent trees and enjoying the warmth of the Third Heaven. In time he realised he had no choice but to go back for The Kingdom to try and stop the evil of the prince with the co-operation of men that could lead to many more millions dying. His thoughts ran to the death and destruction he had experienced first hand in the Blitz. His memory also reminded him of the horrors he had seen on the newsreels of the many dead on the battlefields and the nightmare of the death camps.

James headed back to Teacher Eli's study where he and Uriel were waiting for him. He knocked on the door, entered as he had done so many times before and simply said,

"Here I am. Send me."

XXIII

Over the next three Alphas and Omegas James was given refresher training on his defence and flying skills. In addition, Uriel briefed him on the time period he was about to go back to so that James could fit in as best he could.

"You're being sent back to Austria in 1909 to Vienna which is still the capital of the Austro-Hungarian Empire. At this time, Vienna is a very cosmopolitan city with many different nationalities and is quite the centre of culture particularly with its Opera Houses. Cars do exist but horses and carriages are still the main form of transport. We will give you correct clothing and a map to show what you've got to do. Your commission is to ensure that Hitler sees the Spear of Destiny and history stays the same."

"This is all good stuff Tutor, but there's just one thing......I don't speak a word of German."

"Jerahmeel has thought of that and has made this." Uriel gave James what looked like a miniature hearing aid that fitted inside his ear.

"This is what we call The Pentecost Chip. Once you insert it in your ear, whatever language is spoken to you, you will hear it in your native tongue. So when someone speaks German, you will understand every word."

"Nice but how about me speaking German?"

"You're not easily satisfied are you," Uriel replied sarcastically so James thought.

"It's not called the Pentecost Chip for nothing. All you need to do is listen to the translation it gives you then speak words in reply. The chip will ensure your words come out in the language of the question and those you speak to will hear the words in their own tongue. As you know, not the first time that's happened."

As soon as Uriel had finished he took James down to Jerahmmels lab where he was kitted out with his 1909 clothes. Then up to Teacher Eli's Study.

"You know what you must do," the Teacher asked?

"Yes Teacher."

"There is one more thing that you need to know. You must bring the two werewolves back with you. We can't afford to let them stay back in history because even if we stop them this time, they could still use their knowledge to disrupt what has already happened."

"So let me get this straight. You want me to go back in time, make sure one of the most evil men of all time fulfils his history, defeat two supernaturally trained killers and bring them back to another dimension all without upsetting history."

"Yes."

"Thank you Teacher. Nice to know you've got a plan."

"You James have been brought here at this time to do this work. If you couldn't do it, someone else would have been called. We all have every faith that you can fulfil your task."

"Thank you Teacher. Let's get this show on the road." Eli and Uriel took James to the Stone Room where now there stood armed guards.

"Even us angels can learn new things," remarked Uriel. He then introduced Gedaliah who would sort out James' time transfer.

James stood astride the stone on the raised clear platform. As Gedaliah put the time details in the newly installed panel James shouted, "For The Kingdom!" and all in the room responded by repeating his words.

The transfer took moments and James soon found himself in a somewhat dingy room on the third floor of a large apartment building in Vienna. As he arrived he was met by six armed Guardians ready to pounce.

"I'm Enochim," said James handing over the scroll Teacher Eli had handed him in his study. Having just been caught unawares and overpowered by two Goliathim, these Guardians were taking no chances. Five of them surrounded James with swords flaming as one of their number took and read the scroll.

Dear Juan,

The bearer of this scroll is James Burnett who is an Enochim we commend to you.

James has been sent to you with the authority of the Angel Council to deal with the two Goliathim who have violated the stone.

We request that you give James every assistance and to follow his commands without question.

Yours for The Kingdom,

Eli.

"At ease Troop." The five Guardians extinguished their swords.

"I am Juan, the leader of this troop. Welcome. I accept the scroll from Teacher Eli. I and my troops are at your disposal.

James moved away from the stone and shook Juans hand.

"Thank you Juan. Time is short. I want all of your troop except one, to move the stone immediately to a new location. We can't risk those Goliathim coming back with friends and trying to seize it." Immediately Juan acted.

"Steven."

"Sir," Steven replied.

"Take the troop and the stone to the nearest safe house. Set up a perimeter, have swords flamed and await our return.

"Yes Sir." With that Steven got into action and the troop were gone with the stone.

James got down to briefing Juan as much as he could over his commission.

"Those two Goliathim are going to stop a man from meeting his 'destiny'. We have to stop them otherwise history and millions of people will be destroyed. We must get to the treasure house of the Hofsburg Museum now."

Already at the Hofsburg were two men who were on time but out of time.

"We wait here near the Spear. When we see the Fruher we must stop him getting anywhere near it. If we can divert him from his belief in the spear maybe we can change history for the better for us and the worse for The Kingdom. Do you understand Klaus?"

"Yes Jurgen," Klaus responded.

The two were wolves didn't have long to wait for the wolf to appear. He was a slight man with no real presence. He was dressed in a suit of the day and was following behind as a guide took a group of patrons around the exhibits whilst explaining their history. As the guide came to The Spear of Destiny, he took a moment before starting its story to let everyone, including the wolf, get close enough to hear.

"Now," whispered Jurgen. The two moved forward and each grabbed an arm of their quarry as they marched him away from the Spear.

"What is going on," the little man asked with his shrill voice?

Jurgen answered, "Please don't be alarmed. We are not going to harm you. We have been sent by some friends of yours to pass on a message."

"What message," the man asked as he flicked his drooping hair away from his left eye.

"The message that you better not miss your date with destiny and its spear," James answered before Jurgen could.

"Well Enochim you think you can stop us all by yourself do you?"

"I'll give a go handsome," James answered.

"Two against one? Not fair odds but who said us Goliathim were ever fair?"

As James and Jurgen jousted with words, Klaus found a store cupboard and locked the wolf in it. As Klaus rejoined his compatriot in the armoury display, he realised James was not alone. By now Juan had joined his fellow Enochim.

"Ah, so you're not alone. No matter. Two Goliathim will always beat two Enochim." As he finished, Jurgen grabbed a large mace hanging on the wall and lunged at James. Instantly James reacted with a flying somersault over his attacker whilst lighting his sword and cutting the mace in half. Before Jurgen could think.,James had landed, swivelled on his feet and landed a kick to Jurgens midrift. The Golitahim doubled over in agony as James completed the knock out with a side swipe to his head. Jurgen went out like a candle in the wind before he hit the floor.

Meanwhile, Klaus had pulled a revolver from his jacket and was intent in putting holes in both Enochim. As he fired, Juan swung his flaming sword around like a Catherine wheel. None of Klaus' six bullets could penetrate the fiery shield and hit their target. When Klaus realised he had no bullets left, he tried throwing the gun at Juan who just sliced it in two with one swift swing of his sword.

"Now that's how you disarm a weapon. Now let's see about disarming you." Juan extinguished his sword and reached for his sling and stone. Before Klaus realised what was ahead for him, Juan had hit him square in the forehead and he fell to the floor.

The two Enochim grabbed hands and said together, "For The Kingdom."

"Right, let's get the target back to where he should be. As James opened the door to the store cupboard to find the cowering, bemused twenty year old he hadn't anticipated the feelings he would experience. There in front if him was the man who would plunge the world into a second world war that would cost millions their lives. Not only that but he would lead a regime that would kill tens of thousands of its own people including the disabled, Jews, gypsies and anyone who didn't agree with his warped ideas. Surely taking his head off now would be the right thing to do. Through the mist of his confusion and instinct to act, James heard Juans voice.

"Come on James, we must get him back."

"You do it Juan," James said as he put his Bible back in his pocket and turned his back on a man who would turn his back on humanity.

Juan took hold of the man's arm and led him back to the Spear. As he did so he explained that he and James were security guards who had noticed those two men try to abduct him. Obviously they intervened and hoped he was alright. The man thanked him and re- joined the group who were at the spear. As he did the guide explained about the spears history and its supposed life since the crucifixion. Juan waited to leave with the group as he thought that would be less obvious. As the group and Juan left, the young man stayed behind. Juan thought nothing of it until he got to the door of the treasure house and looked back. There transfixed in front of the spear was the young man.

"Strange," thought Juan but he had always known fact was stranger than fiction. Well you do when you talk, train and work with angels. Juan met up with James who had pulled both of the unconscious men together.

"We've got to try and wake them up and get them out of here. Then it's back to the stone so all three of us can get back to our own time." Juan got some water from some nearby toilets and after having sprinkled their faces, the two started to come around.

"Let's get them out of here." They each took hold of one of the groggy Goliathim and led them outside to their horseless carriage. They put them in the back seat with James in the middle and Juan headed off for the new safe house and the stone. As they travelled, James didn't realise that Jurgen was more conscious than he thought. As Juan slowed to turn left, Jurgen thumped James in the side of the face. He grabbed the door handle and leapt out of the car. As James got over the shock he jumped out of the open door as Juan stopped the car. He stood in horror as Jurgen stumbled across the street not realising a tram was coming. Jurgen was not as lucid as he thought because by the time he realised the tram bell was ringing for him, it knocked him over. James ran towards him as the tram conductor shouted, "He's dead!" James decided it was best if he left the scene and that time rather than risk trying to explain who he was. He raced back to the car and shouted at Juan to step on it. Juan did and soon they were travelling at eighteen miles an hour!

It took about three quarters of an hour to reach the new safe house on the outskirts of the city. Juan parked the car in the grounds of the impressive villa and helped James to get the still groggy Goliathim to the stone.

"Thanks for all you help Juan. You may never realise what you've done but be assured it was for the best." Those words would haunt Juan when in 1937 he saw that young man he had help to save, send bombers to blast his own people in his native Guernica.

James waited for the stone to activate and then whilst helping Klaus to stand, they both entered the rainbow beam and left that time and dimension.

As they came out of the beam in the stone room, James could see the concern etched on Eli's face. Joel and Nathaniel took care of Klaus whilst Eli helped James down off the platform.

"Are you alright," the Teacher asked his pupil.

"Yes," he replied.

"What about the other Goliathim," asked Eli without disguising the concern in his voice.

"Dead," came James' one word reply that meant more than a dictionary of words to Eli. James explained what had happened.

"You're certain he's dead," asked Eli?

"The conductor who found him seemed certain and the way he hit than tram, I don't see anyone surviving that. Eli kept his concerns to himself and led James back to the Enochim house where he would have time to recover.

Sometime later around Omega 5, Joel went to see James. He was much recovered and looking forward to beginning his Guardian training. Joel led him back to Eli's study where he sat down with the Teacher and Uriel.

"Are you rested James?"

"Yes thank you Teacher."

"Good. Now I'm not going to beat about the burning bush. We are concerned over the death of Jurgen as his removal from your dimension in 1950 could have an adverse effect. Not only that, we need to be sure that now you have brought the wolf and the spear together, that they are re-united in 1938."

"What are you saying Teacher?"

Eli looked at Uriel, then back at James.

"We want you to go back to 1938 to ensure history is fulfilled."

"You're not serious," he asked?

"I'm afraid we are. The death of Jurgen concerns us because history could be disrupted so we need to be certain that the spear gets into the hands of The Nazis."

"I don't suppose there's anybody else who could go is there?"

"No. You are here and it is your commission."

"Well, I suppose I better finish what I started. What's the plan?

"I have researched the Enochim histories and found that in October 1938 the stone is in Switzerland. From there it will be moved to Canada and then through South America for the duration of the war." Uriel continued. "We will send you back and some Enochim will guide you across the border and back into Vienna. There you will be given an SS uniform so you can infiltrate the military set up in Austria's capital. On 14th March you must be back at the Hofsburg museum to see the spear be collected and taken to Hitler. Once you are sure the dictator has his talisman in his blood soaked hands you must return to our dimension."

"Have to say it sounds easy when you say it tutor. Right, let's do this thing." Eli gave James another scroll before he left to go and see Jerahmeel to be briefed on the time he was about to enter.

James returned to the Enochim house and against the odds got a good 'nights' sleep. At Alpha 4 he was awoken by Joel, had his breakfast and got dressed in his tweed jacket and slacks. The flat cap was the finishing touch, so James thought. Joel escorted James to the stone room where Eli and Uriel along with Gedaliah were there to meet him.

"Are you set," Eli asked?

"As I'll ever be," his pupil replied.

"Thank you for doing this James. We and history salute you."

"When I took the sword I accepted I would have to do my duty whatever and I'm just pleased to be able to. As a famous general once said ? Whatever, 'I'll be back.'"

The angels hugged their fellow citizen and let him go. James stood over the stone and instantly the rainbow beam enveloped him.

Before he could think about a pot of gold he was in a small alpine village on the Swiss-Austrian border. He shook the trans-dimensional stars from his eyes and was met by the usual six guardians with a bemused look and flaming swords. Without speaking, James handed one of them his scroll. The guardian immediately passed it onto a woman standing over by the window of the cottage. She read the scroll.

"No problem. He's one of us and he's on a special commission." The Guardians and their swords relaxed. The woman introduced herself as Charlotte and she in turn she introduced her five comrades. No time for small talk. James explained that he needed to get to the border by nightfall and showed his host the map on the reverse side of the scroll. He explained Enochim would meet him and take him across the border.

"This won't be easy. The Austrians are on high alert because of all that's going on with Hitler. But if you want to try, we'll give you all the help we can." Charlotte then briefed her troop and decided she and Timothy would escort James to his rendezvous. As it was late afternoon in the first dimension, tea was had and then the three left in one of the troops lorries and headed north to the border. They reached the spot on the border where the railway line crossed into Austria and waited. For over two hours nothing happened until there was a quiet tap on the lorry's passenger door. There outside were two Enochim that James guessed must be shepherds.

"Time to go," James whispered to Charlotte. See you back here at midnight in three days time." James thanked Charlotte, left the lorry and watched as it slowly and quietly headed back into Switzerland.

"I am Hans and this is Deiter. You must follow us and be quiet. No speaking from hereon." James was happy to keep quiet 'from hereon'. Hans led them across the border into Austria and it took them all night to reach his village. When they got to Hans' house, James was treated to a hearty breakfast. After breakfast, Hans took him out into the barn.

"This was sent for you two days ago." Hans handed him a suitcase that when he checked it held the SS uniform for an Obersturmfuhrer, or Lieutenant.

"Thank you for your help Hans. I better leave now, because it's best I stay with you and your family as short as possible." Hans shook James' hand and said he would expect to see him the day after tomorrow. The date was 13th March 1938.

"For The Kingdom" were the last words the two Enochim spoke and the James was gone. He found the train station exactly where Hans had said it would be and brought a one way ticket to Vienna. He didn't buy a return ticket because he wanted to leave as little evidence as possible about where he's been. The last thing James wanted was to put Hans and his family in danger.

The journey took over four hours but was straight forward as James would expect with Austro-Germanic efficiency. He arrived at Vienna's Wien Praterstern Station in the early afternoon and made his way to the Hofsburg. As he did so he sensed the tension in the city and the feeling everyone had that something was about to happen. As he saw the swastika flags fluttering in the wind his heart fluttered for the terror he knew that blood red flag with its white pallor of death and black of evil on it would soon bring to millions.

"Get the job done Burnett or many more millions will die." James tried to re-focus himself on the job at hand. He got to the Hofsburg and found if just as he left it in 1909. There in The Treasure House was the Spear whose destiny he had to ensure. After having a good look around the museum to confirm his escape route he found a small boarding house a few streets away. He had his evening meal and then went upstairs while he was still in Austria knowing that the following morning he would come down to breakfast in Germany. James had a fitful nights sleep and was woken in the early hours of the morning by running, shouting and gunfire in the street below. James decided that it would be safest now to join the confusion as a member of the SS and be around the Hofsburg. He donned his black uniform with the SS logo on its collar that James wasn't sure didn't stand for 'Satans Soldiers'. These runes looked like forks of lightning and James wondered if those who wore them ever thought about the words, 'I saw satan fall like lightning from Heaven.' He couldn't face wearing the swastika armband so he left it off. He slipped out of the boarding house and left his suitcase with a change of clothes in an alleyway just to the left of the building. He headed off in the direction of the Hofsburg and was soon joined by cheering crowds waving swastika flags. When they saw his uniform they treated him like a hero.

"Thank you thank you for coming."

"We're all Germans now."

"This is the happiest day of my life." One after the other they all spoke to James and gave him the 'hiel' salute. To keep in character James responded through gritted teeth and a heavy heart. As he reached the Hofsburg he saw police were already surrounding it. He approached one of the officers and got shown to his superior. James introduced himself.

"I am Obersturmfuhrer Bonhoeffer and I have orders to ensure the safety of the Hofsburg and its treasures for the Greater German Reich." Overcome with elation and hoping to be written of well in reports the 'little hitler' was only to glad to let the Obersturmfuhrer into the building to fulfil his orders. James headed for the Treasure House and waited in the store cupboard that years before had been the 'wolfs lair'. For hours he waited and got more nervous as he did. He could hear people outside and then inside in great jubilation. And then someone said, "He's arrived. The Fuhrer has come home to Vienna." James knew that the time was fast approaching when he would need to act. He listened until he thought it was safe to do so and then he came out of the lair. He joined the crowd that was thronging around the museum and got a position just behind a pillar in sight of the spear. Suddenly, the place was flooded with black dressed SS men like vultures around a carcass. They cleared the room and then one of them opened the case with where the spear was displayed. He took it out and said

"I have it my Haupstumfuhrer."

"Good. Guard it with your life," the Haupstumfuhrer ordered him. The captain turned and looked Obersturmfuhrer Bonhoeffer straight in the eyes. He walked towards him and held out his hand.

"Mr. James Burnett I presume?" James was speechless.

He continued. "Nice uniform but where's your armband. May I introduce myself. I am Haupstumfuhrer Muller. Good to meet you. I was told you would be here and I've been asked to escort you to meet someone." Just about getting his composure back, James answered, "You must have me mistaken for somebody else Haupstumfuhrer. Perhaps I can help you find him?"

"Oh you British with your pseudo modesty. Please Mr. Burnett don't insult my intelligence or that of the Gestapo." Reaching for his pistol and backed up by an armed group of uniformed thugs, the Haupstumfuhrer insisted James accompany him. James had no choice so he complied. He was ushered into the back of a black Mercedes with the Muller and the spear. They raced as fast as they could threw the thronged streets of Vienna and soon reached The Ring and The Hotel Imperial.

The Haupstumfuhrer spoke to the guards who immediately let him, his passenger and cargo through. The car pulled up at the bottom of the marble steps and James was led inside past the five storey high swastika banners swaying in the wind. They past through throngs of uniformed

SS men and the Haupstumfuhrer led James to the second floor. They reached a pair of enormous oak doors with more SS guards outside. The Muller spoke to one of them. The guards parted, the doors opened and James was led inside followed by Muller with his precious cargo. The doors closed behind him.

"So we meet again Mr. Burnett." The words and the person speaking to him were like a spear to James' soul for holding out his hand and smiling was ………….Adolf Hitler.

James couldn't bring himself to shake the blood stained hand of this mass murderer. Hitler was not amused by James' attitude. He broke out in one of his blind rages and shrieked that 'Burnett should show him due respect.' James stood his ground and didn't raise his hand. As he did so, one of the guards in the room whacked James in the back with his machine gun butt. The stunned Enochim fell to the floor on his knees. Hitler calmed himself and joked, "That's better. On your knees before the one who holds your life in his hands." Still James didn't speak as the guards manhandled him into a nearby armchair and stood at either side of him. As he looked around he saw another person in the room he recognised from newspaper reports of his suicide, Heinrich Himmler. Another 'little man' but this one had glasses over his piggy little eyes.

Hitler settled himself into a leather chair behind a desk that was the size of Czechoslovakia. At the same time, Muller placed the spear on the desk in front of his Fuhrer. Hitler waved the Haupstumfuhrer away with a glint in his eye.

"At last we have it in our possession to do with as we will. Now we can really start creating the new world order and my 'supermen' " the little corporal said to himself as he stroked the relic in front of him. As he did so Himmler walked over to his Fruhrers desk to look at the relic himself. Himmler was more into the occult than his leader and so encouraged all the more this sort of relic hunting even sending an expedition to Tibet. The two Nazis looked and smiled at each other.

"You Mr Burnett are privileged to be here to witness another moment when providence fulfils a promise to me. I suppose you're wondering how you came to be here to witness this?" James remained silent.

"Let me tell you with one name............ Jurgen Mayer. You see when you left Jurgen Mayer for dead on the streets of Vienna those Twenty nine years ago you made a mistake. He wasn't dead. No doubt you thought that no normal man could withstand the impact he took and you would be right. But as you know and as I came to find out, Jurgen Mayer was no normal man. His injuries were extensive but he survived. He was taken to a hospital where for months he was in a coma. Eventually he came to and started to talk in gibberish about his mission and the one he had come to protect and serve. The one who would save the nation and the world. The one who would miraculously survive The Great War and from nowhere, lead his nation. It was thought Mayers injuries had caused brain damage and so he was ignored. He was sent to an asylum in the city and eventually moved to Berlins Charite Nerve Clinic to be treated by Edmund Foster. He told foster about his beliefs which the good doctor ignored until he met me at Pasewalk in 1918. When he and I met as he tried to cure my blindness, my words echoed the voice of Mayer and Foster realised something unusual was occurring. He told me of Mayer and his words and I knew they were sent as a confirmation from Providence. From then on I worked to save the nation that had been betrayed in November 1918 by those criminals. In the early 1920's I got to meet Jurgen Mayer just before he died. It was if he was waiting to see me then he could die. He was able to tell me about a man called James Burnett who had thwarted his mission in 1909 and who would return with me in 1938 when I came back to my homeland. Oh yes, he told me the Spear means nothing, but what did he know?" As he saisd this he looked over to Himmler and smirked.

"I've seen what symbols can do to people, whether they be flags, uniforms, rallies, badges and spears. This spear is one more that I and others can believe in.

Jurgen also told me you are not of this time, and that intrigues me. So there Mr. Burnett, now you know."

James was distraught that he had let all this happen. Why didn't he get Mayer anyway, dead or not and get him away from 1909? His anger against himself exploded in anger against those in the room. Before the guards knew it, James had jumped up with fists to underneath their jaws that knocked them out cold. Muller grabbed for his pistol but James had grabbed his iron cross off his jacket and threw it at Mullers hand. The cross stuck in the back of his hand and the Haupstumfuhrer squealed in pain. James flew at him not to give first aid but the anaesthetic off a round house kick to the head. The SS man fell to the floor unconscious. His leader Himmler by now had headed to the door of the office to get help. As a chicken farmer he knew all about how chickens act. Hitler had retreated behind his desk like his army in a Russian winter. James vaulted the desk and got him by the throat.

"If I could I would believe me. But I'll leave you to infamy and righteous judgement." As he spoke Himmler ran through the oak doors screaming for help. Instantly, SS men burst in brandishing machine guns. They opened fired as James leapt for the window and the mighty Fuhrer pleaded with them to stop. James smashed through the glass pane and grabbed the Nazi banner he had seen swaying outside. He slid down it as his pursuers rattled off bullets at him. As he hit the ground he ran over to a motor bike and side car and threw its rider over his head. He revved the machine, smashed through the security barrier and sped off through the streets of Vienna. He was chased by trucks and a Mercedes full of black suited soldiers shooting at him. As he rode alongside the railway track he saw a train heading west. As one of he trucks pulled up beside him he slammed on the brakes, jumped into the back of the truck and proceeded to throw out the guards he found in there. They couldn't shoot him because they had been ordered not to.

The motorbike swerved across the road and took out another truck. As the last SS man was thrown out onto a following Mercedes causing it to swerve into a shop window, James got on top of the truck. As it reached the bridge over the railway he jumped and waited. All too soon the top of the carriage came up to meet him and he was left sprawled out on it like skin on a rice pudding. He threw off his uniform jacket and managed to work his way back and inside the carriage where he sat down. He sat hoping he'd done enough. The train travelled out of the city for some miles until it came to a stop at a small suburban station. Suddenly out of nowhere, were SS troops and leather clad Gestapo. They swarmed over the train like the cancer they were. Without even trying to find James the SS men grabbed a small Jewish boy out of his seat and took him to Haupstumfuhrer Muller who stood on the platform. Muller was not pleased. His chance to impress the Fuhrer had been ruined and now someone was going to pay. The boy or Burnett. To him it didn't matter. He grabbed the boy by the scruff of the collar whilst his mother screamed and his father was set on by the SS men. Muller shouted,

"Come out Burnett or I will kill the boy. Muller pulled out his pistol and counted, "Three, two......"

"Put your pistol away you coward. I'm here," James shouted.

"Thank you Mr. Burnett. Please do not struggle or I will kill the boy." Muller knew that if James wanted to he could take them all on. James was handcuffed and led away as the boy's tearful mother shouted thank you to him. James was hit by Muller but didn't flinch. Muller and James both knew, if Burnett wasn't handcuffed Muller wouldn't have done that. James was bundled into the back of a truck and driven away. He was taken to the central police station where he was beaten up by the guards and left to wallow in a damp cell.

Night came and with it 'night came'. For as James lay in his cell he was woken by another kick to the ribs.

"Get up scum." The Guard lifted James up and set him on his bed. As James strained to look through the blood caped over his eyes he recognised his visitor.................Adolf Hitler. There alongside him was the chicken farmer, Heidrich Himmler.

"So Mr. Burnett you find out that escaping me is not that simple."

"If you're going to kill me get on with it," James snarled at the corporal. "You've done it before and you know you will again."

"No. No, James. You're too valuable to me. You see if you're here from the future then you still exist in this time over there in Britain. Now I wonder what would happen if you met yourself?" For the first time stark terror filled James as he 'wondered what would happen if he met himself'?

"No. I think we'll Keep you somewhere safe and see if we can't arrange a family re-union. I have ordered Riechsfuhrer Himmler to keep you alive at all costs to see if after 1942 we can't get you together with yourself." With that the dictator left with his murderer in chief never to meet James Burnett again.

There was silence as the Holygram finished.

"Is that it? Is there no more," asked Jamie. "What happens to our Grand Dad?"

Anna wasn't sure if angels cried but Teacher Eli seemed to have a tear in his eye. He took a moment to compose himself and then said, "There is more but I have to warn you it is difficult to watch."

"Teacher. We have never known our Grandfather until today and we want to know everything about him whatever it costs. Please will you conclude his story."

"I will because you and your friends need to know the story of a great man of The Kingdom".

The Holygram re-started.

From Vienna James was taken to Sachsenhausen Concentration Camp that had been built in Berlin in1936 just as the Olympic Games were happening. There James stayed for over seven years suffering from beatings, starvation and illness. But more than that, suffering from watching the deaths of the many at the hands of evil men. James believed that things couldn't get worse until in 1943 he was sent to Auschwitz-Berkinow. Because he couldn't be killed it was decided he should work and so he was sent East. What James saw, no twelve year old children should see. But what James saw, every child who comes of age should see. We all need to remember what man is capable of and pray it doesn't happen again. Many times, James saved the lives of those in the camp without their caps. If you lost the cap to your uniform it meant immediate death. James would give his cap to someone who had lost their knowing the guards couldn't kill him. But they could still beat him.

Another concern for James were the activities of Doctor Josef Mengele or 'The Angel of Death' as he became known. This fanatical Nazi was fascinated by twins and how they could be re-produced to populate the new Aryan race. He carried out unspeakable experiments on mothers and twins. Being Enochim James was a twin and this along with his other special characteristics made him of interest to Mengele, but that's another story for another time.

By 1945 the Allies were overcoming the corporal and his fellow criminals so James was moved back to Sachsenhausen. In April 1945 most prisoners were marched away but those to ill to go were left behind. James was one of them. His years of torment had taken its toll and now he was suffering from tuberculosis as many former camp inmates were. When Soviet troops finally liberated the camp James was rescued by Ivan Polokov who was Enochim. He was able to get James away in an ambulance and passed him over to other Enochim in The Allied sector of Berlin. Other Enochim got him away to Britain and then up to Iceland where Enoch's Stone was located for safekeeping. He was transferred back to The Third Dimension where he was taken care of him for many Alpha and Omega.

The problem was he had to go back to his own time and place but he was ill and had aged considerably due to his long stay in the past of the first dimension. A plan was formulated whereby when James returned to the first dimension he would move back up to North Wales where no one knew him and he could be treated for his illness at an established TB Hospital. That's what happened in 1950. James moved back, met his wife and had two daughters. But his tuberculosis took it's toll and in 1973 aged just forty three James Burnett entered New Eden.

Silence returned to Eli's study along with tears. Everyone, including the teacher were crying through what they had just seen. Then Joel, Nathaniel, Micah, Jerahmeel and Zechariah joined them to comfort each other. No one can remember how long they stayed there but eventually the angels took the sleeping exhausted youngsters back to their beds. The children slept but their memories of James Burnett would always be awake.

XXIV

The children were fast asleep after their traumatic previous day. The tutors had decided not to teach them for that first session of their sixth and last season. But something awoke the children that neither they nor their tutors expected. For without any warning there was an unearthly loud toll of a bell. The toll was so heavy that it shook the Enochim house.

Instantly all four children were awake and wondering what 'in heaven' was going on.

"What was that?" Lois asked as she ran into the boy's bedroom with Anna right behind her.

"It sounded like some massive bell," replied Adam but I've never seen or heard of a bell tower here. Where it comes from and what it means I have no idea."

Just then Joel raptured into the bedroom. From the tone of his voice and the expression on his face, the children knew this bell was not good.

"Children, I want you to get dressed and be downstairs in the kitchen as soon as possible. I'll wait for you there and I need you to be there as fast as you can." Joel raptured somewhere else. All four knew this was no time to be winding Joel up so they got dressed as fast as they could and met him in the kitchen in five of their minutes

"Thanks for being quick. I've be asked to get you to All Saints as soon as I can. Let's go." They all went into the park and were staggered to see the angels that were flying about. Obviously something was up, along with the angels, but what? The four mounted their horses and rode across the park to the school with Joel in close attendance.

When they got to All Saints they went directly to Teacher Eli's study. There waiting for them were the Teacher, their tutors and Nathaniel and none of them looked any happier than Joel.

"Please be seated children," said Eli. "We need to explain something to you of the greatest importance and I would ask that you listen very carefully." After all the children had learned over the preceding days what else could shock them. They were about to find out.

"The bell you heard toll a little while ago is known as The Parade Bell. This bell only tolls when there is to be a 'princes Parade'."

"What…..?" Adam was about to ask but the look Zechariah threw over to him suggested he keep his questions for another time. Eli continued.

"There will be five other tolls of the bell. On the sixth toll of the bell the parade will begin. We do not know when the sixth toll will come so we have to be ready from now on. You are wondering what the princes Parade is?" Eli paused for a moment as if he couldn't bring himself to go on. They all knew he had to and so did the Teacher.

"You know who the prince is. He is the one also known as lucifer. At this time, the prince still has access into the heavenly realms when The I Am commands it. One day, Michael will be commanded to banish him from Heaven forever but that day has not yet come as far as I know. So when The I Am commands, lucifer comes. This is one of those times as it was in the days of Job." Eli took a moment.

"What will now happen is that the prince of darkness with some of his evil hordes will be allowed to parade through our city and along Straight Street up to Fairhaven Harbour. From there, they will be allowed to continue onto to where The I Am decrees they must be and for whatever He wishes to say or do to them. Because these evil ones prefer the darkness to the light, they will proceed through our city shrouded in darkness. This means we cannot easily see them nor what they might be doing. So we have to be cautious to guard against any tricks the evil one may try. Let me show you what this means."

Eli motioned for the children to stand up and move over to the window of his study that looked out over the city. The children were taken aback by what they saw. As they looked along Straight Street they saw all the pillars that stood to attention there now on fire. And stood between the pillars were the biggest, strongest and tallest angels you had ever seen. Hovering above the heads of these 'super angels' were many zekes and flaming chariots. All swords were drawn and Adam noticed that the fire missile hatches on the zekes were open. Behind these massed ranks of 'super angels' were myriads of other angels all with their swords drawn and flaming. And flying over the myriads were more zekes and flaming chariots readied for battle.

"The angels you see fronting both sides of Straight Street are the twelve legions, our crack troops. These are supported by all other angels who are available in the city at this time who are not on mission for The I Am. They are all standing ready to guard against the prince who prowls around like a lion to devour whoever he can. The fiery pillars are there to assist in seeing through the darkness............" Eli couldn't finish his sentence because there was another almighty toll of the Parade Bell. The School shook as did the eardrums of the Enochim. The group waited for the shaking to stop and for the ringing in the ears of the children to subside. Eli carried on.

"The fiery pillars are to help us see into the darkness and deal with any tricks the black horde may try. Please come and sit down again." The children did so.

"As you can gather, we are not warned when the parade will take place so we have to be ready at all times. It is rare for Enochim like yourselves to be here but it is not unheard of. What I need you to do is to return to the Enochim house with Joel and Nathaniel and stay there until we know it is safe for you to come out. Joel and Nathaniel will stay with you and if we consider it necessary, others will join them.

Don't be scared. There are myriads of angels here to protect you and up until now no Enochim has ever been hurt in the third dimension." Eli paused as if to let the meaning of his words become as clear as The Crystal Sea in the minds of his young charges And then as an encouragement to overcome the doubts his words may have sown he said, "For The Kingdom."

"For The Kingdom," all in the study replied. The children left with their two chaperones and rode across the park as quick as their horses would take them, which was pretty quick. When they got back, they stabled the horses and then headed into the house.

Sitting around the kitchen table having some breakfast they quizzed Joel as to what they could expect.

"I hate it," he said. "When the parade comes it brings pitch black darkness with it which is not right for our city. You can hear the fallen snarling, growling and cursing us and The I Am. To think that they were once our brothers makes the pain a thousand times worse. It just shows when you reject the way of The Kingdom, evil will abound and bring pain to everyone it touches. The darkness is oppressive and as you look into it, it seems to invade your very soul. You have to stand against it and stand on the promises of The Kingdom. Anyway, you guys will be well away from it and as safe as houses as you would say."

The third toll came as Joel finished. Again the house shook and Jamie hoped they would be 'safer than this house.'

"The best thing is if we all head up to the top floor and wait this thing out. If you've got any books or something to do, bring them with you and I'll get some ...." The fourth toll came, sooner than anyone thought it would, including Joel. Just as everyone was getting over it, Nathaniel raptured into the kitchen and scared the permanent angel city daylight out of everyone, including Joel.

"I do wish you'd use the door like everyone else," joked Anna trying to ease the tension, but it didn't work. The children headed upstairs as Joel and Nathaniel got the goods for a 'midnight feast'. They settled themselves in the boy's bedroom to wait out the storm.

Teacher Eli jumped into the flaming chariot that was waiting for him with Phillip driving. Without any words, Phillip took Eli high over the city to meet with the leaders of the twelve legions. Once the thirteen and their drivers were assembled, the Teacher began the Council of Defence.

"Are your Legions in position commanders?" As one they answered, "Yes."

"We have been through this before and may have to do so again. We know the fallen may try to break out into the city to cause............"

The fifth toll pierced the air.

"Brethren, the time has come. Do your duty and remember we have Enochim in their house. If a break out occurs I want the legion of Judah to head for the Enochim and to protect them is that understood?"

"Yes," came the reply of the twelve.

"To your posts. For The Kingdom!"

"For The Kingdom !" came the echo as the twelve flew back down to the city in their flaming chariots.

As the legion commanders rejoined their troops, Judah reported to his men their special orders. The legionnaires knew where the Enochim house was and that they were stationed as the nearest legion to it.

"If a break out occurs and I consider it has put the safety of the Enochim in danger, I will shout 'Enochim'. That will be the signal for all legionnaires, including cavalry and fliers, to head for the Enochim house. A protective perimeter will be created around the house whilst I and my cohort enter and protect the children. Nothing is to get through that perimeter and to the children is that clear?"

"Yes Commander," came the reply to Judah.

"To your posts." The legionnaires carried out their commander's order and returned to wait for the parade. Silence fell over the whole city as the sixth toll was awaited. Nothing moved or spoke. The usually joyous and active city that never slept was still. The angels knew what was coming, yet they didn't. The prince's parade had occurred before and every time the black hordes tried something new to break out into the city. It was if they felt compelled to destroy the place that had been their home for so long but had turned their backs on. Perhaps it was too clear a reminder of what they had lost as the memory was a festering wound that had to be cauterised once and for all.

The silence reached the house of the Enochim with everyone there now waiting for the sixth toll. They looked at each other wondering when it would come and what it would mean. No one knows how long they waited. But they waited and waited. The silence grew louder and still they waited. Then it came, without warning but with noise, shudders and dread.............The sixth toll.

When the noise had stopped along with the shaking all the angels looked along Straight Street to the Garden Gate.

Slowly, slowly, slowly the massive gates began to open. No creaking just the movement of the giant gates. But instead of everyone then seeing the lovely gardens beyond the gates, all that could now be seen was blackness. The hovering, silent almost enticing blackness moved silently into the City of Angels. As it id so, the angels it came to stiffened in their stance to fight against the darkness that would overwhelm them if it could. The blackness moved forward slowly and then those of the Levi Legion who were stationed first along Straight Street could hear the growling, cursing from inside. As if the darkness wasn't enough to convey evil now it had words.

"Hate. Hate. Hate. You must die. You must die. We will be god. We will be god. The I Am is nothing. The I Am is nothing." The words of evil kept coming but the angels stood firm and did not curse those who were already cursed.

The dark cloud moved slowly along Straight Street sucking the light in its path out of the city but not its citizens. The legions stood firm as did those angels stationed behind and above them. Swords drawn. Minds alert. Hearts at the ready, the angels waited for the assault that they knew would come. Nearer to The Circle the darkness came. Nearer. Nearer. Then they entered the place at the centre of the city and stopped. The curses continued but the darkness stopped. Then silence. Eli looked on almost wishing the cursing had carried on because he now knew with the silence came the danger.

Suddenly black streaks flew out of the darkness like the negative of lightning strikes. The streaks hit the ground and then exploded showering darkness all around. For a moment the angels were blinded by surprise and the darkness and that's when the enemy struck. Pouring out of the darkness like demons from the depth of hell only they were demons in the heaven. They came at the angels these fallen with a hate that had festered from before mans time began. Their hatred gave them strength and encouragement but not victory, never victory. Screaming and waving their swords they came bent on doing harm even if they couldn't kill. They set upon the legionnaires and the battle was joined. The blackness was punctuated by the flash of flaming swords and the sparks they gave off as they hit the fallen's shields and swords. Many fallen fell but still they came.

In silence the angels fought their brothers who now screamed for their defeat. The Legion of Judah was heavy into the battle being attacked on all sides. Judah shouted at his legionnaires to stand firm and they did. But as they did Judah realized that they had been cut off from the Enochim House. He knew now he had to act.

Above the squeals and screams of the enemy he shouted with all his might, "ENOCHIM!!" The Legionnaires heard his words and as one turned and raptured for the Enochim house.

The children, Joel and Nathaniel could hear the battle outside and felt the fear inside.

"Stand firm my young ones," encouraged Nathaniel. "Our brethren will have the victory as they always do." As he spoke they all heard the demonic squeals penetrate the house and then stood petrified as the fallen flew at the windows. The children could see their snarling faces dripping with spittle and what looked like blood. Adam thought they looked like giant locusts with jaws that could snap you in two. Their bodies were scaly like serpents and they had tails with a point like a sword at its end.

The two chaperones had overcome their momentary shook and were now stood in front and behind the children with their swords drawn and on fire. The boys were protecting their sisters and Jamie's mind reminded him how he and Anna had faced this before. Without warning there was a blinding flash of light as one of the windows imploded. As everyone re –acclimatised themselves they saw Phillip hovering outside in his chariot.

"Children! Come to me now!"

Joel echoed Phillips words, "Go children! Go!" Nathaniel couldn't add his invocation before the children had gone to the window. Jamie got Anna into the chariot first, then Lois.

"Adam you next," he shouted! Adam jumped and joined the girls. As Jamie jumped from the sill a horde of fallen came screaming around the side of the house and attacked them. The chariot moved and Jamie headed towards the ground. Phillip immediately engaged the fallen with his two swords and his righteous anger. As he did so, Anna took control of the chariot and swooped down after Jamie. Her brother had managed to hang onto the window sill but a fallen was heading for him.

"Oh no you don't," Anna shouted as she swung the chariot around smashing the fallen into the side of the house. Adam grabbed Jamie into the chariot as Lois screamed 'Fallen' and slashed an enemy across his chest and watched him disintegrate into nothing.

"Nice going sis, but where did you get your sword from?"

"Over in the back of the chariot. All our swords and other equipment are here."

"Teacher Eli must have asked Micah to put it here for us just in case," observed Jamie. "Right, Anna head for the flier port. You two get your gear on." Jamie's tone was enough for all to obey. Not to mention the screaming fallen who were coming after them. The flier port was soon reached and Anna landed the chariot beside the two Enochim fliers they had learnt on. Whilst en route Jamie had explained his plan. "We get into our fliers because two targets are harder to hit than one. We head out to Lo Debar where it's still light and hide out until the angels get this mess under control." Seemed like a plan so they went with it. They got into their fliers and engaged their domes just as the fallen attacked them.

The horrors from hell banged at the domes and screamed for them to die. It was scary but arkov gave them hope. Anna got her gear on and when she was ready Jamie called his comrades.

"Enoch 1 to Enoch 2, do you copy over.?"

"Enoch 2 to Enoch 1 we hear you loud and clear, over"

"Ok Adam and Lois let's get these Zekes in the air. Fly low and fast and don't hit anything or anyone unless it's from the black side. For The Kingdom!"

"For The Kingdom," came the reply from the Iqbals!

The Zekes took off flying straight through the fallen who......fell off. But they kept coming. Both Anna and Adam showed tremendous flying skill by piloting their fliers through the streets of the city. The fallen came after them but were soon reeling under the bombardment of fire missiles being shot with deadly accuracy by Lois and Jamie in their southern seats. But still the fallen came as the fliers broke through into Lo Debar. This part of the city may have been empty for millennia but now it was full of screaming demons and fallen angels baying for Enochim blood. Anna and Adam flew their socks off trying to lose the fallen but there were too many of them. Those they disintegrated and sent back to where they came from were replaced by two more and so it went on. Until………..

Out of the blackness came too more fliers but this time they were flown by fallen. They had no dome and started to fire on the domes of the two Enochim fliers. Without warning a crack appeared right in front of Adam.

"How? What? This can't be happening," Adam thought but it was. Then the dome exploded into thousands of pieces and Adam and Lois were exposed. Anna had seen what was unfolding and headed straight for her friends.

When Enoch 1 arrived they found Adam and Lois fighting for their lives. The fallen were on them because now they tasted blood. Suddenly one of them slashed out and caught Adam on his right arm. As Adam screamed in agony everyone stopped and let the silence take over. The children now knew what they had feared, in this dimension the fallen can harm and even kill those from the first dimension. No taken needed here. The fallen can carry out their evil wishes all by themselves.

Anna took advantage of the lull and flew straight at the pack of killers and right at Enoch 2. As she came along side Jamie disengaged the dome and shouted "Jump" to his friends. Lois grabbed Adam and jumped over cradling her brother in her arms. As they hit the deck of Enoch 1 like a pancake on Shrove Tuesday hitting the floor as dad looked on aghast, Jamie re-engaged the dome.

"Adam are you ok mate?"

"Just a scratch. I'll live," he said as he slumped into his southern seat. Lois wasn't so sure because he was losing a lot of blood.

"I'm not sure if we'll live," Anna said in a matter of fact voice that belied her fear. "Look." The three others did and saw a fallen flier right in front of them.

"Now look 'south'." Anna's request was granted and all of them saw the other flier right behind them.

"I take it if we get caught in their crossfire this dome will be crystal before you can say 'knife' " was Anna assessment.

Adam knew they were powering up their missiles so he didn't wait to explain what he was about to do, he just did it. He leapt forward and as the fallen let fly with their missiles he hit the 'T' button on the north console. Instantly, Enoch 1 fell towards the city slamming the children against its dome. The 'G' force inside Enoch 1 may have been bad but it was nothing compared to the slamming of each of the fallens missiles into each other. The two fallen fliers blasted themselves back to their own place without any help from an angel or an Enochim.

The fall wouldn't break the Zeke but it could make a mess of those inside. All four managed to get themselves strapped into a seat by the time they hit. The fall didn't kill them but now the fallen would. The force of the impact shattered the Zekes dome and now the children were exposed to those who would have them dead. As if to increase their sick pleasure, the fallen waited until all four came around. As they did they found themselves still trapped in their seats and with horrific, dribbling demons filling their vision.

"Time to die," one of the horrors snarled as he raised his sword. The others followed until they heard, "Stay your hand." Suddenly all the children could see were the brilliant white of angels stood between them and certain death. But these were not just any old angels. There were seven. Eli, Micah, Zechariah, Uriel, Jerahmeel, Joel and Nathaniel.

Eli continued with such authority that even his words seemed enough to win the battle. As he looked at the wounded Adam and saw the fear in the eyes of those young children the righteous anger welled within him.

"You fallen have desecrated our place and now you will pay. You have made these little ones suffer and now you will reap what you have sown. Vengeance is mine says The Lord!"

There were no more words only actions. The seven angels set about the fallen with no mercy but utter commitment. Even this horde of what must have been thousands were no match for seven angels of the The Almighty. Fallen were squealing like pigs as they were slashed repeatedly by flaming swords whose speed matched that of lightning. They didn't die that day but perhaps they may have preferred that knowing the judgement that was to come.

As the seven continued overcoming the fallen, The Judah Legion joined them.

At this the fallen knew they were beaten and they headed back screaming curses on the angels. They re-joined the black parade that had been halted in The Circle and was now surrounded by more angels than you could shake a Christmas tree at.

Michael stood on a balcony from the building of the Angel Council and spoke words that would be obeyed.

"You fallen have again be defeated as you always will be. Go now to where The I Am decrees." The darkness slowly moved forward until it reached Fair Haven. Then the angels escorting this brood of vipers stop and watched it moved across the Crystal Sea to a place The I Am had decreed and for a purpose he had set.

As the darkness disappeared there was no shouting of jubilation or joy. The angels had learnt from the start that war does not bring in it's wake happiness but only sad memories to be lived with. Without speaking, the legions returned to their barracks and the angels to their homes.

By now Phillip had arrived with his chariots and two more to bring the children home. Adam was carefully lifted onto the chariot first with Jamie holding his hand.

"Well done Enochim. You fulfilled your duty today."

"Thank you Jamie," Adam gratefully replied. Lois went with her brother back to the Enochim house where he was cared for Alpha and Omega by angels whose calling an and joy is to minister for those in The Kingdom.

Jamie and Anna flew back with Phillip whilst Zechariah and Nathaniel brought back the fliers. The Fishers just wanted to get back to be with their friends. As they entered the room in the house where Adam was lying in bed having been treated by the angels they all sat down. Without any prompting they all held hands and said in chorus, "For The Kingdom."

As Teacher Eli looked on he wasn't sure but he thought he may just felt a tear in his eye.

XXV

For the next couple of "days" the children were given time to come to terms with their experience and Adam time to heal. It must have been something in the air but Adam was soon out and about again with his friends. As Adam found out when discussing his quick healing with Jerahmeel there was 'something in the air'. The tutor explained that the atmosphere in the third dimension somehow enhanced the physical bodies of the Enochim so they became stronger, faster, higher. So that's why they are not allowed to enter the Olympics.

Teacher Eli consulted with the tutors and all decided unanimously that through how the children had acted in what became known as The Battle of Lo Debar they had more than proved they were Enochim. Therefore, no more sessions were needed and the children were allowed to spend their last season in the Third Dimension as they wished. As it turned out, all four carried on their studies because they wanted to. But come Omega 4 they were in Wings giving it large.

On the thirty eighth day the final of Phillips Cup was run between Reuben and Issachar. It was a fantastic race, run in great spirit and at great speed. The four children were given the honour of presenting Phillips Cup to the riders from Issachar who won. But to the great delight of the assembled crowd, the riders immediately presented it back to the four children. As he did so, Ithiel explained.

"Before the race we discussed how you young Enochim had shown yourselves worthy of The Kingdom. We all then agreed that whoever wins would give this Phillips Cup to you to mark your achievement." The children did not know what to say, so Uriel spoke for them.

"Brothers, my students, my fellow workers in The Kingdom thank you for your kind gesture. The memory of it will abide with them for eternity and they look forward to sharing that memory with you in a future day. For The Kingdom!"

"For The Kingdom" all shouted back as Zechariah and Micah lifted the children high on their shoulders. To this day, that Phillips Cup sits in the Lounge of The Enochim House where it reminds all who go there of the Battle of Lo Debar and the young Enochim who fought in it.

The fortieth day soon came. Joel and Nathaniel had breakfast with the children for the last time before they began their work for The Kingdom. Then it was time for everyone to say good bye to the horses. Anna and Lois couldn't hold back the tears and nor could Phillip.

"Don't worry. You will see Milk and Honey again in the coming days." After the last mucking out and race around the park the children said their farewells to the house that but for their parents not being with them, almost became a home. Then after Micah and Jerahmeel had been round to kit them out with their theonology, it was off to meet Teacher Eli and the tutors in the Stone Room.

When they got there Gedaliah was also present and all four knew what that meant. Eli asked them all to stand on the glass platform in their Enochim fatigues and then he began.

"Children the day has now come when you must return to your own dimension to carry out the work for The Kingdom that has been decreed for you. I and my brothers hope you have enjoyed your time with us as much as we have enjoyed it with you. Now it is my great pleasure and honour to ask my four brethren to bestow upon you your Enochim wings that each of you has earned and now fully deserves. Brethren if you will."

Jerahmeel came forward and placed wings on Adam and saying,

"For The Kingdom". Zecharaiah placed wings on Anna and Micah followed placing wings on Jamie. To conclude, Uriel came forward and placed wings on Lois.

"You are now Enochim and ready to fight for The Kingdom." Eli continued, "You know that you have always been gifted but because you have now recognised this and put your gift to use, you are enpowered to fulfil what is asked of you."

As Eli finished Adam and Anna wondered if there was something else to be done. There was and Zechariah didn't disappoint.

"Anna and Adam you're probably wondering who has been chosen to be dualpha pilot." They were, but really neither wanted the job over the other.

"Well I am pleased to announce that the dualpha pilot has a name starting with 'A'. For a second the children didn't realise that both their names started with 'A'. As the realisation dawned Zechariah moved forward and took hold of one hand each of the young fliers.

"Because you have both shown exceptional flying skill and courage it has been decided to nominate you both as dualpha pilot"

The room erupted in applause as Zechariah hugged both of his star pilots.

"Well children it's time for you to fulfil a promise I made to you forty days ago. I said I would send back help to your parents and now I shall. You are that help and I know you won't let me or them down." As Eli finished everyone stated shaking hands and hugging.

"Gedaliah are we set?"

"Yes Teacher."

"Children it is time to go. Please transfigure your swords." The Enochim did as their Teacher bid them. Gedaliah activated the rainbow beam and as Adam went through first followed by his friends, all in the Stone Room shouted, "For The Kingdom."

Samuel couldn't believe that as soon as his daughter had gone, the rainbow beam re-appeared and there in front of him was his son. Then Anna, Jamie and Lois all followed with swords and shields at the ready. The mums and dads just wanted to hug their children but the kids had other things in mind.

"For The Kingdom" they all shouted. The words and the fact they were spoken by these four young children encouraged all who heard them. Suddenly, the Goliathim, taken and their followers were in trouble. The Enochim broke out through the shields and began sending the fallen back to where they belonged. The Goliathim were overpowered and then deheaded by the Guardians. As the Enochim moved outside to join their brothers and sisters they could see their enemies were many but the victory was theirs. The night sky saw flashes of lightning missiles as not one, not two but three Zekes were overhead discharging their devastating firepower that didn't kill but knocked out.

Anna stood mesmerised as one flier in particular performed aeronautic manoeuvres she could only dream off. In minutes the battle was won. The taken were released and the Goliathim brought low. As the fighting stopped the hugging began.

The children were overjoyed to see their parents and that joy was a two way street. The mums and dads knew their children were different but their love for them was just the same. Ruth came over to the families.

"Great to see you kids back and 'fighting fit'. Peter and Samuel why don't you take your families back to The Crystal Sea for a proper re-union and we'll tidy up the mess here."

"You're the boss Guardian Ruth," Peter said as he hugged her.

"Steady, Peter. I do have a sister you know."

The families went over to the fliers that had now landed and waited for the dome on Flier One to come down. Anna couldn't wait to meet the pilot in there after seeing how he flew the thing. The dome came down and Anna realised she already knew the pilot because there sat in all his glory was Ray Leon.

"Nice to see you made it folks," he said.

"And you Ray," Peter said as he jumped into the flier and tried to hug the life out of his old friend.

"Steady Pete, I'm still a bit sore after taking that missile."

By now Rachel had joined them and gave Ray a peck on the cheek.

"How did you survive" she asked?

"That's not important now. Let' just say it'll take more than a surface to air missile to bring this fly boy down." After the kids and everyone else had said their hellos it was off back to The Crystal Sea.

Colonel Ponting was there with Neil and Luke to welcome the warriors home.

First off it was to the Infirmary for checkups and then down to the Dining Room for a late supper. That night all the mums and dads slept together on the Dining Room floor in sleeping bags. Just being together was what counted.

The next day Colonel Ponting insisted on a full de-brief. First of all he was asked how the fallen knew the movements of the Fishers.

"It was Peter," he answered. No one would believe what he was saying most of all Peter who was speechless. Then as the Colonel explained, it all became clear.

"You remember the night the children were attacked and you saved them from Garth?"

"Yes," Peter answered not sure where this was going.

"Do you also remember how when Garth escaped he pierced you hand with his ring?"

"Yes," but Peter was still none the wiser.

"That ring contained a micro transmitter that embedded itself into your hand, the 'mark of the beast' if you will. From then on, the fallen knew exactly where you were at any moment. We only found it last night when Luke gave you all routine body scans as part of your medical."

"So now we know about these micro transmitters we can guard against them."

"That's the idea. I've got to hand it to you Peter..."

Before The Colonel could finish what he was saying, Peter said, "I do wish you wouldn't Colonel."

After the laughter died down, Jamie asked another serious question.

"After what I've learnt over the last forty days, can you explain to me why this Garth was so willing to kill two under twelve Enochim children and be banished for eternity?"

"Do you remember the story of your grandad and Jurgen Mayers who he thought had died in 1909?"

"Yes."

"Well if I tell you that Garths mother's maiden name was Gretchen Mayers and that he's Jurgens grandson would that explain it for you?"

"Yes it would," replied Jamie.

The Colonel continued the de-brief and then let Adam, Anna, Jamie and Lois tell their story. Everyone was amazed by the stories the children had to tell and as they all finished they all realised that for all the Enochim, 'The Half has not yet been told'."

The Beginning.